The Inward Journey

Original Short Stories

James Haydock

authorHOUSE®

AuthorHouse™
1663 Liberty Drive
Bloomington, IN 47403
www.authorhouse.com
Phone: 833-262-8899

Published by AuthorHouse 04/06/2021

ISBN: 978-1-6655-2169-7 (sc)
ISBN: 978-1-6655-2172-7 (e)

Print information available on the last page.

Contents

The Inward Journey

A good story can take you to faraway
places and bring you home again for supper.

— Mark Twain

By James Haydock

Portraits in Charcoal: George Gissing's Women
Stormbirds
Victorian Sages
On a Darkling Plain: Victorian Poetry and Thought
Beacon's River
Against the Grain
Mose in Bondage
Searching in Shadow: Victorian Prose and Thought
A Tinker in Blue Anchor
The Woman Question and George Gissing
Of Time and Tide: the Windhover Saga
But Not Without Hope
I, Jonathan Blue
The Inward Journey: Original Short Stories

1
Erpenbeck and Friend

The dinner hour had come and gone and we were sitting on the veranda of the Hotel Raffles smoking Cuban cigars as evening came. Erpenbeck was speaking in that gravelly voice of his, and I was listening with interest. Always he seemed to have colorful gossip at his fingertips. I found the man amusing and entertaining, a good storyteller, and when he introduced me to Jeffrey Dunn, I merely nodded. I wanted to hear the rest of his story without interruption.

Silas Erpenbeck had been in the past an engineer of sorts, an electrical engineer. Shortly after he came to Blue Anchor he replaced the old gas lamps and jolted the town into the Age of Electricity. The safer electric lights made the streets brighter at night, and for almost a year not a single crime occurred. He worked at the Public Utility for several years. But when a distant relative died leaving him money, he bought the hotel and gave up engineering. Erpenbeck was a small man only five and a half feet tall, rather stumpy, and neither fat nor thin. His hair was closely cut and turning gray. He sported a sparse moustache under a prominent nose. His large eyes despite his age were pools of limpid innocence. His face and neck were splotchy in places from the booze he drank every day.

The hotel he owned, though grandly named after the Singapore Raffles where gin-soaked guests in seersucker suits discussed all manner of dubious deeds, was but a wooden building of four stories managed by his spouse. She was a tall, angular woman in her late forties with a no-nonsense attitude and a commanding air. The owner, often tipsy and excitable, had long surrendered the rule of the hotel to her. Guests of the establishment often heard domestic quarreling from behind closed doors. From it the wife invariably emerged the victor. Sometimes when he drank too much, she locked him in a room and left him there for as long as a day. When seen again his thin face bore marks of grim repentance.

Erpenbeck was a man with an interesting past and could spin a good yarn. So when Jeffrey Dunn sat down beside us as though invited, I was disposed to resent the interruption. I could see the man had been drinking before and during dinner and needed nothing more. Even so, I accepted his offer of another drink when our host excused himself to have a few words with his desk clerk. I scanned Dunn's looks and found nothing truly remarkable. He was tall and thin with a long and sallow face, a weak chin below a Roman nose, and shaggy eyebrows above large gray eyes. He was known as an easy-going and likable fellow when sober but not so likable when drunk. I suspected something was amiss in his life, something that made him not entirely stable. It was a first impression, of course, and first impressions are often misleading. Yet his thoughts seemed jumbled at times and half finished.

He spoke in an accent not belonging to the region. Maybe that's why I noticed. When Erpenbeck returned with a mint julep, Dunn was gesticulating dramatically and slurring his words. They had been good friends in years gone by, and one tried to cap the other with stories of drunken revelry in southern cities. Neither was sober as the evening wore on. But if Erpenbeck was vulgar in his cups, his friend was more refined in language if not in manner. When night came with a chill wind rising from the east, Jeffrey Dunn rose unsteadily and shambled off.

"I . . . I really must get along home," he stammered, as though apologizing for not being home already. "I hope to see, expect to see both of you tomorrow."

"Your missus all right?" Erpenbeck called.

"Of course she's all right! Why wouldn't she be? No problem ever pierces that woman's armor! You know it, old buddy, as well as I do! So why the hell you bother me with asking?"

The passion, coming right after the submissive apology, seemed a little unusual. For several minutes Erpenbeck was silent as he sipped his julep. Then heaving a sigh he spoke to me sadly.

"A good man, that one. Educated and smart. Such a pity he drinks."

"Is he often drunk?" I asked.

"All the time. And when he's drunk he blathers nonsense and wants to fight. Gentle as a kitten when sober. But dead drunk three or four days a week and bellicose. It's this place, you know, and Carla Jean."

"Who is Carla Jean?"

"His wife. Old man Heywood's daughter. Dunn took her away for a while, but she was born and raised on her daddy's hardscrabble farm and insisted on coming back. Dunn resisted, of course, but she was adamant. He's out of his element here and the future don't look good for him. I really believe he's gonna hang himself one day if he don't drink himself to death. When you know him as long as me, you see he's really a nice fellow. Clever and capable but mulish when drunk."

The next day I had business to take my time. I make a good living in the jewelry trade even though it can be dicey and cutthroat. I didn't see Dunn again for three days. Then as I sat on the verandah looking at people in the street, he eased his lanky body into a chair beside me.

"I'm sorry I was plastered the last time we talked," he said, "but I don't know what to do in a place like this. All I can do is surrender to crapulence and forget I ever came to this god-forsaken place."

"Crapulence? I've never heard the word," I said, hesitating. "What does it mean? And why don't you like Blue Anchor?"

"Oh it means drunkenness, just plain drunk. Heard it somewhere and rather liked it. Do you know the English language has fifty-four synonyms for *drunk*? I looked it up once. Any good thesaurus will confirm it. And this town? Well, it's nice in some ways, pleasant with affable people, but dull as dishwater."

I turned to look at him. His watery eyes were somber and filled with anguish. His thin lips quivered before breaking into a timorous grin. The smile displayed white and even teeth. It melted a layer of pain I thought I was seeing as he began to complain.

"I went away three years ago but came back. My wife didn't like England, didn't like the people there, didn't like the weather, or even the shops. Wanted to come back to her little hometown and her old daddy. She was born and raised here, you know."

He fell into silence again and was mute for several minutes. When I didn't speak, he lapsed into nostalgic reminiscence. "I miss London, Rupert, I miss the opera in Covent Garden. Have you seen a performance of *Tristan und Isolde* by any chance?"

Suddenly, or so it seemed, we had achieved a first-name friendship. I thought he was trying to impress me. Glibly he mentioned place names in London and the German title of Wagner's work. I replied as casually as I could that I had seen that bombastic but moving opera more than once. His face brightened and he began to speak of the German more as a friend than a musician from another time. I was disposed to forget what seemed to be affectation on his part and began to see a boyish enthusiasm for good music and literature and the English way of life.

"I wish I could be in London now. Wish I could be in Piccadilly with its well-dressed crowds and fine restaurants and ladies of the night adorning the pavement and the shops all lit up, and a general air of excitement electrifying the street. Oh, I like the Strand too and Samuel Johnson's ditty. Do you remember what he said in that moment of levity? *'I put my hat upon my head and walked into the Strand, and there I met another man whose hat was in his hand.'* Nonsense, of course, but fun! Rhythmic, and the humor is as good as anything we have today. Timeless in fact."

He paused to remember another quote. "Maybe you recall this one from Dr. Johnson. *'Nature has given women so much power that the law has very wisely given them but little.'* Clever, huh? Talking about his own time, of course, but women really do have power. I know the power they have only too well, know it sadly from my own experience."

"Have you read Boswell's *Life of Johnson*?" I asked.

"Not entirely, only parts. The man goes into great detail to fully describe every little mannerism of the great man, every little tic of the fat face and every feeling or thought he ever had. He breathes life into the old gentleman, immortalizes the man. The book is a long one, you know, several volumes I think. Once I wanted to read them all but not any more. I'm sorry to say I haven't met anyone in Blue Anchor who reads anything. People speak of an old scholar who resided here years ago. He lived alone in a quaint little house full of books bound in leather and had read them all. The local library has some of his stuff."

"Oh, you mean Isaac Brandimore. Erpenbeck was telling me about him. He died when the Civil War was ending, I've heard."

"Yes! He was a learned man and a good Quaker. I've heard he hungered to talk to anyone about his reading, anyone from statesmen to tinkers. At parties he stalked his prey and pontificated on politics and poetry. Made a nuisance of himself. People tried to avoid him, the record shows, as they often do with me."

I detected something wistful in Dunn's talk and began to understand why he had come to me. I was well read and had visited the London he loved more than once. I would go there again — my business would take me there — but for him the city was only a memory.

"I'm really at the end of my tether," he said with a vehemence that startled me. "I can't stand little Blue Anchor much longer. It's stuffy and stagnant, and even the countryside is detestable. And the village ladies drawling nonsense in that god-awful Southern twang really grates on my nerves. Also I guess you know Carla Jean and I aren't really man and wife any more. We live apart in her daddy's house. A gang of people she calls her relatives live there. Loud and lazy they are."

"Why don't you pick up and leave?" I asked. "You don't have a job that would keep you here. So why not skedaddle?"

A frown clouded his pallid face and he grew sullen. In silence he stared into the busy street, thinking deeply perhaps or feeling a prick of conscience. He began to squirm in his seat and jerked himself upright.

Then suddenly he blurted: "That's easier said than done. I can never go home again. Too many complications and a lung problem. London air, you know. Sorry, old chap. Gotta go. See you later."

He was gone in an instant. Erpenbeck told me his wife was a handsome woman, athletic with a stunning figure, but solitary in spite of her looks. Dunn had married her when she was sixteen, and she must have been gorgeous at that time. I learned he had come to Blue Anchor from England to manage the estate once owned by Owen Cooper, a swashbuckling spy in business during the Civil War. Cooper had bought the property at auction after a runaway soldier killed its owner. When he died, the land fell into the hands of people in another state. Jeffrey Dunn was hired to manage the large farm, which by then had become a profitable business.

Having grown up in London, living in the American South was a sea change for Dunn. Though at first he couldn't understand the speech of those around him, he liked his job and the sprawling countryside surrounding Blue Anchor. Riding at canter on a good horse down a road with cotton fields on either side, he was moved by the beauty of white under a blue sky. But the spot he liked best, as he told me in one of our endless conversations, was a hidden, crystalline pond fed by a sparkling spring. It was located a mile or two outside of town and surrounded by a thicket of trees. In the evenings throughout the long summers he often went there to relax in the cool water, dig his toes in the sandy bottom, and listen to the friendly silence. Years ago children began to call it Windy Pond even though it had no wind and was always calm and reflective. They went there to frolic in the heat of the day and make a lot of noise, but when Dunn was there the pond was silent and deserted. He lingered in the lonely place, luxuriating in the clean and clear water, and thinking a companion would make it even better.

One evening he went to the pond just as the sun was setting. Tying his horse to a tree, he stripped to his underwear and walked over to the bank. He was ready to swim when he saw a nude girl sitting on a large rock in the middle of the pond. She glanced at him for only a moment and slid without a sound into the water. When he didn't see her for several minutes, he assumed she had hidden among the trees. Then of a sudden she was swimming with powerful strokes toward him. He called out to her, but she turned and swam away. He watched her cross to the opposite bank and climb out. In the uncertain light he couldn't be sure she was naked, and yet her smooth and supple body was stunning.

The next day in his office Dunn asked about the girl. A bevy of local citizens told him she lived with her father, who had worked the land half a century. They said he was an old man with gray whiskers, a weathered face, and yellow teeth through which he spat tobacco juice. He had been a prosperous farmer in his time, but as he grew older life became hard for both him and his daughter. His wife had died of cholera some years before, and the daughter had taken on the duty of looking after him.

It wasn't long before Dunn went again to the pond. Carla Jean was there, and the magic of the place added layer upon layer to her native beauty. He made no effort to speak to her, and she didn't even glance in his direction. She swam swiftly across the water, dived beneath the surface, swam for some distance under water, emerged shaking her long hair, and climbed out shimmering to don her clothes. Again he thought of the sirens of Homeric legend. Surely she was as beautiful as they. When she had strolled into the trees and vanished, he found on the forest floor a bright and beautiful wild flower where she had stood. He picked it up and gently held it in his fingers. For a moment he wanted to keep it as a gift from her. But the sentiment irritated him, and he threw the flower into the water to float away.

Shortly after that he went to the pond every evening,

and each time Carla Jean was there alone. In time they began to talk, just a little, and slowly they became friends. They swam together and sat nude on the rock together. He began to think of her not as a beautiful woman, but as a water nymph energizing the place he loved. When her father invited him to their home, he went with gladness. The house was shabby but comfortable and clean. Though in that setting she didn't exhibit the mystery of the young woman who came every evening to the pool, she was charming in her colorful gingham dress.

"Papa and I are glad you came to visit us," she said. "Won't you have a cool glass of tea and something to eat?"

It was her way of wanting to please him. She had heard that English gentlemen were fond of tea. He was amused. He found the courage to drink the tea and was served a big slice of cake that was too sweet for his palate. It was nothing like the crumpets he had with tea in London. In his room at the hotel he was strangely happy. He had come to love the simplicity of rural life, and though at first he didn't want to admit it, a delightful girl who spoke with a thick Southern accent and lived in a flyblown shack enthralled him. Slowly as time passed he made up his mind to marry Carla Jean. He loved her and wanted her to love him.

For more than a year Jeffrey Dunn was as happy as any man could be. After their marriage he moved out of the town's hotel and rented a pleasant house in the midst of flowering shrubs. Carla Jean was as beautiful in her little house as she had been at the pond, and it pleased him to look at her. They laughed and talked and made love and laughed some more. They went to parties where she became the main attraction, and it did the man good to see his wife happy and radiant. They threw parties themselves and soon found a number of relatives attending, people Carla Jean had never mentioned. Even when not invited they came in shabby clothing, displayed boorish behavior, and ate quantities of food. They were good people but uneducated and plainly the salt of the earth. As they gobbled any food in sight, washing it down with beer or wine, they prattled incessantly. Their nasal redundancy, loud and sometimes argumentative, annoyed him.

"Don't let your folks eat us out of house and home, Love," he laughed indulgently one afternoon in autumn as her kinsmen consumed an entire pig. "Our income isn't all that big you know."

"They're my blood relatives," his wife curtly replied. "We have to welcome them. It's what we call Southern hospitality, and that means stuffing their bellies with good food and drink."

In time, for reasons he never quite understood, their attendance at parties dwindled and ceased. People who had invited them earlier now seemed to shun them, and rumor had it the ladies of the town disliked Carla Jean because she was beautiful and smart and not of their social class. Dunn began to realize that in the American South, as late as the early years of the twentieth century, class distinction was only a stone's throw from the odious class system he had known in England. He tried to laugh it off but found it irksome, indeed painful.

When things grew steadily worse, and when the gleam in Carla Jean's eyes slowly disappeared, Dunn made a decision. He would take her away from her native land to be with his people. In that different world beyond the sea she would shine. He wrote to a cousin, asking him to use his influence to get him a job. As he waited for a reply, Carla Jean boasted to friends and family that she was going to England and would no longer be a simple Southern girl but a sophisticated English lady. She was delighted when her husband was offered a post in a bank south of London, and for a time she got along well with his relatives. Dunn took to his old life again, working hard all day but finding time to read the newspapers, play golf once a week, and tour the island with Carla Jean.

He loved her more than ever as she adjusted to English life, but as time passed he found she was taking less interest in the reality around her. In warm and sunny weather she seemed content. But as autumn yielded to winter and the cold winds howled from the east, she began to complain. She looked pinched and unhappy and that worried him. He tried to cheer her as best he could but to no avail.

"You'll get use to the weather soon," he said to her. "You'll welcome the west wind bringing warmth. When summer comes, you'll have a grand old time. It can be as warm and pleasant here in Surrey as in Blue Anchor. The ladies here go in for flower gardens, but if you want a vegetable garden you can surely have one."

He could tell she listened only to every other word. She was polite but seemed distracted. Her behavior was indolent and lethargic. One day he asked bluntly if she were happy. She replied with a quick affirmative but seemed to be concealing something.

"You don't regret moving here?"

"Oh, no. Not at all. I don't like it here as much as Blue Anchor, but it's better than Daddy's farm. I can tell you this, I'll never go back."

Then one evening in spring as the trees were bursting into tiny leaf, Dunn returned from work to find his wife standing at the window looking wanly into the wet street. She had been waiting impatiently for his return, and she spoke excitedly as soon as he entered the room.

"I can't bear to live here longer, Jeff. I hate it, I hate it! Let's go home! If you make me stay here longer I will just fade and die. I will die like a flower when it gets no water. I want to go home, Love, I do!"

He tried to reason with her, explaining that he couldn't easily give up his job and return. His position in Blue Anchor had long since been filled, and times were hard. There were no jobs there, nothing to allow him to make a living, not to mention the cost of returning. He tried extolling England, its history and culture, its economy, its pretty villages and friendly people. He promised her he would find a way for them to live in an ivy-covered country cottage. She did not respond.

Summer came and Carla Jean spoke no more about going home and Dunn grew less nervous. But one day the local magistrate stopped him in the street and informed him his wife had been bathing in one of the millponds. She had attracted the attention of middle-class citizens who were outraged by the spectacle.

"Public bathing, especially nude bathing, is strictly prohibited here," he said. "And I don't really understand why she would do it."

It occurred to Dunn that the millpond, though surely contaminated, was similar to the pond in North Carolina where Carla Jean had gone every evening in summer to cleanse herself and be alone. In imagination he saw her go to the Surrey millpond, undress on the bank, and slip like a nymph into the cold water. It was much colder than the water at home, but it probably gave her a sense of reclaiming the past. Late one afternoon he went to the pond and saw his wife sitting on the concrete wall that formed the bank. She was looking down at the water, and he remembered the first time he saw her sitting nude on a rock in Windy Pond. She stood up and was briefly hidden from view. Then naked she plunged headlong into the water so adeptly she made no splash. She swam in the cold water as long as fifteen minutes. Then she emerged wet and shining and looking like a water nymph. She was smiling with delight as she donned her summer clothes and skipped away.

At home Dunn didn't mention he had seen her at the millpond but looked at her curiously. He was trying to understand her behavior. Then one day home from work the maid told him Mrs. Dunn had taken a train to London. She wouldn't be home till late. While it vexed him to learn his wife had gone without consulting him, he hoped she would enjoy shopping in the bustling city. He went to meet the last train to greet her and help her with her load of packages, but when she didn't appear he grew alarmed and sped home. He saw at once that most of her personal belongings were gone. Carla Jean had fled.

After a week of sleepless nights and utter misery, Dunn received a letter from her. It was stark and brief. She had always found it difficult to express herself in writing. *"I couldn't put up with Surrey no longer,"* she wrote. *"I'm going home to daddy and my folks. I miss them something awful. Don't try to come after me, Love. It's over."*

There was one thing for him to do. He loved her unconditionally and couldn't lose her. He would have to give up his job and his life in England and follow her. If it meant going back to Blue Anchor to live on a dying farm with vulgar people, he would do it. It hurt to know she had left him with so little explanation, but he would find her again and make things right. His boss at the bank urged him to take a few days off before quitting his job. He was due a raise and promotion, was set to become the manager of important accounts. His future in banking looked bright, but his personal future lay with Carla Jean. Without her nothing could ever be bright. At any cost he would find her and live with her again.

For several days he was half insane with grief and despair. The desolation surged at times into rage. He had done all he could to give her a good life, and she had paid him for his kindness by returning to her sordid roots. The crude life she was living before he met her now seemed more important than the unconditional love he had given her. He quit his job, sold or gave away everything he owned, and traveled third class across the Atlantic. He sent a wire to let her know he was coming. She didn't reply. After a weary voyage that seemed to last forever, he arrived in Norfolk. The next day he boarded a train for Raleigh. A day later he was checking into the Hotel Raffles.

Inevitably before he could leave the hotel he ran into

its owner. Erpenbeck was surprised to see him home again and detained him to ask many questions. Dunn brushed him off as fast as he could and set out on foot for the Heywood farm. He expected to find only the old man and his daughter there, and he hoped with all his heart that Carla Jean would murmur apologies and kiss him tearfully. He entered the yard to find a dozen scraggly people sprawled on the porch and resting in the shade. Most of her kinfolk had moved into the small house and were making themselves at home. Among them on the porch and staring in his direction was his wife. She made no attempt to extricate herself from the ill-clad people around her. Jeffrey Dunn approached and stood in the yard a few feet from her.

"Well, well," she said in that Southern drawl she had begun to lose in England, "look what the cat dragged in."

"I came back to be with you," Dunn happily cried. "I will find a house for you or build one for you, and we shall live happily again."

"I like it here," she replied with a nasal twang "I'm with my own folks now, and I like it here. I don't need no house any better than this. I know I'm still your wife and you got a right to live here too, but I ain't gonna live no place else."

Dunn was dismayed by what he heard and by the way she spoke. She was deliberately emphasizing her Southern roots, the accent and idiom, but he attempted to sound cheerful and friendly.

"Do you have any room for me, Love? On the whole your daddy's house looks a bit crowded. Where in the world did all these people come from, and who are they? Well, you don't have to answer that question. Your relatives, I suppose."

"Oh, we can find room awright, but it won't be no private room like we used to have, nothin' like that. We'll have to bunk in a room with four or five cousins. Guess you won't mind coz you ain't gonna be gettin' me to do the stuff I used to do."

When he married the girl, naively he thought she lived only with her father. Now he was discovering that relatives were coming out of the woodwork. A smelly tribe of them was living in the little house and on the porch and in the yard. For reasons he never understood they had come from all over the state with their meager belongings in burlap bags. No one seemed to have a job, and all day long and into the night they lay about smoking, drinking, playing cards, strumming a banjo with four strings, and jabbering. Dunn found the chatter endless, often droning on when he tried to sleep. The palaver ran through the night when he lay with his wife on a lumpy mattress only a foot or two away from others in the room. For this she had abandoned the large and comfortable flat with a servant in England. He began to spend more and more of his time away from the place. Carla Jean believed he was looking for a job.

He was, in fact, looking for any job that would bring a little money. He knew he couldn't expect to find a position even comparable to the one he had thrown away, but working hard at whatever he could find he thought he might earn enough to buy a house in Blue Anchor.

"As soon as I'm able," he said to Carla Jean, "we'll find a place of our own and get out of here. We can't go on living here with your daddy and kinfolk much longer. We don't have any comfort here, any peace or privacy, and the food is no good."

"I have all the peace I need or want," she replied with a low, trilling laugh that pleased him enormously even as her words disappointed. "As for privacy, Jeffie, who needs it? And the food ain't the best, I agree, but it's good old Southern fare. I like it. You don't."

"Well, there's no need for us to move right away," he said, yielding to the stubbornness he had seen early in Carla Jean. "We can make do here, I guess, till we find just the right place."

A month went by and Dunn found work in a hardware store. He was hired as an accountant to look after the books, and so the pay was more than that of a clerk and more than he expected. Calmly he talked to Carla Jean about moving into town. He had a good job now and things were better. He tried to argue with her. It didn't work.

"If you don't like it here," she said flatly, "get a room in the hotel. You like being alone. Most of the time I don't."

Again he yielded. He hated living with her relatives in cramped and unsanitary conditions, but he couldn't bring himself to go elsewhere and see her move out of his life. So after work, day after day, he went back to the shack in the country. He found it crowded with vulgar people chattering nonsense in a Southern drawl that grated on the ear. The place was grubby, dirty, and smelled of unwashed bodies. In time he got in the habit of dropping by the hotel for a few drinks before going home. Thus fortified, he was able to face the crowd of loafers who gobbled Southern fried food like fat pigs at a trough.

The meal was always starchy and greasy, but everyone smacked their lips, grinned happily, and chattered. He could see Carla Jean slowly slipping away from him. He began to drink more. Every Saturday night he got deadly drunk.

Wobbly and loop-legged he would stumble home, find a mattress on the floor, and sleep it off. Carla Jean and her folk knew inebriation inside and out and laughed at his condition. Though drunk, he could tell they were losing any respect they ever had for him. Moreover, he was not a lovable drunk. In fact when deep in his cups he was quarrelsome and prone to speak the truth as he saw it. That led to a dispute with Gerald Hawkins at the hardware store, and on the spot Hawkins fired him. Several weeks went by before Dunn found another job. During that time he managed to wheedle drinks at the hotel from friends and even strangers but also managed to run up an extensive bar tab.

More out of pity than need Oscar Pinhandle, owner of Darboy's General Store, hired him to stock shelves and keep the place clean. Pinhandle had become owner and manager of the store, a landmark institution in Blue Anchor founded by Jacob Darboy long before the Civil War. Out of respect for the stern old Quaker, the new owner had kept the original name, had made few changes, and ran the place almost as a museum. It was not a proper setting for Jeffrey Dunn, especially when drunk. One day at lunch he had too much to drink, went tipsy back to work, and knocked over a prized vase that shattered on the concrete floor. Pinhandle lectured him, saying he would have to pay for the vase.

"You know the rule of the house, Jeffrey. If you break it you own it. Applies to you as well as to clumsy customers."

Dunn became angry, refused to listen, and stormed out of the store. From then on he managed to stay alive only by doing menial odd jobs. Losing his income and therefore not able to support the wife he dearly loved, he spiraled downward to moan in misery. Because he was so often drunk she ceased to sleep with him on the smelly mattress, and she seldom spoke to him even when he was sober. He began to think something was going on behind his back. When he returned for the wretched evening meal, often Carla Jean wasn't there. Asking why, he was told she had gone to spend the evening with friends. Once he went to the house her father had mentioned and found no one there. Later she explained her daddy was mistaken; she had gone to be with people he didn't even know. She was all made up in her best clothes, and Dunn believed she was having an affair.

"If I find out you're cheating on me," he stormed, "even though you know I love you dearly, I'll break every bone in your body."

"Hah!" she retorted. "You are pathetic! You're a nobody, a gutless drunk! You can't break your own bones either sober or drunk."

Again he buckled to her rebuke, suspecting a quarrel would turn violent. He was silent yet seized with furious jealousy. He believed his wife had become unfaithful and everyone but himself knew the full details. Days later when Erpenbeck at the hotel asked about Carla Jean merely to make friendly conversation, he berated the man with angry, insulting words and lost the only friend he had in the community.

Erpenbeck escorted him outside and cautioned him not to come back. The hotel had become a refuge, and now he had only the wretched hut in the country. So there he went and found Carla Jean dressing to go out. When she refused to tell him where she was going, an ugly scene ensued. She slapped his face and caused his nose to bleed. In a rage he beat her without mercy. Her shrieks pierced him like a dagger, but he went on beating her with a wide leather belt. A few minutes ended a marriage he hoped would last forever.

From then on, nursing cuts and bruises on her delicate body, she despised him and lost herself among her relatives. Although she would have nothing whatever to do with him, they went on living in the same house. She knew he had no other place to go. Both knew the marriage was over and neither spoke to the other. Then one day as she was preparing to go out, he surprised her by asking where she was going.

"What's it to you?" she replied scornfully. "If you must know, I'm going down to Windy Pond. You already took all I ever had from me. You gonna take that from me too?"

He sank into a chair and stared at the rough floor. His shoulders shuddered as though racked by pain. Cold and hard and tossing her head, Carla Jean went quickly outside and walked swiftly to the silent pond. Her need to go there seemed stronger now than ever before. She was drawn there by something mystical in the place, something that calmed and strengthened her, and she went there often. On occasion Dunn went also to Windy

Pond. I don't know what motive he had in going, for he knew Carla Jean didn't want him there. Perhaps he hoped to regain that blissful moment when he first saw her alone and nude and fell in love with her. Maybe he thought he might rekindle the embers of that sputtering lost love. Whatever his reason for going, any time he went there to stand on the bank and look at her, she screamed in anger: "Go away, you worthless bum! Go away!"

As the summer was ending and I was planning to leave Blue Anchor to spend the winter in Brazil, I met Carla Jean at the house of a friend. She was lovely in her gentle, unassuming way, not at all the harsh and vulgar person I was predisposed to imagine. I tried to see something in her that could have driven Dunn to such a devastating passion. I found only a fresh simplicity in the young woman. She was quiet and somewhat shy, not at all coarse or loud or aggressive. I had heard that she and Dunn had knockdown fights with her folk invariably taking her side, but she didn't appear to be capable of violence. I saw only a shapely and pretty young woman who seemed rather unsure of herself. She spoke of England and bragged about the sumptuousness of their living arrangement there. They had every comfort, she said, even a maid. Then with a deep sigh she added, "But I had to come home. I got terribly homesick for my Southern way of life, for my daddy and all."

Some days later as I was sitting on the hotel verandah in the heat of the afternoon, mulling over some papers from my bosses in Brazil, Dunn came up and wearily dumped himself in the chair beside me.

"You're going to South America next week?" he asked.

"Yes. Brazil. Rio and later São Paulo."

"I sure would like to be going with you, Rupert, but of course I can't. I don't have a penny to my name. I've made an awful mess of things. I'm in the deepest, darkest hole I ever dug and there's no way out. And what I don't understand is how it ever got that way. I guess I shouldn't have married Carla Jean, but I loved her more than life itself. Then somehow it all fell apart."

"Do you still love your wife?" I asked. "I met her only a few days ago, and to me she seemed gentle, compassionate, even a little shy."

"She's not a bad sort. At one time I loved her beyond reason and I'm sure she loved me as much, but we lost it. I guess we both lost it. Loss you must know is a terrible thing. It kills. I'm at the end of my rope, I tell you. I'm hanging on, but there's nothing left for me, nothing at all. I'm a drunk, Rupert, a nasty drunk, and I'm worthless."

He got up suddenly, turned on his heel, and left me. I see even now those large pale eyes burning like red-hot coals under the shaggy brows. The man I thought was guilty of peculiar behavior when first I met him had revealed a biting despair to me, and I could do nothing to help him. I grieved for him but could do nothing.

I went back to the veranda after supper to take in the evening. Erpenbeck and a man called Nelson joined me. They suggested we go for a dip in the pond before I left Blue Anchor. It would be a sharing of pleasure among friends said Erpenbeck. The pond was lovely in twilight. We laughed and hooted and tore off our clothes to take the plunge. Nelson, Erpenbeck's man at the hotel desk, dived in first.

In seconds he scrambled to the surface, crying out hoarsely in fright. "There's something soft and cold and heavy down there! I swear I felt something real awful down there!"

"You're drunk!" Erpenbeck yelled, and we laughed.

"No, no! I'm serious. There's something down there!"

Erpenbeck and Nelson went under the water and burst to the surface supporting an object between them. I plunged in to help and we dragged our burden to the bank. Then we saw it was Dunn. In the eerie light his body clad only in underpants was blue and luminous. Shortly after leaving me in late afternoon, he had wandered down to the pond. There he waded into deep water, wrapped a heavy chain around his ankles, and sank to the bottom without a struggle.

Before I left Blue Anchor I heard people saying they were sorry Jeffrey Dunn had to go that way. Then Silas Erpenbeck told me he had gone one evening down to the pond and caught a glimpse of a pretty young woman bathing. Naked and shining in the moonlight, she was sitting on a rock in the middle of the pond and looking into the water. A wreath of wet hair concealed her face, and so he couldn't be certain of her identity. Her slender back and shoulders, convulsing as though in pain, convinced him she was weeping.

2

Ida's Umbrella

When Ida Crabtree's husband Bo died at fifty-eight, she converted their spacious home into a boarding house. As her business began to prosper, she found it necessary to buy insurance. An agent of the Hawthorne Assurance Company sold her a policy that covered the value of the house, should it burn down, as well as items within it should they be damaged, destroyed, or stolen. Ida paid her premiums on time month after month even when the expense was becoming a burden. Every day she cautioned her charwoman to keep an eye on the fireplaces. Her cook took care to see that the kitchen fire never got out of hand, and nothing within the house suffered damage or loss. For years Mrs. Crabtree had no reason to make a claim.

Then one day in late April when it rained cats and dogs, she loaned her prized umbrella to Orville Hastings. The young man was a boarder who worked as a clerk in the hardware store on Main Street. He had just minutes to get to work, and she thought he might lose his job and leave her house if he didn't get there on time in dry clothes. So even though she prized the expensive umbrella and made it a practice never to lend it to any person, on this one occasion she made an exception. Orville brought it back to her after working his ten-hour shift with murmurs of gratitude. All day heavy rain had pelted the store, but he got there and came home again dry as a turtle in its shell.

"Open the umbrella, Orville," Ida said when she saw it tucked under his arm, "and place it gently on the floor. The fine silk covering is wet and must dry thoroughly. My umbrella can't be folded when wet."

He did as he was told and was about to mount the stairs to his room when he heard his landlady shriek. Dumfounded and aghast, she was pointing to a hole in the shining silk as large as a quarter. Reason told her some person with an evil mind had deliberately and maliciously put the end of a cigar to the umbrella.

"What is that?" she cried. "Tell me, Orville, what is that?"

She was trembling as she pointed to her expensive umbrella. She had sacrificed to buy it, telling herself she deserved it. Now it was ruined, utterly and irretrievably ruined.

"What's wrong, Mrs. Crabtree? Is something the matter?" asked Orville Hastings, coming in close to look at the umbrella. The hole was not immediately visible and he saw nothing.

"You or some villainous vandal in that place where you work burned an ugly hole in my lovely umbrella! That's what's wrong! You or some evil villain burned a hole in my expensive umbrella, Just look!"

Overcome by anger and dismay, she thrust the umbrella

in his face, demanding he examine the hole and admit his guilt. He stammered sincere apologies, astonished by what he was seeing.

"I see, Mrs. Crabtree, but I just don't know how the hole got there. I can't believe anyone at the store would do that, and I doubt any customers would do such a thing. Will you let me take the umbrella to work tomorrow and ask about it? I want to get to the bottom of this as much as you do and maybe identify the culprit."

"Well!" she exclaimed, huffing. "If you can find out who did it, maybe you can make him pay. We can't just patch the hole. The entire umbrella will have to be covered with new silk. They don't make them like this any more, and finding a replacement, even if that's possible, would cost a fortune. Take the umbrella and tell me what you find."

The next morning Orville left in bright sunshine with the umbrella tucked under his arm. The manager and assistant manager laughed outright when he entered the store. Some of his fellow clerks already on the job and sorting a shipment of nuts and bolts snickered.

"Oh, you must know the sun will suddenly stop shining to let the rain fall in torrents," the manager laughed. "I never thought you were capable of such elaborate precaution, Orville. Why I learn more about you every day."

"Yessir," Orville allowed. "I know I'm a complicated person. But this here umbrella belongs to my landlady. It's her prized possession. Yesterday someone here burned a big hole in the fine silk. Looks like they used a cigar or something."

"That's most unlikely," said the manager, examining the hole. "You know as well as I we don't allow employees to smoke on the job, and none I know of smoke cigars even at home. Once in a blue moon a customer smokes in here, but we don't encourage it. I think something hot must have rubbed against the fabric. Here, look at this. Between the ribs close to the hole it's scorched like an iron was put on it."

Then, explosively, Orville remembered the umbrella had fallen behind the old stove in the dressing room. He went there every morning to take off his coat and don his hardware tunic. He knew the stove was cold every morning and barely warm before noon. But yesterday it was hotter than it had been for months, hot enough to burn expensive silk. He would have to pay to have the umbrella repaired, and he knew his tiny salary would be hard put to take on another burden.

"I just don't know what to do," he said to himself, "but I caused the damage and will have to pay. I'll have to 'fess up and maybe be turned out of Crabtree's house. I know she's gonna be very angry when I tell her what happened."

There was no doubt about it; he had read Ida Crabtree correctly. She lost her temper when she heard his explanation. With every word of apology her anger increased. How could her clumsy boarder be so careless? For several minutes she fumed and fretted, but then an air of calm swept over her matronly face. She was thinking about something and was no longer furious. With a heavy sigh she told Orville to go wash up for supper. They would discuss the matter later.

That evening when supper was over and done with and the house was quiet again, the two of them sat in the parlor. Mrs. Crabtree urged Orville to ease the nervous twitch attacking his face. She was ready to tell him she might be able to solve his problem.

"We agree," she said, "that since you damaged the umbrella, you will pay to have it fixed. You agreed to do it even when it means you'll have to sacrifice. Another might have tried to weasel out of it, and that person would now be looking for another place to live."

"I ain't one to do that," Orville said as firmly as he could.

"No. You took it upon yourself to accept blame, and you did the right thing. Well, I have insurance on my house and everything in it. I've had the policy for years and never once filed a claim. Tomorrow I will go to the offices of Hawthorne Assurance and do exactly that."

Orville looked at the woman in amazement. It had never occurred to him that she would have insurance on the item he had damaged.

"I will take the umbrella with me," Ida continued, "and insist they cover the damage. I'll keep my fingers crossed 'cause I know how crafty and cunning insurance people can be. All you need do is merely wait and see what happens."

"I'm much obliged," said Orville humbly. "If they won't pay, I will of course. It'll be a challenge but I'll manage somehow. How much do you think it's gonna cost to make your umbrella whole again?"

His landlady paused to think it over. The repair would have to be done by an expert craftsman who would charge for his labor and time, and the silk would have to be of the finest quality. Any repair with new silk would cost a lot, but the exact amount she didn't know.

"I can't say," she said at length. "I can't even guess the cost, but I do know an honest merchant might charge at least forty dollars."

"Oh, my, that's a lot of money! It's a lot more than I thought. I'm sure you know I make only half that much in a whole week."

"Yes, I know," Ida replied, "but rest easy, Orville. I'll pay them a visit, and we'll see what happens. They will know I've paid my premiums and will see it's a good claim. Maybe they'll pay up on the spot. If they don't, I'll get a lawyer. No, I can't afford a lawyer, but we'll see."

When morning came Ida put on her bonnet and best gown and made her way to Evangeline Street where the offices of the company were located. The nearer she got, the slower she walked. At one point she was ready to give it up. What would she say? And what would they say? She told herself she was not an educated woman, particularly in matters of insurance, and they would be able to talk circles around her. Even so, she entered the building to see well-dressed men striding briskly down long corridors with papers in their hands. She opened a door with "Conference" etched on the glass panel and found herself in a room with three men seated at a huge table. They were in heated conversation. After a few minutes one paused to ask if he might help her.

"I have come," she said, her voice faltering, "to file a claim. I've had a policy with your company for years but never made a claim."

"Please have a seat near the window, Madam," the man replied. "I shall speak with you in a moment."

Turning again to the business at hand, the nattily

dressed gentleman picked up the thread of the conversation and went on with it. "I must tell you for the last time, gentlemen, Hawthorne Assurance is not under any obligation to pay the amount you insist upon. You are demanding nine hundred and the most we can pay is four hundred. You can take it or leave it. I am not instructed to offer more."

"Then we shall see you in court. You know our claim is a strong one, and our client, Wilkins and Son, won't accept anything less."

After curt and cold handshakes, the men gathered their papers and left. The insurance executive turned to Mrs. Crabtree.

"What can I do for you, Madam?" he asked courteously.

The tone of the tense conversation overheard by the woman had rattled her. She was nervous and could hardly speak. "I've come because of this," she managed to say, showing him the damaged umbrella.

"It appears to be somewhat burned," said the man in the expensive suit. "Is the fabric genuine silk?"

"It is, absolutely," Ida quickly replied.

He stroked the silk with long white fingers. A subtle aroma of eau de cologne hovered over him. "Why do you bring the item to me?"

"That umbrella cost a lot of money," she answered with hesitation, "and now it's burned with an unsightly hole and scorched."

"Yes, I can see that, Madam, but I'm really not at liberty to help you. Perhaps you should take it up with our Small Claims Department."

Ida was smart enough to know he was trying to give

her the runaround. She began to feel uncomfortable but also insistent. They paid claims in the hundreds but couldn't pay a few dollars to have a damaged umbrella repaired? The very thought incensed her.

"It's badly damaged," she insisted, "and I have a policy that covers it, and I never made a claim. I won't go to your Small Claims Department. Perhaps you see my claim as small but I don't see it small. It's the best umbrella I ever had and now it has a hole in it. I'm sure you know umbrellas with holes are worthless."

"You must understand, my dear lady, that for us it is indeed a small claim. I dare say the cost of putting a new cover on your umbrella, or even replacing it with a new one, would be less than seventy dollars. We deal in figures many times higher. But give me a moment, please, to check your policy."

"Just pay for the repair. Replacing it would cost a lot more."

"I don't have time to read all the stipulations of your policy, Mrs. Crabtree," he said, looking at the fine print, "but I really doubt we can help you. We are never asked to compensate trivial losses such as this. We don't handle household items like brooms, gloves, or umbrellas. Every day such articles are exposed to wear and tear and a chance of getting damaged. You do understand what I'm saying?"

"Oh, I understand all right. Of course I do! But you must understand that my policy covers this expensive umbrella. It is by no means a trivial loss, as you put it. I've always placed high value on this umbrella. I'm asking you to consider my claim seriously. You are not doing that."

Her courage, flagging when she entered the lush precincts of the insurance company, was now in full swagger. She was not about to give up without a struggle, and she was ready to speak her mind.

"You will find I am a policy holder in good standing. I have never failed to pay my premiums on time. I do not have any deductibles you can find in that policy. I make no threats whatever in this matter, but I demand that you live up to your promise to insure."

The gentleman wanted to shuttle her to another department but realized he couldn't. Nor could he convince her that her claim didn't fit their business model. She was wasting his time, valuable time he needed for more important matters, and so he spoke with an air of resignation infused with a hint of compassion.

"Will you kindly tell me how the umbrella was damaged?"

Ida felt she was winning the argument, but decided to make her case as strong as she could. "This is how it happened, sir. I put the umbrella in its stand but realized it was still damp. So I opened it to dry near the fireplace. A cinder popped out to burn it. My foolish charwoman put green wood in the fireplace, and it was popping like you wouldn't believe when I went to make myself a cup of tea."

The claims manager was now becoming just a little impatient. She heated a large boarding house with wood? He was aware her neighbors had switched to more efficient coal.

"What value would you place on the repair," he said with a sigh. "It wouldn't be an ugly patch but a new cover of high-grade silk. All the hardware seems in good condition."

"I don't know," she replied. "I will have to leave that to you. All I know is I sacrificed to buy that umbrella."

"You will have to get a quote from a good artisan."

"I can do that. I'll have the umbrella repaired and bring the bill to you. Is that acceptable?"

"It is indeed, and there will be a small adjustment in your favor to cover inconvenience. Our cashier will cut you a check for the amount shown on the bill plus a little gratuity for your trouble."

Ida Crabtree thanked the man and made her exit as fast as she could. She wanted to be out of his sight before he changed his mind. She went directly to a well-known umbrella maker who advertised his services frequently. It was a first-class shop catering to the wealthy. She entered with high confidence and asked whether the man behind the counter were the owner. With reserve and a little bow he said he was.

"I have a job for you," she announced imperiously. "I want this umbrella repaired with your best silk. Work carefully with it and use the strongest and most durable silk you have. I know the repair will be expensive, but money is no object. Please have it done in a few days."

Home again, Ida explained that because Orville was responsible for the burn and because she was compelled to consume an entire day to solve a problem he caused, he would have to pay for the repair. However, and she paused to let it sink in, he would not pay the entire sum. She was willing out of the goodness of a generous heart, and because she liked her boarder, to accept only five dollars for six weeks.

At the end of that time Ida Crabtree had turned her loss into a sizable profit. Orville Hastings paid her thirty dollars. The insurance company gave her more than a hundred, and the umbrella man charged fifty for an excellent job. As it happened, the good woman endured a painful experience but gained a tidy sum. She spent the money to improve the comfort of her boarders. When another downpour pelted her house, she offered to lend her expensive umbrella once more to Orville. He politely refused, explaining he had bought at reasonable cost a good raincoat with a hood.

3

Eddie in Limbo

If you had been living in Blue Anchor during those turbulent days after the Civil War, you might have seen in the early morning a thin and halting man pushing the wheelchair of a frail but attractive woman through the narrow streets. Repeated day after day, the scene in time became so common that not even the hawk-eyed sheriff, or the men idling their time away in front of the barbershop, bothered to notice any more. The couple performing the ritual each morning had become a fixture of Blue Anchor and part of its life. Their clockwork activity was woven into the social fabric of the village. All who lived there had seen an old man hobbling behind a wheelchair, tending its occupant with care. Anyone could see he listened closely to every word she spoke.

"My dear Eddie," she would say in that soft, purring voice of hers, "what would I do without you?"

Looking embarrassed and shifting his weight from one foot to the other, invariably he responded in monosyllables or remained silent.

In his youth Eddie had been a Southern soldier in a

regiment of the Civil War that called itself the Fighting Falcons. He lied about his age and was shouldering a tall and heavy rifle when he was sixteen. The recruiting sergeant knew Eddie wasn't old enough to fight, but needed to fill his quota. With reluctance he signed up boys intent on becoming men. To become a man was to die if need be in a grisly war. Eddie fought in battles that killed his friends but somehow managed to survive.

Then one day as he lay recovering from a bullet buried deep in his left shoulder, he met a dashing young warrior named Robert Crawford. A second lieutenant in the regiment, Crawford saw promise in the boy and enlisted him as an orderly. Though it was not a position many soldiers envied, Eddie preformed his duties as instructed and got along well with his officer. Crawford rose rapidly in rank and soon became a captain leading a hundred soldiers.

However, at a pivotal turn in the war he marched his troops into a deadly battle that didn't go well. General Longstreet had warned General Pickett that it would be suicide to charge well-armed Union forces dug in on Cemetery Ridge outside Gettysburg. His soldiers would have to cross an open and unprotected field, climb the slopes in the face of withering fire, and fight the enemy hand to hand. Thousands of men in their prime would be killed, mowed down like blades of grass. With General Lee's approval, Pickett charged the Union troops despite Longstreet's advice. Captain Crawford with his company of poorly trained infantry bravely engaged the enemy and was severely wounded. Half of his men were slaughtered.

Pickett had sent 15,000 foot soldiers across open terrain into Union fire. Fewer than 6,000 survived.

Attended by Union physicians, Captain Crawford lay in hospital at Gettysburg for several weeks. When the worst was over they sent him back to Richmond. There he slowly recovered and thought he might be able to fight again. An ambitious soldier, his dream was to behave with valor, be noticed by superior officers, and be rapidly promoted. It did not happen. When the war ended, he was not the colonel he hoped to become but still a captain.

Eddie in the rank of corporal continued to serve Crawford as a competent and caring orderly. After the war both were discharged on the same day and went home to Blue Anchor. Crawford had a wife there and a big country house. Eddie with no family and no home of his own was given a room and a miniscule salary. Hardly without knowing it he became in civil life a servant to the man he had served in the army. He remained at the beck and call of that man for thirty years.

As the years passed Crawford became bitter and vindictive. It was all Eddie could do to serve a man who often required infinite patience. He would have given notice had he not been assigned to looking after Mrs. Crawford after she fell from a horse and injured her spine. The outing each morning encouraged a tête-à-tête from which a guarded familiarity arose between them. Fragile and needing his care, she needed his companionship as well. Her approval of the devoted servant was always expressed in soft and affectionate murmurings that he could barely hear. Whether he understood her exactly or not, his replies were always prudent and deferential. They talked almost as equals, and Eddie frequently managed to give her good advice. The foremost subject of their conversation was the uncertain disposition of the captain.

His wife and servant couldn't help but love the man, but now as they were moving with the years into uncertain old age they were finding his caustic temper intolerable.

"My dear husband was certainly not in the best of humor today, was he?" Bertha Crawford observed as they began their morning junket. "In recent months little things set him off and he explodes."

"You might say, dear lady, his anger grows each day within him. I seem to recall he was angry the day we left a defeated army. Now it threatens to consume him."

"Let's give the poor man the benefit of the doubt, Eddie. He's unfortunate. Before you came to know him he had shown himself a brave and capable soldier, got to be a captain fast. He expected a commendation and promotion after Gettysburg but got neither. He was brave but didn't win, and the brass just shunted him aside."

"Well, you might admit some of it was his fault. When I became his orderly I felt the sting of his arrogance every day, and so did his superiors. They would have done better by him if not for that. If he wanted so dearly to advance in rank, he could have been more humble. I can't understand why he deliberately rubbed people the wrong way."

"And now you and I are stuck with him. Anyone else would never put up with the man, but we have no choice. It seems we are victims of circumstance, Eddie, as well as victims of the captain. And the big irony here is that he himself is a victim."

"It's natural you make allowances for him, my lady. I

know you love him. But try to see the truth of the matter. We're the only poor souls in all the world willing to remain with him. Anyone else would have left in a hurry a long time ago. Oh, there's our bench! Perhaps I can sit on it for a few minutes and rest the old legs and feet?"

"By all means, dear Eddie. These morning jaunts must be very tiring for you. I sit here at my ease while you must push this heavy chair, and you're not a young man any more."

"I forget my age when I'm with you, dear lady, and your chair really ain't heavy. I'm pleased to push it so you can breathe fresh air and see the village wake up. Ah, this old worm-eaten bench feels good here in the shade. Almost like an easy chair, comfortable."

"I've been thinking, Eddie. I've been wanting to ask you this for a long time. Why have you stayed with Robert all these years? Why in the world didn't you leave him when he became irascible and short of temper and abusive? Your loyalty and love seem extraordinary."

"Well, I didn't have any folks to go home to, and when he said come and live here, I just felt it was the right thing to do."

"I married the man, Eddie, and so the laws of this nation as well as society demand I stay with him. In the early years he was handsome and attentive and I loved him more than you will ever know. But when he became self-centered and withdrawn and demanded I live in isolation, the love I had for him slowly began to fade. I still love him, I guess, but in a different way. I tell myself I'm all he has really."

"I don't like to admit it," Eddie muttered, stroking his

thinning beard with some embarrassment and hesitating before finishing what he was thinking, "but it seems to me he sort of owns me too."

"Oh, my! That's only in your mind! You can leave us any time you wish. He doesn't own you and neither do I. We have no slaves any more in this country. I'm sure you are fully aware of that. And it seems demeaning that a military man like yourself, a proud soldier, should think of himself as being owned by another person. I must admit we haven't treated you well at times. Robert demands so much of you, and we pay you so little. I can't understand why you've remained with us all these years when you could have left, married, and had a family."

"But Bertha, you must surely know! It's all so different with me."

When they were alone in private conversation he had fallen into the habit of calling the lady by her first name. Humbly he had asked if he might, and she had said it didn't offend her at all. In fact, she rather liked to hear her name on his tongue. Her husband had ceased to call her Bertha, and people in the village called her Mrs. Crawford.

"You are not a simple farm boy," she said, pursuing thoughts not quite in harmony with his. "You have an education. Your speech shows refinement. I know you read a lot in that little room of yours."

"I do. I like to read, and I like to study too. I never had a formal education like you. I went into the army when I was only sixteen. But after I got out and came to be a servant in your house I spent lonely hours every evening searching all manner of things in books. You and Captain Crawford have a grand library, and you were so good to let me have the run of it. He's been edgy at times, even ugly I might say, but you've never treated me badly even once. I've had to put up with some harsh words from him when he gets in one of his moods, but I just tell myself that's in the order of things and live with it."

"That's all good and well, Eddie, but you could have left us long ago, could have found a well-paying job to challenge your intelligence and ability, could have had a much better life than you've had here. So why did you stay with us and blast any hope of securing a good future?"

"It's the fault of my personality," he stammered, "my disposition or whatever you want to call it. My old mama used to scold me for not standing up for myself. She said I was weak but I proved her wrong. I was a soldier and I fought in bloody battle. I killed young men. I'm not proud of that, mind you, but warfare demands you kill or be killed. I managed to live when most of my buddies in that barbaric war died, or went home dazed and daft with limbs missing."

"War is a terrible thing, Eddie, but you were never weak. Surely you must know that. You're the strongest person I've ever known, and I've known you for many years. But why do you blame your disposition for giving up so much to be with us? I don't understand."

"When I become attached to a person it's like glue. I mean it's like someone slathered glue on us and stuck us together. When I become attached, I stay with that person through thick and thin. Attached, you see, completely and permanently attached."

Bertha Crawford began to laugh. It was a lilting kind of laugh, and he laughed with her. He liked nothing better than sharing laughter with her. Spontaneous and unexpected, it gave meaning to his life.

"You're not going to tell me our captain's sweet and lovable personality caused you to become attached to him all these years. Now be honest, Eddie. He was never sweet and lovable, and you know it."

Eddie was becoming visibly embarrassed. The bench was hard under his thin buttocks. He squirmed to attain comfort and laced the fingers of his hands together in fidgets. Behind his gray beard, speaking incisively in the still air, he gave away his long-kept secret: "I was never attached to him, my lady, never at all. It was you!"

The woman in the wheelchair spun around surprised to observe her servant carefully. "I, my poor dear Eddie, I? What exactly do you mean? Oh, you must tell me, please."

He looked up into the air and trained his gaze on the tree tops. Then he began to study the gravel that surrounded his feet. How clean it looked. How could it be so clean when people walked on it every day? He turned his head so as not to look at her, as timid people do when forced to reveal a shameful secret. Then he summoned his trooper's courage, that same feeling he had when ordered to the front line in ferocious battle, and spoke clearly.

"I will explain, my lady. It happened this way. Don't you remember? Captain Crawford was wounded at Gettysburg and lay in hospital there before the Union physicians sent him back to Richmond. In that city in convalescence he composed a love letter and bade me deliver it to you in person. You gave me a silver dollar and a smile that went to my heart. I wish I could say I still have that dollar, but I don't. I had to spend it for a new shirt. Anyway, I never forgot the look on your face when I gave you that letter. Now you understand what I'm saying?"

"I must be turning dense in my old age, Eddie. I am sorry to tell you I do not understand. I need more details."

He looked into her face as if searching for something. His little blue eyes had a look in them she had never seen before. She could feel her heart begin to flutter, and the palpitation made her nervous. In her lap she found her Japanese fan and cooled her face with it. Then Eddie was speaking louder than usual, louder and with excitement as though confessing a hideous crime.

"I fell in love with you, my lady! I fell in love with you! It happened when your hand touched mine receiving the letter. There! Now you know! Maybe you don't believe in love at first sight, but I do. I thought I would never have to tell you, Bertha, but now you know."

"Oh, Eddie! Why didn't you tell me this twenty years ago?"

That good and gentle woman hung her head and said nothing more. In seconds it all became clear to her. This poor creature, moved by immense devotion, had given up everything life had to offer to be near her, to serve her, and say nothing of the enduring affection he held for her. She wanted to cry. She wanted to press her face against his chest and sob without restraint. Sadly and with deepest resignation, she asked her servant with all the politeness she could muster to take her home. He rose and with a sprightly step began to push her chair homeward.

4
Bradshaw the Miller

In the summer of 1861, when Matthew and Catherine Kingston came to live with her widowed father, Jeremy Clay, his barn had several cows, an aging pony, a gentle mare, and a steer. In 1862 errant Confederate soldiers killed the cows for food, slaughtered the mare for grease, and harnessed the steer to an ammunition cart. Even though the pony seemed worthless, the soldiers thought it might yield some grease to lubricate firearms, and so the squad made ready to kill the animal.

"Stand down!" cried the sergeant in command. He was young, only twenty, but spoke with authority. "We're not scavenging in enemy territory, men. It's a Southern farm we have here, and we can't hurt them people inside that house no more than we have to. I say spare the pony and hang on to a little humanity."

"I'm with you, Sarge," said a lanky private lowering his weapon.

"We're with you too!" yelled the entire squad. "Spare the pony!" And they did, though little else was spared.

Prowlers in the night came later, searching for anything

they could get their hands on. They found nothing of value beyond the pony. Desperate men and women, they decided to hitch Peg to the cart they found in the barn and drive away in grand style. They were thwarted when they found the cart had a broken wheel. Anticipating the theft, Jeremy Clay had removed the good wheel and replaced it with a broken one. The subterfuge sent the ragtag scavengers, homeless and hungry, to another farm a mile away. They found it deserted.

Peg remained in her stall unharmed and was used sparingly in season to pull the cart to the local granary and mill. One fine morning in early May, Matthew flicked the reins to guide the pony to the loading dock in back of the mill. Finding no one there, he brought the cart to the front of the building and looked for other customers doing business.

"That's strange," he said to himself. "There ought to be activity here, people and wagons. Looks like something happened here."

He jumped from the cart and went through the open door. Though the sun was already above the horizon, the building was cold and dark and very silent. In one of the work rooms he found the miller, Samuel Bradshaw, crouched in a corner behind empty barrels. The rotund man was in his flannel nightshirt, distraught and shivering. Confederate soldiers had come in the night looking for his three sons. With papers showing the Bradshaw brothers had been officially conscripted into the army, they ransacked the house and the mill. When they found no sign of the brothers, they demanded to know where they were hiding.

The full story of the disturbance, as Matthew prodded for details, came vividly from the miller.

"The penalty for aiding and abetting enlisted men who will not serve," said the burly sergeant, "is death. You can be shot, old man, or do you want to be hanged?"

"I know nothing, Mister, nothing. My sons are farmers only."

"Address me as Sergeant! You identify as Samuel Bradshaw. These papers show your sons are strapping, grits-eating, Southern recruits. They are soldiers now, and the army needs 'em. If they run and hide like rabbits, they'll be hunted down like rabbits and shot."

With typical stubbornness Bradshaw told the violence-prone soldiers nothing. They slapped his face, pulled his hair and jabbed him roughly in the ribs, but he refused to tell them what they wanted to hear. A private found a length of rope, fashioned a hangman's noose, and tossed it over a rafter. Two soldiers put it around the miller's expansive neck and lifted him squawking from the floor. When he began to claw at his throat in terror, his eyes beginning to bulge and his mouth foaming, they let him down.

"Speak, dammit!" the sergeant shouted.

Bradshaw remained silent. He was lifted again, and again they let him down to recover. Then for a third time they hoisted the cringing old man. His nightshirt was soaked with urine and soiled; his feet pointed downward. The moment he ceased to kick they lowered him to the floor. The miller's middle-aged wife came running from the house, her nightgown above her knees. Hysterical and sobbing, she pleaded.

"Please don't hurt my old man, please! He don't know a thing! Our boys left us five days ago. We can't tell you anything."

"You will tell us, Mother Hubbard. You know where your sons are hiding, and you will tell us. We have ways of making you tell."

A soldier grabbed her by the shoulders and stood behind her. Another threw her gown over her head, revealing her voluminous bloomers. They hooted and howled at their little joke and demanded to know the whereabouts of her sons. She could not or would not tell them anything. They were about to lash her to a post and whip her with a thong when an officer rode up to intervene.

He told the woman to go back into the house and ordered the soldiers to release her husband. They threw their victim bodily into a stack of barrels. As he lay there groaning, grasping his burning neck, the officer asked if he were the owner of the mill. Bradshaw, barely able to speak, named Josiah Bosh, a local Quaker, as the owner. He himself was merely an employee, the manager.

"That Bosh is the one we should be stringing up," said the mouthy sergeant. "Them Quakers have scores of strong sons that ain't serving. They call themselves Southerners and breathe Southern air and eat Southern food and own land all over hell and creation but won't do a damn thing to help us win this stinking war."

The lieutenant, though calm and polite, was inclined to agree.

"The Quakers," he said to Bradshaw, speaking with only a trace of anger, "by keeping good men out of the army are making it very difficult for you and me. They could help the Confederacy enormously by simply putting their faith in their pockets until the war is won. They could be leaders, those people, but they refuse even to serve."

The miller thought it unfair that his sons would have to fight and perhaps die while the big and strong son of Josiah Bosh, simply because he was a Quaker and able to pay the exemption tax, would experience no pain. At that moment he might have indicted his employer but said nothing. He knew that if Bosh got in trouble with the authorities, he too would be in trouble, would be out of a job. The officer urged Bradshaw to persuade his sons to come forward and face their obligation like men. In the dank and dark corner, his body quaking with cold even as his neck burned to blisters, Bradshaw groaned.

He lay there shivering among the barrels, sleeping on and off, until Matthew arrived early that morning. They went into the house to find his wife Maggie cowering under a bed. They had to lift the bed to one side and coax her from her hiding place. She was terrified but had suffered no harm except for a skinned knee. Bradshaw fixed a breakfast for her as Matthew calmed her with quiet talk. She drank bitter chicory coffee, ate some griddle cakes fried in bacon grease, and slowly regained her composure. She spoke not a word.

Matthew left the mill with three sacks of cornmeal, Peg pulling the cart. The day was cool and quiet under brilliant blue skies. Pale morning glories beside the road were in full bloom. Their heart-shaped leaves were as green as green could be, and Matthew couldn't resist plucking one for his wife. An amber-crowned kinglet, startled by a human hand probing its domain, screeched a high-pitched note of alarm and flung itself skyward. A bumblebee, browsing among the flowers seeking nectar, didn't appear to notice either bird or hand.

With a gallant little bow and a flourish, Matthew presented the verdant heart-leaf pasted on a yellow piece of cardboard. He knew she would be upset when he revealed what he had seen and heard, but maybe the little gift would calm her. She received it with a gracious smile and fondly kissed his cheek. As she listened to his story, the smile dissolved into a frown of dismay.

"The Bradshaws today," she said with growing alarm, "the Kingstons tomorrow. You and Jesse, God forbid, and even your father."

She paused, trying to read her husband's reaction. Her brown eyes were bright with tears and her voice shaking with anxiety.

"Don't worry about us," Matthew cautioned. "It's not a good thing to worry about something that might never happen."

"When things spiral out of control, how can I not worry?" she asked. "How can I not be anxious? Your little brother learned that a large detachment of Rebel soldiers is on its way here. They will grab anything they can use, anything. He and his sister are in the south pasture right now, looking for a better place to hide the heifers."

"If anyone can find a better place for them, Jesse and Anna will do it. And don't you worry about Confederate soldiers moving through. They won't be on a rampage like

Northern soldiers. They are not the enemy, Catherine, and they will not harm us."

"They won't harm us? The word is out that Confederate soldiers raped a black woman in Atlanta and shot her husband dead when he tried to stop them. I heard another rumor too, one even worse. White women are now being raped, and shot when they scream."

"Atrocities happen in wartime, but maybe the worst is over."

The worst was not over, not for the Bradford brothers. They came out of hiding and were briefly trained as infantry soldiers. They died in the first battle they fought near New Bern, North Carolina. The miller and his wife didn't receive news of their passing until well after the war. Stilted military language told them their sons died as valiant soldiers resisting a massive invasion of Union forces. Later the old couple learned they died by accident when canister shot exploded.

Catherine Kingston made it a habit to pray every evening for the war to end soon. It did not. It dragged on until the spring of 1865. Some units were in deadly battle as late as the end of August. In Washington, Abraham Lincoln was assassinated by a well-known actor in league with the Southern cause. The assassin was hunted down and shot dead by a Union soldier twelve days later. The soldier was arrested for disobeying orders but later released and honored as a hero. The Kingston pony, grandly named Pegasus but feeble with age, stumbled one morning while grazing and fell into a ditch. Matthew had to shoot her.

5
That Lonely Place

When the time came to make the hard decision, Matthew Kingston refused to pay the tax that exempted Quakers from military service in the Confederate army. After his induction, he was given three days to put his affairs in order. As he did so, his wife and mother raced against time to create for him a durable shirt. His friends and relatives in Blue Anchor promised to look after his family while he was away. Little brother Jesse would care for the heifers hidden from scavengers and forage in the swamp to fill the wood box for winter. Quaker friends would help his father-in-law harvest crops he might be able to salvage, and the women would assist his wife in her daily routine.

At the general store Matthew was expected to discourse at length on his reason for joining a North Carolina regiment but said little. His wife, looking stronger than she felt, stated flatly the war would soon be over. Her husband would be home again before anyone missed him. She was trying to make a joke even as a tear appeared in one eye. It trickled down her cheek, revealing her struggle to hide her misery.

Near the end of the day Jesse came over to the little house under the sprawling live oak to milk the heifers he had hidden behind bushes in the long sweep of pasture. As he was picking up the milking pails, he hesitated a moment and fumbled in his pocket.

"Here," he said abruptly to Matthew, "I want you to have this."

He held in his hand the precious pocket knife his father had given him when he turned twelve. Smiling acceptance, Matthew received the knife without hesitation. He knew at once that Jesse had chosen that way to express an awkward love for his big brother.

"I'll take good care of it, Jess. One of these days you'll have it back, I promise. I may need the knife for all sorts of things. Thank you."

It was an uncomfortable moment for both, but the boy slipped away without a word and trotted to the meadow. The two heifers came to meet him as he crept through the broken fence. A strong fence could attract the attention of marauders looking for booty hidden away from the house. They wouldn't be looking for livestock behind a decrepit fence, and so it was left in disrepair.

The rich, thick grass was becoming wet with dew and released a damp and musty odor when disturbed. Crickets in the bush began to chirp, emitting a metallic trill that resonated in the still air. Jesse squatted on his haunches and worked at the udders of one cow as the other grazed nearby. Streams of milk squirted from under the boy's capable hands and made a slurping sound as they filled the metal pail. The second cow swung her head around as he milked her and snorted. He could feel her breath on his face and its smell in his nostrils. The profound repose of the place alerted his senses.

After the milking he drove the heifers to the sheltering clump of alder bushes and rearranged the jasmine that concealed the entrance. As he did so he thought he might be able to chase away some of Catherine's anxiety with a bouquet of flowers. He reached out to pick a stubby branch of the fragrant plant. Just as his fingers closed on the flowers, two ragged bats darted from the bush. Their tightly strung wings nearly brushed his face as they hurled themselves skyward, and they startled the boy. He uttered a loud cry that was not quite a scream. Instantly a scratchy chagrin rose in his throat, and he chided himself. He would soon be a man, and a little thing like a bat shouldn't scare a man. He chortled uneasily, picked up the pails, and headed for the fence.

A gaunt and shadowy figure was standing on the other side. In the lingering twilight, Jesse couldn't be certain whether the person was a man or a woman. He approached cautiously, the flowers tucked in his wide belt and a pail of milk in each hand. He was thinking that maybe he had given his knife away too soon. He doubted he would ever use it in a rumpus, but to have it now would be a comfort. Loosely clothed in rags, the man looked like a scarecrow. Jesse had heard that deserters, some driven crazy by the horrors of war, were roaming the countryside. Just such a person had shot and killed their neighbor, Thomas Bolton. Was this another? Was he dangerous? Though his courage was flagging, Jesse went onward to the fence and set his pails on the ground. The scarecrow-man was laughing, cackling, and dancing a little jig.

"I heard you cry out, you fraidy cat! Fraid of your own shadow, you are! And flowers too! Oh, how girly sweet! Gimme that milk, boy! Harland Ebrow loves milk! Harland Ebrow's the name and fighting's my game! But now I'm on the run hiding from the sun! I'm a poet, don't you know it? I can make a rhyme any time. Woooeeee that's good!" It was the warm milk he was praising. He drank deeply.

The evening air becoming cooler, the skinny rawboned figure was shivering. He wore no shirt and his trousers were slit and torn. On his right foot was a military boot, but the left foot except for a ragged sandal was bare. Lean of frame with bony shoulders and long arms, he was so thin that in half darkness Jesse could count his ribs. Since he carried no weapon, he was no threat to the boy, nor to anyone but himself. Out of his mind, he was running from the horrors of war, and he was hungry. Jesse gave him the milk without hesitating. The derelict drank the entire pail, the thick liquid flowing from his swollen but grinning mouth to his sunken chest. He put the bucket down, wiped his mouth with a skinny arm, and smiled from ear to ear. In the dark face Jesse could see teeth that were gleaming white although two were missing.

"Gimme that other bucket," he demanded. "Harland Ebrow loves warm milk. It's better than a warm quilt or crazy guilt. I been hungry and cold and sometimes bold, but now I'm told I'm old. I'm tired too, and I ain't had no milk in a long time. You can keep the flowers, pretty boy. They don't bring no joy. But don't you never tell nobody you saw me here. Do I make it clear? Answer me, boy! No fear."

"Yes, sir," Jesse meekly replied, "I won't tell nobody."

The boy was shaken but not frightened. He knew the difference between jabber and threats and was inclined to pity the poor wretch. He obeyed the deserter because he had been taught from the time he was a toddler to obey adults who spoke with authority.

Harland Ebrow was unhinged but not free of anger. He thrust his haggard face forward, scowled for a moment, and laughed with a loud, cackling, croaking sound. His face was dirty and his forehead above the right eye lacerated. His lips were cracked and blue. A trickle of blood came from the dirty wound. Harland Ebrow had once been a soldier, perhaps a brave soldier, but something terrible had happened to him. It made him a comical harlequin figure bizarre and crazy.

The boy passed the second pail of milk over the fence to him. With grotesque facial distortion and jerky movement of his frail body, the man drank part of it, wiped his mouth with the back of his hand, cackled, and said he would keep the rest for later.

"You don't mind losing the bucket, do you, boy? Well, I don't mind if you do mind coz I'm not a bit kind! To hell with you, boy. Go home!"

Then hesitating as he turned to leave, the fugitive swung around and blurted, "Gimme that belt! I can use a good belt!"

Jesse gave him the wide belt but kept the flowers. The wraith fastened the leather around his skinny waist and loped eastward along the fence, swinging the pail in one hand and cackling. Harland Ebrow was on his way to find shelter in the swamp and meet other fugitives hiding there. If he could trust even one of them, he would perhaps trade the belt for a bit of food or a shirt.

There in the swamp dwelt men of all ages, from scraggly teenage boys to gaunt old men who had lost all their worldly possessions late in life. They were called swampers and were rarely seen, except when stealing corn or potatoes near dark. Troubled by calamity and often desperate, they were tolerated by the farming community. No one knew exactly where in the huge swamp they came from, nor where they were going. They were seedy-looking characters, and the villagers avoided them. However, at times a compassionate farm wife would place food on a stump for them. After the war some of these men attained high position in the costly bureaucratic effort to restore the South. They were called leaders, and yet to the end of their lives they wore their hangdog look even when wearing a frock coat and top hat.

Jesse, who knew as little about the larger world as about the horrors of war, climbed through the wooden fence and scooted in the opposite direction toward his brother's house. Clouds hanging in the western sky suddenly opened, and it rained hard. He ran in the rain until his first wind was gone. When his second came, he ran even faster until he was breathing hard again and forced to dog-trot. He trotted across the meadow and through a clump of damp woods until the house came into view. Then he broke into a sprint, swinging the empty bucket, his shirt and trousers wet as new wash on a cloudy day. The scarecrow-man had taken his milk and belt but in return had given him the speed of an antelope. Matthew saw him tearing into the yard, the flowers clutched in one hand and the pail in the other. The boy stopped near the kitchen door, breathing hard, and scurried inside.

"The heifers had no milk?" his brother asked incredulously.

"They had plenty," said Jesse, gasping. "But a crazy man got it. He was thin as a rail, half-naked, tall as a stove pipe!"

Now reviewing what had happened, he felt a cold uncertainty running through him. Was the runaway really all that tall? Was it right to obey him with no resistance and give up the family's milk? Was it a wise thing to do, or cowardly? He had endured a time of crisis.

Matthew heard the story, quickly told in few words, and invited the boy to sit for a big slice of pecan pie made with honey. He relaxed at the kitchen table to recover from his ordeal, and his brother assured him he had done the right thing by the crazy man. After gulping down the pie and a tall glass of milk, the boy shyly gave the sprig of flowers to Catherine. She thanked him graciously but with an air of worry.

"It was scary meeting that fellow in that lonely place," he said. "But I guess he needed the milk more than us. He called himself a poet. Made rhymes and danced a jig and spoke rough. Then he stole my belt! But I'll find another somewhere."

"You can have this one," said Matthew, removing his own. "Keep it and wear it till I get home again. I leave for the army tomorrow."

The shower had moved onward. Standing on his porch, Matthew could see Jesse running home to repeat his story.

6

Ready to Ride

Five Confederate soldiers on horseback were riding up the narrow lane that led to a farmhouse near Blue Anchor. A horse without a rider trailed behind them. Clad in signature shades of gray, their weapons and trappings glinting in the patches of light between the trees, they projected raw power not to be resisted. Their horses were sleek and shining in the sun and snorting as they entered the sandy yard. A strong man with broad shoulders dismounted and sprinted to the porch. Unmistakably in charge, his knock on hard wood was neither gentle nor hesitating. It sent David Kingston to the door.

"Good afternoon, sir, I am Captain James Dawson of the Fifth North Carolina. Your name, I take it, is David Kingston?"

He bowed slightly and touched his fingers to the brim of his hat. It was a smart-looking slouch hat with impressive insignia and a golden cord encircling the base of its crown. Dawson was not a young man but appeared to be in fit condition. His eyes were tinted blue and under his nose was a mustache with specks of gray. A proud and capable officer, he wore on his chest several ribbons of valor.

The dignified, simply dressed owner of the house, taller than the captain, calmly inspected the man in gray.

"Yes, that is my name."

"These papers tell me, sir, that one Matthew Kingston, your eldest son, is ready to ride with us. According to what is written here, he must come with us to Richmond at once. If he cannot provide a horse of his own, we have a temporary mount he may use for the journey."

David stepped aside as Matthew pushed forward to face Captain Dawson. "I am Matthew Kingston. I'm ready to go with you as instructed. But I must tell you I cannot and will not bear arms. I will do your bidding constructively but will not destroy."

"I've heard those words before," said Dawson. "Your papers identify you as a Quaker. Well, my advice is to put your Quaker notions in your pocket for now. You can dig them out later if your God allows you to survive and prosper. Join the army like the man you appear to be and fight like the rest of us. If the South is to win this war, every man among us will have to fight."

"I must repeat, Captain, I wasn't born to kill or be killed in a senseless war that most certainly could have been avoided."

Dawson looked a little tired. He pointed to a thin, stiff-legged horse that had once belonged to a farmer. A lanky sergeant with a sardonic grin on a long face covered with stubble held its reins.

"There's your mount, Kingston. Do you have traps? A bedroll? Extra clothing? Make haste, man. You will not waste my time with specious argument. Save that for a tribunal or judge if you must."

Catherine Kingston emerged with a knapsack full of clothing she had prepared for her husband. The dismay she felt on hearing the knock had now become a palpable calm. Though a nervous twitch made a mockery of pretty lips, her face was serene, her large brown eyes sorrowful but dry. Determined to control her emotions, she found strength in Quaker injunction handed down through the centuries. A good and loving wife, she was determined to appear strong.

Matthew slipped his arms through the straps of the knapsack and shouldered it. He kissed his wife and child, embraced Jesse and Anna, and bade a fond farewell to his father and father-in-law. He murmured something to Sarah, the faithful cook, as she withdrew to the kitchen dabbing her eyes. His mother followed him into the yard, looked sternly into his face, and kissed his cheek.

"Don't worry, Mama, I'll be all right."

"Of course you'll be all right. We all know that. But take care."

"I will, Mama. It's a promise."

"When you get home again, we'll have a big celebration."

All was quiet in the yard as mother and son spoke in private. Only the whinny of a horse, impatient and hungry, broke the silence. The soldiers shuffled their feet and looked on but said nothing. Then with a ring of authority a full-throated masculine voice issued a command.

"Sergeant, bring up the horse for this man. Now, Matthew Kingston, take your weapon and give it care.

It could save your life some day. Take it now and treat it well!"

The captain thrust a long Enfield rifle-musket into the hands of the man who had asserted he would carry no weapon. Carefully made in England for the Confederate army, it fell with a thump to the ground.

"That's no way to treat a friend you will soon depend on," said Captain Dawson, carefully controlling his anger. "Pick it up! Remember you are under orders now. You may not ignore a direct order."

Matthew didn't want a scene in front of his family, and he didn't wish to have his behavior interpreted as insolence or arrogance. So he picked up the heavy rifle and handed it to the captain. With its butt on the ground it stood nearly five feet tall. The officer put his hand around the thirty-nine-inch barrel to keep it from falling to sandy soil again.

"We have no time to waste, Kingston. I will not argue with you. For the second time I order you to take your weapon, mount your horse, and ride with us. You will not hear a third order. I will not explain to you why you must obey official orders."

"I'm under orders from a commander higher than you, Captain. He tells me not to shed blood. That command I must obey at all cost. I don't wish to appear rude or discourteous, but I'm not able to obey an order that may involve violence or death to another human being. I will ride with you but without the weapon."

"You speak nonsense that will get you killed. You must know I could have you executed at this moment for disobeying a direct order."

"I will ride without the weapon," Matthew quietly repeated.

Captain Dawson viewed himself as a reasonable man in full control of any emotion that might arise to trouble him, but now he was angry. To suppress the anger, to relieve exasperation he turned away from Matthew to survey the family the young man was leaving behind. They stood on the porch as witnesses and wisely did not interfere. Honest and hardy people wresting a living from the soil, they must have seemed to the captain eerily similar to his own family. His father, a small planter in Georgia, traced his roots to England as did the Kingston family. A church-going Baptist with religious feeling but with no creed strong as that of the Quakers, he readily became a volunteer early in the war. With his family's blessing and with no hesitation he went off to war.

He joined the army for the adventure it would bring and the chance to be a man among men. He quickly became an officer and within two years rose to the rank of captain. He felt as though he had found his calling. He wanted to command men but do more than that. He wanted to save what he considered a venerable and gracious way of life, and he was willing to lay down his life in that cause if need be. He deeply resented people calling themselves "conscientious objectors" because the war didn't jibe with their religious beliefs. "Put your religion in your pocket," he had said to more than one.

"You are not obliged to go with us," he was now saying after a long pause. "I am authorized to exempt you, for the present, if you pay the exemption tax. Are you not able to pay the fee and stay home?"

"I'm able to pay the tax," Matthew replied. "But I've chosen not to pay it because the money collected helps to fund the war. My religion forbids me to support this war or violence of any kind."

"I see that your wife is heavy with child. The papers I have here say you have another child. As a father and a Quaker the law allows you to stay home and look after your family. No able-bodied man should be exempt from doing his duty in these dangerous times, but the law is the law and I shall obey it."

"Thank you, Captain. But I've given a good deal of thought to the matter and don't feel easy buying my way out on religious grounds. I've heard that young men of other religious persuasion, Methodists and Baptists, can't buy exemption. Also the tax buys weapons that kill. I will have none of that."

Matthew sprang easily into the saddle and waited for the next command. The old horse trembled under his weight. Again when offered the rifle he wouldn't hold it or shoulder it or even touch it. Bemused and angered by the Quaker's stubbornness, and knowing that any moment the situation could spiral out of control, Captain Dawson turned to his sergeant and gave an order.

"Take the rifle and strap it across the saint's back. Strap it tightly, mind you, but don't assault or confront him. He will follow commands gladly when the time comes."

Sergeant Thompson obeyed with alacrity. Catherine's eyes flashed as she saw her husband wince involuntarily under the rough handling. He said nothing but sat tall and calm on the weary horse, peering into the eyes of the angry sergeant. When Dawson saw no further resistance, he allowed the man a moment with his wife.

She ran into the yard to say goodbye. Matthew's father went with her. She clung to the horse's stirrup, looking upward in anguish, but remained strong. She mumbled words of hope and encouragement and stepped away. With permission from the captain, David Kingston stood beside the docile horse and spoke to his son.

"Listen to me now and look at me. All that you encounter will leave a mark upon you for better or for worse. Let it be for better. Keep your mind open and calm. Take care, observe, absorb, and remember. If you do that, my son, today will serve you well tomorrow."

The family waved as the horses broke into a canter and moved swiftly down the avenue of live oaks. Grasping the reins with one hand, Matthew raised his left arm in a farewell salute. Steeped in biblical imagery, it flashed into the minds of the onlookers that the long rifle the man bore on his back had become a heavy wooden cross.

7

They Also Serve

The South fought hard that second day at Gettysburg but failed to breach the North's defensive line on Cemetery Ridge. More than a hundred soldiers in Matthew Kingston's infantry unit were slaughtered that day. They fought with courage, resolve, and purpose but fell blasted like clay pigeons in a shooting gallery. Their torn bodies littered the battlefield and became obstacles impeding the ranks of the living. As he stumbled over the dead and dying, the young Quaker was ordered to grab a rifle and fire at will. When he refused, firmly declaring he would not bear arms, Captain Daniel Thacker issued another order.

"Shoot him!"

Instantly two long rifles were leveled at the young pacifist, and the riflemen waited for the order to fire. However, before he could issue that order, the captain had second thoughts. If the Quaker wouldn't shoulder a weapon, he could and would attend the wounded.

"They also serve who bear litters!" Thacker shouted over the din of battle. "You will do that now, my young friend, or die!"

It was an order to help and not hurt his fellow man. In minutes Matthew began removing broken bodies to a field station behind the lines. It was hard and hazardous work but altogether necessary, and he could do it without compromising his beliefs. He was tired to the bone and suffering pain in every muscle when that second day at Gettysburg was over but survived the onslaught uninjured.

That night, though his aching body cried out for rest, he slept fitfully. Too soon the next day came. On that third day he was one of thousands in Pickett's infamous charge. Hapless soldiers marched double time across an open field to the slopes of Cemetery Ridge. Knowing full well they were easy targets, but knowing also they could do nothing about it, they ignored enemy fire as they sprinted over the fallen. Running with them with stretcher ready for use, Matthew was able to view the horror of strong men shattered.

Through the acrid smoke he could see crouching figures in blue firing point-blank at gray-clad figures hurtling toward them. The men in gray spun like whirling dervishes when hit. They were men in their prime, boys not fully grown, old men pushing sixty. Ripped apart and screaming as they fell, their precious blood stained the ground red. Most of them, thrashing in agony, held on to life as long as they could. Soldiers rushing behind them stumbled over the dying and were themselves trampled. Others vaulted over the dead and charged onward.

The air was pregnant with discordant sound. Matthew heard large-caliber bullets whizzing past his head. He heard them splat with a dull thud into human flesh, and the screams of dying men drowning all else. In a moment he was forced to decide whether a man was dead or alive before placing him on the stretcher. If a fallen soldier cried out, he and his assistant (a boy he knew only as Tom) tried to render aid. If the soldier lay still, they judged him dead and went for the living. Corpses so cluttered the field of battle they became a hindrance. An obscene number of young Americans died that day. So many fell on the stricken when they themselves were struck, it took many hours to clear the battlefield. When night came, crows circled the bloody ground and landed on the bodies of fallen soldiers to gorge themselves.

Though facing impossible odds, Southern troops somehow reached the Union forces to engage in hand-to-hand combat. Captain Thacker was one of them, and in minutes he was killed. Fewer than half of Pickett's force of thousands managed to survive. While Matthew Kingston was lucky that day, his assistant was not. The boy from South Carolina, not more than sixteen, caught a bullet in his right eye and spun to the ground, his young blood spurting skyward.

"If I don't make it," he whispered, "tell my papa I died in the midst of battle doing my job. And tell him this, please . . . dying ain't so hard."

In that instant Matthew deeply admired the boy even as heart and mind told him Tom was wrong. Dying *is hard*, especially for the young. Any leaf turning yellow in autumn cries out in silent pleading for sap.

The young Quaker shouldered the boy to the medical tent, stepping over contorted bodies but not attempting to duck the bullets. One came so close to his neck it tore his collar. Another ripped off the heel of his boot. His gray shirt, lovingly created by his wife and mother, turned smelly and red that day. Blowflies gorged themselves on the thick, warm blood that oozed from the boy's gaping wound.

A sharp and salty tang of something monstrous and ugly was in the air. Caustic battlefield smoke, hanging thick and blue-gray, burned Matthew's nostrils. A cloud of green vapor, its origin unknown, whirled, broke, and vanished. The reek was so strong the young man found it difficult to breathe. Gasping for breath, he stumbled upon a cot and placed the boy's limp body on it. Tom's blonde hair, matted with blood, glistened like crushed strawberries in the sun. Matthew looked into his distorted face and tried to speak to him. In the heat, stench, and rampant confusion, he asked for a last name but got no reply.

General Lee with his usual show of gracious magnanimity took full responsibility for the slaughter. "All this is my fault," he muttered. "I must surely take the blame. I alone am to blame for this terrible loss of lives." Racked by dismay at so colossal a failure, he was distraught and with good reason. He had trampled human understanding and left it bleeding. Though he would live to fight another day, the war that divided a nation was lost at Gettysburg.

8
We Have No Pigs

Rachel Kingston was setting the table for breakfast. In early morning April sunlight flooded her kitchen. "I do hope the quiet in Virginia means the war is winding down," she said as her husband entered the room. "Maybe our son will be coming home soon."

"Many Southerners," David Kingston replied, "are happy to know Confederate troops are fighting on despite being defeated at Gettysburg and Vicksburg. They don't want to believe the South is running out of men and supplies and teetering on the brink of defeat and disaster. For them losing the war is unthinkable."

"It's an attitude of quiet desperation," Rachel said, "or maybe not so quiet. I truly believe the South will fight to the last man. The soldier-scavengers will grab every pig, calf, sheep, and chicken they can lay their hands on. The recruiters will take every male above four feet who can walk. I worry about Jesse. He's underage, but they tried to lure him away once and will try again. I worry about you, David. They could take even a man your age."

"They won't if I pay the exemption tax," he said with a

half smile, "and that I won't do. Our son Matthew did the right thing standing up for his beliefs. If push comes to shove, I will do the same."

This was the first time Rachel Kingston had heard so radical an idea coming from her husband. Alarmed, she was about to tell him that under no circumstances would she see him leaving home to become a soldier. In normal times she placed God and religion first in their lives, but only in normal times. In a time of danger and distress, people of free will had to act on their own to insure their safety. That's when religion took second place to survival. Before she was able to put her thoughts into words, Sarah the cook called out from the parlor.

"Sojers here wanting somethin' to eat. Jes' two sojers in blue. They look kinda down in the mouth. Should I send them away?"

"We can't do that," said Rachel, leaving the kitchen for the parlor. "Enemy soldiers can't be dismissed with a flick of the hand, Sarah. We have to give them something, or they could tear the place apart. The cornbread you were ready to put on the table will go to them. I will invite them inside and hope they leave with no trouble."

"Did Sarah say they're wearing blue?" asked David.

"Bluecoats," Rachel answered. "Union soldiers, tired looking."

"I don't remember seeing bluecoats in the area," said David sotto voce, "but let's invite them in and get rid of them soon as we can."

The soldiers were already walking through the door and removing their caps. Rachel had heard that Union soldiers never bothered to do that. Later she learned the two removed their head gear to hide insignia that might identify them. Natives of New England, they were not observing Southern courtesy. Northern soldiers were known to barge into Southern homes wearing muddy boots and dirty clothing. They made themselves comfortable in any room they chose. These two had intentions of doing exactly the same.

Sarah brought in a platter of golden cornbread, and Rachel followed with a pitcher of milk. The men were young, rangy, and thin. Lines of exhaustion and stress creased their soiled and weathered faces. They were polite but cautious. In the same situation Southerners had killed Union soldiers. They thanked their host for the food and eagerly drank the milk while wolfing down the warm and tasty bread. It was not a time for table manners, only a chance to fill hungry bellies.

"You got some eggs?" asked the younger man.

Exhausted from hiding in enemy territory in unkind weather, his blonde hair was greasy, his pale blue eyes tired and bleary, his hands dirty. Clean and rested he would have looked like any young man in the village of Blue Anchor. He spoke the same language, but with an accent that Sarah found amusing.

"I really could eat some ham 'n eggs, Ma'am. I need ham and a dozen eggs! I could use a bath too, but I know I ain't gonna get it."

"We have no pigs," David bluntly replied. "Those were taken from us a long time ago. We have some hens that lay eggs, but the few we had on hand went into the cornbread. As for a bath, wouldn't it throw you off guard?

We're peace-loving people and would never assault you, but as good soldiers I doubt you want to believe it."

"You talk good, old man," said Gabe, the older of the two. "Just don't pay no heed to Luke. I'm convinced he's not all there. The war you know, it gets to some of us. But hens, you have hens. Well hens are chickens and I been told southern fried chicken is the best in the world. I want somebody to get out there and catch me a fat old hen and make us some fried chicken. Then after we rest a little we'll be on our way."

Sarah was looking at the soldier with mixed feelings. He was a dangerous invader, but his talk was strange and funny and causing her to smile broadly. Curiosity had gotten the best of her, and she had not retreated to the kitchen. She glanced at David and Rachel as if for permission to kill a hen and cook it. Rachel's look put her at ease.

"Hens are no good for fried chicken," David asserted, "too tough, you know. Old hens have to be boiled. I do wish we could offer you ham and eggs, or fried chicken, but our condition won't allow it. This war is a terrible thing for you, but it's taking its toll on us too."

"You do have milk," Gabe replied with a cunning smile, "and good milk too. That means you got a cow, a fine healthy cow."

"Sure does mean that!" said Luke, grinning widely.

As they spoke, Sarah eased away from the wall to return silently to the kitchen. The children were playing outside and she wanted to be there when they bounced into the room unaware of the visitors.

"Oh, no you don't!" Gabe cautioned. "You can go back to

yer kitchen, but don't you try to sneak no cow away from us. Our unit is gonna take us back gladly when we show up with a healthy cow that gives good milk. Now, listen up, all of you. No one leaves this room till Luke here goes out and gets that cow."

He drew his pistol and placed it on the table. It was a big and heavy revolver and even David shuddered as he stared at it. Gabe was more experienced than Luke and clearly the one in charge. Without waiting to receive the order, Luke was exiting the house to search the barn. He hoped to find a good cow they could take as a prize.

All this time Jesse and Anna were somewhere outside, and now they came into the kitchen with cheerful chatter and the usual clamor of young feet on the oaken floor. They were noisy children and seemed even more noisy now.

"Shusssssh, chillen," warned Sarah, her finger on her lips, "we have bluecoat sojers in the house!"

"Bluecoat sojers?" asked Anna, wide-eyed and curious.

"Union soldiers!" Jesse blurted, flying through the back door.

Anna remained in the kitchen, but Jesse was in the yard and running toward the barn as fast as he could. He didn't have to worry about the heifers. They were in the pasture and hidden, but the horse and mule were in the barn. He thought he might be able to hide them.

Suddenly Luke appeared in the boy's path, laughing at his efforts to reach the animals and make them secure. Though thin and exhausted, injured and losing strength, Luke was on a mission and menacing.

"That ain't gonna do at all," he said calmly, grabbing Jesse's arm. "The mule you can keep but me and Gabe really need that horse. I'm surprised to see such a fine animal after three years of war. Can't believe you still have him. Anyway the horse belongs to us now."

"That horse belongs to Colonel Cooper," Jesse solemnly replied, "He won't be pleased to learn you took him."

"Cooper?" queried Luke, his pale eyes blinking. "You say Colonel Owen Cooper? We heard of him. Told not to mess with him. Told he has connections in Richmond and Washington too. Chats with Jeff Davis and Abe Lincoln and has power from both. We won't tangle with Cooper. What proof you got the horse belongs to him?"

"Here," said Jesse, pointing to a small yellow tag attached to the horse's right ear. "He don't brand his animals like some do, says it's cruel to do that. He tags 'em and this right here is the proof."

The rogue soldier scrutinized the tag, and quickly returned to the house. Jesse could see he was nervous.

"No heifers in the barn," he said in an undertone to his companion, "and no horses we can ride. We need to get outta here fast."

"Sojers!" Sarah called from the kitchen. "More bluecoat sojers! I declare! At least a dozen on horseback and looking mean!"

Through the parlor window David could see a squad of bluecoats moving with purpose. He judged them to be scouts of some kind reconnoitering the region. If that premonition were true, a larger force would come behind them. Quickly he walked into the yard to greet them, hoping they wouldn't enter the house. Gabe and Luke, not at all happy to see their fellow soldiers, ran helter-skelter to the cellar. In the yard the squad stacked their rifles to make a cone and placed their kits in a ragged circle around it.

The brawny sergeant pushed past David without saying a word, entered the farmhouse as though he owned it, and made himself at home. In the tight little kitchen he smelled of sweat and leather and raw strength. His cap, which he didn't remove, was broadcloth with a leather visor. Above the visor and visible to David and Rachel were brass letters identifying the man's regiment and company. Placing his hand on a big pistol in a sturdy holster, he warned the enemy not to make any sudden moves. Then he asked many questions. By then the entire squad was in the house and looking it over. They were chasing deserters, the sergeant announced, two men on the run for more than two weeks.

"By now they are ragged, hungry, and dead tired," said the sergeant. "Have you seen them? We got reports they are in this area."

David remained silent, but Rachel expressed dismay. She was certain her house and yard would become a battleground should Johnny Reb happen to come that way. The bluecoats, leaning against the kitchen wall, assured her she had nothing to worry about.

"If any pathetic butternuts step foot on yer property," they said in simultaneous utterance, "we'll blast them to smithereens!"

"But you're only one squad," David observed.

"No matter," asserted the sergeant. "We got plenty behind us. But enough! We're here, looking for two low-down deserters. We got wind they're hereabouts and we gotta search this place."

David and Rachel as good Quakers believed in the sanctity of human life. They wouldn't lie to protect Gabe and Luke, but no religious principle demanded they expose them. They knew the penalty for desertion in those latter days of the Civil War was execution, and they shuddered at the thought. Both hoped the pair had managed somehow to leave their property without notice.

In the cellar the forlorn figures had found a small window. Glad that deprivation had made them bony-thin, they crawled through the window and ran like foxes for the woods. Savoring the excitement, Jesse ran with them. He told them to go eastward and hide in the swamp. When he turned to go home, he said they could sleep in a logger's shack for shelter. In early April it was chilly at night and often rainy.

"This sure is poor country to forage in," said Gabe, staring straight ahead and clicking his tongue. "I reckon your mama wouldn't care to see the likes of *us* again."

"I reckon not," Jesse replied, casting a friendly glance at the man and speaking the same idiom though with a different accent. "I reckon not. But maybe you'll do all right in the swamp."

9
The Changeling

If you had been able to examine Thomas Bolton's walking stick in those tumultuous months before the Civil War, you would have seen engraved on the handle a Latin motto expressing Bolton's world view: *Sine Labore Nihi:* "Nothing Without Work." Incessant labor had made the Southern planter a wealthy man and one who prized his possessions. No strain no gain was the philosophy he lived by, but fast-moving events threatened to take everything from him. Walking homeward from the Kingston farm that evening in autumn, and mulling over problems that defied solution, he felt frustrated and angry. *All the fruits of his labor,* he was thinking, *all those years* . . . but he did not finish his thought.

Suddenly from a cluster of trees came peals of derisive laughter. Stopping in amazement to listen and look, Bolton fastened his eyes on a vine-encrusted sweet gum tree near the road. In the silvery moonlight he could see a person high in the tree wearing only a loincloth. Standing on a limb and clutching a vine, he looked like a revenant from beyond the grave or a visitant from some other world. Though not a timid man, Bolton couldn't help being startled by the half-naked figure. The eerie sight glued his feet to the ground.

He took a deep breath, stared at the scene, and finally identified in the shifting darkness the changeling son of a former slave named Bupee Mwewa. A free woman, she had once been called Sally Search but now went by her Nyanja name. She lived with her wayward son in a rent-free cabin on the Kingston property, and they were known to every person in the village of Blue Anchor. Bolton knew the boy by sight, for often in the fall he would bring small game to the planter's kitchen to be dressed and cooked. When offered money, invariably he shook his head and mumbled guttural sounds. Offered a brightly colored toy or trinket that moved, he gladly received it with joy.

Ethan Search was known far and wide as a strange but harmless boy who took great delight in being close to mother earth. Bupee Mwewa proudly called him *Nature Boy* or *My Wild Child*. He had in fact many names. Some of the blacks called him *Thunder Man* after seeing him emerge from the Great Dismal Swamp near Blue Anchor in crashing thunder and pelting rain just as a storm was breaking. Others in the community called him *Wonder Boy* or *Bupee's Boy* or *that Changeling Child*. Isaac Brandimore, the learned village scholar, once called him *a polysemous person lacking full development.* Whatever the name he went by, Ethan Search was one with nature, in harmony with natural law, and joyous when not upset. Rarely unpleasant, at times for no apparent reason he cloaked himself in a dark mood and became explosive. At that moment he would find his voice and cry out in a high-pitched, animal-like call so eerie it grated on the nerves of all who heard it.

The boy could run like an antelope and swing from tree to tree on wild grape vines. In the sweltering swamp he displayed amazing agility, observers who happened to see him reported. Legend had it he could swing across several miles of the Great Dismal Swamp without touching the ground or stopping to rest. If he did rest, it was always on a limb high in a tall tree. He was thin as a rail but strong as a bear, and he seemed to have an uncanny knowledge of the swamp. Though judged by some as mentally disabled, many believed he could identify on sight all the plants that flourished there and name every animal living there.

In the labyrinth of the dark and mysterious swamp he never got lost, the old-timers at the general store insisted, and yet few were there to see him. Grizzled swampers eking out a living gigging frogs and trapping small game lived in or near the swamp and seldom talked to people in the village. The word got around, however, that every swamper to a person admired Ethan Search from a distance. Though known to everyone, the boy had no friends unless one named creatures of the wild as his friends. His mother reported that bears seemed to recognize him and gave him no trouble, bees refused to sting him, and mosquitoes never bit. Snakes sunning themselves on tree limbs coiled in readiness when they heard him coming, but never harmed him. The deer stood and blinked as he came and went, nodding their heads as if they knew him, and they never ran from him.

He had a special understanding of all wild things, of birdsongs for example, and some believed with a shrill whistle he talked to the birds and wild turkeys. The heat of summer made his ebony skin glisten, but the cold of winter never seemed to touch him. In the chill autumn air Thomas Bolton shivered in his heavy woolen coat, but Ethan's bare skin seemed not to feel the cold. Though the boy rarely made a sound, at times he cackled with high-pitched laughter that became his signature. When upset and unhappy, he spoke as clearly as a classical orator. On this night he was shaken and talkative.

"Thomas Bolton be an angry man! Thomas Bolton be a sly man! Thomas Bolton try to beat da clock! Hickory dickory dock! Try to beat da clock! But ol' clock keep on ticking, keep on ticking!"

He cackled in the still air and swung in a half circle on the vine. His feet came close to the planter's head as he swung to a limb nearby to squat on it. Again came the shrill, rhythmic incantation repeated three times without pause.

"Thomas Bolton try to beat da clock. Try to make da time stand still. Don't believe a cold, cold wind's gonna blow 'im over da hill!"

The wealthy planter stood transfixed, listening intently to every syllable. He was not afraid but suddenly felt heavy and cold. The lanky visitant rattled on and on, squatting on the limb and laughing. In the still night he uttered a piercing cry as if in pain and broke into a mocking singsong. He sat like a Buddha on the limb, pressing his palms over his ears. He released them and pressed again. Then of a sudden he became eerily serious, his voice curt and crisp in the autumn air.

"You won't never see Edna Becker again," he taunted.

"You done lost da best cook you ever have! Edna done gone to Canaan's happy shore, to Canaan's happy shore! You done lost her, Mars Bolton, and none too soon. People run from you now but not da ol' stranger at the doh! Hear what I say, Mars Bolton, hear it real good. Massa gonna sleep in da cold, cold ground! Massa gonna sleep in da ground!"

His words rang and sang in the moonlit darkness. Catching their cadence and swaying to their rhythm, he repeated them over and over.

"What does he mean by a stranger at the door?" mused Bolton. "And how could he know about runaway Edna? What on earth could his jabbering mean, if anything? And me sleeping on the cold ground? Hah! That's a laugh! I have a warm bed in a very comfortable house waiting for me. The little ape's an idiot and babbling nonsense."

The boy clutched the vine with one hand, swung in a wide arc, and dropped nimbly in front of Bolton. His burnished face just inches away, he stared into the troubled man's eyes. With perfect enunciation, as if carefully schooled, he repeated his bizarre diatribe.

"Edna is gone, my dear fellow, gone! Edna is gone to Canaan's happy shore. And a pale stranger waits for you, dear man, waits for you at the door! A pale stranger waiting, waiting! And you will sleep, Thomas Bolton, oh my goodness yes! You will sleep in the cold, cold ground!"

A moment later he turned to swing away. At that instant Bolton aimed his heavy cane at the vine. He brought it down with all his strength, intending to thwart the boy's escape. He didn't intend to injure Bupee's son. He wanted only to know what he meant by a stranger waiting at the door. But the cane missed the vine, smashed into the boy's skull, and laid him low. Surprised but snorting contempt, the planter stooped to examine the limp form. Although blood trickled from the back of Ethan's head, he appeared to be alive and breathing. As calm and still as the silence that surrounded him, he lay relaxed on the damp autumn ground as if asleep.

"It's a good thing his head is hard as a rock," Bolton said aloud. "He'll be all right. He'll wake up and find his way home."

The silent moon yielded and went behind a cloud. The countryside went dark and quiet even as a breeze rustled dying leaves. Except for Ethan Search, clothed only in a loincloth and lying peacefully at his feet, Bolton was dreadfully alone. For an instant he thought of covering the boy against the cold. But with what? He had only the coat he was wearing, and that he couldn't spare. Moreover, to leave such a clue behind for someone to find was lunacy.

He won't feel the cold, Bolton was thinking as he walked onward toward home. *The leaves will cover him like a blanket. He'll be all right. He'll wake up and go home before morning comes.* And so a nebulous doubt concerning the boy was galvanized into firm belief.

The next morning Leo Mack found Ethan Search half covered with fallen leaves lying near a vine dangling from a tree. The mother had waited in her cabin all night long, chanting an African feel-good song she hoped would bring him home. Though he was wayward and capricious and unpredictable, she loved the boy dearly. Later that day when they told her he was dead, something inside her died too. In solitude at home, Thomas Bolton drank a tumbler of brandy in two or three gulps. With a clean handkerchief dipped in turpentine, he wiped a red stain from his walking cane and went to bed.

Three years later when the war was raging and Bolton was on the brink of losing everything he had worked all his life to acquire, a Confederate deserter put a pistol in his face and pulled the trigger. An old servant in another room heard the soldier cry, "I'm sorry, sir! I'm sorry! You abruptly opened the door!" The deserter fled and Bolton's son, a Confederate major on his way to do battle, came upon the wounded man. He gave the servant money to look after his father and asked her to seek help from a midwife. She left in haste with all she could load into a cart.

Nine days passed in summer heat and the flies swarmed. A ragged vagrant, attracted to the empty house, stumbled upon Bolton's bloated body. It lay stinking on the floor near a soiled and stinking bed. Beside it, half hidden by a reeking, urine-soaked nightshirt, lay Bolton's expensive cane. The beggar seized it, struck the dead man with it as if defending himself, and ran like an animal being chased. *Sine Labore Nihil,* etched in gold and flashing in the sun, meant nothing to him.

10
Gone to Glory

In the afterglow of sundown the big stallion trotted with ease as the young woman clinging to her husband's waist bounced on the pillion. Saddened by sorrowful news heard that afternoon, they were on their way to open the Quaker Meeting House in Blue Anchor. In the distance they could see torches burning red and yellow as slaves from nearby plantations converged for the ceremony. The news that Ethan Search was dead had spread faster than a brush fire, and the slaveholders were allowing their workers to pay last respects to the half-witted boy. They had heard that when he was alive many blacks viewed the strange wild child as having mysterious powers and close to God. He was pure and innocent, they believed, and knew all the best places in heaven. Now they were saying he would live eternally as a harp-playing angel resting on fleecy clouds in sunshine and walking golden streets.

Thomas Bolton permitted his workers to honor the memory of the boy he called *the changeling*. He even supplied wagons for transport but with overseers on horseback. He knew it would be an emotional ceremony punctuated by weeping, clapping, and singing. It was worth the trouble and expense if it soothed the agitation of the black community. His overseers would look after his people — no worry there — and have them back on the plantation to begin work at the break of dawn. Not a single person in Blue Anchor suspected he had anything to do with Ethan's death. Of that he was certain, but one had to be cautious.

Matthew and Catherine Kingston, riding at a leisurely pace on Caesar, arrived to find the yard of the Meeting House filled with flickering and sputtering torches. Phantom-like faces darted and bobbed behind them. Dusty forms gyrated in the glare and smoke and seemed to be dancing to unheard music. Men and women dressed in their best clothing chatted in small groups, asking how could God allow Ethan to die so soon. Not a one could remember he had ever been sick, and all of them knew how adept he was in the forest. Matthew hitched Caesar to a post, slowly made his way through the crowd, and unlocked the entrance to the big white building. Four young men stood nearby ready to carry the feather-weight coffin inside.

In double file the mourners followed the coffin-bearers to the head of the middle aisle. The men rested their burden on sturdy sawhorses in front of the gallery. In the cavernous room families and friends fanned out to find seats. Some of them sat as close to the coffin as they could. The torches had been stacked in brightly burning pyramids in the yard. Their flickering, uneven fire threw eerie shadows on the yellow-pine interior walls.

Candelabra at the head and foot of the coffin struggled to throw light on the boy's face.

A steady flow of silent figures filed past to take a last look at Ethan. Often screwed to a grimace when alive, his face was now relaxed and almost pretty. A little girl said later that when she paused to look at him, he winked. Mystery had always surrounded the boy who could fly like a bird on a grape vine. The mourners passed in front of the coffin, looked at Ethan in a white muslin shirt, mumbled a few words, and took their seats on the brown benches with tan cushions. The sound of their shoes on the bare wooden floor blended with a low murmuring that ceased when the service began. Bupee Mwewa, and the tall preacher stood near the coffin. The mother seemed almost childlike in the black dress Catherine had given her for the occasion. She looked like a little girl craving solace under heavy misery. Above them were the unoccupied benches of the gallery. Except for a cough here and there, profound silence filled the room. The service was about to begin.

From her seat Catherine could see diaphanous shades jostling one another in the gallery. As the lean and stringy preacher rose to speak, the figures floated upward from their seats, loomed from the ceiling and swooped downward. When a cold chill ran down her back, she remembered something her father had said when she was a little girl: "*There's some folks that see things, sweetie, and there's some that never see even the stars. It's all right to see things others don't see. It's all right.*" That remembrance brought a feeling of comfort to the young woman. Most of the time her eyes were open to see the thing as in itself it really was, but sometimes she looked beyond the thing to see the marvelous and unexplained. That was happening now.

When the preacher turned, while sermonizing, to stare at the space above him, she caught her breath with surprise and wonder. She was certain that he too had seen and recognized the visitants and was acknowledging their presence. As he stared at the gallery benches, seats that everyone else saw as empty (for no dignitaries were in attendance), he must have seen the dream-people too. Surely he saw blue and purple apparitions meld into a smoky mass, rise to the ceiling, hover there for a moment, break from one another, and sink back into separate seats. With knowing eyes she had seen them, and it pleased her to know this man had seen them too, but when she looked again they were gone.

A nocturnal wind was rising, soughing in the moss of the live oaks, blowing the pungent smoke of the torches through the half-closed door and down the aisle. In the blue haze the baritone voice of the rangy preacher rose and fell in measured cadence. The sweet chariot, he said, had swung low to take one of God's gentlest children to and through them pearly gates, leaving the sorrowful mother behind to mourn. He spoke with his thin arms outstretched until he could sermonize no more. Then a large man with a large voice began a hymn. One by one the others picked it up, accompanying the swelling chorus with a muffled tapping of feet. Their bodies swayed back and forth as the old hymn grew louder and more animated. When the singing ceased, the angular preacher rose again. His voice was soft now, curiously at peace as he spoke of the grave and the eternal life beyond. Gazing once more into the gallery, Catherine saw only a wisp of blue vapor hovering above the benches. Resin in the torches was sending a stream of smoke.

With the preacher's last word the ceremony ended. The men in charge of the coffin stepped forward to close it and nail it shut. They paused for a moment to allow Bupee Mwewa, resting her head on the pine box, to move aside. They waited with a show of patience and courtesy, but the woman did not stir. The preacher gently touched her arm and took her elbow to lead her away. Again she didn't move, her head remaining on the coffin close to her son's face. The preacher nudged her shoulder to encourage her to move away. Instead of walking with him, she began to slip downward to the floor. At that moment the preacher saw what had happened. He looked to the ceiling, raising his hands to the rafters, and cried out for all to hear.

"Oh my! Oh my, good folks! Looky here! The good Lord done come and took Bupee to be with her son! She done gone to glory, gone to them pearly gates here and now with Ethan waiting!"

A movement like a rogue wave in a tempest told Matthew that unless something were done fast, there would be a wild rush to look at Bupee's face. It could turn into a stampede, injure or kill people, and make a mockery of the ceremony. If the mounting excitement were not contained, pandemonium would surely break out with force. Something had to be done to calm the mourners and keep them in their seats. Quickly Matthew left his place beside Catherine and went to the coffin.

"Start a hymn," he said to the thin preacher with the big voice.

"But we must care for Bupee," said the man of God. "She done gone to her heavenly reward and we got to respect her remains."

"Start a hymn at once," Matthew repeated. "Please do it now!"

Sensing the urgency in the young man's words, the preacher opened his hymnal and asked the congregation to turn to page 117. They would sing of traveling glory bound to sweet Canaan's happy shore. And they would sing "Amazing Grace," a hymn everyone loved. For the length of the hymns, the collective feeling to view the miracle up close was kept in check. As the singing ended Matthew hesitated, unsure what to do next. To ask the preacher to start another hymn would impede the progress of the ceremony and frustrate the audience. A delaying tactic so obvious was indefensible. The ceremony had to continue.

Then came an idea, in outline so simple and so beautiful Matthew wondered why he hadn't thought of it earlier.

"Can we bury them together?" he asked a pallbearer.

The man looked at him with wide eyes and shifted his weight on the wooden floor, taking time to absorb the question.

"I think we can," he answered. "Bupee is small and this box is uncommonly wide. It was built for a man, not a boy like Ethan."

Matthew asked the preacher for his opinion. The man could think of no similar event ever occurring in his ministry, but was certain no person in attendance would object. Bupee had wanted desperately to remain close to her son, and she would now have her wish. He was delighted that he could help her in this small way. Just as the assembly was becoming restive, two men lifted the tiny woman gently and placed her beside her son. A little girl in her Sunday best, one who had known them both all her life, placed two small handkerchiefs over their faces. In her mind the pieces of delicate fabric, glowing against dark faces, were the gowns the two were wearing as glorified angels in heaven.

The baritone preacher, smiling approval, now led the gathering in prayer. Then standing and swaying and lifting their voices to the heavens, the friends of Bupee Mwewa and Ethan Search sang a soulful resurrection hymn. As the last strains of the hymn hovered above the congregation, the coffin was closed, nailed shut, carried out by men at each corner, and placed in a cart. The burial plot was nearby, and a lengthy ceremony was conducted there. The entire community believed Ethan had lost his grip when swinging on a vine and fallen. In his comfortable bed at the Bolton estate, the man who had killed him by accident, by a sorrowful twist of fate, slept soundly.

11
Dueling at Dawn

Not a person in the village of Blue Anchor knew that Thomas Bolton, the wealthy Southern planter who lost it all as the Civil War was ending, once fought a duel. It happened some years before he bought one of the largest plantations in the region with many slaves to work it. The year of the duel was 1846 and the season was summer. Young Bolton belonged to a prominent North Carolina family but was living temporarily in New Orleans. He had met and married in that city a Southern belle named Henrietta Bibideaux. She was pregnant that muggy evening when they had dinner at a fashionable restaurant with friends. A good-looking woman, she became more beautiful as her pregnancy advanced. That caught the eye of a gentleman seated at a table nearby.

In those days Bolton had a voracious appetite and was deep in a dish of red beans and rice when his wife touched his hand, brought her lips to his ear, and whispered: "That man over there, dear. He keeps staring in our direction, staring at *me.* Do you know him?"

Her husband turned to look. "No, I can't say I do know him. Rather handsome young fellow. Is he bothering you?"

"In a way, yes. He's making me feel a tad uncomfortable."

"My dear, he's paying you a compliment," said her friend. "You must know men don't usually look twice at a pregnant woman."

"You must know as well," said the woman's husband, "that if every ill-mannered person we see in public places were to offend us, we wouldn't have time to do anything but complain. Wouldn't have time even to enjoy this splendid seafood."

Bolton was inclined to agree with that sentiment but also felt it was his duty as an honorable man to confront the gentleman. Known even then for a fiery temper, abruptly he stood up and went to the man's table. He felt he couldn't allow some insolent fellow to leer at Henrietta and spoil a delightful evening with good friends. It was up to him without hesitation to preserve the honor and dignity of his attractive spouse and set the fellow straight.

"My wife, sir, tells me you've been staring at her and making her feel uncomfortable. She's in the family way as you can see, and perhaps that makes her a bit more sensitive than usual. As far as I'm concerned it's a small matter, but I'm asking you to direct your gaze elsewhere. You may look at some other woman if you are so inclined, but please direct your eyes away from her."

"Oh, ho!" the man exclaimed, jumping to his feet. "Now you listen to me! I will look at your wife or any other woman as long as I please. It's a free country, sir! And there is no law that forbids a man to look, even leer at a woman if he so chooses. Now leave me, sir!"

"I will ask you again, my good man, as politely as I know how. Leave off staring at my wife. It's indelicate and makes her uncomfortable. If you're not looking for trouble, you will direct your gaze elsewhere."

"Well, old boy, perhaps I *am* looking for trouble. I'm responding to your silly insistence politely but losing patience. Get out of my sight!"

That was the tipping point. Bolton seized the man by the shoulders, spun him around, and pressed his face hard against the wall.

"I will not brawl with you in a fine restaurant," he hissed in the young man's ear. "You and I will settle this matter at a later time."

He flipped his card of identity on the table. His antagonist glanced at it and presented his own. In one motion Bolton accepted the card and slapped the man hard. The slap across well-toned cheeks made a sharp, crisp sound for everyone to hear. Paul Johnson, the name on the card, did not retaliate. A waiter nearby quickly led Bolton back to his table. For a moment the restaurant was eerily quiet. Then polite chatter resumed mingled with the sound of silverware on good china.

Home again Thomas Bolton knew he was in for a duel. The state of Louisiana had outlawed dueling as early as the eighteenth century, and yet driven by Southern codes of honor the practice persisted. If the duel were to take place, Bolton would have to find an isolated locale somewhere near Lake Ponchartrain. Forty miles long and twenty-four wide, its shores had many isolated places suitable for illicit activity. He and his friends would have to find a dueling site and follow centuries-old rules. Carefully chosen "seconds" would be on hand to guide the combatants in protocol and choice of weapons.

After Henrietta went to bed, amazed and saddened by what had happened, Bolton strode up and down his well-appointed parlor for an hour. No longer angry but agitated, he talked in undertones to himself. He had done what honor required him to do, had proven himself a Southern gentleman. News of the duel would eventually emerge, and he would be the talk of the town. Some of the most powerful men in the city would meet him in the street or drawing room and congratulate him for correcting the behavior a boorish, arrogant lout. Influential people would see him not as an outsider from another state but as one of their own, a denizen of New Orleans in good standing.

Under the stress of the moment he was speaking out loud to himself. More than once he had scolded a friend for doing that, for didn't it mean losing one's grip on reality? But now he was saying as if to another person, "what a poor excuse for a man, that ignorant oaf. He chose to start this ugly little affair. Now disgusted I will have to end it."

For seconds he would select well-known men of means whose names would look good in the newspapers. If he showed himself brave and steadfast, as indeed he would, his opponent might offer an excuse to back down. Then he would be acclaimed the winner by default with neither man hurt and no blood shed. Pacing the room, he looked again at the man's card: *Paul Johnson, Rue de Saint-Honoré 39, New Orleans*. He had traveled that street. It was a pleasant avenue with attractive houses made even more pleasant by shade trees and flowers.

But who was this man? What did he do for a living? Why was he in the restaurant that evening seated at a large table all alone? Why had he stared with such effrontery at Henrietta and not at some other woman? And why did he react as he did when asked to cease and desist? Were dark thoughts running through a depraved mind as he sat there staring at a pregnant woman? Was he perhaps a stalker and dangerous? A stranger had barged into Thomas Bolton's world to cause him and his wife distress. In no way could the stranger's conduct be excused. The matter would have to be corrected on the field of honor at whatever the cost. Should it be with swords or pistols? The sword presented less risk. A duel with swords was seldom fatal. Pistols, on the other hand, were a serious risk. He could lose his life or kill the other man and be charged with murder. After all, duels were illegal.

Then suddenly a feeling of unease seized him. What if his opponent were a better shot or a better swordsman? He was a younger man and would have more stamina and perhaps courage as well. Bolton was fit and strong and determined to fight without flinching, but could it be this unknown man was stronger and better? No, he couldn't be; he did nothing when slapped. He could have returned the slap but merely smiled like a silly baboon. Bolton's heart began to race, beating rapidly as he yielded to worry. Again he spoke as if to another person, and the sound of his voice was metallic and grating.

"At this time two days from now I could be dead."

He went to bed and slept fitfully a few hours. Through the curtains of his bedroom window he could see the dawn breaking. The new sun glowed intensely, promising a hot summer's day. Although Bolton's mouth was dry at breakfast, he forced himself to swallow a few bites of bacon and eggs with coffee and juice. Later he couldn't be certain he had eaten breakfast at all. He knew he would have to leave the wife he loved dearly for most of the day to select his seconds. He chose a military man of rank and a well-known merchant of irrefutable reputation.

"You are really serious about this, my friend?" asked the colonel.

"Yes, absolutely. Honor demands I do it even though my wife urges me to forget it. A little thing she calls it, but I don't see it as little."

"You say you've chosen pistols?" asked the merchant. "If so, I have a fine pair of dueling pistols specially made in France. They will level the playing field for you."

"All other arrangements will be in our hands," the colonel added. "We'll get in touch with Johnson's seconds to select the field of honor and discover whether he finds the use of pistols agreeable. You know the procedure to follow, do you not?"

"Twenty paces," Bolton hoarsely replied. "Weapons to be raised at a given signal. Shots to be fired by one gentleman and then the other until one man is dead or wounded."

"It's well known that you are a good shot," said the colonel. "There is little doubt the outcome will be in your favor."

As night was coming Bolton's seconds came to his house to tell him all arrangements had been made. "We found a heavily wooded island in Ponchartrain," the colonel confirmed. "Hunters go there to shoot quail. Your adversary accepted your conditions at once. He seemed unusually calm, almost nonchalant. His seconds are capable men. One I'm told is a journalist for a leading newspaper."

"Were you able to learn more about my antagonist?"

"Not a thing, I asked about his background but got no answers. He's as much a stranger to me as to you."

"We shall have to find a reliable doctor," said the merchant. "The duel won't be over until the bullets do their damage. I would like to have it take place near a house or hospital, but we had to choose a locale away from houses and hospitals. Pistol shots ring out, you know."

It was all painfully clear. Bolton would be fighting perhaps to a violent death a total stranger named Johnson. The reality of the situation now hit home, and it made him nervous. He told himself it was all right to be nervous, but as a man he couldn't show at any time even one ounce of fear. He would have to face Johnson again, not merely to scold him as in the restaurant, but to kill him or perhaps be killed. Was he an expert with a pistol? Wouldn't that explain why he readily accepted all conditions set for the duel? Again, rising in Bolton's parched throat came the acid taste of anger spiced with not knowing. The man calling himself Johnson was insufferable!

On the other hand, his perverse behavior might only be for show. Privately he could be afflicted with doubt too. Perhaps attempting to show manly bravery, he was really a fraud and very afraid. That bit of chicanery Bolton could understand, for he felt the same way. But if he didn't maintain in the presence of all involved the bravery expected of a man of honor, he would be ruined. His lovely wife, already looking at him as though she didn't know him, would despise him. His friends in positions of power would reject him. Every person in the entire city would stigmatize him as a coward. That, of course, was a condition too painful even to think about. He would fight the nasty little duel and win. If not, he would die with unimpeachable honor.

The time was set for one hour after first light. The early morning was cool and quiet. All participants were on the scene and appeared rested and fresh. When Bolton looked at the gentleman who had become his mortal enemy for reasons he saw as frivolous, the man seemed larger and more menacing than in the restaurant. Johnson stood his ground without saying a word, displaying no hint of backing down. He wore a hat with a wide brim that obscured his face. All Bolton could see was a moustache, white teeth, a strong chin, and the shadow of a grin. He concluded in an instant that Paul Johnson was a formidable opponent demanding caution and respect.

The seconds began the procedure, calling out loudly and waiting for their orders to be executed. "Turn opposite back to back! Walk twenty paces! Turn and fire when ready!" A cooling breeze came from the east, and yet both men were already sweating. With exaggerated confidence they strode the twenty paces and turned. Johnson quickly fired his pistol and grazed the left arm of Thomas Bolton. The bullet tore his sleeve and stung like twenty hornets. Right-handed, Bolton could now take careful aim. The rules called for an alternate exchange of shots.

Johnson stood with one hand against his chest staring fiercely at his opponent. Bolton cocked his pistol and aimed carefully at the man's feet, taking his time. Then before he could pull the trigger, a gunshot rang out loud and close. Grievous thoughts raced through his head like a herd of wild horses. *"Oh my god! The idiot is breaking the rules! He's shooting a second time before I can get a round off! No dueling pistol either, a revolver! Six bullets! Oh my merciful god, I'm dead!"*

Bolton stood frozen, confused by what was happening. A moment later through sweat streaming from his forehead, he saw Paul Johnson lying in a heap on the damp ground. Blood was gushing from his head and turning the ground red. The man had placed the death-spitting end of the revolver's barrel against his temple and pulled the trigger. That instant of self-destruction haunted Bolton for the rest of his life. Why did the young man do it? Did he die because negative emotions got the best of him? Did he believe when he pulled the trigger he was already dead? Bolton wanted only to wound the man and visit him later in the hospital to prove his worth as a gentleman.

The journalist on the scene wrote a sensational story about the event. It appeared that same day in the evening news. It set the whole city chattering. After a cursory investigation, charges were filed against Bolton. Indirectly he had caused the death of a high-ranking politician's eldest son, and the politician wanted justice. The duel was illegal, Bolton's lawyers conceded, but it was Johnson who had killed himself after failing to kill his opponent. Bolton had suffered a wound but had not harmed the governor's son, had not even fired his round. In time young Bolton paid a hefty fine, and all charges were dropped. A month later Henrietta delivered a healthy baby boy. They left New Orleans never to return. Governor Isaac Johnson, mourning the death of his son, wore black for six weeks. In a lengthy interview, he said Paul had been for a long time troubled, self destructive, and looking for a fight.

12

The Cavalry Charge

The Battle of Chancellorsville began with heavy fighting on the first of May, 1863. It didn't end until the sixth of May when Union forces retreated across the Rappahannock River. Casualties on both sides were horrendous. Instead of open terrain, the battle was fought in a forest. Infantry, artillery men, and the cavalry got lost in a maze of trees and undergrowth. Horses stumbled and broke their legs. Fires broke out and the wounded were burned to death. Late in the evening a Confederate general, fondly known as Stonewall Jackson, was hit by friendly fire. He suffered for a week and died of his wounds. Another soldier not so well known as Jackson died when trampled on that first day.

More than two decades before the battle, a man named Thomas Bolton married a young woman with whom he hoped to sire a large and loving family. She would give him sons, and he would give her in return a life of wealth, leisure, and privilege. Early in their domestic life they were guardedly happy. Thomas worked many hours each day and didn't see his young wife as often as he wished, but to show his affection he gave her expensive trinkets. Then a miracle occurred though at the time he didn't recognize it as such. Henrietta Bolton in pain that wracked her frail body delivered a healthy baby boy.

"This is the first!" Bolton crowed triumphantly. "After this, we shall have more! I want five sons to keep the Bolton name alive!"

Henrietta loved children and wasn't at all reluctant to help her husband realize his dream, but she had trouble conceiving. Two long years went by before she became pregnant again. Then in the middle of a dark December night she gave birth to a blue baby girl who couldn't breathe properly. The child died before they could name her. After that the poor woman suffered one miscarriage after another until all the juices of life dried up within her. She wanted desperately to give her husband the children he craved, but what appeared to be a hostile destiny decreed otherwise. Even so, after he bought a huge cotton plantation, money poured in as if fortune favored them. The faster the money came, the fonder Bolton became of the things it could buy. Everything was for the large family he hoped to have.

They named their son Richard Thomas Bolton. He was bright and eager to learn, but also strong and healthy and athletic. He learned to swim and ride soon after he learned to walk. In his teens he could run a mile on a hot day and not feel tired or winded. When he was twelve his father gave him his first rifle. He used it to bag squirrels and other small game in the Great Dismal Swamp southeast of Blue Anchor. As expected, he became as sure a marksman as any person in the region. At the local sporting events, invariably held in late summer, he earned a reputation for hitting his mark with uncanny accuracy.

By then the girls in the community were beginning to notice Richard Bolton. One in particular observed him closely and made diary entries concerning the way he conducted himself. Years later a newspaper published parts of the diary. She had said in one entry, rising poetically to extend a simile, that when he made up his mind to do something he flew to it exactly like a snipe. By that she meant he would dart in one direction and then another before flying straight to his chosen target. She admired how he held his course tenaciously once he found it. Everyone said Richard would be a good catch for any girl, but he seemed always too busy to pay attention to the young women of the village. He was being educated at home, and that consumed several hours of each day. His father had brought in a capable tutor from Richmond to help him with his studies. His mother, housebound and a semi-invalid, taught him to love books and music and good art.

For balance the boy's father encouraged his interest in the outdoors. In a small skiff with fishing gear and rifles slung over their shoulders, they explored the bogs of the Great Dismal Swamp. Thomas Bolton had been drawn to the sprawling natural wonder as soon as he settled in Blue Anchor and quickly learned to navigate its intricate waterways. In time he taught his son the mysteries of the huge swamp. They spent happy days and eerie nights there, but as Richard grew older he was expected to help with the family business. It was a productive plantation with numerous slaves to supervise. Richard became the chief overseer, keeping an eye on workers who toiled from early morning until the sun went down. Though he rode a tall horse and never stooped to manual labor, he worked from dawn to dusk as they did. In the evenings and into the night he struggled with paper work.

One evening in the summer of 1861, some years after his mother's untimely death, he sat with his father at dinner. The large mahogany table, a dozen feet in length, reflected rich hues under the crystal chandelier. It was set for a formal dinner and yet for only two people. They sat at opposite ends of the table facing one another, drinking good burgundy and sharing a variety of broiled and baked meats on glistening china rimmed in blue. The conversation was genial with good-natured banter and the mood relaxed. Then suddenly without notice Richard announced he would join the Army of the Confederate States of America as an ordinary soldier in as little as two or three weeks.

Surprised and angered by the announcement but struggling to remain calm, his father protested, imploring him to reconsider. He was needed at home. He was needed in the fields. He was needed to help run a large and complicated enterprise. A man no longer young couldn't be expected to do it alone. It was an appeal to reason as well as emotion, but Richard's resolve stood firm. Reluctantly, when all argument failed, Thomas used his wealth and influence to secure a commission for his son. The young man was inducted into the army as a first lieutenant and quickly rose in rank.

He held the rank of major when he rode that day with Jeb Stuart at Chancellorsville. A cavalry commander under Robert E. Lee, General Stuart fought well in that horrific battle. He led his troops with splendid decision that first day. On a gray-white horse adorned with red and gold trappings, Jeb Stuart was in the thick of battle for hours but survived. Richard Bolton did not survive. At Darboy's General Store in Blue Anchor, addressing a group of young Quakers, he had made a stern prediction: "When war comes it will swallow you and your kind. You smirk as I say this, but you will lose everything if you refuse to participate. You will lose your land, your freedom, even your lives." Later he became a cavalry officer to fight for the way of life inherited from his brusque father. He didn't say he was ready to die if necessary to defend the venerable Southern way of life, and yet he might have.

At Chancellorsville Major Bolton led a cavalry charge against the enemy when the thick and heavy woods gave way to a clearing. On a splendid horse, himself a dashing figure, he urged his men forward. He raised his saber high as the signal to move faster, and the curved blade glinted in the shimmering light of a sunny spring day. He could feel the hot blood rushing through his body, and he was more alive than at any other time in his life. He saw himself as a man among men fighting with valor for a just cause. At last he would prove himself a courageous and dedicated soldier as other men had done. Young and brave, he was a promising leader but not immortal.

As he was riding fast and hard to engage the enemy, a bullet struck his mount in the neck. The horse pitched forward, swinging its head, and threw the hapless rider to the ground. In minutes he was trampled by a dozen horses. His broken bones pierced his flesh, and his vital organs oozed out on the ground. As the field doctors struggled to save Stonewall Jackson, the blood of Richard Bolton stained the forest floor crimson. His handsome face was battered beyond recognition, his head broken, and his stomach ripped open. Two exhausted men placed him on a dirty cot to wait for medical attention. Too many others needed attention and rank no longer mattered. His vital juices soaked the stinking canvas and attracted a swarm of flies. His bowels released their waste, and the flies pounced upon him like a whirlwind.

A soldier nearby cried out in pain. It was a heart-rending cry that no one seemed to notice. A man in a uniform reduced to ribbons, perhaps another officer, stood leaning against a tree. He was bleeding profusely, his left arm torn off at the shoulder. He stared blankly at nothing, his blue lips quivering. Death came within the hour to free him of pain. Major Bolton struggled to live but died the next morning. With not one person to mourn his death, he died on the bloody cot as the sun was rising to the tree tops. His commander, General Stuart, gave the order to bury the soldier on the field of battle. A flight of raucous crows settled for an instant on the deadly ground and whirled off like a dark storm cloud to sink behind the trees.

As a youth Richard Bolton had been too proud for his own good, they said at the General Store. Yet every person in conversation there was saddened by his untimely death. He was a promising young man in the prime of life, all agreed, and he died too soon. The army declared he died a hero in fierce battle, bravely charging the enemy line and urging his men onward. Leading his troops into battle and riding ahead of them in a daring display of courage, so the bulletin read, he quickly became an easy target. Mortally wounded but clinging to a galloping horse, he continued to charge headlong into the fray.

The official bulletin was riddled with extravagant lies. To speak the truth and set the record straight, while admitting the first casualty of war is truth, Major Bolton died before the battle began and not from a blast of bullets. A handful of military inspectors, investigating weeks later, came to know from a single witness that the young officer was thrown to the ground and trampled by the horses of those behind him. Not able to find corroborative evidence, the inspectors made no attempt to change the official report.

It was filed with a thousand documents ultimately sealed. Rapid and careless handwriting, surely done under stress, disclosed the young cavalry officer suffered bullets to the neck, back, and shoulder but rode on. The bullets actually pierced the neck of his mount. A few men riding with him at full gallop in acrid smoke with weapons firing or ready to fire, may have seen the incident. They did not live to report it.

13

George Henry Jones

Private George Henry Jones lived in Massachusetts when the Civil War began. With no small amount of trepidation he became a soldier in the Fifth Infantry Regiment of that state. In 1862 his regiment entered eastern North Carolina with a voracious invasive army fighting hard and occupying towns and villages. Morale among the Union troops was high as they moved from town to town, fighting with little resistance a ragtag force of Confederates. Yet from the time he entered enemy territory Private Jones considered himself the most unfortunate of men.

He was a large man with stumpy legs that made walking difficult, and he suffered terribly when required to run or march double time. He told himself he wasn't cut out to be a soldier even though in a moment of regrettable patriotism he had volunteered his service. A peaceful man wishing no harm to anyone, he was the father of three children who laughed at his clownish behavior and adored him. His wife was a gentle and long-suffering woman who loved him deeply in spite of his girth. He returned her love in full measure and they were happy.

But a civil war suddenly burst on the scene, and Jones had to leave home. Every evening in bivouac thoughts of his family brought trenchant agony.

Though not exactly a lazy man, Henry Jones (as everyone called him) had always been one who loved his sleep and rest. He liked to retire early and wake up late for a good breakfast. Stuffing tasty food into his massive body was a simple joy he shared every day with his robust family. But when he relaxed afterwards and smoked his pipe while reviewing the day's events, he liked to be alone.

Military life allowed none of that. The officers pushed their men, especially on campaign, to exhaustion. At night the soldiers slept in their uniforms, their rifles beside them, on hard pavement or damp ground not more than a few hours. Breakfast was something only civilians enjoyed. The chow prepared by untrained military cooks and flung upon a tin tray was often so bad it wasn't fit for pigs. Sometimes it cut the lining of the stomach and caused a man to retch. Soldiers often went hungry when fighting. And no one could expect to be alone for long in the army. Life for Jones and most of the soldiers in his regiment, some as young as fourteen and some pushing fifty, was so miserable they often thought of desertion and even spoke of suicide.

Of course it was a joke and a macabre one at that. No man wanted to die, not even to save the United States of America. They went to war to kill or be killed, and yet every one of them wanted desperately to live. And so it was with Jones. He soon discovered war was a dangerous game. He could be killed or severely wounded as they moved against the Confederates, and then what would happen to his family? Instinctively and with good reason he feared and hated the weapons of war. Merely the thought of cannon, rifles, revolvers, and swords made him shudder. And the thought of hand-to-hand combat was too much to bear. Should that ever happen, he would never be able to dodge or defeat a rangy Rebel intent on laying him low. And so he thought long and hard of the dangers before him. In several skirmishes his fellow soldiers had seen what they called his courage, but possibly they saw only a coward's courage. In desperate battle, would George Henry Jones run as fast as his bulk could carry him? He didn't know and he didn't want to know.

He knew only when battle was eminent his fat legs became so weak he wanted to sink to the ground. He surely would have fallen if not for the certain knowledge that his comrades in hobnailed boots would trample his fat body as if it were a bump of sodden earth. He came to know and hate the stench of battle, the smoke and the noise, the clamor of cannon, and the whistling of bullets. For months he had been able to tolerate the palpable horror of war, but had lived in terror. Then one fine day in summer as his unit moved along a narrow road in the quiet countryside, all hell broke loose.

A Confederate assault, a fusillade from a corn field, halted his regiment in its tracks and killed thirty men in fewer than ten minutes. Surprised and bewildered, Jones stood like a statue not able even to fall to the ground. An easy target, he felt he could do nothing and was already dead. Then suddenly he was seized with a wild desire to survive. Running was out of the question. That he couldn't do. So with legs stiff and feet together he jumped into the first ditch his eyes fell upon. It was covered with bramble, and he gave no thought to its depth.

He fell like a boulder through prickly blackberry bushes and landed heavily six feet down. A trickle of blood came from thorny scratches on his face. Looking upward, he saw a clear-blue sky through the hole he had made. An enemy soldier passing over could shoot and kill him with one blast, and so he crawled along the ditch to escape the hole and the fighting. For what seemed an eternity he heard the cries and groans of battle and covered his ears to shut them out. In time all was quiet.

No longer quaking with fright, Private Jones began to think about getting back to his unit. But how? And in what direction? Again the gnawing terror, fatigue, and suffering he had known for months began to overwhelm him. He had lost all courage, all strength. He wouldn't be able to endure the agony of long marches and the alarm of another sneak attack. But what to do? He couldn't stay in the ditch until the war ended. He could stay no longer than a day or two. He had to eat. His over-grown body demanded food and drink.

He was wearing a Union uniform in enemy territory. His unit had gone on without him, overcoming the Rebels or retreating, and he was alone. A cold shiver ran down his back when he realized he could be shot on sight by any Southerner. He had heard the stories of Northern soldiers killed by hatchets and pitchforks and shotguns by peace-loving villagers. If he were not very careful he could be one of their number. He had heard too that on rare occasions a man detached from his unit was taken into the home of caring people, given food and rest, and turned over to the local sheriff. To become a prisoner would solve his dilemma, alleviate his misery, and allow him to get home again when the war ended. Southern military prisons were no paradise — rumor had told him that — but certainly better than the battlefield. In prison, even a harsh one, he had maybe a fifty-fifty chance to survive.

He made up his mind to become a prisoner of war. He would travel by night in an unmarked shirt and muddy trousers until he reached a village or town. In morning light in full uniform he would surrender to the first man to see him. The weather was warm and he could easily do without his cap and coat but not his boots. He smeared mud on them to make them look like clodhoppers and began walking. The night was dark and silent, and he was alone. A nocturnal creature in the brush startled him to a sweat, and the cry of an owl wounded him with fear and anxiety. He imagined he heard someone walking behind him, and that made his trek even more painful.

When dawn came he could see in the smoky distance a little village. Half an hour later he could tell by the chimneys that people were cooking breakfast. Merely the thought of hot food — bacon and eggs, sausages and fluffy biscuits — made his big belly growl. He was hungry, very hungry, but found it necessary to hide in thick bushes until night came again. He felt he couldn't walk into the village in broad daylight for fear of being shot. His blue trousers with their military cut would surely give him away even when dirty and smeared with mud. He would have to approach after sundown as night was falling.

He curled up in his bushy retreat and slept fitfully, his big and heavy body demanding food but not getting it. Now a new fear nagged Henry Jones, plain and simple starvation. He saw himself lying on his back with eyes wide open, unable to move as creatures of all kinds fed on his carcass. A big crow landed on his sweating face. He wanted to swat it away but couldn't move or cry out. With its razor-like beak it pecked out his left eye and flew triumphantly away. He could feel the pain; it woke him up. Quickly he touched his face to confirm he was dreaming.

As soon as twilight came he emerged from his hiding place and set his course, stumbling as he went, toward the village. He found himself standing in front of a low, squat building called "The Cat and Fiddle." It was obviously the village inn. He had seen places exactly like it at home. He could hear the squeaky strains of a fiddle and people talking inside. He could smell, wafting through a window, the enticing aroma of roast pork as Southerners cooked it. Abruptly he walked inside.

Tired and hungry and so drained of energy he thought he might faint, he slowly made his way through a crowd of old men to the long mahogany bar. Had he been thinking clearly he would have realized all the young men were at war. Behind the bar stood a fat man, the barkeep, with a florid face made pleasant by a wide and crooked smile. He was polishing a glass with a white towel.

"What will you have, ol' buddy?" he asked.

The way he spoke was husky and familiar, and Jones noted a thick Southern twang. He sat looking into the bartender's face without saying a word, and the query came to him again, "What will you have?" He was starving.

All he could think of was food and drink and whether he would be arrested as soon as he spoke. He tried hard to disguise his New England accent and managed to speak.

"Food and something to drink, please. Some of that roast pork, please. But I must tell you I can't pay for it."

The bartender gave him a quizzical look as though suspecting something out of the ordinary but seemed friendly. "Aw, that's all right, ol' buddy. I can see you're down on your luck. You look like you been sleepin' in a rabbit hole. You got plenty of girth like me but look a mite down in the mouth. Hold on, I'll getcha somethin'."

He placed on the counter a tall glass of beer and went to the kitchen for a plate of steaming pork with corn bread, black-eyed peas, green beans, and thick slices of tomato.

"Dig in, friend, and don't worry about paying. It's on the house! We're in this together, and I sure hope it ends soon."

Thanking the man warmly, Jones ate until his belly against the bar cried out for him to stop. By then three or four men were standing behind him and looking him over. His clothing seemed a bit strange to their eyes. Moreover, he was young enough to be serving in the army. They asked if he were by any chance a military man lost from his unit and trying to get back to it. If so, which side was he on?

"You just can't be Johnny Reb," one of them said. "Our boys wear gray, and I never seen a fat graycoat wearing blue pants and a-talkin' funny. I don't mean no insult, but ever last one of our boys is thin and rangy. They wear gray and say they gonna fight till they die."

"I felt the same way when I volunteered up North," said Jones quietly, making no attempt to conceal his accent.

"But after seeing what war is like, living for months in hell and seeing I was fighting people that looked like me, I changed my mind. I'm a Union soldier from New England. Massachusetts is a long way from here but not very different from these parts. Anyway, I'm your enemy and I surrender officially to you. Please take me to your jail and lock me up. As of this moment I'm your prisoner, and I will not attempt to escape."

"Well, bust my britches!" exclaimed the talkative man. "A fat bluecoat eating and drinking in The Cat and Fiddle and wanting to surrender to a bunch of old yokels. I swear I never heard of such a thing! I guess we better get ol' Sheriff Higgins in here to do it up right."

"He just walked in," said the barkeep. "He's here now."

"What's all the fuss about?" Higgins demanded.

"This man here is a enemy soljer. He wants to surrender!"

"Is that so, Mister? Are you really a soljer?" asked the sheriff.

"I'm a federal soldier from Massachusetts, and I am now your prisoner," Jones announced for all to hear. "I'm at your mercy, a prisoner of war. Do with me what you will, but please don't execute me. I have a family back home. They depend on me."

"And where did ya say is home?" queried the sheriff.

"Massachusetts."

"You don't say, Massatoosetts! I have a brother that was living there when the war broke out. A barber with a wife and kids, an ol' Southern boy like me. Guess you never met a barber named Caleb Higgins? Don't know where he's living at present."

"I wish I could say yes, Sheriff, but I never knew a Higgins."

"Didn't expect you did. You'll go to jail for tonight. Tomorrow maybe I can find something better for a prisoner o' war. I'll get a letter off to the governor in Raleigh to tell him of what's going on here."

The letter was written in a fine hand by his daughter, a student of English in a school for girls. *"Sir,"* it read, *"I am in possession of a Federal Prisoner, one Private George Henry Jones of Massachusetts. His Regiment was obliged to retreat, carrying with them their Dead and Wounded, after a Desperate Encounter with brave Confederate soldiers. Because at the present time (owing to the War and all) we are short of field laborers, I ask we keep the man in my Custody and require him to work on a Farm here. If you or your people have Objection or a different Opinion, please inform your humble servant at your earliest Convenience."*

The office of the governor in wartime was a nest of confusion. If the letter from Higgins was read by anyone, it was tossed aside, forwarded to the War Department, or ignored. No answer came from Raleigh and it was just as well. Instead of falling into the hands of bureaucrats or a military force, Henry Jones was safe in the company of a competent and compassionate rural sheriff.

Safe at last, Jones spent several nights in the village jail. Every other day he ate his fill of fried chicken cooked and delivered by the sheriff's wife. Village elders decided he would become a farmhand until the war ended. Farm labor made Jones leaner and stronger. Shortly after the war he joined his family in Massachusetts in better health than when he left.

14

Gwendolyn's Confession

In Ida Crabtree's boarding house in the village of Blue Anchor lived an unhappy woman who had left her husband. Her name was Gwendolyn van Buren and his name was Charles. Except for the evening meal she remained alone each day in her room. Then one morning when rain was falling hard and fast and making a noise on the tin roof like a dog chasing a cat, she came into Ida's kitchen for a cup of coffee. Sensing she wanted to talk, Ida sat with her and encouraged her with a sad little smile of concern. Primly sipping her coffee, Gwendolyn spoke in hurried sentences about people in the neighborhood, the parson of the church, the butcher at the meat market, and finally her husband.

Half an hour later the rain fell lightly and ceased altogether. When Gwendolyn paused in her narrative, Ida put some bread in a skillet to toast, spread some butter and cinnamon on it, and placed it before her. She was twenty years younger than her landlady but looked almost as old. Her face was drawn with worry, and one could see the woman was miserable. Talking might alleviate the misery. She poured her thoughts and feelings into Ida as though the woman were a pot as large as a washtub. It was her way of easing her pain after a long silence. Everyone in the boarding house knew she had come there after breaking up with her husband, and some were saying she had suffered abuse from him or some other terrible calamity.

Gwendolyn went on talking, and from time to time a fleeting smile crossed her face, the smile of a woman confused and heartsick.

"You mustn't take this thing so seriously," said Ida attempting solace. "I know how you must feel. When my old man up and left me, I moped around this house for days and days and finally got over it. Time is the great healer, you know. Tell me exactly what happened."

Two pearly tears appeared in the corners of the woman's round blue eyes. Subdued and speaking softly, she murmured: "I have . . . well, I'm not sure I can say it . . . I have a lover!"

Shyly she glanced at her landlady, put her head on the table, and began to sob with such force it shook her entire body. Ida waited patiently, remaining silent until the woman grew calm. Then trembling with emotion, Gwendolyn began to unburden herself. With some reluctance but in ringing tones she cast away her secret. Her clipped sentences created a rapid staccato in the quiet kitchen.

"It shouldn't have happened. If I had known myself better I would not have let it happen. But it did! And since that day I'm mad with misery. How quickly we yield! How quickly a woman's heart responds. It takes so little really.

Just a glance, a casual and open glance, and a moment of tenderness. Then like floodgates we open our hearts. We long with passion to love and be loved."

"Now listen, Gwen," Ida softly interjected. "What you describe is the way any woman capable of true feeling behaves. I know that feeling, and I know it will diminish as mine did. And you need not feel guilty."

"Oh, but I do! I do feel guilty even though I think I know why it happened. You know my husband, Mrs. Crabtree. He's a sensible man, but I will tell you this: he has no understanding of a woman's heart. He is always so self-assured — urbane, calm, in control — always self-centered and unflappable. A thousand times I've wanted him to take me roughly in his arms and kiss me hard and hold me so tight I couldn't breathe. In the beginning he did that at times but not any more."

"It's because Charles is older than you, dear. You must know men become that way as they grow older. They become more distant, sort of sink into themselves, and live in their own little world."

"I could tell he was growing older and colder the longer we lived together, but the thought of having an affair, loving another man, never once entered my mind. Then it happened, all of a sudden, probably because Charles was so indifferent to the natural beauty all around us when traveling. Plainly, it was calm and cold indifference! Oh, I shudder even now as I recall it. That cold indifference paralyzed my enthusiasm, robbed me of natural ardor and delight. Golden fields, green woods, and sparkling streams thrilled me but meant nothing to him."

"He was probably thinking about how to solve some

problem in his business. You told me he has nineteen employees. Just one can create all kinds of problems. You must know a boss's life is not an easy one. Just one unruly boarder in my house can bring turmoil and misery."

"No, no! I'm sure it wasn't that. He was simply oblivious to beauty. I squeezed his hand to share my excitement, exclaiming 'Look Charles! See how beautiful the countryside, so beautiful!' Nodding in feigned agreement, he unfolded a newspaper to read about the stock market! His behavior froze my heart. When people love each other, shouldn't that love become more intense in the presence of beauty?"

"Well, maybe, Gwen. But you must know by now there's no understanding men. No real understanding at all. We women live on one planet and they on another."

"We visited a gorgeous resort nestled against foothills under blue skies. It had rolling green lawns, blooming shrubs, fresh and fragrant flowers, and a small lake. We were there six days, and most of the time Charles remained inside with his nose in a newspaper or some such thing. I found pleasure taking long walks on the grounds and sitting beside the water. Every few minutes the lake changed its appearance. Do you know lakes are living things? Its surface differed one moment to the next, reflecting the changing colors of the sky and kissing the wind. It glittered with diamonds, with *diamonds* I tell you."

"Well, you know our lake right here in Blue Anchor has that kind of beauty too, and people go there to fish but also for pleasure. I guess while you enjoyed your stay in that grand place, Charles was thinking about business or some other matter. You can say he's a realist while you embrace the romantic view of life. Guess that's why you quarreled and left him and came to live here. But go on."

"Oh, we didn't quarrel, Mrs. Crabtree. Nothing so mundane as that. At first I sat on a bench to view the lake. Then I sat down on the cool grass and got lost in a vision. A strange feeling came over me. I was seized by an insatiable desire to love and be loved. I knew even then I was revolting against the dullness of my life. I wanted to walk arm in arm beside the lake with the person I loved and who loved me. I wanted us to laugh and joke and discover little things to bring delight into our lives. And I wanted to share that delight with a hug and kiss."

"You have the soul of a sensitive poet, my dear. This crazy world we live in, especially the way we've made it in these times, was never meant for the likes of you. I understand but feel helpless to help you."

"I was so alone and so miserable and burst out weeping. Something was stirring behind me as I walked the path, and when I turned to look I saw a man in dark clothes gaining on me. He startled me and for a moment I thought I might run in fright. Then coming closer he asked, 'Why do you weep, lovely lady? In this beautiful place is it for joy?' I had seen the young man more than once in the lobby of the hotel, and recognition calmed my fear. But taken by surprise and not able to find a clever retort, I told him I felt ill."

"It's good you knew the man. When a stranger approaches a woman like that, walking all alone in a secluded place, nothing good can come of it. We read about it in the papers all the time."

"He said he would go with me to the hotel, taking care

that I would be all right. In a very natural way we strolled side by side, and he asked about my trip to the resort and what I had seen along the way. With some hesitation I spoke of the beauty that somehow touched my heart and soul and thrilled me. All that I said he understood even better than I myself. His remarks could have come from me but in better language and with more incisive thought. He caught every nuance of feeling I had and rode with it. Oh! Did my heart flutter! And then of a sudden he was quoting marvelous lines from Lord Byron's *She Walks in Beauty*. You won't believe it, but I found myself on a fleecy cloud floating in a clear blue sky caressed by a breeze ineffably sweet. Then it happened. I don't know how or why, but it happened. I fell in love with that man! I fell deeply in love with that man, head over heels in love!"

"Oh, my! You poor thing! You were vulnerable, ripe for the plucking as they say. I do hope he didn't take advantage of you."

"Take advantage, you say? He did indeed! He stole my heart! But sadly even now he doesn't know it. He gave me his card reading Percival Seagrove. Such a pretty and poetic name! I didn't see him again until the morning he departed. He was young and healthy but not really handsome. He wasn't tall and dashing. He was round and pudgy and shorter than me, but it didn't matter. I loved him! He came when I needed him most, and I love him still. I think I shall always love him. I went directly to our room, packed my things when my husband went down to buy a newspaper, and left as soon as I could. I scrawled a brief note to explain: *I love you, Charles, but love another more. I am leaving you. Please take the necessary steps to dissolve our marriage."*

"Oh my! You really did make a fast decision, didn't you? Oh my!"

"I thought I might find Percival along the way as I traveled to my aunt's house some distance from the resort. I didn't. I sent a letter to his residence, the address on the card he gave me, asking him to write to me. A woman calling herself his protective sister replied succinctly on lovely engraved stationery: *"Mr. Seagrove is currently unavailable to you or anyone stateside. He is preparing to travel in Europe and cannot respond to your request."* I didn't write again. A few days later my husband found out where I was living and came in a huff, demanding I explain my behavior. As we talked I could see he was placing all the blame on me, a frivolous and silly woman losing all control. So I dismissed him with as much civility as I could manage, apologized to my aunt for disturbing her, and came here. I've been told he is trying to find me. I can't say whether we shall live together again or not."

Gwendolyn van Buren ceased talking, shrugged her thin shoulders and looked meditatively at the empty coffee cups. Ida Crabtree offered to fill her cup again, but she declined. The older woman knew Gwendolyn expected a response, something profound and philosophical to make her feel better. But Ida was no philosopher, only the keeper of a boarding house. For more than two decades she had run a well-kept house and was known for her good common sense. That she drew upon as she put the finishing touches on a sad, ingenuous, and remarkable confession from a woman she liked.

"I will tell you what I think, Gwen. Very often when a woman is emotionally charged as you were, it is not a man she loves but Love itself, the concept. Your real lover as you sat on the grass that day and later strolled with Percival back to the hotel was that living lake in all its beauty. I advise you to go to your husband and tell him there is something about him that displeases you. He won't be able to change his ways, but I think he will treat you better. At heart he's a kind man but stubborn and practical, the salt of the earth we say. I really believe you'll be less miserable in your own house, my dear, than here in mine."

Again Gwendolyn placed her weary head on the kitchen table and sobbed as women often do when their hearts are broken. The noise on the tin roof told her it was raining again. She let Ida know she wanted to go to her room and be alone. Her friend went up the narrow stairs with her, uttered a reassuring remark, and left her. She believed it was good for Gwendolyn to take refuge alone and have a good cry. The salty tears that streamed from the woman's round eyes would have the power to wash away her pain and leave her pure.

15
Old Mortimer

Fall had come and the odor of fields lying fallow made the stagnant air of late afternoon thick and heavy. Mortimer Birkenstrap and his son Gus had managed to bring in a good harvest on their sixty acres and were preparing the brown land for the next season. They lived east of Blue Anchor in a farmhouse that was slowly falling apart. The woman of the house, Maddie Birkenstrap, had died of pneumonia one cold and dreary day in December. So for six years father and son got by as best they could. Both toiled to cultivate the land and care for the livestock. Neither paid attention to amenities or comfort. It was time for a woman to stem the tide of decay and make the house a home again.

Gus had reached that time in his life when he wanted a wife and family. He talked it over with his papa, saying he had come to know a buxom young woman he might be able to marry. In time she would bear children to help out on the farm, help they really needed. A woman in their daily lives would change things for the better, Gus insisted, but old Mortimer resolutely shook his head. He was losing his hearing and wouldn't be able to get along with someone new, and he was too old to put up with a woman's bossy ways. When Maddie died he felt sad for a while but soon adjusted to the silence and began to feel relieved. She was a talker, and a new woman in the house would talk and talk. That would create problems and he was too old for problems.

After a supper of potato soup flavored with slabs of bacon, Gus sauntered over to the neighboring farm to chat with the woman old Mortimer knew only through hearsay. He found her some distance from the house gathering firewood to be cut and stacked for winter. Hilda Ross was a big girl with broad hips, strong legs, and full breasts. She wore a smile most of the time, and her reddish-brown hair framed a pleasant freckled face. Walking beside Gus and talking with him, their stride was the same and so was their height.

"Well, how's it going?" she asked.

Her companion, a broad and muscular fellow with blonde hair, blue eyes, and strong hands answered softly.

"Nothing to report, nothing at all. He's an old mule."

"He won't listen to you?"

"He's hard of hearing, but that ain't the problem. He won't listen to reason, won't hear me out, shuts up to everything I say."

"What are you going to do?"

"What do you think I should do?"

"Go to a Quaker elder and ask for help."

"All right, I'll talk to Jeremy Clay."

"Go tomorrow."

"I will."

As they walked, Hilda was bouncing a small child on her right hip. Now as they approached her house, the little boy held out his arms for the man to take him. Though not his father, Gus liked the toddler, held him tight against his chest, and nuzzled his plump face. They rubbed noses, and the child giggled happily. Gus kissed his forehead, lifted him high in the air, and gave him back to Hilda.

In the fading daylight they could see a man working in a nearby field. The horse and plowman moved along as one, and the plow turned up the rich, moist soil to shine in the autumn air. Gus and Hilda knew the man — his name was Jonah Wolverson — but Hilda knew him better. He was the father of her child. She gave him a quick glance but went on talking to Gus, asking questions.

"What did your old daddy say?"

"He said he would have no part of it, absolutely no part."

"Why? I really would like to know why."

"The boy, Hilda. The boy is yours but he's also Jonah's."

"So what? Everyone knows little Adam is Jonah's child. You might say he took advantage of me one evening when I drank too much cider and turned giddy. Later it happened when I had no cider at all and wasn't giddy. So now in your old papa's eyes I'm a slut not worthy of a poor farmer living a hardscrabble life in a ramshackle house. I didn't want anything to happen between me and Jonah, but it did. Your old man don't like me for something I couldn't help, but that's his problem, not mine. I got over it a long time ago."

"I like you, Hilda, I like you lots and you know it. I like

your little boy too. It's my pa, my starchy old pa, that's standing in the way. But I'll find a way to get it settled."

"See that you do, Gus, and don't shilly-shally."

She didn't kiss him as they stood in front of her house, but entered as she was speaking and closed the door. With a heavy tread and shoulders slumping, the young farmer made his way homeward.

He wanted to marry Hilda Ross. But his father, old Mortimer, opposed the very idea. The child, born out of wedlock and belonging to another man, could never be a true member of the family and would be just another mouth to feed. The son by contrast had deep feelings for Hilda and wanted her in spite of her indiscretion. With her he was stupid with happiness. He loved her and her son and had no hate for the man who brought the boy into the world. But old Mortimer had other feelings. He would not have that woman in his house and certainly not her bastard child. Staunchly he opposed his son with the obstinacy of a deaf and crusty old man. He even threatened to sell the farm if Gus got out of line. That would leave him no inheritance whatever.

"She will take good care of you, Papa!" Gus shouted in the one ear that still heard a few sounds. "She's a good girl, strong and healthy, a good cook, and thrifty too. She can make things here better for us."

"You can't marry that woman," the old man muttered with mulish insistence. "That woman ain't wholesome and she's bossy. If something happened to you or me, she could end up owning this place, and it's been in our family three generations."

Old Mortimer stubbornly stood his ground. No appeal

to head or heart could make him waver. Only one hope was left for Gus, the magic that Jeremy Clay in his office as Quaker elder might exert. So after several days of hesitation the young man implored Jeremy to have a talk with Mortimer Birkenstrap.

"So you want me to speak to him? One old man to another?"

"Please, sir. Everyone knows you have strong persuasive power."

"And what am I to tell your father?"

"Tell him I love Hilda and she loves me. Tell him we need each other. Tell him she's a good girl and thrifty, but don't say she's smart."

"I can do that," said Jeremy, extending his hand.

"Much obliged, sir. I'll plow your back forty come spring."

"I won't hold you to that, Gus, but I'll keep it in mind."

Mortimer and Gus owned their sixty acres but were not rich by any means. They paid a young girl seven dollars to come in twice a week to tidy up the house, make the soup, look after the chickens, milk the cows, churn the butter, and keep the place warm in winter. Gus helped her with the chores whenever he could. The old man didn't work any more but deluded himself into thinking he did. Bent double with rheumatism and leaning on his stick, he observed all that was going on with a keen but jaundiced eye. Sometimes in good weather he sat under a broad tree and remained there for hours. He dozed from time to time in the warm air, but when awake he thought of the price of pork, eggs, and corn and whether the harvest would be a good one.

When the sun dipped behind the trees and the shadows grew long, he made his way home, favoring his weak left leg, and took his place at the end of the kitchen table. Without a word he waited for his soup, and when it was set before him he placed his crooked fingers round the bowl to warm them before eating. He did that summer and winter, for his hands were always cold. He slurped the soup with a noisy smack of his thin lips and used a piece of bread to swab the inside of the bowl for any morsel he might have missed. The coffee he drank at noon came from the grounds of the morning coffee. His mission in life was to make the most of everything and lose nothing of anything. The older he got the more stringent and miserly he became. Shortly after his supper, stubborn and mute, he climbed into the loft where he had his bed.

The two men seldom made an effort to talk to each other. Only when doing farm business, selling a crop or buying a pig, did the young farmer ask his father's advice, and that was a hard procedure. He was forced to bawl into the old man's good ear and wait several minutes for a response. Then from the depths of a sour stomach came hoarse and hollow words. That's how it was that evening when Gus loudly announced his plans to marry Hilda Ross. Papa Mortimer had thought his son wanted to talk about the purchase of a horse or a heifer, or another pig. He bristled with anger when at length he understood Gus was expressing his desire for a woman. The lout wanted a woman to live with them and eat their food, a loose woman no less with a bastard child, and the child would also eat their food. With meticulous accuracy the old man calculated how much soup the little fellow would slurp before he could work the farm, how much bread and butter he would devour, and he groaned in agony at the results. Louder than usual he let his son know he didn't approve of Hilda Ross and would never allow her to come into his house.

"My god, my boy! Have you lost your mind? All you say is just plain crazy. I won't allow it! It just won't happen, it can't happen!"

For three months the same argument was repeated with the same results. Then Hilda advised Gus that evening in autumn to seek a solution with the help of a Quaker elder. Arriving home, he found his father already seated with spoon in hand, waiting for his soup. In silence and just a glimmer of light, they ate some buttered bread after the soup, drank a swig of cider, and went to bed. The next day Jeremy Clay talked with old Mortimer when Gus was tending the livestock. His work was made easier by thoughts of a red-haired girl urging him to act.

"I must have her," he kept saying to himself. "She's a fine girl. It's a pity she laid with Jonah, but I love her all the same and her son too."

But what if the Quaker didn't succeed? He would have to defy the old man and marry Hilda anyway. His father in anger might actually disown him and wrest away his one thing of value, the farm. He crossed his fingers and kept them crossed until he heard Jeremy's pleasant voice on the graveled path from house to barn.

"Good news, Gus. We ironed out the kinks in your problem. It's smooth enough now. I'm hoarse from shouting into his ear, but your papa finally came around.

He's stubborn as a mule, cold as winter rain, but not all bad. I believe God will find a place for him in heaven."

"Thank you, sir! Did he really agree to the marriage? Ah, Mr. Clay, you're a miracle worker! Come spring you can count on me for doing that back forty! God already has a special place for you!"

The wedding at the beginning of the new year was a civil ceremony with Jeremy and Hilda's friends attending. Mortimer was there as witness but said nothing. At home with four occupying the small house instead of two, he spoke only a few words when necessary. He spent his days outside in good weather, often leaving after breakfast and not appearing again until supper. Then he would slurp his soup in silence, eat the sugary dessert Hilda was fond of making, climb to his bed in the loft, and sleep like a puppy.

Mortimer didn't like Hilda but did like her cooking. The food was better now, and he made it a point never to miss a meal. But the boy at the end of the table, sitting on his mother's lap and nibbling on every morsel she put in his mouth, disturbed the old man. He stared weakly at mother and child, his watery old eyes riveted on them. He had lost his hearing, but his eyesight was as good as ever, and he didn't like what he saw. He suffered pain with each mouthful the boy swallowed.

The year went by well for the newly married couple. Their crops grew thick and strong to make a good harvest, the apple trees promised an abundance of fruit to lay in for autumn, and the livestock flourished. To save the expense of hiring men to help them, Gus and Hilda toiled from morning till night, working very hard each day. Then one day her husband went to the fields as usual but came back in the afternoon all weak and dizzy and fell into bed. He was ill with a high fever for several days. Early one morning when Hilda went to the sick man's bed to comfort him, she found him unresponsive. She touched his face and found it cold. His eyes were open and she closed them. Her young husband was dead of a mysterious disease that was killing others.

After the burial ceremony Mortimer and the woman he despised but depended on for life found themselves alone in the farmhouse with a noisy child. While Hilda had good reason to be cruel to the old man, she looked after him with the same care she had given her husband. She kept the little house clean and warm and served him soup with buttered corn pone at supper. Always while eating he warmed his stiff and bony fingers by placing them around the bowl. When the bowl was empty, he whimpered for his sugary dessert.

There came a day when the old man was off his feed. He was not feeling well, he managed to say. Hilda kindly urged him to eat. With her help he slurped his soup, ate a piece of corn pone slathered with butter, and drank a glass of cider. Rubbing his belly, he rose from the table and hobbled outside. It was a warm and pleasant afternoon, and wearily he went for a walk. He came to the pond he had fished for many years and sat near it to be alone. As night was coming he got up to return home but faltered. Some villagers found him the next morning leaning against a tree, his old face turned upward to the sky.

16

Spenhoffer's Special

The innkeeper at Blue Anchor, Jules Spenhoffer, was a tall man in his late forties with little hair on a large round head and a pot belly. He had operated the inn profitably for a dozen years and was seen by the villagers as a good businessman. One afternoon in late summer he stopped his buggy in front of the farmhouse owned by an elderly widow named Jolene Waterford. Hitching his horse to the fence surrounding the yard, he went to the front porch where the woman sat shucking corn. Jules owned land adjacent to the widow's farm and wanted to purchase several good acres from her. Each time he broached the subject she refused to sell him even one square foot of her land.

"I was born on this farm and I mean to die on it," she had said to him. "As long as I live I will keep my farm as it was when I was born. Nobody will get his hands on any part of it. That promise I made to my husband before he died, and I intend to keep it."

Jules was a man of optimism and stubborn persistence, and so he thought in time she might relent. She was in her seventies, wrinkled and bent over, but as active as any woman. The visitor touched her thin shoulder in a friendly way and sat down beside her.

"Well, Miz Waterford," he said in the unctuous tone he always used with her, "it seems you are as hale and hearty as ever! I'm glad to see you doing so well."

"Well, thank you, Jules. I have a few aches and pains but can't complain. What about you? Seems to me you put on some weight."

"Stomach got fat, Miz Waterford. When a man gets my age the fat goes to his belly. Instead of going to my chest it falls lower."

"Yes, I can see that. Sure did fall lower. A little round belly you got there, Jules. Well, not so little I might say by way of correction."

Jolene said no more and went on with her work. The innkeeper watched her knotted fingers, hard as steel, seize the ears of corn and shuck them rapidly and skillfully. The naked corn fell into her lap while the husks went into a tub at her feet. When her task was done, she gathered the corn in her apron to take to her kitchen but waited for her visitor to say his piece. She had an inkling it would be the same old spiel she had heard a dozen times.

"I know I've said it before," Jules began, "but are you absolutely certain you don't wanna sell me a few acres? It ain't the whole farm."

"Well, you know, the parts go to make the whole. I'm not selling any part of my land. I thought I made that clear. Ever so often you come out here to pester me with the same old question."

"I know how you feel, Miz Waterford. You love the land

and so do I. At the same time we have to reckon with change. Now I've come up with something that just might suit us both real good."

"Oh? And what is it, Spenhoffer? You have some sort of scheme up your sleeve?" She made no effort to hide her suspicion.

"You can sell the land to me and keep it at the same time! You can sell me the whole blessed farm and yet keep it as your very own for as long as you live. That's what I'm saying!"

"I don't believe a word of it. You're trying to bamboozle an old woman, Jules, and you ain't gonna do it."

"Let me explain. Every month I will come here and give you a hefty sum of money. You will not have to pay back even one dollar. All you have to do is take the money and spend it. That sound good to you?"

"No, it don't! I smell a rat in a stinking hole," groused Jolene scornfully. "People don't give an old woman money, and not a young woman either, unless they expect something in return."

"Oh, you think it's some kind of scheme, and I don't blame you for being cautious when you hear it, but it's all legit. You can remain on your farm as long as you live with no worries whatever. All you need do is sign a paper showing I'm the rightful owner after your death. Because you don't have nobody to inherit your place, it will go to the county. But with my plan you can keep it with plenty of money to live in clover till you die. I pay you every month and the land is mine when you go. You'll have no worry of any kind. It's gain with no pain, Miz Waterford."

"I'll think it over," the feisty woman replied. "Come back in a week or so and we'll talk about it."

The innkeeper went away happy as a lark, but Jolene had trouble sleeping. All night she thought about the deal offered her, suspecting there was something in the offer not to her advantage. Then on the heels of other thoughts came the one about the money, a lot of money every month falling into her apron from the sky, manna from heaven and nothing done to earn it. Who could resist such an offer?

By the time all this was taking place Blue Anchor had a law firm on Main Street, and there she went for advice. The young lawyer listened carefully and told her to accept the offer but demand a larger monthly fee based on her age and the value of her farm.

"You could live fifteen years longer than expected," he said, "and even then Spenhoffer would not have paid you the full worth of your farm. So demand larger payments and put it all in writing."

Getting a lot of money every month, enough that would allow her to live almost as a wealthy dowager, made Jolene feel young again. Yet she was suspicious, fearing a trick, and had trouble making up her mind. At last she allowed the lawyer to put the deal in writing. While she couldn't be sure Jules would agree with the new stipulation, she returned home dizzy with thoughts of a grand future.

Within a few days the innkeeper came again. He sat across from her at the kitchen table as they shared a jug of cider. She insisted she wasn't able to make up her mind concerning his proposal. But she feared he might get up and leave before she could mention the deal the lawyer put in writing. At last when Spenhoffer grew impatient and began to fidget, she named the higher monthly figure. Carefully she explained it was based on the value of her farm, and she couldn't take less.

Eyes blinking and fat lips shining like ripe cherries, Jules mumbled his disappointment. "Can't do it, Miz Waterford, can't do it. Can't pay you that much every month. I'm not a rich man."

To get him to change his mind, she began to talk about how long she might live. "Five or six more years? I'm nearly seventy-three and ailing. Only last night my joints hurt so bad I could hardly crawl out of bed."

That brought a laugh from the innkeeper. "Come now, old lady, you and I both know you are plenty spry and strong as a bull, and you'll live to be a hundred. You'll live to see me six feet under."

She laughed at that, a high-pitched titter. He was making a joke. "If that belly gets any bigger," she chided, "I just might."

They spent the afternoon discussing the proposal and finishing the jug of cider. Jolene opened another jug and they went on talking. Finally, disgusted with himself but seeing no other solution, Jules consented. He would sign the papers drawn up by the lawyer and pay her the figure shown in the papers on the first of every month.

Three years passed and Jolene seemed to be getting younger rather than older. She splurged on a fancy horse to draw her new buggy, hired a coachman to drive her, and bought for herself a new wardrobe. Every summer all of Blue Anchor saw her proudly on display in new dresses. In the past she had been a taciturn woman living in isolation, but now she was gay and talkative in a social setting. The money she received each month from Jules Spenhoffer was an elixir for her. It prolonged her life and gave her the will and energy to live it fully.

From time to time Jules went out to see Jolene Waterford, just as one goes to the barn to check on the livestock. She met him with a cunning look that soon became a smile, her little blue eyes glinting. Seeing how well she was, invariably he left muttering imprecations.

"Will that old granny never die? I just gotta find a way to hurry things up." So he began to think about some means of getting rid of her.

Visiting Jolene a week later and hoping to confront a very sick old woman, he found her as healthy as a newborn heifer. After chatting a few minutes he asked her why she never came to his place.

"People are talking and saying we ain't on friendly terms. You know it's a lie. I'm fond of you in my way, Miz Waterford, and to show it I'm willing to treat you to dinner and drinks on the house at my place."

"I will accept your invitation, Jules. I have to go into town on market day and I'll have my man drop me off at your inn for some good eating. You are known to serve good food and spirits."

The innkeeper showed her to one of his best tables and treated her like a true lady. He himself stood by her table to receive her order. When she seemed undecided, he recommended the best the house had to offer: roast duck, a leg of mutton, roast beef. The table sagged with good food, but she ate next to nothing. For most of her life, she averred, making small talk, she had lived on tiny portions of meat and vegetables with only a morsel of bread and butter. Sometimes she would have a glass of buttermilk with her food, though mostly she drank water.

"Well, now listen, Miz Waterford, at my place you'll have something stronger than water to drink!" the innkeeper cried. "A drop of brandy perhaps? Emily, bring out my special brandy, Spenhoffer's Special!"

The waitress put on the table a magnum of strong brandy and two snifters. Her boss filled the glasses half full, laughing as he did so and asking Jolene to sniff the golden liquid before sipping. "It's the best we have," he said. "People say it's the best in the whole state."

The good woman sipped the amber nectar with pleasure, a twinkle in her little blue eyes. She drank as slowly as she could, swishing the brandy across her tongue and holding it before swallowing to make the pleasure last all the longer.

"Umm, yes!" she announced, smacking her rouged but wrinkled lips, "that *is* good, real good!"

"Yep, it's my special recipe. That's why we call it Spenhoffer's Special. I'm real proud of it. Whole community loves it."

Jules poured her another glass, and slowly she drank it. He wanted to pour a third, placing the bottle to her snifter, but she refused.

"Oh, drink up!" he said. "It's the mildest thing you can drink. It melts in the mouth before it goes down the gullet, and it tastes so good."

When she refused a third glass, he very generously offered her an entire magnum, a bottle large enough for a week of pleasure. At first refusing, she had second thoughts and took it away with her. A few days later Jules rode out for a visit with a keg of the strong brandy. The old woman, having finished the bottle he gave her, accepted the keg with an eagerness that pleased him. Later he brought another keg, and they shared a few glasses. For the first time ever Jolene Waterford called Jules Spenhoffer her good and caring friend.

But then a problem raised its hoary head. Some ladies in Blue Anchor made it known to all who would listen that Jolene was getting drunk just about every day. Her hired man, the only person on her farm besides herself, found her loop-legged in the kitchen, on the porch, in the yard, and at times in village streets. The ladies expressed their concern, for she was becoming a spectacle. To guard his reputation and keep it clean, the innkeeper ceased to go to her place. He mailed her stipend to her each month, and her man every week or so picked up a keg of brandy, declaring she was in good health but often drunk.

"It's a pity Jolene Waterford took to drink at her age," Jules said with a look of distress at a town meeting. "It will be the death of her if she don't receive help from somebody soon."

It was indeed the death of her. She died alone in the middle of winter smelling of Spenhoffer's Special. She had finished the current keg and had sent her man to buy another. She felt dizzy while he was gone and went to bed for a nap. He found her dead, her little blue eyes wide open and a half smile on her thin face.

Looking over his newly acquired farm to make sure all was in order, Spenhoffer spoke to the hired man in words dripping with compassion.

"The community is sad to lose a worthy lady like Jolene. We grieve for her dying so sudden like. If she had laid off the booze, I'm sure she would have lasted ten, maybe fifteen years longer. But she couldn't resist old Spenhoffer's Special before bedtime. Too bad, too bad."

"Yessir," replied the hired man. "Too bad, really too bad, but she was old when she went, and everybody knows she had a good life. I do hope you'll let me go on doing my job, sir. I'm a good worker, dependable and loyal. With me on the job you won't have to worry about nothing."

17

The Girl in the White Raincoat

After all this time, dear daughter, you want me to tell you again about the girl in the white raincoat. She sat in the back seat of my car one dark and stormy night when I was a student. Her wet blonde hair was a bit darker than her raincoat. Both hair and coat absorbed the colored lights in the wet street. She sat surrounded by a rainbow of color for ten minutes or more. Then the rainbow turned blue and she was gone. She didn't open the door and leave the car and say goodbye as any normal girl would do because this girl, to my way of thinking, was anything but normal. Smiling wanly and saying nothing, she suddenly disappeared. She vanished like a ghost in a scary movie.

You remember I told you this story when you were a little girl with a toothy smile and flaxen hair. We hiked through the woods one summer afternoon, and you sat beside me on an old dock we came upon while walking beside the lake. We took off our shoes and dangled our feet in the water. The sun was shining hot and warming our backs, but the story was about a cold encounter with a strange being, and you listened to every word with an air of surprise. A few days later you repeated the story to your friend at a sleepover and laughed with glee when she begged you not to tell her more. Though you were little in those days, you only half believed what happened. It was similar to your half belief in the existence of Santa Claus. You wanted to love a jolly and generous old man who gave you presents, but somehow you found it hard to believe he was real even when I said he was.

Now you tell me the girl in the white raincoat wasn't real either. She was only imaginary, something an overactive imagination might produce under stress. Or maybe I was tipsy that evening, having visited the punch bowl at the party too often. No, I wasn't seeing a white elephant in a white raincoat. I drank very little of the spiked punch because I knew I had to drive home in bad weather. So the girl was no illusion born of too much booze. She was a phantom, I tell you, but real.

I was returning to my dorm from a party in a nearby town. The streets were wet and slippery, shining and reflective in places, dark and foreboding in others. The rain was pouring down in sheets that splattered against the windshield and cut visibility to a hundred feet. Then suddenly, in front of my headlights, I saw a slender figure in a white raincoat standing in the middle of the road. I slammed on the brakes and skidded to a halt. Shaken, I got out and looked for what I thought would be a horrible sight. For a terrible few minutes I thought I had run down the woman in white. I looked under the car and to either side but found nothing. Shivering from shock, or perhaps the wet and cold, I got back in the car and went on down the street. At the next intersection I stopped at the red light and waited for it to change.

That's when I noticed I was not alone. My rearview mirror framed a girl in a white raincoat. Her blonde hair was wet and draped across her cheeks and neck. Her face was wet with a bluish tint and shining. She wore a half smile below large and liquid eyes. The red light turned to amber and then green and the white raincoat absorbed the colors. Her skin, shining blue like the flame of a gas stove, didn't change color. I went beyond the light, parked and looked into her face. In the heavy silence I blurted questions I hoped she would answer.

"How did you get in my car? I thought I struck you back there! Why were you standing in the middle of the road in the rain?"

She smiled sweetly but didn't speak. I asked again. She pointed with a long index finger shining blue in the darkness.

"That way," she murmured, "take me that way, 2326 Diablo Drive." Her voice sounded like a newly minted bell. It was pleasant but metallic. It rang with authority, with something like a command.

"Where the devil is Diablo Drive?" I asked. "I'm new in this city and never heard of it."

"That way," came the answer, "that way."

She sounded impatient, even petulant, yet somehow soothing. "You must take me that way," she said, her voice smooth as silk.

I coaxed the old car into running again and sped off. Though I fastened my eyes on the dark street, I managed to glance in the mirror. She sat quietly behind me, her blue hands in her lap, a delicate smile animating a gaunt face. I felt nervous and flustered.

"She really has her nerve," I was thinking. "She got in my car all of a sudden and now tells me to take her somewhere. I wonder if she thinks this old Plymouth looks like a taxi."

In silence I drove on down the street. The night was getting darker and darker, the rain was pelting harder and harder. The windshield wiper was doing a bad job of keeping the wet off. I stopped at an intersection and waited for the light to change.

"Where exactly," I asked, "do you want to go on Diablo Drive? You gave me a number, something like 666, but that's creepy and probably not real. What's the real number?"

I got no response. In the mirror I saw a bluish light, but when I turned to look at her, she was gone. You won't believe it, but she was gone, evaporated! I never heard the door open, never heard it close, but the girl with the wet hair, smiling face, and shining blue skin was gone.

I stopped the car, got outside and looked around, and got all wet again. I saw nothing but the wet street and shimmering lights and felt a cold, slanted rain on my face. In the street late at night in uncertain weather and longing for bed, I was puzzled by the wonder of it all and the mystery. How could it happen? How could a pretty girl get inside my car and make herself at home and then leave as suddenly as she came? I went on down the street, tapping the steering wheel and trying to regain my composure.

From the radio came an eerie male voice: "The girl in the white raincoat. A girl with blonde hair and blue skin and a sad but smiling face. Ah, we know her well! Ah, hoo! Ha-ha-ha!"

The laughter was diabolical. It made me cringe. *"What is this?"* I thought with growing alarm. *"Am I going crazy? Did someone at the party slip me a cautionary drug? Or was it the punch? I tasted nothing."*

"You must go that way," a chirpy female voice instructed, "that way, 2326 Diablo Drive."

In the darkness a lightning bolt skittered across the wet street. The radio shrieked with static and went dead. It didn't matter because I had the number and the street stenciled on my brain. I would find the address despite the bad weather just to see what might happen.

Then suddenly it was there. On a hill sat a small house with 2326 over the doorway, the letters shining in blue light. I climbed the steps and knocked on the door. I knocked again. It was well after midnight, near two in the morning. Would anyone answer? And if they did, would they be holding a shotgun ready for use? I was about to knock a third time when the door opened. A slight woman in night clothes, with tousled gray hair and tortured eyes, stood in the doorway. She looked old and tired but vaguely resembled the girl.

"I'm sorry to bother you Ma'am," I said, "but I need to talk about something very strange that happened to me tonight."

"Oh, yes!" she answered knowingly. "You are not the first. You saw a girl in a white raincoat standing in the street. She got into your car, sat in the back seat, and pointed that long, slender, white finger in this direction, mumbling in a lyrical voice 2326 Diablo Drive."

"No, Ma'am," I said. "Not white. Her finger was slender and long but not white. It was *blue* and *shining* and so was the rest of her!"

"Yes, others say that. It's always a bluish light, isn't it? You turned to say something to her, but she vanished. She slipped away into the night, into the rain and dark as always. Every year at this time, from when I was thirty-six until now at forty-nine, it happens."

"Every year it happens? And this goes on with other people too? I thought I was the only one. I'm certain it just has to be some kind of crazy joke. Are you in on the joke, Ma'am? Is she standing there behind you? Is that a snicker I hear?"

"No, no, young man. It's no joke. It happens every year and always in bad weather. On this night thirteen years ago a train struck and killed her on the railroad tracks. She was walking home from her work at the diner. She's been trying to come home ever since. You were crossing the tracks when you saw her standing in the middle of the road?"

"Well, yes," I stammered. "The tracks really jarred my old car. But are you telling me she's dead? Ah, c'mon, lady, I wasn't born yesterday. You can do better than that!"

"Goodnight, young man," she replied politely. "And thank you for telling me my daughter is trying to come home. Maybe next year she herself will knock on this door."

The porch light went off. The letters 2326 went dark. As I settled behind the wheel to drive away, a blue vapor flashed in front of my headlights and bounced across the street. Well, that's the story you wanted to hear again, dear girl. It's the same as when I told it to you twenty years ago.

18

The Clock Struck Nine At Noon

It was summer and his wife urged him to rest and go fishing. With some reluctance, because he wanted to finish an experiment he was working on, he drove to his favorite watering hole with fishing gear. There he sat on the bank for two hours, had no luck whatever, and decided to go home. When he climbed into his truck and turned the ignition key, he heard only a soft grinding sound. He turned the key again, heard the battery struggling to start the engine, and then heard nothing. He would have to hire a mechanic in the nearby town to get the truck running again. He wanted to be home working in his laboratory.

Setting off on foot, he walked down a dusty road under an orange sky that slowly turned purple and then blue. On either side was a bucolic scene heavy with silence. He expected to hear birds chirping or at least the wind, but all around him the air was silent. In the distance he could see a low, squat building set back from the road, and when he reached it he went inside. It was an old-fashioned diner with a long counter featuring chrome stools with red leather tops standing in a row like sentinels. Two or three booths were near the windows. A jukebox in the corner flashed colored lights as it played a country tune. He saw no customers in the place, no waitress behind the counter, no fry cook in the kitchen. He tapped his fingers on the fly-specked counter and called out to anyone who might hear him.

"Hello!" he yelled. "Anyone home? You got a customer out here!"

When he received no answer, he waited for a minute or two and called out again. Only the jukebox responded, repeating the tune it was playing when he entered. In a throaty, gravelly voice a male singer complained of troubles on the farm: *"Three hungry children, a crop in the field, and you chose to leave me, Lucille."* In no mood to be entertained by some poor farmer's misery, he unplugged the machine. It fell silent and no longer flashed. He called out again, louder.

"Hello! Anybody here? You got a customer at the counter! He's got money to spend on a juicy burger!"

He turned and looked at one of the booths. On its table was a cup of coffee with a ribbon of steam rising from it. On a shiny white plate was a breakfast of bacon and eggs half eaten. From the piece of buttered toast someone had taken a bite, and the small glass of orange juice was half empty. Something cool like a sudden breeze brushed his face.

"What's going on here?" he asked himself. *"Looks like someone got up and left in a hurry. Where is everybody? Maybe in the kitchen? Outside in back for some reason*?"

He went behind the counter and into the kitchen. On the grill was a fat hamburger and on it was a slice of cheese. The grill was hot and the burger was sizzling, but the cheese wasn't melting. Grease on the grill was popping but gave off no odor. No cook was anywhere in sight,

He called out again, "Cookie! Your hamburger will burn to a crisp in two minutes if you don't get to it fast!"

It wasn't burning. It was simmering in its own juices but not burning to a crisp and neither was the cheese. He pushed open the screen door to look outside but saw nobody. He had found not one living soul inside or outside the restaurant, only signs that people had recently been there. Outside in back he saw the usual garbage cans. They were full and stinking in the sun, but no insects swarmed around them.

He went back inside, vaulted the counter, and paused before going through the front door. There was little doubt people had been in the place only minutes before he got there. Now they were gone, erased as an artist erases a superfluous line, as a schoolgirl erases a wrong word in her diary. What was happening? What was going on? Suddenly the jukebox, its cord unplugged, began flashing again. Then as he stared in amazement the machine began to play an old tune he liked as a teenager. The same male voice who sang of Lucille and betrayal when he first entered the place, was now singing another mournful tune: *"You are my sunshine, my only sunshine. You make me happy when skies are gray."* It was country music with a sad little twang.

He left in a hurry and went on down the road. The day was becoming hot and yet in the middle of his back he felt something cold. Then to his happy surprise he discovered he wasn't entirely alone. A stray dog a hundred paces from him was crossing the road, a dog with wooly white fur and a lame leg, or was the creature really a dog? He rubbed his eyes and looked again. The animal was gone.

"I'm sure I saw a mutt," he said to myself, *"but where did he go? Maybe to the cook who deserted his hamburger? Or to the customer who didn't finish his breakfast?"*

He chuckled at that, amused by the image of an invisible man owning an invisible dog and living in an invisible world. In a moment he was somber again, walking fast enough for shortness of breath.

Ahead he could see the town, a pleasant little town with neatly arranged buildings and clean streets. Within minutes he was in the main square with its bank and shops and clock tower. He glanced at the clock to know the time of day and found it had no hands. Later as he began to look for people, the clock struck nine even though the sun made the hour close to noon. Something was dreadfully wrong with the timepiece. He would have to tell someone the clock was damaged and have them set it right. He strolled along the main street, passing a hardware store, a bookstore, and a bakery with succulent pastries in the window. Peering inside each store, he saw and heard no one. The town was as vacant as the diner and silent. He told himself he was suffering nightmare and would soon awaken.

Suddenly burdened by a feeling that someone was watching him, he looked across the square and saw a woman sitting in a sedan. It was an old Buick, exactly like the one his father owned when he was a kid. Gladdened by the sight of another person in that forsaken place, he ran over to speak to her. She was sitting primly on the front seat. Her large eyes in an eerily white face were wide open and looking straight ahead.

With an open palm he slapped the closed window, expecting her to roll it down. She didn't move. Abruptly he opened the door. She fell out in her white dress and lay as if injured on the dirty pavement. For an instant he thought the woman was playing a cruel joke on him. Then he saw she was a facsimile of a woman, a mannequin only, sprawled on the pavement with her thighs exposed. He pulled her dress down, crouched on his haunches beside her, laughed in a casual way, and spoke tender words to her. It was all a joke, of course, a joke that stung the senses, and yet it brought comic relief to make him feel better. He scooped her up and put her back in her seat. He looked for the driver, for wouldn't he soon be delivering the mannequin to a department store? The driver was nowhere to be seen. A blast of the car's horn might bring him. He pressed its button hard but got no sound.

In the square, only two hundred feet from the sedan, was a public telephone booth. Its door was open and its phone began to ring. He ran to the phone, lifted the receiver from its hook, and spoke into it rapidly and loudly. He was uncomfortable now and sweating. His day had become anything but a quiet day of fishing.

"Hello! Hello! I'm glad you called. Hello! My name is Sydney Nordstrom. I have a problem here. Please, hello!"

Whoever was calling suddenly hung up. He jiggled the instrument with some force, hoping to hear a human voice.

"Operator! Operator! Put your supervisor on the line

and let me speak to him or her. I must speak to someone in charge! Please!"

His pulse quickened when a female voice, clear but shrilly metallic, sounded harsh in his ear. "Dial your number, please. Dial your number, please, and deposit your coins. Dial your number, please."

"Operator! Operator! I have a dire emergency here! Please don't cut me off! I must speak to someone, I must!"

"Dial your number, please, and deposit your coins."

Hanging on a hook inside the phone booth was the phone directory of the town. Immediately he recognized the name. It was the town where he had spent his childhood, where he had graduated from high school before going on to college, where he had met and married his high school sweetheart. His father's name, Gregory Robert Nordstrom, was listed in the N section with a phone number beside it.

He wanted to call that number, any number in the book, but fumbling in his pockets he found no coins. Without coins the telephone was useless. Then as a cold despair washed over him, he saw the police station across the street and thought surely he would encounter someone there. Inside he found only a warm chair. Moments before someone had been sitting in the chair. A lighted cigar smoldered in an ash tray. The office was empty and only a ceiling fan moved. The jail cells were empty. A heavy cell door threatened to close on him. He sat down under the fan, his aching head in his hands, sweating in an artificial breeze.

He was tired and hungry. He went to a drugstore nearby and fixed himself a strawberry sundae. The store had within its walls every single item a thriving drugstore could have except for one thing. It had no life, no people, no clerks and no customers. It was well stocked with all kinds of merchandise and a soda fountain filled with goodies. In the middle of the room were circular racks for paperback books. Idly he spun a rack only to see another nearby spinning all by itself. He went over to examine it and found the rack had in its slots many copies of one book and only one book. Its title was *A Mode of Linear Extension*. Flipping through its pages, instantly he saw a scientific work of sorts written by one Sydney Nordstrom for a popular audience. That was his name!

"There is reason to believe," one paragraph read, *"that behind the reality we know through our senses is a parallel reality. Some day, using a mode of linear extension now being developed by scientists, we may be able to transport men and women into that other world. We could be living in what might be called a bubble close to another bubble. If we can find a way to merge the bubbles, to integrate one with the other and thus create a portal, we may be able to open fantastic new frontiers."*

Shrugging his shoulders, he quickly judged the book a piece of wild speculation by a man with the same name as his own. He left the drugstore in late afternoon. The shadows were long and the day was cool. For half an hour he sat on a concrete bench in a silent park with stubby purple grass and pink trees. He thought about the book he had seen. Perhaps it made sense after all. He glanced down the long, deserted main street reflecting on its pavement a glimmer of light from the shops. All day he had seen no sign of life, except for the dog that may not have been a dog. He had heard only three sounds: the jukebox in the diner, the telephone in the square, and the town clock. The car horn when pressed made no sound at all. He had found the presence of people at the diner and in the town but no breathing, visceral life either animal or human. He had eaten an ice-cream sundae in a well-stocked drugstore that was rich and cool to the tongue, but like the burger that emitted no odor when fried on a grill the ice cream had no taste.

Even time itself was out of whack. What clock without hands strikes nine at noon? He walked across the square to fetch warmth and shelter for the night. Perhaps he could find a comfortable couch or even a bed and a bathroom in one of the shops. His wife would worry when he didn't come home, but what could he do? Though brightly lit and apparently open for business, all the shops were closed. He tried to enter several; their doors were locked. Knackered and no longer resisting, he sat down on the curb under a street lamp and rested his weary head on his knees. Inside was confetti swirling in blind confusion.

A moment later to his surprise he heard in the still air a whooshing sound that lifted him skyward like a dry leaf in autumn. Looking downward he could see in the light of the lamp a whirling column of dust particles sparkling like rare gemstones. In a moment Sydney Nordstrom, a cutting-edge scientist proposing theories for others to chew on, was back in his truck. Heaving a sigh of relief when the engine turned over, he drove home tapping his fingers on the steering wheel. Though he felt a little dizzy as the headlights danced on the road, he was strangely calm. His legs ached dreadfully, as if from too much walking. On his tongue was the taste of strawberry ice-cream, his favorite flavor. In the distance he could hear church bells tolling, dogs barking, and the hustle of everyday life as night fell. Though racking his brain to remember, he couldn't recall how his day had gone. But of one thing he was certain: he had caught no fish.

19

The Goblin at Miller's Landing

They said they didn't believe in goblins. When John Tawdry who taught eighth-grade English read Christina Rossetti's "Goblin Market" one evening at a town meeting before it all began, they nudged each other and winked. Oh, they thought the poem entertaining, but the story it told wasn't believable. The frisky goblins Rossetti created were not genuine goblins at all. They were symbols of temptation, Tawdry had to admit, demons badgering the poet even more than the girls in the story. So the practical-minded villagers left the meeting chuckling. Goblins could people the imagination of a troubled poet, but no goblin would ever inhabit Miller's Landing. Or so they thought.

It was summer and hot. The water at the landing was turning green with algae and attracting flies. The air was flinty and hard to breathe. No cooling breeze came from any direction. Ingrid Baxter was sitting on her porch fanning herself when Gabe Crawford rode up on his bicycle with two bags of groceries. Sweating under the blazing sun, he parked his bike in the shade, lifted the groceries from its basket, and trotted toward the house. In the middle of the yard under a towering elm tree, the little blue-eyed boy everybody called Mr. Bangs was on his plump knees poking a frog with a stick. Agile and slippery, it jumped when poked and hopped away. A moment later the creature lay dying in the hot sun. Mr. Bangs had flashed a mind wave at it.

Gabe hurried past the boy and went to the porch. Under his breath he was singing some kind of song. Always he did that when coming near the Baxter house. Every person in the village did that, even little girls not much older than Mr. Bangs. They sang nonsense verses and jumbled their thoughts so the boy couldn't read their minds, and they tried to think of silly things apart from themselves. Should a clear thought come to Mr. Bangs, he might decide to act on it. Sometimes if he liked you he might do something good to enrich your life. If he didn't like you it could be something bad. Sometimes when he tried to make a good thing, it got out of hand and became a bad thing. But no one could blame the child. He was only six, and how can you blame a chubby little kid with blonde hair and blue eyes even when the eyes don't seem normal?

Crawford put the groceries on the porch and stopped his chanting long enough to speak. "That's everything you ordered, Miz Baxter. Think we got it right this time."

He was the delivery boy for Henry Hawkins at the general store. He was already nineteen and no longer a boy, but that was his job description. When not stocking shelves or sweeping the floor, he took on the duties of delivery boy.

"Thank you, Gabe," said Ingrid airily, "and how is your

mama? I sure hope she's feeling better. My, it's a terrible hot day."

"She's well again, Miz Baxter," said Gabe with a nervous chortle. "She can't see all that good after what happened, but she's just fine. And please don't say it's a terrible hot day. It's as good a day as we ever get around here. It's a good day, Miz Baxter, a real good day."

Ingrid Baxter was a round little woman neatly dressed and always busy. On the porch she was shelling peas. Her fat hands worked fast as she smiled wistfully at Gabe. Only a month or so earlier she had scolded her son for turning their long-haired dog into a rug and for causing Mrs. Crawford's eyesight to falter and fade. In response he grew sullen and lashed out at his mother with his mind. That was the end of Ingrid's sweet smile and bright eyes, and the end of a strong personality that usually subdued her son. The word spread in the village that even members of Mr. Bangs's family — his real name was Bobby Baxter — were not safe when the little boy lost his temper.

Her fingers working mechanically, Ingrid looked at Gabe with unblinking eyes and a blank face. "Land sakes, Gabriel, you don't have to go carrying on like that with me. Bobby won't hurt nobody, especially you. He likes you, told me so himself. You like Gabe, don't you Bobby?"

The boy was looking at the frog turning stiff in the sun. "Don't call me Bobby, Ma. My name is Mr. Bangs and you don't have no right to call me nothing else. Sure, I like ol' Gabe all right. He's a goofball, a goofy goofball, but I like him all right."

Gabe Crawford, wearing a nervous smile, pedaled off quickly. He wanted to get away from the Baxter place before Mr. Bangs decided to make something happen. Then because Bangs liked him and didn't want to hurt him, he found himself pedaling like never before, moving faster than a race horse down the dusty road. Bangs knew Gabe wanted to get back to the store. So why not help him a little?

Inside Ingrid Baxter was putting the groceries away. It wasn't hard work and yet in minutes she felt exhausted. Wearily she went back to the porch, sat down in the rocking chair, and picked up the pan of peas. She wasn't old, but from the time Bangs had flung something at her with his mind something had gone wrong with hers. She was tired all the time too, especially when the weather was hot. Her husband Grover came up, and she told him Gabriel had brought the groceries.

"Good, very good," he said in reply. "Very good, indeed."

Everybody in the village said that because they feared upsetting Mr. Bangs. Every day and every thing, terrible or not, was very good.

"Oh my!" the round little woman sighed. "It's just too hot even now in late afternoon. I wish Bobby would do something to make it cooler."

"Now Ma, be careful what you say!" cautioned her husband. "He's there in the yard, and he can hear your thoughts if not your words. You know as well as I do we gotta be careful."

Bangs didn't have to be near a person to know what the person was thinking. Most of the time he was lost in his own thoughts and didn't care. But if for some reason someone attracted his attention even for a moment, his strange preternatural mind would bristle and deliver . . . well, you couldn't be sure what.

"This weather today is real good! It's just fine," piped Ingrid.

"Yep, it sure is!" Grover was quick to reply. "It don't get any better than this. Couldn't ask for a better day!" Then bringing his words to a whisper, he asked, "Did Gabe bring us good meat for the roast?"

"He sure did," Ingrid softly replied, "and we gonna have a fine gathering tonight. Good eats for all the guests and some good piano playing too. We'll be celebrating Steed Hanover's birthday."

Bangs stepped on the dead frog to be certain it was dead and shuffled off toward the cornfield. He moved near the house like a crab, sort of side ways, and didn't say a word.

His mother, sweating and uncomfortable, fanned her ample bosom vigorously without relief. "Just a beautiful day, dear, it's very nice!"

"Fine day we're having, Mr. Bangs," chimed his father. "Fine day!"

Ignoring his parents, the boy went to the cornfield. He walked between the stalks breathing deeply the fragrance of the ripe corn. He had made it rain during the night, and so the field was fresh. On the other side was a grove of trees with mossy rocks and a spring-fed pool. He lay down in the shade and looked up at the cloudless sky, all copper instead of blue. His mind had turned it copper, and it had made the spring that fed the pool where a furry creature wanted water.

A fox with sleek fur was drinking at the pool. A smaller

creature blundered nearby. The fox grew tense and made ready to spring. Bangs caught the currents of the animal's mind, didn't like what he heard, and instantly sent it scalded with oil to the cornfield. A couple years back some of the people in the village had waited in ambush for the boy-demon to come out of the grove. Their aim was to render him harmless, and they were bent on doing whatever it took to achieve that end. He read their thoughts and sent them all to a grave in the cornfield. Now because the people who remained deliberately confused their thoughts to protect themselves, he tended to ignore them.

He liked being alone. That way he could experiment with goblin power and explore ways to use it. Home again, he went into the basement. It was cool and damp there and had a musty smell he liked. Also he could play tricks on the mice that scampered across the floor and the spiders too. It was fun to stop a mouse in its tracks and make it move in slow motion. He could strip it of its fur if he so desired, or send it a hunk of cheese. It all depended on his mood. Sometimes he drove an army of flies into a web, but only if he liked the spider. He could hear his mom preparing food for the party. She and his dad were talking.

"Where is Mr. Bangs?" he heard his father asking. "He oughta come in now and wash up."

"I seen him out in the yard a little while ago. Don't know where he got to. Maybe went to that grove he likes or to the cornfield."

"Well, it's been a nice day," his father said. "And I think

we'll have fun this evening, a nice evening after working hard in the fields."

"Nobody told Steed Hanover it's gonna be his birthday party?"

"Nope, not a soul. It'll be a big surprise, a real big surprise."

"Especially when we put that new sheet music on the piano for him. Thelma Windsong found it in her attic."

"He's always glad to get new music. Can't find it much any more."

"I know, I know. Been that way since Bobby didn't like Kenneth Horn and sent him off to the cornfield. His store with anything you wanted just went under after that. His wife and boy couldn't keep it running and had to close it."

"Don't call him Bobby, Ma. Call him what he likes. It's a real good thing to call Mr. Bangs what he likes."

"Yes, yes! It's good and Mr. Bangs is good. My boy is a good boy."

"Of course he is! Everything in this place is good 'cept one thing maybe. When I came up I saw a million flies swarming around a dead frog out there in the hot sun. Why do we have a frog baking in the yard and stinking up the place?"

"I dunno, dear. I never saw it. Maybe Bobby, uh Mr. Bangs, brought it up here from that place he likes near the cornfield."

"Well, it'll dry up quick in this heat. And so it's good."

When it came to living with Bangs everything was good. Everything had to be good even if it wasn't. One couldn't risk getting on his bad side, for he could make things not so good, indeed not good at all. He could do things that were unspeakable. Every person in the village knew that, even the children. You couldn't tell what he was likely to do.

The guests arrived near eight. The day had been extremely hot, but when the sun fell a frigid cold wrapped itself around their world. Grover Baxter got a sputtering fire going in the fireplace, and his wife set the table in the dining room and lit the candles. Bangs slumped in a chair near the fire. They had no electricity in the house because Mr. Bangs got rid of it when he decided he didn't like it.

Otto Pettinger and his wife were among the first to arrive. He was a farmer like all the others and strong. In the past he had tried to persuade Bangs to make things to stock the village store, things like clothes and canned goods and even meat to be butchered. But Bangs turned temperamental and sent the store's owner, Kenneth Horn, to the cornfield. Since then no one had tried to reason with the boy. After all, he was only a child of six. No one had the nerve to ask him to do anything, not knowing how he would take it. They tried to avoid him.

Sally Pettinger immediately began to help Ingrid with the dinner. A few minutes later all the guests were making small talk in the big parlor. They were adults with healthy children, but no children had come with them and for good reason. Little Evie Wickham on a dare had tried to play with Bangs, laughing as she approached him. Then her laughter turned to a long, high-pitched screech and she was gone. Like dew in sunshine she evaporated, and no one ever saw her again. In grave whispers the parents explained to wide-eyed children that Ingrid Baxter's little son looked like a normal boy but was really a goblin who despised children. They cautioned their offspring not to go near him.

It was true. Bangs didn't like children. As he slouched in his chair eyeing the activity in the room, he wasn't sure he liked adults either. But Steed Hanover was all right, a straight shooter. Tall and good humored, he sat down at the upright piano and ran his fingers over the keys. He was a good musician and began to play a tune from memory softly and with feeling. Rich chords rolled out of the piano like sparkling streams. The rhythm was good enough to cause some foot tapping, but no one sang. Bangs liked Hanover and the music he could draw from the instrument, but not the human voice. Once someone had tried to sing, and then a bad thing had happened. So with trembling fingers Steed played tunes that would put Bangs in a good mood.

He played until his hands ached, and then when the boy seemed to be nodding off to sleep he played a lullaby with its phrases becoming softer and softer. When he stood up to move away, everybody in the room wished him a happy birthday. They whispered their good wishes because Bangs was snoozing and would awaken angry if they spoke as people normally speak. Bangs didn't like any kind of noise.

"Well, I can't believe it!" said Hanover softly. "I sure wasn't expecting a birthday party. Thanks, good people. Thanks to all of you."

They gave him small presents, things they had made by hand or things of sentimental value — a pipe, a pair of socks, some chocolate-chip cookies, and a scarf. And then with a flourish Ingrid Baxter gave him the new sheet music, knowing he would prize it above all else. With a show of vast pleasure he slipped off the ribbon and opened the cylinder. Rather than wrapping it, Ingrid had rolled up the music like a medieval manuscript with a ribbon around it. Steed was flabbergasted. His round eyes grew rounder and he smiled from ear to ear.

"Thanks a million," he murmured, stepping quickly to the piano. "It's maybe my favorite piece! Do you mind if I try it out?"

Grover Baxter's face grew stern and so did Ingrid's. "Well," he said, "looks like our little boy is fast asleep. The music could wake him up, you know. Do you think you can wait till after dinner?"

Steed was clearly disappointed but said as if by rote, "It's good I can't play that beautiful music just now, it's good to wait. Of course I'll wait till after dinner."

They ate while Bangs slept. They ate every scrap on the table. Tender roast beef in delicious gravy. Peas and carrots and country biscuits and big slices of banana cream pie for dessert. It was good that Bangs was sleeping. He would eat his own food in his room where he liked to be alone. But the group couldn't allow their chatter to become too loud. It wouldn't be good to awaken him of a sudden. He might cause something to happen and ruin the party.

After dinner Steed eagerly looked over the sheet music, his gift from good people. He glanced at the piano and then at Ingrid and the little boy near the fire. Bangs was awake and glowering at the flames.

"Maybe I can play it now?" Steed asked. "Mr. Bangs

ain't sleeping any more. He's sitting there now, looking at the fire."

"Why yes," said Ingrid. "Play your birthday present now so we can all enjoy it, and I'm sure Bobby is gonna like it too."

"Don't call him Bobby, Ma," Grover Baxter whispered.

Steed began to play the opening arpeggios of *Für Elise*, softly and with a delicate touch. Everyone in the room moved closer to the piano, eager to hear every note of the famous bagatelle. With eyes riveted on the score and swaying just a little as he played, the pianist seemed entranced by the music. Then without warning the hands of the man at the piano, severed at the wrists, flitted across the keys to turn Beethoven's music into raucous jazz. When the keys became bloody, the hands jumped to the top of the piano, bowed grotesquely to the audience, and fell with a thump to the floor. Mr. Bangs with eyes blazing was either angry or having fun.

"Now listen, Steed. You must never play that dirty kraut music again! Not ever again! I'm gonna put your hands back on and you gonna play twenty tunes that I like. *Twinkle Twinkle Little Star* is the first and *Chopsticks* is gonna be the last."

On a keyboard no longer bloody with hands nimble and talented, the man played nineteen popular tunes. He swayed and rocked as he played, and sweat poured down a face frozen in a grimace. Then suddenly he collapsed and fell heavily to the floor. Strong and fit from hard farm work, it was horrible to see him pale and white and hollow.

When his friends lifted him to a chair he seemed as

light as a feather and stiff as a mannequin. All that was good in him was gone. Mr. Bangs had wanted twenty songs but got only nineteen. That caused him to send Steed Hanover to the cornfield. The goblin at Miller's Landing was being naughty again. Not a single person at the party, not one man or woman, had the will to do anything about it.

"It's good, Mr. Bangs," someone finally said. "It's good you put Steed out of his misery. He had it coming. He was a bad man. You did good."

A blizzard came in the night while the villagers slept. The next morning the water of the landing, all green with algae and seething in the heat the day before, was crusty with ice and snow and frozen solid. Geese that had flourished during the hot weather lay dead on the shore. Smaller birds had also perished and cluttered the snowy streets. The crops so carefully tended all summer and promising a rich harvest, shriveled and died. The corn field with many corpses lay in ruin. All the stalks with ears of sweet corn were reduced to rubble.

Two days later the entire community became a minuscule stain on the sands of the Mojave Desert. A lone fly sniffed at a sticky and smelly substance in the middle of the stain. It quickly drew back, licked its feet, and flew away. The goblin at Miller's Landing had outdone himself.

20

A Town Called Ashland

Richard Maitland was driving down a country road in the summer of 1979. New York City lay a hundred miles behind him, and he wanted to get even farther away. Going there just out of college at twenty-three, he was certain New York was the city of his dreams, the one place in all the world where he could accomplish what he wanted to do with his life. His dream was to become a writer, but the dream faltered when he found himself in advertising. He wasn't sure he liked what he was doing but rose in rank from copy boy to senior executive, his present position. The job paid well but demanded long hours of dreary desk work. Factory workers gave forty hours a week to their jobs, working eight-hour shifts for five days. Maitland, living alone in a Fifth Avenue apartment and wearing Armani suits and Gucci boots, was expected to put in sixty. The job was consuming too much of his time, too much of his life. He had to get away for a few days.

His sleek convertible was new and should have been a joy to drive, but Maitland didn't have the peace of mind to enjoy the car or the scenery it passed. All he could think about were board meetings, contracts to examine and sign, self-important lawyers pontificating, prattling ad men extolling the virtues of worthless products, and the happy happy tone each TV commercial must have. The fresh air was touching his face like a kiss when something under the hood began to rattle. Even though he knew the fuel tank was almost full, the car seemed to be running out of gas. Ahead was a service station. He would pull in, find a mechanic, and pay him handsomely to solve the problem without delay.

Near the pumps a fellow was fixing a flat tire. Maitland pressed the horn of his new car to produce a loud blast. The man looked up as if to say, "Hold your horses! I heard ya!" He went on applying a patch to an inner tube. Maitland sounded another blast.

"I'll be with you in a minute, Mister," the man calmly called. "Gotta hold my thumb on this patch and let the glue cure. Takes only a minute. Everybody in a hurry these days, but this glue ain't in no hurry."

"A little service, please! I don't have all day. Something's wrong with my engine. The thing is brand new and gold-plated but already causing me trouble. Will you check it and tell me what's wrong?"

"Your fuel pump's no good, Mister. These pricey imports got fuel pumps worse than yesterday's family jalopy. It's gonna take a couple hours to fix it, and that's sayin' I can find a replacement."

"What am I to do in the meantime, Jack? As far as I can tell, you don't even have a waiting room. And if you did have one, it'd be dirty and swarming with flies and smelling of grease and old tires and the food you left uneaten last Thursday."

"The name's Alfred, friend, but people in town call me Al. And you're right about that waiting room. We had one a long time ago but turned it into a storeroom. Served us better as a storeroom You can walk to town if you feel like it. Only a mile down the road."

"Fine! I'll walk into town. Need to stretch my legs. Need to break in these new boots. I'll be back in two hours. I'm hoping you'll have the job done by then and I can be on my way,"

"I'll try, Mister, but can't promise nothing. I work as a mechanic but have to pump gas and check oil and clean windshields and check tire pressure any time a car pulls up to the pumps. All that takes me away from repair jobs. Hey, you got some good-looking boots there."

"Yes, Alfred. They're Gucci. If the name means nothing to you, it's okay. Your job sounds tiresome and boring but not half as bad as mine. Tell you what, I'll trade you. Take my job in New York and I'll stay here and do yours. I'll look over the town first. Treat the car kindly."

"It's a great looking machine, friend. I'd love to drive her. Never drove a fancy car like that. Don't see many like her round here. You're joking about jobs, but you wouldn't like mine any more than I'd like yours. The town, in case you wanna know, is called Ashland. Only about a mile thataway and pretty nice."

"Ashland? I grew up in a town by that name. Haven't been back in thirty years. Went off to college and then moved northward to New York and a hectic way of life that grinds a man down. Often thought it might be nice to go home. But in New York you can't go home again."

"Well, if you're looking for no grinding, you came to the right place. I'm sure as shootin' we don't have any of that here. No grinding and no rush, just an easy way of life from day to day."

The closer Maitland got to town the better he felt. Worry and stress fell by the wayside as he walked. Alfred, known as Al by all the townspeople, had it right. It was a pleasant place and "pretty nice." The day was sunny and clear with a cooling breeze that was absent at the gas station. The street was shaded with narrow-leafed elms, and the houses set back from the street seemed to glow in late summer. He came to what appeared to be the main street and entered a drugstore. It flashed into his memory as the one place where he had spent many hours as a teenager. In the corner was an old-fashioned jukebox. It had the same songs he remembered from his high-school days. At the soda fountain he ordered a sundae with three scoops of ice cream.

"I remember," he said to the smiling girl behind the counter, "when a sundae with three hefty scoops was only a quarter. Now I guess you charge at least a dollar."

"No, sir," the girl replied with a friendly smile, "it's still a quarter." And she pushed across the counter a strawberry, vanilla, and chocolate sundae nestled in a crystal dish. "That'll be a quarter, please."

"You mean you're still selling sundaes for a quarter? Your boss must know he can't make any money that way. Can't break even that way or pay you a decent salary. An ice-cream sundae costs at least a dollar a few miles from here and more than two dollars in New York."

"Always been a quarter here in Ashland," the girl said, "and I get paid enough to buy new stuff now and then and go to the movies once in a while. Where you from anyway?"

"New York City, but I'm pretty sure I grew up in this town. Been away a long time, but everything seems strangely unchanged. Even your face, all fresh and smiling, is familiar."

"Oh, I have the kind of face everyone thinks they've seen before," the girl replied, a broad smile showing good teeth. "A man from Atlanta said I look like his ex-girlfriend. Tried to get me to go home with him. Gave it some thought but decided I couldn't. Never lived any place but here."

Rising from the stool, the ice-cream flavors lingering on his tongue, Maitland flipped a crisp new dollar bill on the counter. Expecting a coin, the girl looked puzzled.

"A dollar," she exclaimed, "paper money! I'll get your change."

"No, no, you keep the dollar. Best sundae I've had in years, delicious! Worth every penny of that dollar. Now I think I'll try to find where I lived a long time ago. It was only a few blocks from here."

He walked down the shady street with houses on either side and saw right away the house he lived in as a boy. In front of the sprawling, two-story house, gleaming white with green shutters, two boys were shooting marbles. He paused to watch.

"I used be a pretty good shooter," he said when one of

the boys looked at him as if to ask what he wanted. "I used to live in that house and I hated mowing that big lawn. Had only a push mower back then."

"You lived in the Maitland house?" the boy asked.

"Why, yes. Is it still called that?"

"Called what?"

"The Maitland house. I'm Richard Maitland and I used to live there. Used to have friends over on weekends. Played hide and seek in that rambling old house. It has lots of rooms and closets and a secret room in the basement for lots of fun."

The boy quickly rose to his feet, visibly upset by what he had heard. "You're not Richie Maitland!" he blurted fiercely. "I know Richie Maitland and you ain't him!"

"I am and I can prove it. Will my driver's license convince you?"

He fumbled in his wallet to find the license with his name and photo, but the boy was already running away. His companion quickly scooped up the marbles and ran too, yelling as he did.

"You ain't Richie Maitland! You're a stranger here and crazy as a coot! You're bad and Mama told us never to talk to people like you!"

Startled by their reaction but chuckling, Maitland strolled into the nearby park where people were enjoying the fine weather. A boy was climbing a tree and his mother was begging him to come down.

"Willie, Willie! Get down from there! Please, come down. You're liable to fall and break your neck. What am I going to do with you?"

"I'm gonna climb higher, Mom. I wanna climb higher!

I'll come down when I get way up there on that highest limb. I wanna climb real high."

Maitland coaxed the boy down and caught him as he dropped from a lower limb. The flustered woman thanked him with good humor, and he fell into conversation with her.

"Nothing so good as summer and being a boy in summer," he said with a twinge of nostalgia. "And that merry-go-round. I grew up riding that thing every summer. It hasn't changed a bit in all these years."

"Well, it's still looks new," the woman said hesitantly, "even though they put it here in the park three years ago."

"Oh, you are mistaken, Madam. That merry-go-round was here when I was a boy of ten or eleven. I rode it all the time, and I carved my name on one of the wooden horses. Guess the horses got refurbished with a new coat of paint. That post over there, see it? I carved my name on it that same summer when I was eleven."

As he was speaking he glanced across the green and saw a boy gouging the post meticulously with a pen knife. Amazed and curious, he went over for a better look. The kid was carving a name in block letters into the soft wood. The first name, *Richie*, was finished and half of the last name was there, *Mait--*.

"You're Richie Maitland?" the man asked incredulously.

"Yessir, but I didn't mean no harm, Mister. Lotsa kids carve their names here, honest. You not gonna tell on me, are you?"

"Yes! You really are Richie Maitland! That's exactly the way I looked, and talked, thirty years ago!" Maitland was scrutinizing the boy's face, barely controlling strong feeling. He reached out to pat the top of his tousled head. Frightened, the kid folded his knife and scurried away. Maitland called out, "Wait a minute! Let me explain!" But Richie Maitland was soon out of sight.

"I really have to get to the bottom of this," the advertising executive was thinking as he stepped on the porch of his boyhood home and rang the bell. An older man appeared behind the screen door. Though the screen obscured his face, his voice sounded very familiar.

"Yes?" the man asked. "Is there someone you wish to see?"

For a moment Richard Maitland was speechless. With some effort he muttered, "Pops? Pops? It's me! Richie! Don't you know me? I'm Richard! You never called me Richard but I'm your son!"

The man quickly closed the heavy front door. Perplexed and frustrated, Maitland pounded on the wooden door and cried out: "Don't you know your own son, Pops? I'm your son! I can prove it! I'm here from New York." The door remained shut.

Next door a teenager was polishing a shiny car. "How do you like her?" he called out as Maitland was walking away. "She's brand new! My dad just bought her for me! Graduation gift! Can you believe it?"

"Brand new?" Richard asked, approaching the car and touching the forward-thrusting fender. "Brand new? Looks like a 1950 Ford to me. Great condition, though. I'd say expertly restored."

"No, no, mister. She's right out of Detroit, brand new. Look at them white-wall tires and that hood and them headlights. Look at that split windshield and that grill with an airplane propeller right in the middle. Ah, man, she's a sweet little car, a convertible! And she's all mine!"

Confused, Maitland struggled to understand. Then it hit him. Like a rabbit punch in the stomach, it hit him: *"A 1950 Ford, not restored but new. I'm not in the late summer of 1979. I'm in 1949 and that was the summer when I was eleven! Oh my God, somehow I went back in time!"*

"What did you say, mister? You don't sound right. Can I get you a glass of water? Maybe you'd like some lemonade. You're sweating too much. You're white as a ghost and saying screwy stuff."

"I'm in the summer of 1949! I can't believe it, but it's 1949!"

"Yeah, I guess so, mister. August 28, 1949, new cars just come out."

"I was eleven in 1949. I'm older now, as you can see, but somehow I'm in the year 1949. I went back to where and when I grew up! Don't you see? Something happened as I tried to escape a dull and stressful present. Something miraculous threw me thirty years back in time! But it didn't make me eleven again."

"I don't getcha, mister. You seem to be talkin' funny. You sure you're all right? Heat ain't gettin' to ya? It's been a hot summer here. Let me get you a cool glass of lemonade."

Maitland declined the boy's offer, thanked him kindly, and returned to his car. He had a long way to travel and time was short.

21
Rivertown's Phantom Ship

Our village in South Carolina, aptly named because of its broad and fertile river, lies forty-nine miles from the sea in farm land. It's not a big and busy place, and strangers who find it by accident call it a one-horse town of little interest. We who live in Rivertown find it pleasant enough. It's because most of the time we mind our own business and live without friction. Though folks from Charleston and other big cities sometimes call us hicks, we just chuckle and shrug it off. Our weather is often wet, but Rivertown is a good place to live and we like it.

Dull? Well, you can say that, but a lot depends on what you see here. If you were to sit on one of the benches in our little park just as night is falling on a Saturday in summer, you might not think our village dull at all. That's when the ghosts of the lads who died in that terrible war — we lost seventeen men at Gettysburg — come looking for the girls of past generations who lie in the churchyard. We don't interfere with their amorous activities. We just let them come and go and don't make a fuss about it. They walk along the graveled path that circles the park, and the only difference between them and any young lovers is no footprints. They can have a little fun in Rivertown without the living prying or complaining. Even ghosts know a good thing.

But what I'm about to tell you was unusual even for our neck of the woods. It happened the year we had two of the worst storms anybody had ever seen. I remember the first one well because it lifted half the roof off my barn and put it in a neighbor's fish pond. I went to the village inn to tell Langley the innkeeper about it, and he said it was awful to suffer a damaged roof but nothing compared to what the tempest placed in his turnip patch.

"It looks like an old ship, the kind you see in illustrated magazines, like the ones the pirates sailed a long time ago. It's big, real big, and it's sitting there on dry land, and the turnips don't mind at all coz it seems to be a phantom ship light as a feather."

Well, that surprised me. I had never heard of a storm strong enough to blow a ship from the ocean all the way to Rivertown. Then Langley said again it was a ghost ship with no real substance. That made me think maybe the wind had blown our resident ghosts out of town and they would have trouble getting back, and I was right. For days in calm and sunny weather they straggled footsore to their old haunts again. Judge Peterboro said his son had never looked so dead since he stormed the Union troops at Gettysburg. Langley had a worried face and wanted me to come with him to see the ship. Because he's one of the leaders in our village and I can't afford to cavil with the man in matters of importance, I felt I had to go along with him.

Sure enough there was an old-fashioned vessel in the middle of his field. It was a ship no one had seen since the days of Blackbeard, and he roamed the seas until he was killed in a sea battle with Virginia sailors in 1718. The hull was made of wooden planks caulked with oakum and painted a rusty red. The unpainted deck planks (we found out later) were of durable wood and scrubbed by seamen every day. At the stern was a great bay window, and later I learned it opened on the Captain's cabin. The ship carried two masts and a mizzen, and the rigging all taut and graceful was in fine working condition. She had a full complement of sail, but in the turnip patch, of course, the sails were furled. From several portholes I could see the barrels of black cannon, and the prow of the vessel had a long bowsprit with forestays attached. Under full canvas on a deep blue sea the ship was surely an eye-popping sight, but here she lay not on even keel but tilted in Langley's turnip patch.

We moved in close, and tapping my knuckles on her hull, I said, "She appears to be real solid for a ghost ship."

"It depends on the way you look at her," said Langley in that instructive tone he uses from time to time. "If she really is solid, and we have no proof of that as yet, she's gonna spoil my turnip crop, and the missus ain't gonna like that at all."

Now I don't claim to know much about ships, but that ghost ship blown in by the wind had the appearance of weighing a few hundred tons. She was certainly no feather, no dry leaf in an autumn wind to blow away at any time. It seemed to me that big and heavy ship was there in Langley's field to stay, and I sort of felt sorry for him.

"I have to say one thing," he said to me. "All the dray horses in Rivertown won't be able to haul that thing out of my turnip patch, and my old lady is gonna have a fit when she finds out."

Just then we heard a noise on the deck, and looking upward we saw a tall man looking downward. He was slim and handsome and dressed in some kind of uniform, or so it seemed, and he had a gleaming cutlass dangling from his left hip. He smiled and spoke cordially.

"Avast there! I'm Captain Sebastian Yoke," he said loud enough without shouting. "I'm here to take on some new sailors, but I think I possibly misjudged the size of your harbor and came a bit far up."

"You say you misjudged the harbor?" cried the innkeeper. "Why, man, you're fifty miles from the sea! Even though our river is nearby, you're on dry land in my turnip patch! My wife is partial to turnips, I must tell you, and will have a fit."

The Captain drew from the pocket of his waistcoat a silken handkerchief and wiped his brow with it. The sun was beating down pretty hot that day, and the deck of that ship just had to be hot. He tucked the handkerchief away with a genteel flourish and spoke again. "I'm only going to be here a month or so, my good man, and I shall be on my way when my business is done."

"Well, I don't want to be a bad neighbor," Langley replied, "but I worry, you see, about how my wife is gonna take all this."

The Captain probed inside another pocket and pulled

out a golden brooch that shined in the sun like a beacon at night. With an expert movement of hand and wrist he tossed it down.

"I hope this will pacify your gracious wife," he said in that resonant voice of his, "at least for the time being."

The village innkeeper was taken aback by this development and let the brooch slip through his fingers as he tried to catch it. In the dust it glittered like finest gold and felt heavy in his hand.

"I can't say she don't like trinkets of this kind," Langley yelled. "I'm sure its value outweighs any inconvenience you're causing here."

"Tut, man. Forget it!" said the Captain. "There's plenty more where that came from. Your wife, I warrant, will like my little gift?" And with that he turned on his heel and went inside his cabin.

Langley held the golden brooch close to his chest as we walked homeward, and he mumbled how much his wife would like it. "That tempest sure did blow me some luck. The missus will love this thing. She'll wear it to church every Sunday."

Well, Gertrude Langley liked the brooch very much and wore it to every social event she attended in our village. She wore the trinket as proud as a peacock and said to anyone who would listen that a few measly turnips couldn't hold a candle to a golden antique brooch fashioned expressly to make a woman beautiful.

I should tell you the people in Rivertown didn't have much time to bother with the ghost ship or its Captain and crew. Also it's just not our habit to meddle in things that don't concern us. So we went our way and they went theirs, and Captain Yoke stayed longer in that turnip patch than he said he'd be staying.

Time moved along at its usual pace, and our shoemaker told me something over coffee one morning that really surprised me. He said his great-grandpa, known to me as a quiet and courteous spirit, had got in the habit of coming home drunk as a skunk at three o'clock in the morning and waking up the whole house.

"Why, it can't be Jeremiah!" I exclaimed. "He's one of the most respectable ghosts in the entire village."

"It's him all right!" said the shoemaker.

I could hardly believe a steady young ghost like Jeremiah had taken to drink, but then in a hustle the butcher came in complaining about his ancestor who fell in one of the last battles of the Revolution. He too was coming home drunk, hooting and howling. After that I kept my ears open and found out there was hardly one young buck among all the ghosts of Rivertown who wasn't straggling home all tight and tipsy and prone to noise in the middle of the night.

And we soon found out where the young reprobates were getting the sauce, the demon rum that made them daft. Langley wanted to give the Captain notice to clear out of his field, but each time he worked up the courage to confront that ghostly gentleman he remembered his wife would never part with her brooch. So things went from bad to worse until our parson, a very persuasive man, knocked on my door early one morning with a stern look in his dark brown eyes.

"I must have words with Captain Yoke about all this drunkenness in the village," he said. "I'm ready to put a stop to it, and I want you to come with me. Dead or alive we must have exemplary conduct among our citizens. If the rowdy behavior doesn't cease, we will certainly lose our reputation as a nice place to visit."

"Well, after all, it's only a bunch of ghosts," I replied, grinning. "It's not like your maiden aunt getting drunk at a tea party."

The parson is a good man but lacks a sense of humor. He didn't seem to understand my remark and ignored it.

So to the ship we went on a rainy day. When the Captain taking the air on deck saw us looking up at him, he doffed his hat politely and invited us on board. We climbed a slippery rope ladder that scraped the side of the ship, and he took us into his cabin with the bay window. It was a fantastic place. It had heaps of gold and silver coins scattered on black velvet and big chests thrown open to show they contained many more coins. And he had a chest with rare gems just pouring out it. It seemed to me the ship had been everywhere because neatly placed on shelves were many curious items from every corner of the globe.

Parson Rumley didn't complain when the Captain handed us ornate silver cups filled with thick rum. He sniffed at his before sipping it, but I drank mine in one or two gulps. I couldn't blame our ghosts for guzzling so much of the stuff. It filled my veins with honey and my heart with song. I wanted to dance a little jig to music that came pouring from the sky. The rum was out of this world.

In that giddy state I didn't listen much to what the parson was saying, but I guess he was telling Captain Yoke to leave off supplying rum to the younger apparitions in our village 'cause they were setting a bad example for the older ones who might be inclined to ape them. The Captain listened politely with full attention and only put in a word now and then. When the parson was done, he filled our cups again and quietly informed Rumley of his intention to leave us.

"It will please you to know, sir, that I will cause no more trouble. It will please you even more to know that I shall put out to sea tomorrow night. My plan is to sail eastward from here. Now I ask but one favor: wish me a good voyage with a hearty toast."

We readily obliged the Captain, and when we left the ship we wobbled to and fro in the muddy field trying to avoid the turnips. Parson Rumley rolled along in a funny sort of way, sloshing through the mud and laughing and telling off-color jokes. I had never seen the man behave like that, but I blamed it on the rum, that brave sweetly medicated draft, and not him. His merry babbling was like the music of mermaids in love and sort of moving. I was mumbling stuff too, and then I heard the parson say distinctly.

"If I were you, my friend, I would go home to bed and say nothing of this. Tell yourself it never happened." He has a way of putting things real straight, you know. So I did as I was told.

The next day before dawn the wind piped up strong. Before I finished my breakfast it was gusting real high and shaking my roof again. I feared the breeze might bring down the whole house. So I took a shortcut through a clump of battered trees to the inn. Langley and a stout man helped me shut the door. It seemed to me a dozen goats were pushing against it, eager to come in out of the storm.

"It's a powerful blow," Langley said, pouring me half a glass of rum. "I hear some chimneys are down already, and someone said the new roof on your barn is in your neighbor's pond."

That made me feel real bad because I had paid dearly to have the roof replaced after the first storm. But all I said was this: "You know it's funny how sailors can predict the weather, how they seem to know when a blow is coming. This tempest is even stronger than the first, and so their ship should go tonight with good speed."

After a few drinks and tall tales that took us through the day — Langley's rum is certainly not as good as the Captain's — we had trouble with the door. The wind burst it open like a bullet blasts a bottle. It didn't seem to bother Langley, for up in the sky was a sight to behold. Sailing quite comfortably among the windy stars under full sail and like a delicious white cloud in a black sky, was the ghost ship, the one we thought had taken up permanent residence in the turnip patch. Her portholes blazed with light and we heard music and singing from the deck. And then we heard a stentorian blast as though from a trumpet.

"Get to it, ye sea dogs! Into the rigging! Shorten sail! Make haste! The ship's heeling by thirty degrees!"

The crew must have jumped to it, for the ship righted herself in minutes and sailed swiftly away. We never saw her again.

When morning came we examined the storm's damage

and found it moderate. Trees were down all over, and the centuries-old elm in Oliver Thatcher's yard barely missed his house. Some chimneys were down too and some roofs damaged, but the report that mine blew away was exaggerated. Only a few shingles landed in my neighbor's pond, and that I was glad to see. However, our insubstantial ghosts were blown away, and this time only a few returned. That's because most of the young men, lured by rum and adventure, had sailed with Captain Yoke. That really upset the ghost girls, and we could hear them bawling and howling like old banshees even in the day time. Families lost their ancestors, and the ones who had complained the most about drunken behavior went about lonely. The butcher and shoemaker grumbled the loudest, but I didn't have much sympathy for them.

Then one day some months after all this happened a ghostly young man who had sailed with Yoke came stumbling up Main Street and sat down on a bench in the park and told us a fantastic story. It seems the Captain turned out to be not a gentleman at all but a bloodthirsty pirate on the prowl for Spanish loot.

"We anchored in the lee of an island," said the young ghost, an ancestor of a lawyer in town, "and we waited for a ship on the horizon to come closer. When her colors told us she was Spanish, we fought them bastards like fury and seized their valuables. I got a brooch here to prove it, and some others got doubloons worth a fortune."

To the amazement of all who saw it, the brooch was heavy and golden and exactly like the one Captain Yoke gave Langley's lady. Today we display the piece in the town library, but when asked to place her brooch on display beside it, Gertrude Langley adamantly refused. She insisted she would keep her bibelot and hand it down to her daughters as a family heirloom. Rivertown don't have no ghosts any more and no ghost ship with a swashbuckling Captain to get them drunk. The town is a bit boring without them, but maybe you would like it. You're welcome here at least for a day or two. Come see us.

22
The Walker

The times were hard and I was on the road again. For several months I had worked as a carpenter for a construction company in Raleigh. They promised when the project was finished they would have more work for me, but that didn't happen. A pimply straw boss smelling of cologne and cheap gin told me one day I was no longer needed. I would have to pack up my things in the shed where I slept and move out. He gave me the nine dollars I had coming, ordered a yes-man to escort me off company property, and left me to shift for myself. I had a girl in town but had to leave her without notice, and that bothers me even now.

With no income and only a few dollars in my pocket, I heard of a good thing in Richmond and decided to walk a hundred miles to get there. I would walk if I had to but was hoping people more fortunate might give me a lift. In the first hours walking beside the road a score of Buicks and Chevrolets went whizzing by. Not a single driver even bothered to look in my direction. Then at last a farmer in a rusty truck with a wobbly front wheel stopped in the roadside dust. I shouldered my knapsack containing everything I owned and ran to meet him.

The year was 1933 and surely you know it wasn't a good year. A lot of things were happening in 1933, good for some people but not so good for most. Shirley Temple wasn't yet a movie idol, but Greta Garbo (real name *Greta Gustafsson*) was a big film star and so was one-in-a-million Mae West. A popular movie was *King Kong*, and *The Lone Ranger* was on the radio. Several construction companies began building the Golden Gate Bridge that year, and people hoped work like that would bring us out of the Great Depression. Sadly, it didn't.

The headlines of the time were ugly. Adolf Hitler was appointed Chancellor of Germany in 1933 and by the end of March had become dictator of the German people. Some disgruntled nut in Miami tried to gun down president-elect Franklin D. Roosevelt but killed the Mayor of Chicago instead. In Washington desperate measures were taken to stem the ravages of the Depression, but the bread lines in spite of the New Deal were as ugly as the headlines. Millions were out of work and thousands stood in line for a crust of bread and a bowl of watery soup. The nation and all the world seemed to be going to hell in a hand basket. I had to live through it all, and somehow I managed to survive.

In March at about the time the Nazis were beginning to persecute German Jews, the Civilian Conservation Corps (CCC), was created by Congress to relieve rampant unemployment. I was working at the time and so didn't pay much attention, but in the fall when I lost my job I got to thinking maybe it wasn't a bad idea to look into joining the Corps. Some of my friends had already signed up and told me I should go to Richmond and be inducted. From there I would be sent into rural lands owned by federal, state, and local governments to improve them with manual labor. For me it seemed the right thing. Though often hungry, I was young and healthy and needed to work. So I went on the road again. I would walk from Raleigh to Richmond if I couldn't hitch a ride. The first to show me a bit of kindness was the man in the truck.

I thought he didn't see me because he rumbled past me some distance before stopping. I could smell the exhaust as the truck sat idling. An old man with a scraggly white beard was sitting in the cab. He was chewing tobacco and spat a dollop of brown juice at my feet while telling me to get in. I don't think he was aiming at me with that stuff, and yet I couldn't help but think it was an unfriendly gesture from a man who had the heart to give me a ride. He asked me where I was going, and we talked about Richmond. He reminded me it was once the capital of the Confederacy, and he said a relative of his died at Gettysburg. Over the years he had raised a big family on a big farm, but lately his wife had died and now he was all by himself with no one to work the farm. His three sons had joined the Navy, and one of his daughters died of dehydration due to cholera. The younger girl, only seventeen, moved into town when she married a car salesman.

He was hungry to talk, and I rode with him down that highway for at least twenty miles. Then we came to a country road, and he said he had to go that way to get home. He stopped the truck to let me out, and again I could smell a strong odor of exhaust, like the muffler or something was leaking. I said maybe he oughta get it fixed and he said he might, but maybe I should go on to his house for a good supper.

"I ain't the best of cooks, mind you, but you look like you could use a some meat and potatoes to stick to them ribs of yours. I'd like someone to chat with for a while. It gets sort of lonely out there in the sticks."

I asked how far did he live from the main road, and he said eight miles, and I knew he expected me to walk back to the main road after eating his vittles. My belly yearned for a good meal, but my brain told me walking eight miles for what might not be a good meal just wasn't worth it. So I said goodbye to the old fart as gently as I could, and we parted company. I could smell his truck as it chugged away.

Night was coming and the fall air was turning nippy, and so I walked at a good pace just to keep warm. Every now and then a car with blazing headlights would pass and I would stick out my thumb. They didn't notice and I kept on walking. When I began to feel more tired than hungry, I looked for a place to spend the night. Though I had some beef jerky in my bag to tide me over when food was scarce, I would have to sleep without any supper. Then I heard shuffling footsteps behind me, boots lightly scuffing the pavement.

I spun around and saw a skinny little girl not five feet tall limping along and lighting a cigarette. She was cupping her long hands in the wind to keep the match from sputtering out and puffing. She wore no overcoat, not even a sweater, and she looked unspeakably fragile in a thin summer dress. In the moonlight I could see she had a lame left leg. Her face, half hidden by an unruly mop of dirty blonde hair, was ghostly pale. Her eyes were black, larger than normal, and filled with the pain of living. I was about to ask how she happened to be on the road at night in the middle of nowhere when she spoke first.

"You walking this road, Mister? You been walking this way long? You on the road maybe to Richmond?"

"Yes, I think I am," I answered curtly.

"Well, if you don't mind, Mister, I'll walk with you but don't go too fast. My legs ain't very good any more. You know it's sorta lonesome walking the road this time of day."

"It's night," I corrected. "The day is over and I gotta find a place to sleep, but I can walk a mile or two with you. You live around here? You left home without a coat? That's a fool thing to do in late October."

"No, I don't live anywhere close to here. And I don't own a coat. I had to pawn it this summer when I needed to eat. I been on the road a long time, and I can tell you it ain't always easy. The police picked me up a few times and slapped me around when I wouldn't go home. I kept running away. I said to them police guys, *'Why don't you leave me alone and go looking for Bonnie and Clyde? I ain't doing nothing wrong.'* They laughed at that. Now I don't have a home except the roads, and they all look the same. Sometimes I wish I could be riding with Bonnie and Clyde, getting my name in the papers. I'm eighteen, you know. Bet you think I look younger."

"Fifteen," I said. "You look no older than fifteen. And it ain't no good to be wanting to ride with Bonnie and Clyde.

They're getting in the papers all right, but they gonna die young."

"Well, you're wrong. Mister. Them two will live forever and so will Pretty Boy Floyd, and I was eighteen in August. Walking in that month is murder, just too damn hot. My dress keeps sticking to my bum leg when it's hot and wants to work its way up. I wouldn't mind if I had pretty legs, but I got nerve damage in one, and both too skinny."

"You could use more weight all right. Guess you don't eat as good as you should when you're walking like this in all kinds of weather."

"I never did eat good, and I been on the road a long time. Now I don't have a home to run away from, just the road. I'm a walker."

She puffed on her cigarette, inhaling deeply and smoking the butt to less than an inch before flipping it away. It was the only one she had.

"I don't have a home neither," I said to her, "but I'm hoping to have one a few years from now. I expect to work for the government and save some money in hard times. I don't know why I'm telling you this, but I hope to find work as a CCC man."

"CCC?" she asked in a monotone. "I never heard of that. What does it mean? I can't understand why people think initials are words."

"Civilian Conservation Corps. Single men can join and get paid and work at building bridges and roads and planting trees and stuff. You live close to the work site, and you get paid pretty good."

"Oh, then you expect something at the end of the road. You have a reason for walking here at night. You have something called *hope*. I don't have that any more. I did have a lot of it when I started walking, but now none at all. Any hope I ever had just slipped through my fingers and fell to the ground. Crushed at fifteen. I'm eighteen now, no lie."

For her to be talking like that sort of puzzled me, and I didn't know what to say. I was beginning to lose my patience with this strange, inquisitive, talkative and lonely vagrant, and I muttered, "Well, I'm always expecting something. It's human nature, ain't it?"

"Not with me," said the girl gently, "coz I'm dead."

The remark carried no drama with it at all. It was plainly spoken and matter of fact. I had to strain my ears to hear it, and yet it split the night air like an axe striking a hunk of firewood.

"I'm beginning to feel that way too," I replied after deciding to take what she said as a joke. "I'm dead-tired and gotta find a warm place to sleep but don't see no barns anywhere, only fields and forest. It's not a good place for people like you and me."

"I'll tell you something," the girl said hoarsely. "People like us are the unfortunates of the world. It was never intended for us to live like other people and be happy. We're always hungry and thirsty and tired and sick and walking. I'm on the road now coz I can't help it. I'm tired to the bone and sick but proud to be walking."

She stopped in the middle of the road, overcome by a dark, insistent cough that put her on her thin knees shivering. This strange waifish stray alarmed me, and yet I felt sorry for her too. I took off my coat and tried to put it over her bony shoulders.

"Here," I said. "Take my coat for a little while. You need it more than me. That cough of yours sounds real bad and you're shivering."

"You go to hell!" she replied, glaring fiercely at me. "I don't take no charity from nobody. You're my brother because you walk the road with me, but I want nothing from you, especially pity. Another thing, you won't molest me neither. Too many already tried. They'll burn in hell!"

I backed off and just as I did she slumped to the pavement. I pulled her limp body to the side of the road, looked in all directions for help, and saw nothing. As I was trying to revive her, pumping her sunken chest to get her breathing easy, my luck changed. A Ford roadster, bright and shiny, in better condition than me or the girl, came up swiftly. The driver jammed on the brakes and stopped.

"What's the trouble?" asked a gentleman with a gray mustache and a worsted suit that had to be expensive.

He was out of the car in seconds and kneeling beside the girl. He held her wrist for a pulse and put his ear to her chest. Looking at me with concern, he said her labored breathing appeared to be a symptom of pneumonia or tuberculosis or both. She needed professional care.

"This girl's in sad shape," he said. "She needs to see a doctor and fast. I'll take her to a hospital down the road. It's only a few miles. You can come along with us."

Well, I don't like hospitals and I shy away from them whenever I can. It was late and I had to find a place to sleep, and so I said I'd walk on alone. We lifted the girl, light as a feather, into the car and it sped away. I'm certain she wasn't conscious when we placed in the front seat, and yet I couldn't help but notice the large black eyes as

I tried to make her comfortable and what looked like a playful wink.

I went to sleep on a bed of leaves. Morning came with an autumn sun that later gave way to rain. I didn't feel the rain until I was out of my nest and standing up. I knew it was going to be a wearisome day trudging along all wet and hungry and not knowing where or when I would eat. Then to my surprise I found an apple tree with fat, over-ripe apples still on it. I went on down the road, moving slow at first and then faster to stay warm. It wasn't all that bad a day until I heard a familiar, high-pitched voice coming from behind me.

A figure as thin as a shadow had slipped out of nowhere to confront me. "You walking this lonely road, Mister? You on the road maybe to Richmond? Well, if you don't mind, I'll walk with you but don't walk too fast coz I got a bum leg. It's lonesome walking this time of day."

We walked the first mile slowly because she was limping as before. Near the end of the second mile she went off to some bushes to relieve herself and never returned. I never saw her again. In the distance surrounded by fields in need of farming was a house. I hoped she went inside to find food and shelter but never found out.

Walking with her on that road was like a nightmare remembered at noon. Yet from time to time even when busy at work I can't help but think about her. To this day I wonder what happened to that lunatic girl addicted to walking and proud to be a walker when millions were suffering. Maybe she died the next year like Bonnie and Clyde, or maybe she didn't. Maybe, for all I know, she was already dead when I met her that chilly autumn night on the road.

23
The Merchant

Boston on a Sunday morning in the middle of November was damp and cold. From the gray sky came a threat of icy rain or snow. A bitter wind whistled through the streets, and people on the pavement turned up their collars and bent their heads low to push onward. In their chilled faces I could see marks of misery not caused by the weather. I was getting settled in the city after a long sea voyage, and I can say with certainty I wasn't very cheerful either. I had thought the ship would dock in the warmth of a southern port, but in mid ocean the captain received word to dock in Boston. I like to make the most of the hand fate deals me, and so in November I was racing against winter to find a job.

Now prowling the streets in bleak weather, I tried to convince myself I was only a spectator of the human condition. But when a heavy vehicle splashed icy street water on my trousers from ankle to knee and above, I began to feel that I too had fallen victim to a world grown uncaring and ugly. I looked around and saw no sun to flood the streets, no warmth and no laughter, and I wondered why. What had become of the children, hooting and hollering and warming hearts? Where indeed was the faithful dog affectionate and wagging its tail? I saw only the sad faces and hunched figures of weary pedestrians in a hurry. I heard only the hacking cough of an old man and the sound of feet on pavement.

The wind blew hard down dreary streets that were named long ago (believe it or not) in alphabetical order: Arlington, Berkeley, Clarendon, Dartmouth, Exeter, Fairfield, Gloucester, Hereford. The bitter wind chilled me in every sinew and made my teeth chatter. Yet my brain, warm under a woolen cap, was amused by the Boston street names. I didn't know how they came about. Did some wag with a whimsical sense of humor manage to pull a practical joke on the entire city? Or did a committee of pompous men at a big table make the decision? My thoughts were suddenly interrupted by a strange little man who sidled up to me, thrust a leaflet in my face, looked me earnestly in the eye, and insisted I take it.

"No!" I said to him with some impatience. "I never read those things. Save it for someone more gullible."

"But, sir, you must have it! Ignore the small print, if you will, but read the bold print. Your destiny — your destination more exactly — requires you to know what my leaflets contain."

"What they contain I don't really care to know. I have no interest in what you're pushing, no interest whatsoever in the tired drivel I'd find there. Also I'm fairly certain they're not your leaflets, as you say. Didn't some hack prepare them for a fee, and were you not hired to pass them out? I advise you to get out of the cold, old man. You seem to be limping and shivering and your lips are blue."

"You think I'm a tramp, a good-for-nothing doing this for a few pennies. I assure you, my good man, I'm not. For many years I have been a successful merchant, and the leaflets I hold in my hands I myself prepared especially for men like you. The first paragraph will tell you exactly what you have done with your life. The second will tell you what the future holds for you."

The man spoke in good English and seemed educated. I observed him with new-kindled curiosity. His clothing was by no means that of a prosperous merchant. The thin overcoat he wore was greasy-looking and ready for the trash bin. The hat, pulled down over dark eyes with bags under them, was old and battered. His shoes were in no better condition than his hat. Yet he claimed to be a successful merchant?

"I'm finding your comments hard to believe, old fellow, but if it makes you feel any better I'll take one of your leaflets. I can't say I'll read it in this cold and windy street but will look at it when I get home."

Quickly the little man thrust the sheet of paper into my hands and with a bow of quiet civility made ready to walk away. "You are thinking I'll be working all day long to get rid of my leaflets," he said, struggling to smile, "but not so. I give a leaflet only to each person who needs it. You won't regret receiving it."

I watched him shuffle down Berkeley with its shops on either side and the steeple of a nearby church hovering over the street like a child stomping on a toy. The sky was turning less gray, and I glanced at the flyer he had given me. Then with a low whistle of astonishment I looked at it carefully. In the left top corner was a detailed drawing of an ornate casket. Under it in bold and black letters was this injunction: *"You Will Soon Be In The Market For A Coffin."* A smaller inscription read: *"At 312 Blackstone, D. B. Agincourt & Co. will fill your order promptly. Come see us at your earliest convenience."*

"Strange!" I thought with some amusement. *"I'm thirty-four and will soon be needing a coffin? For me? Or for my no-good brother struggling to make a living somewhere in the South? Could it be a portent warning me of impending calamity? Nah, I don't believe in such nonsense."*

In my tiny apartment as I read the Sunday paper, the leaflet lying on a table nearby became the focus of my thoughts. In imagination I began to see an undertaker attempting to drum up business by passing out flyers fraught with scare tactics. It seemed on the surface a brainless endeavor, even a joke. Then reason told me the man who gave me the leaflet wasn't brainless at all and not capable of joking.

"You Will Soon Be In The Market For A Coffin." The words vaguely suggested some kind of threat. Had I made an enemy of someone rabid enough to kill me? I had perhaps an enemy or two among rough people in other places, and I had far-flung relatives who could have a grudge against me. Yet not a one knew my whereabouts after crossing the Atlantic to return home. Also, I was young and healthy. It was unlikely I would need a coffin any time soon.

In the afternoon my friend Horace Rye who lived in the same building came to my apartment to ask if I would have dinner with him. He had been working long hours all week and needed to relax over good food in a good restaurant. I showed him the curious leaflet. He read it with a serious look on his thoughtful face.

"It could be nothing more than a joke," he said, "but in the wrong hands, say a high-strung person, it could be a mite dangerous."

"I'm inclined to agree. I'll pay a visit to Mr. D. B. Agincourt tomorrow. I really need to get to the bottom of this."

"You have his invitation," Rye laughed. "So it's only polite of you to go. Why don't you come by my place later and tell me about it?"

"I don't expect to find a gargoyle or griffin, probably nothing more than the sad little man I saw this morning, but I'll let you know."

Monday was a gorgeous day, one of those rare days in a New England winter, with blue skies and sunshine. Instead of taking a cab, I decided to walk to Blackstone Street and speak to Mr. Agincourt at the address on the flyer. The place was only a few blocks from my neighborhood and not at all like an ordinary funeral home.

The window facing the street was draped with heavy black curtains, and I saw nothing to identify the business. I opened the heavy oaken door and stepped into the vestibule of an old mansion. To the right was a large room carpeted in white with an enormous coffin on display. To the left was a smaller, less impressive room with a counter and chairs. It appeared to be the office of the establishment. I stood at the counter and rang a silver bell. Within minutes a little man came blinking like a mole from a hole. He was dressed neatly in a well-fitting suit and vest. I detected no limp, and his lips were no longer blue with cold.

Though I knew him immediately as the man who had given me the leaflet, he appeared not to recognize me.

"May I help you, sir?" he asked pleasantly. His voice was higher in pitch than when I met him in the street.

"I want to know about this leaflet you gave me yesterday. In the wrong hands, it could be quite disturbing, even dangerous."

"Oh, I should hope not!" he said with an air of surprise. "I believe our representative made it clear to you that we distribute these leaflets only to persons who need them, and we are very careful to avoid mistakes."

"Your *representative* as you put it was you, sir. Furthermore, I think you can see I have no need for a coffin."

"Oh but you do indeed," the man suavely replied. "You will soon need a coffin, sir, no doubt about it. We have information, special information to that effect. If our representative gave you that little advertisement, it was because you really need to read it."

"You appear to be a reasonable man," I said, "and yet this babble you give me isn't reasonable at all. You speak of a *representative* but you gave me this flyer yourself only yesterday, and you know it. Now I want to know why you think I need a coffin."

"It's a sentimental profession, you must know, based on long tradition. The dead don't really need coffins. You and I both know that. Cremation is cleaner, faster, less expensive, and more efficient."

"The dead? What are you trying to say?"

"I was coming to that. Life is so very short and we must always keep in mind that death comes soon. Sometimes it comes when we least expect it. Your name is Horace Rye?"

"No, no. That is *not* my name. My friend and neighbor who lives in the same building goes by that name."

"Oh, my! I see! I said we seldom make mistakes but apparently I was speaking with too much confidence. I must look into the matter immediately. We have no time to spare. Our special intuition tells us that when a person needs a coffin it's usually within twenty-four hours. Oh, I must correct the error posthaste. You can rest assured nothing in this leaflet applies to you, sir. Oh, my! I must look into this without delay. Please pardon the inconvenience. Please forgive us for any unrest we may have caused. It won't happen again. I do apologize."

The sun had dipped behind dark clouds and the breeze warmed earlier by sunlight was now colder. On the pavement again I tried to recall exactly what the strange little man behind the counter had said. His firm had made some kind of mistake and he was sorry. He was beside himself with anxiety and quickly left the room. He didn't have the courtesy to show me out of the dimly lit place but apologized profusely.

The short November afternoon quickly grew dark and cold. I walked briskly westward toward my residence, but denizens of the pavement blundered into me, almost knocking me down. A light drizzle began to fall. I hailed a cab and went home. There beside the window looking down on the wet street I sat for an hour, resting calmly before going to the kitchen for a cup of coffee. Glancing at the clock on the mantelpiece, I remembered Rye had asked me to come to his place to tell him what I discovered when visiting D. B. Agincourt.

"Perhaps, if you go there, you'll find the solution to your riddle," he had said. "Either that or a cuckoo bird chittering and chattering."

I had found no solution at all and no bird, only a suave little gentleman perhaps of French descent named Agincourt. He had given me the double talk of his profession and had quickly retreated. One thing of real importance I did discover. I was not in their business ledger, not in the market for a coffin after all. I felt somewhat relieved.

At nine in the evening I went to Rye's apartment. His door opening on the hallway stood ajar, and that led me to believe I was expected. I entered, shut the door, and turned on the light. My friend was slumped in a chair near the window sound asleep. I can't forget that look of calm and peaceful serenity on his rugged face. His eyes were closed and a barely perceptible smile lifted the corners of his mouth. I knew the man was much in need of rest, and so I decided not to waken him. I left him where I found him and returned to my own rooms. For several days I was busy with job interviews and saw no sign of my neighbor. Then I read in a newspaper that the Boston Harbor Patrol had found the body of a man in his early thirties in the water near the docks.

A day or so later the landlord of our building gave me the full details. Horace Rye, who worked on the docks as a shipping agent, had become the victim of a tragic accident. Inspecting the cargo of an Indonesian ship, he slipped and fell into freezing water. Although three brave men risked their lives to drag him out, he was dead by drowning when they got to him. My landlord added, after telling me this, that Mr. Rye had been a good tenant and would be sorely missed.

The next day was frigid, but I went again to see D. B. Agincourt at his place of business. He had identified me as Horace Rye, and I wanted him to explain the connection between him and my friend. Viewing me as Horace Rye, he had said I needed a coffin. Then days later I learned that Rye had drowned by accident. Was his death coincidence, or something more sinister? I went to Agincourt's place to talk at length with him but was sadly disappointed. On the street where the solid old funeral home had stood, I found a vacant lot. In it were only a few gray bricks. Near the sidewalk a rose bush caught my attention. Deep within the faded leaves was a crimson rose defying the weather.

24
Eugene the Conjuror

The audience in one of New York's finest theatres was restive. Marco the Marvelous, known in Europe and now in America as the greatest magician of his time, was slated to perform but had fallen ill the day he arrived from Paris. Frantic, the producer of the show sent his people searching for a replacement. They found Eugene the Conjuror, a struggling magic maker who had never performed before an audience so vast, particularly one that had paid dearly to see the world's best.

They had come to see Marco's levitation act in which he placed a shapely woman stiff as a board between two chairs. They knew that after a bit of fanfare he would kick away one chair and then the other to have her rise in thin air. To prove there was nothing under or above her, no hidden strings or supports, he would pass a large hoop around her body and move it from head to toe. For several minutes while the audience gawked and the magician bowed with an oily display of suavity, the pretty woman would defy gravity, serenely floating in midair. Then in a cloud of blue smoke and blast of trumpets, she would find herself gently placed on her feet to the sound of wild applause.

That signature act made famous by Marco the Marvelous the well-dressed audience would not see that night. Instead they had before them a little man with a worried look on a pale face juggling brightly colored glass balls. In a red jacket and yellow trousers, he looked more like a gypsy clown than a magician. Lacking even a cheap imitation of Marco's black cape, he appeared to be a simple juggler and nothing more. People began to chatter and chuckle as they realized he was not even good at juggling. He was nervous, unsure of himself, and not in full control of his art. That was because Jennings, the dynamic theatre manager, had told him he would have a contract for an entire year if he managed to please the disappointed audience.

Much was riding on the Conjuror's performance. Though he struggled to do his very best, nothing at all went well. In the opening part of his show he had tried to saw his assistant in half, an act sure to please when well done. But fate, chance, hap, bad luck or an unkind power caused the blade to jam in its slot. When he tried to pull it out, the entire structure fell with a bang and a clatter to the floor. His assistant sprang to her feet and did a little congratulatory dance, as if the collapse was part of the act, but the audience knew better. From the gallery came hoots and cat-calls and derisive laughter. Even though his ears were burning and his tongue dry and parched with embarrassment, the juggler-magician laughed along with his audience, smiled broadly, bowed gracefully, and went on with his act.

Now as he juggled the fragile balls, he seemed to be losing the all-important edge, as jugglers call it, the supremacy of eye over object. He couldn't keep his eye on the one ball that kept all the others in motion. It missed his hand and seemed to explode when it hit the floor. Tiny shards of glass, glistening in the limelight, flew out in all directions. Musicians in the orchestra pit winced and touched their faces for blood. Men and women hissed and booed and threatened uproar. Jennings in the wings was shaking his head and mopping sweat from his brow.

"I've lost it, Molly," the magician said to his wife who served as his assistant. "I've lost any talent I ever had, and I've lost even a peon's contract with Jennings. I can't do anything right this evening. We may as well exit the stage and let the curtain fall. The audience will demand their money back and the manager will see that I never work again, but I can't go on with this ridiculous farce. I just can't do it."

"It's all right, dear," his wife whispered, bravely attempting to smile. "Gus is sweeping up the glass and we'll continue our performance whether people like it or not. We can't quit, it's not an option. So think of something good, something magical and mysterious."

"Think of something good?"

"Yes! Something like the liver and onions I'll cook for you when we get home tonight!"

He loved her for coming up with that. She had that special knack of saying something witty when wit was most needed. She was braver and more determined than he could ever be, and she was beautiful. If he gave up and quit, if he walked off the stage as a hangdog loser, he felt certain she would leave him. He knew she would never tolerate a loser. With big round tears bathing her face, she would tell him gently in that tone of voice he always found soothing that she couldn't be his wife or assistant any more. He would lose her. The one thing in his life he valued most he would lose, and he would die without her.

With the distinctive aroma of liver and onions tickling his nostrils, he summoned the strength to prepare in minutes the one act that could save the evening, his career, and even his marriage.

"The disappearance trick," he said. "We'll do it and do it well. We didn't rehearse it because I didn't plan to use it tonight. Now, after all that's happened, we have to do it."

"We've tried it two or three times, you know, but it didn't come off the way we expected. We have to get it right this time."

"We will amaze that pompous audience tonight. We'll execute the trick with stupendous aplomb. You, my love, will adorn the act with grace and beauty, and they will love you."

He had regained his old confidence and was boasting. She smiled encouragement as he turned to his audience, more restive than ever.

"Ladies and gentlemen!" he said in a strong but slightly unsteady showman's baritone. "I now present for your entertainment, edification, and mystification the last act of the evening. You will speak of it with awe and wonder at breakfast tomorrow morning and for the rest of the day. With no contrivance, with no mechanical device whatsoever, I will vaporize this lovely woman before your very eyes. She will disappear not to be seen by any of you ever again."

It was showman's banter, of course, patter the audience had heard before, and yet every person sat up to take notice. He had caught their attention, and they were willing to give him one last chance to please them. It was not a rare or fantastic illusion — many in the audience had seen other magicians perform it — but they wanted to see in what way his might differ. And they were thinking it might fall apart to bring down the house with peals of laughter. Those inclined to mock were now silent, and those ready to leave decided to stay.

To place her front and center, the conjuror took his lady by the hand and felt it tremble. She stood looking down at shadowy figures, a host of people she couldn't really see. In the glare of the limelight they could see every detail of her: the smooth and shapely shoulders, the graceful neck, the slender figure, and the pretty face surrounded by an abundance of dark hair. A ripple of applause went through the audience. Eugene felt supremely proud of her. It seemed to him that her beauty filled the vast auditorium, and all who saw her adored her.

"We must get it right this time, dear," she murmured.

And they did get it right. With a flourish he waved his magic wand above her head. Then slowly he pointed the instrument at his assistant, and poof! The lady was gone! Somehow, hidden by the puff of smoke that came from his wand, she had moved in seconds to the screen arranged to conceal her. But when he checked she was not behind the screen. The audience must have seen her scurry off the stage like a frightened puppy, and he expected them to laugh their heads off in unrestrained mockery. His last act had gone terribly wrong.

He had failed big time. He was ready to exit the stage as fast as his legs could take him when suddenly from the entire house came a burst of wild applause. They were mocking with applause instead of laughter, and their cruelty made him sick. How could they be so cruel? He thought of running off stage but couldn't move. He was ready to drop to the floor in a quivering heap of humiliation. He closed his eyes and stood transfixed, waiting for his knees to give way. Again and again applause broke out from every corner of the house, and the orchestra began to trumpet strains of praise. The curtain rose and fell and rose again. Opening his eyes, he couldn't believe what he was seeing and hearing. He braced himself and bowed. Then came more applause.

When the curtain was lowered for the last time, muffling the uproar, he staggered offstage to be supported by Jennings himself.

"Good for you, my good man! You have a job for at least a year, maybe more! See me in my office tomorrow and we'll sign the papers. That last trick of yours was uncanny, as good as any I've seen. I don't suppose you want to tell me how you did it."

"Did it with magic, sir, magic!" the conjuror replied.

"I daresay you did! No doubt about it! There she was one minute, then gone the next. Damnest thing I ever saw! She went poof and evaporated! For as long as a minute, some are saying, her shadow remained glued to the floor. Then as if to follow her it rose as a blue mist and vanished.

Can't imagine how you did it, but there's money in it for sure. I'll draw up a contract tonight and have it ready."

It was news he thought he would never hear, but if Jennings didn't know what had happened neither did he. So he went in search of his wife for an explanation. With sweet emotions churning within him, he searched the theatre, wondering whether even she could explain. Did the trick really come off as perfectly as people were saying? And what had become of Molly? When he asked about her, the stage hands laughed and laughed, convinced he was joking.

"We can't tell you where," they cried, "and neither can anyone else! Only you know where the lady went. You vaporized her, man, a terrific magical trick! Fantastic! Bravo!"

But he didn't know. Always in control of anything affecting her, Molly would know and tell him. Then with joy and a hint of mystery he would tell her about the contract Jennings was preparing.

He would find her in their dressing room. She would be there in her street clothes, waiting for him. He knocked on the door and getting no answer, entered abruptly. She wasn't there. The room was empty and cold. Her street clothes lay exactly where she had left them before going onstage. Seeing them alarmed him, but quickly he calmed himself. In spite of the mishaps, he would have a contract for a year with good pay. He had to find Molly and shout the good news. By now she would be home cooking that supper of liver and onions. But why did she leave in theatre garb? She had never done that. It was all so very strange.

He hailed a cab and sped home. Molly was adroit and

clever. She had fooled even the man who had taught her the trick. He would find her at home, and he fumbled nervously to unlock the door. He stepped inside to find only a night light in the living room. In shadowy darkness he called out for his wife. Turning on the lamps as he ran from room to room, he found the small apartment cold and vacant. From the tiny kitchen came no warmth or light, and no odor of onions sizzling with liver. Molly wasn't home. He saw only reminders of her.

"Oh my God!" he muttered, speaking emphatically to mute walls. "What is happening to me? What is happening to her, to us?"

He ran out with all the lamps blazing, leaving the door wide open, eager to get back to the theatre. What a fool he had been to suppose she left unnoticed to come home. Now he was certain she was in their dressing room waiting for him, and he would take all the blame. Half an hour went by before he could flag a taxi. The theatre was dark and deserted. He pounded on the stage door, waited for a minute or two, and pounded again. The old night watchman slowly opened it.

"My wife!" he cried. "I'm looking for my wife. She didn't return home. She just has to be somewhere in the theatre."

"There's not a living soul here, sir, nobody but me — only me."

He spoke respectfully, for even the watchman had been told that a new star in the business of entertaining people had risen that night.

"Take me to her dressing room," the magician urged. "Please, I must know whether she went there while I was away."

The watchman with night lantern in hand led the way through a long and narrow passage. He apologized for not moving faster.

"I'm getting old, you know, and I have a bum leg. But trust me, sir. Your wife can't be any other place but here." He was sensing agitation and wanted to sound sympathetic.

"I've been looking for her from the moment my show ended. I don't understand what's going on, just don't understand."

"It'll all come out in the wash," said the watchman, "and be as plain as day. They say you made your lady disappear better than anybody ever did it, and it brought down the house. Total disappearance. *Evaporation* the word I hear. But don't you worry, sir, we'll find her."

In the glaring light of the dressing room Molly's clothes lay neatly folded exactly where he had seen them earlier.

Then with some trepidation, for in a strange way he was beginning to believe in his own marvelous magic, the conjuror thought he might find her exactly where she disappeared the moment he waved the wand.

"Please take me to the stage," he said to the old man. "The task will make you richer by twenty dollars. I must stand where she stood. That's the key to solving this mystery. I'll stand where she stood and find her there demanding an apology for all the inconvenience."

The watchman was thinking the magician was becoming slightly unhinged. But for twenty dollars he readily led the man to the vast auditorium where a happy audience had witnessed and applauded an amazing feat on the brightly lit stage.

In an eerie green glow that cast strange shadows on the walls and ceiling and even made the old watchman breathe harder, the magician stood in the exact spot where two hours earlier he had performed his disappearance trick.

"Molly!" he called, "come back! The trick unfolded better than we expected. We have a contract for a year! Come back this instant, dear Molly, I conjure thee!"

The cavernous room, stripped of the humanity that had warmed it earlier, returned nothing but an echo. The magician, distraught and almost weeping, cried out again: "Molly! Please, Molly! Please come back! Come back now, this minute!" Again only a mocking echo.

The ancient watchman led the magic-maker outside, thanked him for his generous tip, locked the door securely, and went to his bunk in the basement to sleep. Eugene the Conjuror went home to empty rooms and fell asleep confounded and weeping.

A year later when all hope was gone and Eugene was working as a delivery man for a trucking company, he received a beautiful postcard of sea and sky. It came from a villa on the Isle of Capri. Blue ink in a feminine hand beckoned him: "I'm here, my love! Come to me!"

25
The Traveler

"Fascinating peregrinations you've experienced, Mister!"
"Indeed! Perambulations too!"

People sometimes refer to me as an Irish Traveler. I severed all contact with the Travelers some time ago, but traveling is in my blood. Even though I'm a hick from an odd little town in South Carolina called Kelly Junction, I figured any number of people in New York were no better than me. Thousands from Ireland had come there to live, fleeing the potato famine, and weren't they my brothers? There's an old saying among the Irish. Maybe you've heard it, maybe not. It claims we're the children of one mother because no other mother would have us. We're an ornery lot but like a good joke, and we know how to survive too.

In only a few years near the end of the nineteenth century Irish folk made up a third of the population of Boston, New York, Philadelphia, and Baltimore. New York had the largest number, and so I didn't have any trouble at all fitting in and finding a place in the Bronx. The city had Irish neighborhoods all over — Brooklyn, Queens, Staten Island — but I preferred the Bronx close to Manhattan.

The weather was real good that summer in 1880, and so when I wasn't looking for a job I was exploring the city. I looked for a job one day and explored neighborhoods the next. Leaving my cheap hotel room early each morning, I walked mile after mile through colorful streets. I was in no hurry and stopped to look at anything that caught my eye.

One day I strolled through the commercial district all the way to Mulberry Street in lower Manhattan. The street was listed on maps as early as 1755, and for many years it teemed with all kinds of people. It goes right through the middle of Little Italy, and walking that part I had to be careful not to bump into another pedestrian or step on someone's heels. In all my life I've never seen so many people, mainly from Italy and Sicily, crowding the street and sidewalks. Most of the time I had to dodge wagons, carts, horses, dogs, goats, and children as I moved along. On the edge of the sidewalk were green-grocer stalls tended mainly by heavy, middle-aged women. Children were everywhere.

Scores of men didn't seem to be doing anything whatever except standing in the street with their hands in their pockets and chatting. Every swarthy man wore a mustache, a hat, and dark clothing in need of a good cleaning. The women were in short sleeves but wore long and colorful skirts that swept the pavement. Barefooted children played games in the street. One little boy with long hair was running through the crowd chasing after a hoop. He wore only a grimy white shirt that barely covered his belly button. Two young men were throwing pennies at a line in the dirt (a gambling game my ancestors played in Ireland), and two boys grabbed apples from a vendor's cart and ran with them. Shouting threats of perdition, the vendor added his two cents to the noisy congested street. A hullabaloo of sounds and strange odors came from all directions. I had to be careful not to breathe too deeply the atmosphere of the street. It struck me as tainted air.

Another time in September I went to Mulberry Street to participate in the festivities surrounding the Feast of San Gennaro. The celebration began as a one-day religious ceremony by immigrants from Naples. Then overnight it became something like a fair lasting three days. Mulberry Street was the center of the celebration, and it was closed to traffic for the occasion. Everybody for miles around, decked out in their finest, poured into the street. A mob of perspiring bodies surged along laughing and hooting, their collective breath smelling of garlic and tomato paste. The scene was loud and happy, pregnant with festivity. Hard-working people free of labor for a brief time were having fun. Italians know how to make celebrations memorable. Though sometimes painful and uncertain, they celebrate life because they love it.

The festival featured parades honoring the saint, street vendors selling food and souvenirs, games and trinkets for children, Italian pastries that melted in your mouth, and other attractions. I was there to gawk at the Grand Procession that came near the end of all the festivities. They carried the saint's statue from one church to another down Mulberry Street. The faithful tossed coins into a container at his feet while others kissed his outstretched hand and pinned bills to his robe. I liked being there in the midst of all the activity, and I thought about sunny Naples I was never able to visit when I was a seaman.

The southern end of Mulberry Street sort of loses itself in New York's Chinatown. I went there and spent a couple of days jostling hordes of people. I stood out like a sore thumb in Chinatown because of my height and fair skin, but the Chinese are polite people and made me feel at home. If they noticed me (and I'm sure they did), they didn't make a show of it. They went about their business and let me to go about mine. I looked with interest at the window displays and all the street activity. Eateries along the way, not more than mere stalls, were serving up scallion pancakes, wonton soup, fried dumplings, tapioca bubble tea, taro-filled sticky buns, candied crabs, and more. The Chinese love to cook all kinds of stuff and live to eat it. But strangely, I didn't see fat women as I did among the Italians.

The street was crowded with grocers, butcher shops, fishmongers, and vendors of live geese and goats. Standing large above the street was an array of brightly colored signs in Mandarin. People on the pavement were speaking Mandarin or Cantonese or whatever, and I felt like I was in a foreign country. It was a noisy place and smelly but it dazzled my senses. I stopped to sample some of the food. It was cheap and good. Once or twice I got jostled and thought of pickpockets, but I had nothing they could pick and must have been a disappointment. I heard about the Lunar New Year that Chinatown celebrates with eye-popping parades near the beginning of February and thought I would like to be there, but I knew by then I would be in another locale. An old man with one eye touched my arm and mumbled in broken English, "You wan' opyum?" He held on to my sleeve even after I declined his offer. In time I made my way back to my room in the Bronx.

When October came, I had to think about moving on down to a warmer climate and finding a job. My search for work in New York had turned up only one hard and dirty job at low pay, washing dishes in a Greek restaurant, and I didn't bother to take it. I liked being in the big city for the summer and walking the streets most of the time, but the money I had when I arrived was almost gone. I didn't want to find myself somewhere in winter with no job and no place to sleep and nothing to eat. Just the thought of that made me shudder. So near the end of the month with all my belongings in a rucksack I hitched a ride on a military caisson headed for Washington. When I said *caisson*, maybe you thought you didn't hear me right but you did.

They were a convoy of vehicles moving southward to the capital to participate in some kind of military exercise for the benefit of politicians who like to be entertained richly at government expense. I was straggling along beside the road, struggling with the weight of my rucksack, and a soldier asked if I wanted a ride. I gladly accepted his offer, and to keep him out of trouble I hopped on the back of the caisson. I didn't even know what a caisson was until they told me it was a cart for hauling ammunition. They bellowed with laughter and claimed it could blow at any minute. I took it to be a joke and didn't move an inch and got a free ride all the way to Washington.

You probably want to know what I thought of Washington. It's a pretty city with a lot of imposing buildings but a bit too grand for me. And I never did have much use for politicians. They claim their only reason for living is to help "the American people," but I'm pretty sure most are in the racket to help themselves. I remember the local politics back in Kelly Junction and I know how nasty the wheeling and dealing got to be at times. Even in a place like that we had a cockalorum — a word my grandma taught me — who went about telling people how to live their lives. Well, that wouldn't be so bad if you didn't have to pay money to be told how to live, but even in Kelly Junction we paid taxes.

The politicians were always into graft and corruption and just plain old greed. Oh, I guess you could say it was on a smaller scale than in a city like Washington, but it's still the same. As an Irish Traveler, I know for sure how some of them self-important little men, swaggering around in fancy clothes, fleeced even their own mamas and laughed about it. Oh, they lived high on the hog all right, for a time, until someone smarter took them down. It happened all the time in Kelly Junction and surely in Little Italy too. Though I never learned much about the Chinese, it just had to happen in Chinatown as well. The politician's cast of mind just ain't the same as yours and mine.

But you wanted to know whether I liked Washington. I can't say I despised that well-planned city with all its fancy buildings that look like they were shipped over from ancient Greece, but I was glad to leave it before the weather got cold. However, instead of going on southward, I decided to do a little backtracking. I got to thinking I wanted to go back to Baltimore. I had been in that port city years earlier but never saw much of the place. On the waterfront when I was young and seeking a way of life other than being an Irish Traveler, I had sold my horse and wagon and boarded a ship for New York hoping to become a seaman. So maybe nostalgia took me back to Baltimore, or maybe I was feeling I needed a partner in life and could find her there. I don't recollect exactly what my feelings were at that time, but I do know I was beginning to think I should settle down and maybe start a family.

And you guessed it, I was feeling kind of lonely too. In the midst of all the crowds in Chinatown and Little Italy I felt lonely. I was a solitary traveler enjoying myself but not sharing the good times with someone I cared about. All the people around me seemed to be in groups joshing each other with give and take and having fun together. I knew I didn't belong there with my fair skin and blue eyes and brown hair, and all that sweaty togetherness made me feel even more like an outsider. I remember a funny little girl in Mulberry Street. She was dressed all in white and came running up to me and caught my hand, crying Papa! Then she looked up at my face and saw I wasn't her papa. To judge from her reaction I might have been a monster hiding under her bed. Suddenly aware of her mistake, she let out a high-pitched screech, a really loud scream, and scurried away like a rabbit.

Some people in the street were thinking I had abused the child, and that sort of scared me because men have been lynched for less. Then her real papa, viewing what happened as a joke and laughing in a friendly way, quickly explained the situation and got rid of the gang around me. I didn't see it as a joke at all. The whole thing was sort of scary and got me to thinking. Could it be I was wasting my life bouncing from pillar to post? Shouldn't I find a steady job and a girl willing to marry me and settle down and maybe have a big and loving family?

Nah. I like living in my own little world. It can be lonely at times but never boring. I don't eat as well as I should, but who does? I like being on the move. I like seeing new things and different places and going to a new place when the spirit moves me. Come spring I'll be on the road again. I'm a peregrine traveler. Perambulation is in my blood.

26
Marvin Delgado

I was not an old salt by any means when I signed on as crewman of the *Sea Cloud* that day in late October, 1879. I knew almost nothing of nautical folklore and was embarrassed when the crew found out I had never heard of Mother Carey and her chickens. They had fun with my ignorance but offered an explanation. Mother Carey, they said, is responsible for storms and shipwrecks at sea and sends doomed sailors to Davy Jones's Locker. She's not a witch but flies above the boiling seas on her broom surrounded by storm petrels, her chickens, and laughs at the misery of sailors beneath her. No one likes her, all respect her. Her story is one of many nautical tales I learned while on the *Sea Cloud*.

As it happened, a seasoned sailor was injured in a drunken brawl the night before the ship was to sail. Though I had no experience at sea, I was chosen as one of several wharf rats to take his place. I found myself on call as an ordinary seaman twenty-four hours a day, answering to any officer at any time. The ship was scheduled to sail from New York to Gibraltar and on to

Naples. In less than a week I learned the ropes, got my sea legs sooner than expected, and did what I was told. Though dangerous work, particularly in the rigging, I liked being at sea.

During the early weeks of a mild November I had the morning watch from four to eight (0400 to 0800). When I came on deck one morning, all drowsy from not enough sleep, I found the seas almost calm. Stars in a black sky were like diamonds and seemed so close I thought I could reach up and touch them, or even snuff them like candles. A cool breeze touched my face to make me feel alive. I stood at the rail on the weather side of the vessel (the side hit by the wind) viewing the approach of dawn. It was a sight one can never see on land. Dawn at sea, as any sailor will tell you, differs markedly from that on land.

To the east I saw the first streaks of daylight. A bank of low clouds released dazzling beams of light the moment the sun touched the horizon. Those silver streaks wait for the rising sun and suddenly bring color to a gray sea. It stirs one with a sense of unease. Maybe it's the dying night or the new day struggling to be born that causes foreboding. You look around and all you see is a gray nothingness, the murky water merging with a murky sky and your tiny boat so small in the midst of it all. But then comes the dawn with silver and the sun with gold and the sea day begins. No longer ill at ease you feel a kind of joy.

Just as the dawn was breaking I noticed a cloaked figure sitting on the lee side of the cabin house shielded from the wind and smoking a meerschaum pipe. Because it was my watch, I had to identify the person and warn him to be careful with his ashes. The man seemed to be singing a strange little song. I paused to listen . . .

Oysters and rocks,
Sawdust and socks,
Grandpa made clocks
Out of cellos!
Blow us a breeze,
Now if you please,
Blow us a breeze,
With your bellows!

Marvin Delgado, our one paying passenger, greeted me with a friendly hello. He said he couldn't sleep and decided to come on deck and smoke his pipe and watch the dawn break.

We chatted for a while and I asked him about the song. He said his grandma taught it to him in Spanish when he was a very little boy. Later he came across the English version, liked it better, and memorized it. He had booked passage on our ship because he was told Gibraltar would be a port of call that would place him close to Spain. From Gibraltar he would go to Segovia to meet relatives not seen in many years.

Because his extended family had fallen on hard times, he would give them a heavy bag of jewels set in gold to sell for a handsome sum. It would allow them to live in comfort for the rest of their lives. He was glad to help them get back to a good life because they had helped him when he went off to America as a young man. He said he was not afraid to tell me all this because his valuables were well protected in the captain's safe. Even so, I wondered why a passenger would be so talkative with a common sailor. I guess he was a mite lonely. An order from the second mate interrupted my thoughts.

"You, there! No time for lollygagging! Look sharp! Rig the pump and swab the decks. Make them shine! Get some help."

Four of us pumped water from the sea and began washing the decks. It's an operation performed every morning. It takes about two hours and can be real hard on the back. When the job was over and the pump put away, I sat down to wait for seven bells, the call to breakfast. The second mate issued another order.

"You, there! Check the braces and rigging on the topgallant mast. Check every fitting from the royal masthead downward. Look for any worn stay or shroud, any tear in a sail, and be quick about it."

I was hungry and my empty stomach was aching, and I wanted to ask if I could do that dangerous job after eating. Yet I knew I couldn't disobey an order from this man who refused to call me by name. So up the mast I went, climbing gingerly on swinging ratlines. The higher I got as the wind picked up, the more the vessel rolled. It seemed to me I was on the end of an upside-down pendulum swinging back and forth. It was quite a ride and what a sight! From the royal masthead I could see a tiny white spot far out on the horizon. Because of the curvature of the earth, only I could see the object from my great height. Half an hour later when breakfast was nearly over, came the cry: "SAIL HO!"

I was off duty by then but went on deck to see clusters

of sail approaching slowly. Two ships larger than our brigantine were moving westerly. It was the first time I had seen other vessels at sea at such close range, and it seemed to me an artist had carefully painted them to exceed in beauty anything the human mind can imagine. I've heard it said that in all the world there is nothing more beautiful than a frigate under full sail on the deep blue sea, a galloping horse kicking up clouds of dust, and a dancing woman in skimpy costume swiveling her hips. The woman is pretty but the frigate is gorgeous. When I close my eyes I see a triple-masted square-rigger flaunting an abundance of white sails, scudding across a blue sea under a bright sky. Then of a sudden the ship becomes a gigantic bird all white and lifted into flight.

These two passed to leeward of us and out of hailing distance, but Captain Spooner using his glass could read their names when their sterns hove into view. They were both out of Boston and headed home. I've been told a sailor must have no regrets when on an outward voyage, but I wanted to be with them. The ships were raw and powerful but beautiful and moving fast. Within minutes, or so it seemed to me, they came and went, propelled by a stiff breeze from the southeast. Not long afterwards we dropped anchor in the Azores, remained there in the lee of an island for a storm to pass, and then moved out. In the open sea the breeze turned colder. I went to my sea chest in the fo'c's'le to get my pea jacket. That's when I heard a rumbling in the hold and men shouting. Instantly I knew something wasn't right.

I wanted to run toward the trouble to find out what was happening, but instinct took over and drove me to the deck and open air. On the quarterdeck, his wife and child beside him, Captain Spooner was ordering three men to release the tender from the doghouse and get it ready for launching. He explained that several small explosions had gone off like firecrackers in the hold, and he feared our cargo of raw alcohol might go with a big explosion. He couldn't be sure what would come next, but thought it prudent to abandon ship and wait to see what might happen. We were carrying a volatile cargo that could explode like a ton of gunpowder and blow the ship sky high. In minutes we got the tender over the side. The Captain's wife, his little daughter, and Dan the cook were in the boat as we lowered it. The rest of us soon followed.

Twelve of us crowded into the small boat towed by a line of about a hundred feet. Our capable Captain in yellow wet gear stood calm and tall beside the ship's wheel. As we looked up at him, he seemed the very picture of a Gloucester fisherman on a rainy day putting out to sea. To this day I believe he had decided to go down with his ship but had second thoughts when his wife cried out for him. The sky above us was blue and the wind was light, but to the southwest dark clouds were scudding low on the horizon. With her wheel lashed, the *Sea Cloud* under short canvas was moving slowly southward. She was towing thirteen tired and bewildered people in an open boat designed for nine.

We waited for something to happen, waited for the alcohol to explode. It didn't. Then as Captain Spooner decided to draw in the towline and climb back on the ship, a fresh wind filled her sails and she picked up speed. A yellow squall line lay on the horizon. The storm moved in with winds so fierce we could do nothing but hold on with white knuckles. The ship and our boat behind her moved faster and faster. Quickly the tender exceeded its hull speed and its prow began to rise and fall in rough water. As we crashed through building waves, seawater splashed over us and began to collect along the centerline. Dan with furious energy was bailing with his cap when the towline broke.

Abruptly we were set adrift in a dangerous sea. The *Sea Cloud* went on without us. Rowing hard with oversized oars, we tried to catch her but plowed into a wave and capsized. Eleven men, one woman, and a toddler three years old, were thrown into the water. The lifeboat turned turtle, floated upside down for a few minutes, and sank. I could hear the shriek of a woman's voice and a child screaming. A masculine voice I took to be the Captain's was entreating the woman to remain calm, but she was saying her clothing was dragging her down. The Captain tried to rip off the long skirt as she dipped beneath the surface. He dove under the water to save her, but I never saw them again. Dan seized the child and tried to hold her above water. In terror she squirmed out of his hands, was hit by a wave, and sank. A few human heads bobbed in water made rough and turbulent by the strong winds. One by one they slowly disappeared, their frantic last cries muffled by the wind.

I looked around and saw no one, heard nothing but the howling of the storm and the screech of heavy rain. Islands lay to the northwest not more than ten miles away. That helped to even the odds with the sea. It wasn't like being in the middle of the ocean losing hope and strength and waiting to die. I was near land in water almost as warm as the air. Wind and waves were moving in the direction of the Azores. I kicked off my shoes and trousers and began to tread water. Then to my surprise I heard a man's voice only a few feet away. It was our passenger, Marvin Delgado. He was holding in his capable hands the large oars of the tender, but a wave hit one of them hard and thrust it away from him. When it came floating near me, I furiously swam for it.

"Are you wearing a belt?" he yelled over the turmoil.

"Yes! My wide seaman's belt. I never go anywhere without it!"

"Take it off and lash the oars with it! Lash them tightly together."

I did that and found the wood could almost support our weight. All I had to do after discarding my boots was hang on and kick just a little. Delgado was doing the same thing but appeared weak and drooping. Blood was streaming down the left side of his head.

"When the boat capsized, I was injured," he said. "Something sharp jabbed the side of my head. I'm losing blood and losing strength. I may not be able to hang on much longer."

"You can do it and you will. Both of us will hang on long enough to reach Santa Maria. The island ain't far from here."

"I'll try, Amigo, but if I don't make it I want you to have this."

Beneath the water he was pushing something against me. It was a leather bag the size of a pumpkin. It held the precious jewelry he was taking to his relatives in

Spain. Early in the voyage he had said in a moment when his guard was down that he had valuable items in the Captain's safe. Somehow before abandoning ship he had managed to get to them. Now he was saying if he didn't survive, all the valuables in the bag were mine. It contained a fortune I could live on in comfort for the rest of my life, but somehow I didn't want it. I wanted him to keep it, feel the firmness of dry land, and give it to his relatives.

"Hang on!" I yelled. "You have to get that precious stuff to your kinsmen. They will celebrate your name for being so generous."

He did hang on through the remainder of the day and into the night. But when dawn came I found myself alone. Exhausted, I must have dozed in the darkness and didn't see or hear him slip beneath the water and sink with his treasure. Even now, years later, I sometimes think he might have made it had he not been weighted down by that sodden leather bag made heavy by water and precious stones. It brought no comfort to anyone and probably cost him his life. Yet he had a deep puncture in his temple and may have bled to death. All I know is sometime in the night he let go the oars, let go the heavy bag, sank downward, and drowned. Of the thirteen people on board the *Sea Cloud*, I alone remained alive. How long I would live I couldn't say. Yet the weather was good and I was not in mid-ocean.

27

The Fortune Teller

At eighteen Leo Connor married Caitlyn O'Hara, a blossomy girl of sixteen, in a ceremony with friends and relatives attending. Caitlyn's family came with a dowry of food and clothes and three bottles of red wine but no money. Proud of her son and beaming, though aching in every joint, Sarah Connor was present and so was his sister Lena. His father and brother, Liam and Luke, were on the road moving northward with a dozen Irish Travelers. They had left early that spring in wagons they would live in while traveling. Trailing behind them were horses and mules they planned to sell to farmers. Also they expected to earn money doing odd jobs as carpenters, floor scrapers, and roofers. Then finding themselves in a northern state near the end of summer, they would hit the road again and return to South Carolina. It was not an easy existence for any of them. Because they were in the habit of fleecing the inhabitants of every town they visited, they were often in trouble with the law. It was their way of life and that of their ancestors.

Newly married, Leo didn't go with the Travelers that

year. After four months of marriage, he and Caitlyn rented two rooms above a barbershop in Kelly Junction and made the tiny apartment their home. Until then he and his bride had lived in the cramped Connor house and later in a camp set up in the woods. They liked the free and open camp, and Leo often smiled to see Caitlyn swinging in a hammock and listening to bird songs in the trees overhead. She was a pretty girl with clear skin, large eyes, and blonde hair. She was delicate, even fragile he thought, but smart and self-sufficient. It was a pleasant time for them both, but in late summer it became necessary to find shelter in the village.

That first summer of their marriage they went hungry at times. It worried him that Caitlyn went to bed with an ill-defined emptiness under her navel, but she declared it didn't matter. To him it did matter. In their sitting room she nestled her head against his shoulder and murmured she would love him forever. He laughed at that, saying forever is a long time. She made a little face and said they would live each day as a special gift. They would cherish every moment even when life was hard and food scarce. She had faith in her husband, and her loving support made him find jobs of any kind to put food on the table.

Their new living quarters, two rooms rented from the O'Keefes who had prospered, were clean but barren. The smaller room had a bed and dresser but needed a tallboy and closet. The sitting room, doing double duty as the dining room, had a couch by the window and a small table with two chairs. In the little alcove that served as the kitchen an old black stove worked well enough to cook simple meals and warm the rooms in winter. It didn't matter that the place had battered furniture, no carpeting, a tiny niche in the wall for a kitchen, and only two dingy windows fringed with fly-specked curtains. They could live with the roar of laughter and banter that often came from the barbershop below. Barking dogs were no bother either, and the odor of garbage in the alley seared their nostrils only when the windows were open. They were two against the world, and for them that was all that mattered.

Morning came and the happy couple awoke to the clanging of a bell. Leo in high spirits threw off the counterpane and jumped out of bed. Caitlyn sat in the middle of the bed with only a pillow in her lap. Her long blonde hair flowed like a waterfall over her shoulders, and she looked very white and clean. Her big blue eyes darted doe-like around the room and settled on her husband beside the window. Leo was jumping into his trousers to pursue a bakery cart making its way past the building. It had rained during the night and the unpaved street was muddy. The vendor was ringing a cow bell to let people know he had bread and pastry for sale.

Leo scooped up some coins on the table and ran downstairs. With no time to put on his boots, he went barefooted in the chill of the morning. He picked his way through the mud to reach the vendor and bought two gigantic rolls with little tubs of butter. When he returned, flaunting the golden rolls as a captured prize, Caitlyn was ready with a wet towel to clean the mud from his feet. They ate the buttered bread at the table in their sitting room, washing it down with black coffee. They laughed and joked as they ate, delighting each other.

As they began to talk about the future, Leo got to thinking how Caitlyn might look at sixty. Would she gain weight with age and become matronly? Or would she remain slim and trim in her sixties and beyond? He leaned across the table and kissed her forehead.

"I feel so light and limp this morning!" she exclaimed, sipping her coffee. "Limp as a wet noodle and sort of lazy like. But I do want to go romping through a meadow today and gather some wild flowers. They would look so pretty in the purple vase your mama gave us."

Leo lost the reserve his bully of a brother had branded upon him in years gone by and burst into a great bellow of laughter. The sudden eruption startled the girl and she almost spilled her coffee.

"Hush!" she cautioned. "You'll disturb that old barber below us. If he complains to the O'Keefes, we might have to find another place."

"Laughter and chatter and racy language often come from his shop," Leo replied. "So why can't we give him back a little of what he sends up to us? It's only fair, you know."

"Shhhh," she cautioned, putting her index finger across her full but pale lips. "Now, please, Leo Love, no more of that."

He was in love with her sensitive face and the blonde hair that enhanced it and the way she walked and talked. When his sister Lena emitted a high-pitched giggle from time to time, it annoyed him. But Caitlyn's giggle was throaty and pleasant, even amusing. He could see she was not altogether perfect, but she was young and fresh and alive. She was lovable and funny, as sensitive as a leaf in the wind, and she was his. He ceased his laughter, seized her tightly in a comical bear hug, and kissed her mouth gently and then hard.

All night long in the amber light of a sputtering candle they had made love. The release he felt when their tryst was over was engaging, relaxing, expansive. Now this girl he adored was saying she felt limp and lazy even as she wanted to romp in a meadow. He understood, and he wanted to tell her she had made him feel limp and lazy too but more than that. He couldn't put it into words, but somehow he felt . . . well, more than that. Perhaps no words were necessary, for in that one vivid phrase she captured not merely her own feelings but his as well. Then her mood changed even before they left the table. She complained of a headache and wanted to lie down. She lay in bed still as a statue while he ran errands. As soon as he was home again, they sipped cups of tea and ate thick soup flavored with cheese and onions.

Early the next day Leo went looking for work. Caitlyn remained in bed till late in the morning. Rising hungry and looking for something to eat, she found on the shelf behind the stove half a loaf of brown bread, a rancid dollop of butter, and some stale coffee. She nibbled on the buttered bread and thought of the man she loved. He would return exhausted and sad with nothing to show for his effort. Yet he would quickly assume a cheerful air, kiss her lightly on both cheeks, make a joke and ask about dinner. How could she tell him they had none?

Somehow she would have to find a way to make some money to buy food. She knew women and girls in the colony had ways of earning money, and she told herself she could do it too. She would never sell her body as some had done to bring disgrace on themselves and their families. That was out of the question. She would starve before doing that, but why not try her hand at fortune telling? Her mother had taught her the art of reading palms, had required her to memorize what to say when tracing the creases of the mark's hand, had even taught her when to look into the person's face with deep compassion and concern and offer words of comfort while hinting at something awful.

As a little girl, breathless and fascinated, she had watched her mama read the cryptic palm lines and foretell the future. The ritual went far back in time and was always the same. It followed an arcane formula tested and used by generations of Travelers, and her mother had passed on to her the carefully guarded procedure. All she needed now was the signature costume of the fortune teller: a red blouse and black skirt and a scarf to cover her head. The clothing was in the yellow pine chest where she kept most of her things. She put it on and viewed herself in the mirror. In minutes she looked the part of a bona fide fortune teller, a bit too young for the trade perhaps but genuine.

Some distance from town, half a mile from the main road and set deep in a thicket of tall cedar trees, stood a sprawling stone mansion. A retired chandler known as George Harris owned it, having inherited the property from an uncle. He had lived in the vast, dark entrails of the house for a dozen years and rarely went outside except to walk in the garden near evening. Everyone in Kelly Junction knew of his existence but had seldom seen him.

Word was out among the women of the village that he was a very wealthy man but eccentric, reclusive, and miserly. He was an old man becoming older each day and taking no interest in anything that didn't directly concern him.

Caitlyn reasoned that even sick and near death he wanted to know what the future held for him. Her husband wanted to know about the future and often talked about it. Didn't every man want to know the mystical scheme laid out for him by powers unknown? She convinced herself that George Harris in spite of his age wanted to have his fortune told. She had heard he lived with many servants who kept the rambling old house in order and lived there as if they owned the place. Someone had said the man wasn't always in his right mind, and the older and feebler he got the more power the servants gained. Should he die without a will, said village gossips, the help would claim to be relatives and take ownership of the fine old mansion.

These stories piqued Caitlyn's curiosity. She wanted to entertain the chandler and learn more about him, and she hoped the old man would be generous with her. It was a long walk to the mansion, but shortly after the noon hour she knocked on the massive door and waited for a response. She knocked again, bruising her knuckles on the ebony wood and drawing her hand back quickly. Again no one answered, though she could hear someone moving inside. Then she saw mounted on the heavy door a bronze apparatus for sounding a very loud knock. She lifted the ball-shaped knocker and pounded it against the plate. It made an elaborate sound like a hammer striking an anvil.

Immediately a hard-faced, middle-aged woman in gray and white answered the door. She opened it just wide enough for Caitlyn to see her leathery face and dress with its white collar. Uttering not a word, she seemed to be asking with supercilious impatience, "Who are you, Missy, and what do you want? Why have you come to bother us here?"

Summoning strength she didn't know she possessed, Caitlyn spoke first. "If you please, Ma'am, I wish to see the master. I'm here to have a private meeting with Mr. George Harris."

"The master does not see anyone," the woman replied, a note of cold contempt creeping into her voice to underscore the scornful gaze that surveyed the girl from head to foot. "You must go away now. My employer does not see anyone, and certainly not the likes of you."

"You assume incorrectly, Madam. George Williston Harris will see me. It is a matter of grave concern for him as well as for you. Please announce my arrival and allow me to enter." The words came from Caitlyn as from an oracle, and the housekeeper looked stunned.

"Wait here, please," she mumbled after some hesitation. "The master is real sick and may not be able to talk to anyone, but I'll send a girl up to check on him."

"You alone will show me to him," Caitlyn said evenly, leveling her gaze upon the woman's bemused face. "He will talk to me even though I will do most of the talking. Do not require me to wait."

The door was now open. The housekeeper, becoming defiant, placed her hands on her plump hips and blocked any passage the visitor might attempt. "You're one of them gypsies in the village, ain't you? I can tell by the way you're dressed and by the way you walk and talk. Master Harris has no use for gypsies, absolutely no use. Now if you know what's good for you, Missy, you'll go away fast."

"I will say this once more and only once more," said Caitlyn, her voice calm but her eyes blazing. "If you value your position here, you will take me to George Harris as fast as your fat legs can move you. I will not argue with you, Mistress Housekeeper."

Defeated, the woman reluctantly gathered her skirts on one arm, and trundled sullenly down a long and gloomy hallway with Caitlyn close behind. At the end of the hallway they ascended a barren and dusty staircase that led to a room meanly furnished. On a narrow, rumpled bed pushed up against the wall lay an exhausted old man. Though his eyelids flickered when the two women entered, he said nothing to acknowledge their presence.

"This young woman claims you will see her, sir. She's one of them Irish gypsies in the village. Shall I send her away?"

"Eh? Eh? What is it you say? Gypsies?"

"I am not a gypsy, Mr. Harris. I am an Irish woman newly married. You probably have Irish blood in your veins too. I belong to a nomadic people called the Travelers, and the country people who surround us in these parts confuse us with gypsies who travel, but that is all we have in common. My roots are in Ireland; gypsies come from India."

"She is dressed like a gypsy," said the housekeeper, "flaunting that red top and black skirt and swinging them hips. I dessay she'll steal anything she can get her hands on if I leave her alone with you."

"Now listen to me, Bessie, and listen good," said George Harris attempting to sit up. "You and your kind have already stolen everything I own, and so I'm sure this woman, this gypsy or whatever she is, can find nothing left to steal. Go from us now and have the cook send up lunch for me and for the young woman too."

"Of course, sir, if that's your wish," snapped the housekeeper, edging her way out of the room and descending the stairs.

Caitlyn had made a turban of the colorful scarf and was assuming the pose of fortune teller. But on hearing she would be having lunch with the owner of the mansion, she removed the turban to display her blonde hair with an air of easy informality. In a vibrant voice with girlish overtones she spoke kindly to the old man, and he liked the sound of her. She propped him up on huge pillows. He looked at her as if she were a long-lost relative, smiling weakly. In the tired, flinty old eyes under shaggy brows, she could see a satirical glint that amused her.

"Are you a gypsy?" Harris asked, forgetting in his dotage that he had asked the question just minutes before. "I want you to know I have no use for gypsies. They make a living plundering people. I don't like gypsies. They stole a wagonload of premium wax from me once and sold it to a competitor for half its worth. When I was younger I was a candle maker, and a damn good one too."

"I know, sir. Your reputation is well known in the community. But listen to me. I am not a gypsy. As I said to you earlier, I am Irish. My skin is fair and my hair is blonde. My eyes are blue and I speak a fine Irish brogue. Gypsies, as you must surely know, are dark of skin and eye, swarthy people. They have black hair and speak a language unknown to me and my people. Their blood differs greatly from ours."

"Yes, yes! Now I see. You are young and fair and speak with a soothing, musical sound. You may entertain me if you wish, but let's have lunch first. So very nice to have a young girl talking to me."

A maid came clumping up the stairs with a large tray, placed its dishes on a bedside table, and left. It was a generous lunch of sliced cold ham, biscuits, fruit, and buttermilk. With no vestige of an appetite, Harris nibbled on a morsel but Caitlyn ate her fill. The biscuits were fresh from the oven, and the ham was expertly seasoned. The thick buttermilk with flecks of butter on the surface had a tangy taste and quenched her thirst. No longer hungry and thirsty, Caitlyn felt alive and happy and was hoping her husband had eaten well too. The visit with George Williston Harris was showing itself as better than expected. He was lonely and sick and needing kind attention, and she was giving him that. Far from rejecting her, as the housekeeper fervently wished, he found her amusing and charming. She brightened his day.

"Take this key and unlock the drawer of my dresser there," he said to her when they had chatted amicably for an hour. "If the servants in this old house didn't pilfer the key while I slept, you'll find a wad of money in the drawer. I want you to take it, all of it. If you don't, they will in time and I want you to have it."

"But I've done nothing to deserve it, Mr. Harris. I came

here to tell your fortune and maybe earn just a little money."

"I will say it again, Missy. I don't like gypsies but I do like you. The air in this little room is fresher because of you. They moved me here from the master bedroom, and I don't know why. Now take the money and go with my blessing. I feel just a little weak from the excitement of your company. I want to rest now."

Caitlyn left the old chandler's mansion with enough money to buy provisions until summer's end. Also there was enough for the rent and for new clothes. Three days later she heard George Harris was dead. A nephew with papers to prove identity and ownership took over the old mansion, ousted the servants, and hired a caretaker. The nephew's lawyer found no will, no legal papers of any kind. But in the drawer of the bedside table was an unfinished draft of something that might have become a will. Scrawled by a shaky hand on thin paper and almost lost in a jumble of smudgy words, it raised an eyebrow: *"To my pretty Irish girl, my fortune teller who gave me comfort and raised my spirits, I George Harris . . . I George Harris do . . ."* The remainder was indecipherable.

The wily lawyer quickly tore the piece of paper in half and burned it. It couldn't possibly be seen as a will. Should it come to light it would cause only trouble. He decided not to say a word about it to the nephew, who paid him a handsome fee for his service, or to anybody.

28

Like a Polished Apple

In that tropical prison where men came to suffer and die was a man we called "La Pomme." His real name was Marcel, but he got the nickname because his head was as bald and shiny as a polished apple. He was not a big man, not even muscular, but strong as a bull in a fight. Moreover, he had more strength of will than any man I ever knew. He was one of the most daring convicts ever to trouble any prison, and all he ever thought about was finding a way to live free again. La Pomme had tried escaping several times, and for his latest abortive attempt he was sentenced to three years in solitary confinement. When he found himself in a stinking cell so small he could pace only six steps before turning, he had but one idea. It quickly became an obsession.

Somehow in that hellish complex called Devil's Island he had to find a way to leave Isle Saint Joseph and get to the hospital on Isle Royale. For several days he smoked hand-rolled cigarettes stoked with quinine. The result when the doctor examined him was a towering temperature. Marcel thought that would get him sent to the hospital, but the doctor sensed the sham and sent him back to his rat-infested cell. A day later he stuck a needle through his cheek, rubbed fecal dirt in the wound, and slowly got his face so inflamed and swollen he looked to be on the brink of death. When the doctor came on his weekly visit, this time he sent La Pomme to the hospital. The first step in the man's scheme to escape had succeeded on the second try.

Sprawled on the white hospital bed in nothing but his underwear, Marcel now pondered his next step — how to get away from Isle Royale and do it before the doctor pronounced him well again. He would have to construct a raft to get to the mainland, but out of what? Then one afternoon his eye fell on a pile of boards in the corner of the ward, twenty of them neatly stacked and ready to support mattresses. His raft was there before his eyes waiting to be built. The next morning, under the pretext of changing the urine-soaked boards on his bed, he was able to put aside just the ones he needed for the raft.

The problem now was how to get the planks out of the hospital and hidden in a safe place. The ward was on the second floor, and that made the job even more difficult. But when he found out that beneath his bed was a room on the ground floor in which old mattresses were stored, he knew exactly what to do. In the night for several hours, he patiently cut a hole in the decayed floor with the knife he carried for protection. The following night he dropped the selected boards through the hole. Landing on the old mattresses, they made not a sound. Then he pushed a blanket and a sheet through the hole. An hour later after making the hole bigger, he let himself down. Within minutes he was in the yard running for the wall. He folded the blanket and threw it to the top as a cushion against pointed pieces of glass, barbed wire, and nails. Then he made four bundles of two boards tied with strips of cloth from the sheet and threw them over. He climbed the wall where the blanket lay across the barbed wire and slithered down the other side.

Lashed with strips of strong blanket cloth, the raft was easy to put together. In but an hour he was struggling against the surf to get past its waves to the sea. The night without a moon was very dark, and so he didn't have to worry about being seen. Suddenly a big wave lifted the raft free of the rocks and placed it in deep water. Sleek sharks grown fat from feeding on human bodies circled the contraption. He was daring rough seas at night on a flimsy raft in water bristling with sharks, and he didn't know how to swim. One false move and he could drown or be torn apart and eaten. To insure a bit of safety he tied himself to the raft. As the shore receded, he was thinking maybe he had made a mistake. Except for the pounding surf, all was quiet.

Morning came and La Pomme was missing. All the convicts were questioned, but not one knew anything. Guards combed the island but found nothing. Through binoculars they examined the sea. They saw no raft nor anything else on the horizon. The news of the escape ran like wildfire through the prison population. Every person who heard the story had his own theory on how the escape was accomplished. Then word came that a battered raft had washed up on the rocky shores of Devil's

Island. Marcel's partly eaten body was carrion stinking in the sun. It was a creative rumor full of detail but false.

When day broke, the islands were out of the man's sight. As luck would have it, he had drifted toward the mainland. His mouth was dry and the sun was already scorching his skin, but the taste of freedom was sweet. The raft moved slowly toward shore until he was fewer than a hundred yards from land. Then he noticed the thing had come to a standstill and was beginning to drift seaward. Low tide was setting in and taking him out to sea. With oars he might have resisted the tidal tug, but he had none. It took him so far out he lost sight of the mainland. He lay on his stomach and wanted to sob but couldn't.

The next day, hungry and thirsty, he drifted back to within a few hundred feet of the coast. Had he known how to swim he would have made it to shore in a few minutes. Despair set in to compete with desperation. He released a board from the raft at the risk of having it fall apart and began to paddle, but the tide was pulling the flimsy structure back out again, and he was too weak to fight against it. That night, once more, he was on the open sea and staring exhausted at the stars. Day came and he was sick with hunger and thirst and parched by the tropical sun. Four days passed and then seven. He slipped into delirium. Sharks bumped against the raft, trying to flip it over. He had tied himself tightly to it, and they caused him no harm. But he was slowly dying of thirst, starvation, and exposure. When the raft came within a few yards of the coast one night, he thought he might slip into the water and wade ashore. He was too weak to move off the raft, and the tide swept him out again far away from shore.

On the seventh day a group of Indians fishing off the coast of Dutch Guiana saw a naked white man burned severely by the unrelenting sun. His bald head was beet-red and blistered. He was lying unconscious on soaked boards falling apart. They approached cautiously and with their paddles drove away two circling sharks. Finding the man just barely alive, they brought him to their village as a curiosity for all to see. Except for soldiers who sometimes came looking for escaped convicts, they tolerated no white men in their territory. They expected this man to die before sundown. But an old Indian woman named Peche took it upon herself to care for the stricken man. She applied cooling wet cloths to his burning skin, dribbled water down his parched throat, and fed him a mush of sea-turtle eggs to quell his hunger. In a few days Marcel was awake and resting and regaining his strength.

A week later an Indian girl named Leywa took him into a hut where six women and four men were living. She hung a hammock wide enough for two. Marcel lay in the hammock alone for only a few minutes before she came and snuggled beside him. He understood he had been adopted by this village of Indians, and she was to be his keeper. She touched his face, his ears, eyes, mouth, and chest. Her fingers were long and tapered but rough with small cuts from the coral where daily she dived for oysters. He kissed her full lips and she returned the kiss with a painful bite, her way of kissing. They found an empty hut, set up housekeeping, and lived as man and wife. She cooked dishes strange to his taste, but he ate anything she gave him and quickly gained the weight he had lost during his ordeal on the raft. They bathed each other every day in the sea and lay on the beach to dry themselves.

Marcel had escaped the brutal penal colony in French Guiana to struggle against natural forces and almost die. He was now living an idyllic existence with a beautiful girl who called herself his wife. This went on for seven months. They made love and she found herself pregnant. Her younger sister grew jealous on seeing her swollen belly and wanted the same. One day when he was resting in the shade after bathing, Leywa placed her naked sister beside him and waited for natural impulses to take over. He let her know he was her man and unwilling to have relations with her sister. That made her happy, for she was beginning to think because she was no longer slender he was losing interest in her. For a time she was overcome with happiness, and then one day as the rain poured down in torrents grief struck her down. Soldiers on assignment came and took her husband away. Two days later Marcel, known by all as *La Pomme*, was back in prison.

Within a month he was again on Saint Joseph in soul-shattering solitary confinement. By order of the chief guard a sign was put on the bars of his cell: *"Prisoner 46511 suspected shammer and dangerous. To be sent to hospital only in extreme emergency."* Marcel could see it would now be more difficult than ever to get himself back into the hospital where he might flee again. Then one night the guard found him writhing in pain on his cell's dirty floor clutching his stomach. He poured water on the prisoner's face, gave him a dose of paregoric, and left him there. The next morning when the doctor was making his rounds, Marcel told him he had suffered an attack of appendicitis during the night and needed an operation. Ignoring the sign on the cell door, the doctor sent the convict back to the hospital at Isle Royale. The chief guard, a Corsican named Carpetate, assured the doctor that absolutely nothing was wrong with La Pomme. He was guilty of another hoax. Carpetate's complaints were harsh and loud but went unheard.

"Do you believe La Pomme will have that operation the doctor is planning?" Carpetate asked a fellow guard. "He told me to give the old rat nothing to eat and just a little water from time to time."

"Yeah, I think La Pomme will get that operation. Why not?"

"Well, I for one believe he has nothing wrong with him. He's here in the hospital to do what he did the last time he was here — escape."

"Maybe this time he won't be coming back. Took him a long time to get back the last time he left. I heard he lived with Indians."

"Yeah, I heard it too but how true is it? I'll bet you three bottles of beer ol' La Pomme won't be operated on," said the chief guard.

"You're on!" said his friend. "It's an easy way to get beer."

A day later the prisoner lay on the operating table waiting for the doctor to clean his instruments. The hospital, notorious for its lack of good medicine, had no chloroform. The doctor had to use ether, and he may have used too much. The patient quickly became unconscious, his feet beginning to jerk. Seeing that something was wrong, the doctor delayed the operation. At the time indicated, his patient did not wake up. The news spread with great speed through the wards and barracks. The man called La Pomme because his bald head was as shiny as a polished apple was dead! There would be no more trouble from him. Was the doctor responsible? Possibly, some inmates said, though maybe not. For years Marcel had been a sour, sour apple.

That afternoon, where sharks circled in a frenzy, we eased his body into the sea. La Pomme the Magnificent, who had defied the creatures day after day in boiling and turbulent water, in the end became their feast. We made a wreath of flowers and palm fronds for the ceremony. I tossed it gingerly into the foaming and bloody water.

"At last," said my companion, "that man of strength and will is free. No guard will chase after him ever again."

Back in the barracks as we discussed what had happened, a three-hundred pound man we called *Tout Petit* said maybe La Pomme had planned it that way. We laughed at that. Then as night was coming on and we prepared for bed, I got to thinking maybe he did.

29

Albert Foley's Night Out

At fourteen Albert Foley managed to sneak into the Hereford Avenue Dance Hall to attend a gala wedding. He knew full well he had not been invited, but he was curious and eager to have fun. With big saucer eyes he surveyed the scene. On a makeshift stage were four musicians in gaudy dress, hired to make music for the guests. In the hubbub of laughter and merrymaking, they performed like warriors in battle. Two squawking fiddles were trying to conquer each other when drums and a bass fiddle charged into the fray. The boy beamed on hearing this and tapped his feet to rhythms never taught by a music master. Though the evening had just begun, the musicians were already mopping their brows. A blonde woman wearing dangling earrings and a red skirt encrusted with sparkling sequins gave them heavy mugs of dark beer.

Two long tables laden with food caught the boy's eye. He had never seen food in such abundance, and cautiously he made his way to it. His mouth began to water as his nostrils caught the aroma of roast beef, baked ham, and steamed potatoes flavored with bacon. Fascinated, he stared at boiled rice with almonds, macaroni in a golden cheese sauce, sizzling sausages, ripe and colorful fruits, wedges of cheese, and platters of pastry. Some of the guests were already munching on the goodies, chatting as they ate and unaware of the boy in their midst. At one of the tables he bolted down cold ham, spiced beef, and fat sausages until his belly could hold no more. Then he drank half a bottle of beer and gorged on pastry for dessert. No one bothered to notice.

He stuffed meat and cheese into a large golden bun, wrapped it in a dirty handkerchief, and put it in his pocket. At home in the middle of the night, or maybe the next day, he would eat it with gusto. But now fully satiated, he wanted to take part in the festivities, maybe dance with one of the pretty girls. Then he realized he had to resign himself to watching. Not dressed for the occasion, he knew his appearance would give him away. His gray shirt was soiled, his trousers frayed, and one shoe had a ragged edge. Even though he knew he didn't belong, his young senses thrilled to the sights and sounds around him. Living for him had never been easy, but in the Hereford Avenue Dance Hall, surrounded by joyful people hell-bent on having a good time, he was happy to be alive.

In a trice he forgot every pain he had ever suffered and immersed himself in the excitement of the scene. He throbbed with delight, his senses as keen as a tuning fork. Everyone around him was laughing, singing, chattering in rising clamor, and eating with both hands. The musicians were playing in a mad frenzy, and couples in their Sunday best were dancing riotously. It was the music that turned that barren room into a wonderland, a mansion in the sky. The person leading the little band was a laborer by day but a poet and music-maker by night. Donnelley was his name, and he had taught himself at night how to draw music from an old and battered instrument after working all day. His dilapidated fiddle was out of tune and its bow was sawing the thing in half, but from it came raw and raucous music to warm the soul.

Donnelley stamps his booted feet as he plays, sways, and swings with eyes half closed. With hand signals he beseeches his companions to pick up the pace. As they remain on the stage, he moves to the table where the bride and groom sit too excited or too uneasy to eat. A cry rings out for a fast and rhythmic tune to celebrate the beauty of the bride and the joys of young love. Standing now in front of her table, waving his fiddle-bow wand in her direction, Donnelley creates magical, mystical, melodic music that hangs in the air and tugs at the heart. The melody rushes forward on a siren note and conquers the girl. Tears flood her large blue-gray eyes and run down her powdered cheeks. Her girlish face flushes deep and turns scarlet. In her white wedding gown with its flowing train she wants to run away, but this is her wedding day, her moment of glory to remember forever.

When her closest friend stands on a little stool and begins to sing, a few minutes of respite come her way. The girl's voice is throaty on the low notes and unpleasantly shrill on the high notes. She sings a dolorous ballad of love found and love lost, and she almost chokes on her own love sickness as the gaudy musicians sweat to produce a musical fantasy. When the song is over and the applause dies down, the father of the bride comes forward to give a little speech and offer a toast. He is a man of middle age but looks older. His life has not been an easy one, but now as he speaks he places all emphasis on the many good things that make any life worth living. Customarily a man in his position took his speech from a book and learned it by rote, but Arthur Brody is a poet at heart and delivers his own speech.

His oration is bombastic and boastful, but on the whole a bundle of heartfelt congratulation. Even Albert Foley draws near to listen. Some of the women wipe their eyes and whimper when Arthur touches upon the hardships of his life and expresses fervent hope that such may never occur in the lives of his daughter and new son. Of late he has come to believe that he may not live much longer. When he brings that into his speech, the women begin to cry in sympathy for the poor man. Even some of the men turn their faces to the wall to dab their eyes.

Then abruptly a fat and jolly little man only five feet tall and proud to be the father of the groom, is on his feet to give a speech. He looks at life through rose-colored glasses, insists the present may not be as bad as it seems, and paints a sunny picture of the future. He showers congratulations on the newly weds and predicts intense joy for them. He bases his prediction on particulars that delight the young men but cause the bride to turn her gaze away and blush. He sits down congratulating himself on having made a superb speech, not aware that some of his words had a double meaning to cause discomfort.

Now the tables are taken from the room, and the revelers pair up and dance as if competing in a contest.

That's when the musicians really begin to earn their fare. As midnight approaches, some of the dancers leave the floor and find their coats. Their long workday begins early, and they must sleep off the festivity of the evening and gain some rest. The younger folk go on dancing, urging the fiddlers to play fast and loose. In time only a few remain, and by then Albert Foley is on his way home. He prances along in the middle of the street, dancing a little jig of triumph and joy. His evening has been much better than he ever expected, and he is pleased with how well it went. Stooping to pick up a rock as big as his fist, he hurls it fast and hard at the trunk of a tree. The sound of the stone whacking the wood pleases the boy. When he reaches his poverty-bitten house, he enters quietly and stealthily.

Home for Albert Foley was some distance from the Hereford Avenue Dance Hall. He lived with his obtuse and abusive father, oppressed and silent mother, a worthless older brother who was always teasing him, and a younger sister losing her eyesight. The house was in a shambles and falling apart. His family and the house were much in need of repair. In his rumpled bed he slept with sweet memories of a fantastic evening. He dreamed of a bright future too, but life kept getting in the way.

30

I Remember Myra

I traveled up the east coast that summer all the way to New England. In Boston I found a boarding house in a neighborhood near the business district and devoured the abundant food on its sagging table. It was tasty and filling, and I found myself growing stronger by the day. My mama and sister in Kelly Junction were wondering what had happened to me. My brother and old daddy had never given a damn about me or anything I did. It didn't bother them at all when I left home without a word, but Mama worried. When I was growing up, she worried I wasn't getting enough to eat. So in a long letter to make her feel good, I described the boarding-house table.

"We have many kinds of vegetables, Ma. At dinner on various days we have squash, white potatoes, sweet potatoes, tomatoes, corn on the cob, spinach, beans, cauliflowers, turnips, and something called kale. It looks like turnip greens but is more tasty and tender. Some of the vegetables I never saw before and had to get used to them sort of gradual like, and now I like them all except cauliflower. Mrs. Craigenstock — she's the portly widow that owns the

house — will have no one go hungry. She loads each plate with meat, vegetables, two kinds of bread, and fruit. A side dish has what she calls a tossed salad.

"We eat cranberries with our meat, and sometimes we have a very sweet dessert, and her cook fixes potatoes more ways than mashed. I never heard of so many ways. Did you ever taste cranberries, Ma? They're so tart they shrivel your tongue, but if you sprinkle sugar on them you get a nice fruity taste sort of like a strawberry. When I first tasted them I wanted to spit them out fast. Then I tried them with sugar and they're not bad. Hope you can try some.

"For breakfast, and you won't believe this, we have meat and potatoes with eggs and waffles and coffee. Sometimes the good woman puts a pitcher of thick milk on the table, and I always drink a big glass. Then she wants to fill it up again! I sure wish Lena could be here to drink that milk and eat the big breakfast every morning. In no time she'd put on weight and feel a lot better. Good food might even help her eyesight. I'm here to tell ya, Ma, it's a first-rate boarding house, as good as it gets. There are about a dozen people living here, all very pleasant." I signed the letter *Your Loving Son, Leo.*

I liked living in the Craigenstock boarding house though eventually I had to move on. Even now I think about the place and the people who lived there. One person in the house was a woman who asked me to call her Myra Medlock. She was tall and plain but had a nice smile. A year or two shy of thirty, she was the daughter of a city official and worked long hours in a milliner's shop. Her dark hair was neatly parted in the middle and fell to the nape of her neck in tight ringlets. Her pale cheeks were artificially colored, and her dark eyes were more restless than any I've ever seen. Her full lips were a curious contrast to a straight and severe nose and a chest as flat as mine. She smelled of lavender when you got close to her. I mean when I sat beside her at dinner I caught a whiff. She told me she got her clothing wholesale, and so she dressed more fashionable than the other lodgers. Better educated, she affected social graces some of the others didn't even pretend to have. She took a liking to me and always tried to sit next to me at dinner.

"I do believe you hail from the South," she said, glancing at me shyly and smiling. "I can tell by the accent."

I was filling my plate to satisfy a hearty appetite and looking at a mix of vegetables I didn't recognize. It happened often during my first weeks at the boarding-house table.

"Oh that's succotash!" she explained. "It has sweet corn, lima beans, sweet peppers, carrots, okra, salt pork for flavor, and maybe a soupçon of sugar. Go ahead and try some, I think you'll like it."

I put a helping of the colorful vegetables on my plate and passed it on to her. She smiled primly and placed a little beside a big, black, juicy hunk of pot roast.

"I like succotash," she remarked, shrugging her thin shoulders, "but I never eat large portions of anything. Do you know the dish goes all the way back to the pilgrims?"

Well, I didn't know that but I did know she had a big chunk of meat on that plate of hers but not many vegetables.

"How long have you been in Boston, Mister. . . ?" she paused.

"The name's O'Connor, Miss, but call me Leo. Not very long. I came up from Kelly Junction. That's where I live in South Carolina. It's a town a lot of people talk about 'cause most of the people there are Irish Travelers. The men travel in the summer time doing odd jobs for country folk. That's how we got the name, but our roots go back to the old country. I'm sort of traveling on my own and looking for work."

"What kind of work are you looking for, Mr. Connor?"

"Oh, call me Leo, please. Nobody I know ever called me Mister unless they were angry at something and wanted to box my ears."

"Oh, I didn't mean to offend, Leo. Of course I'll call you by your first name. We don't stand on tradition or formality here. I expect you to call me Myra. You're under no obligation, however, to call me Miss Myra! Isn't that one of your charming Southern customs?"

"Well, I guess it is," I said with a chuckle.

It seemed funny to me that this woman in faraway New England would know stuff like that, and I could certainly remember hearing young, unmarried women in Kelly Junction called Miss Kathleen or Miss Emily or Miss Sophie or whatever their names happened to be.

"If you call me Miss Myra," she said with mock aggression, "I will have to pinch your cheek! It would imply you see me as a lonely old spinster, and I haven't reached that stage yet."

"Oh, don't worry. I would never offend a young lady like you. I'll do as you say and call you Myra. It's a nice name, sort of unusual."

"It's an old name in the Medlock family, belonged to a

distant cousin. We're an old family and proud to live in one of the finest cities in America. Boston will treat you well if you treat her well."

"I like Boston even better than New York. People are more friendly here, cold and distant there. And Boston has many Irish people. More Irish here than you can stir with a stick!"

I hadn't remained in New York long enough to make an accurate comparison but felt she wanted to hear good things about her city, and so I lied a little to make her feel good.

"We're proud of our ethnic neighborhoods and our public facilities," Myra offered. "We have the free library, of course, but also excellent museums and art galleries and parks when the weather improves. Perhaps in good weather I can show you some of the sights."

"That would be warm and friendly of you," I said as I glanced at the woman's thin face. "I'd like that."

I got the impression then and there that she was lonely and sort of aching for companionship. When a little frown creased her brow, I attempted to muffle my Southern accent and choose my words more carefully. I was using expressions seldom heard so far north, and maybe she was thinking it was deliberate.

"Do you know about the telephone?" she asked, abruptly changing the subject. "It's a marvelous invention. People can talk to each other several miles away. They even say it may supersede the telegraph, make it antiquated in a few years."

"Yep, I heard about it. Before long this boarding house will have a telephone in the kitchen, and Mrs. Craigenstock will use it to buy groceries from her grocer and meat from the butcher. She won't even have to leave her house. People will write their letters on that new-fangled typing machine I've been hearing about, and in our lifetime you and I will watch photographs that move."

"Well, I can't believe that will happen anytime soon!" she replied with a trill of laughter. "But science and the arts are improving every day. Boston has become a testing ground for all the new things before they go out to the rest of the country."

In a way Myra Medlock so proud of Boston was like my people back home. Outsiders often cussed our village, saying thieves and swindlers lived there, but we thought it was a good place to live. The old folks were always saying it was heaven compared to the old country. I wasn't sure I liked Myra with her quirky little mannerisms, but she seemed a good soul. As time passed I found out she loved nature better than anything. When the weather turned warm we walked in the parks, and she would ooh and aah over every little flower and plant peeking up from the soil. She'd squat on her haunches and stroke the petals of a little flower and murmur tender words. I couldn't be sure she was actually talking to the flower, but it sure seemed that way at times.

She never had much to say about her family or work or personal life. She did tell me once she wanted to go off to art school and become a famous artist and sell her pictures for thousands and live high on the hog. Well, she didn't put it exactly that way.

She said, "I dream of living grandly in a splendid house

and proving my worth as a woman. I'm working hard to achieve the dream."

Her father couldn't see spending a lot of money on art school, and so in time she had to earn her living as a milliner. She told me she designed women's hats when she wasn't selling them, but her secret desire was to be close to nature and paint its beauty. I think another secret desire she had was to get a fellow and be his wife. When the weather was good we walked in the parks a lot and talked, but our friendship never went beyond friendship. Sometimes I wonder why.

I do know one spring day she just up and left the boarding house where she had lived for three years and took up with a traveling man. Mrs. Craigenstock told us at dinner one evening that he was a salesman of barbershop supplies, and Myra had known him for only a short time. He went up and down the eastern seaboard visiting barbershops in towns big and small. He had no home as far as anyone knew and lived out of a suitcase, as the saying goes. Most of the time, burdened by a large black sample case, he traveled by train. On occasion he went by cart or wagon to places away from the railroad. He had a schedule to follow and worked many hours to meet his quota in cities and towns south of New York City. He never got as far as Boston again.

In the beginning Myra traveled with him, but after a few weeks he deposited her in White Plains. She found a job in a shop and looked forward to his arrival every other month. But his visits gradually became infrequent and finally stopped altogether. In time Myra found another man, an industrial engineer, and married him. He had a good income and she wanted to start a family, but her husband was a brusque and solitary man and often lost his temper. The last I heard she was living in a boarding house in upstate New York.

Life for Myra Medlock was never easy but somehow she found the courage and strength to live as best she could and endure. She never got what she really wanted in life but managed to hold up her head, square her shoulders, and speak cheerfully to anyone who would listen. At least she was that way when I knew her in Boston. Any time I'm feeling low, and it happens more than I would like, I remember Myra.

31

A Greek in Troy

"I do wish we could buy another story from you," said the editor of the newspaper, twirling a yellow pencil in his fingers, "but at present we can't buy any more. Also I can't advance you money on stuff we've never seen. I suggest you take a year off to gather material, perfect your style, find your voice as we say, and submit material to us again."

"I thank you for the good advice, sir, but there's no way I can do that. The world won't let me. It demands I find food, shelter, and clothing even when I can't find work. I sent you stories because I needed money to survive. I thought you might laugh at my poor attempt at literary labor, but I was desperate."

The editor looked at me with obvious concern, twirled his pencil faster, and glanced at papers on his desk. "The economy has tanked, you know. We're in a deep depression. People are hurting. Even the *Tribune* is hurting We had to let people go." It was an awkward situation.

I had come to Chicago to find work and was almost

penniless. I pounded the pavement looking for anything to tide me over. A burly foreman offered me a job killing cattle in a slaughterhouse, but that I couldn't bring myself to do. A kindly bookseller in a shop with "Cheap Books" emblazoned on its window said I might send a story to a newspaper and get paid for it. I wrote several stories and sent the best to the *Chicago Tribune*. To my surprise they accepted the piece and sent me a small check. That encouraged me to write more. They rejected several but soon began to send me a check for each submission. Then suddenly the dribble of money ceased.

So instead of trying to do business by mail, I decided to go there in person, explain I was working on a story that would be ready soon, and ask for a small advance. I felt ashamed for asking, and was about to leave him when the editor offered a suggestion.

"That first story you submitted was reprinted in a paper in New York state. A town called Troy. It's a long way from here, but maybe they were impressed by your work and might offer you a job. It's really the only help I can give you."

I seized upon his suggestion and left the windy city at the bottom of Lake Michigan to travel eastward to Troy, New York. The journey of 800 miles was memorable for its discomfort. Children on the train were rowdy and unsupervised. Fat men with fat cigars filled the car with a haze of acrid blue smoke that burned my nostrils. An old man with a gray beard, hacking cough, and runny nose was hugging a burlap bag filled with live chickens. Every few minutes the bag seemed to jump off his lap with a flurry of cackling and a roar of laughter from the other passengers. It gave us some comic relief.

A frowzy woman with yellow hair in clothes that looked like they belonged to someone else was eating fried chicken and other goodies. She took each piece from a large tin bucket, gnawed it to the bone, licked the grease from her stubby fingers, smacked her lips, and began working on another. The odor of fried food had always made me ravenous. I was faint with hunger, and for an instant thought I would ask her for a biscuit. She had several in her bucket and could surely spare one, but something inside me stood in the way. When I was growing up my mama often said she would rather starve than beg. So I guess, following her example, I was too proud to beg a biscuit. Also I thought the woman might cause a scene or something worse.

In the trash can of the toilet I found a discarded apple with one bite taken from it. I could see the imprint of teeth in the white flesh, and I dribbled water over it to clean it. I ate the apple to the core and then ate the core. I told myself I would have to save the few dollars in my pocket for a rainy day. After paying my fare I had almost nothing left. I would have to eat whatever and whenever I could. So with some reluctance I put down natural impulses and tried to convince myself the apple was filling and tasty. It was big and juicy but hard and sour, not tasty at all. That's why someone threw it away.

In Troy I rented a room for one night and slept like the dead on a lumpy mattress with urine stains. I made myself tidy the next morning and went immediately to *The Hellespont Herald*. Clean and neat after a week without a bath but in clothes beginning to show wear, I asked the chief editor for a job. I said I would take anything available and work hard. I explained by way of credentials that I had some skill as a writer and had published some of my work in Chicago.

"We have nothing for you," the man replied. "Work is very slow in this city right now, jobs are scarce."

I said I would work as an office boy, run errands, sweep the floor, and empty waste baskets. With growing impatience he repeated they had no work for me. Only a week before I came, he said, the paper was forced to lay off two people because of sagging revenue.

"You published my story, the one the *Chicago Tribune* bought and printed for its readers. Doesn't that mean something?"

"It means we pick up a lot of material from other newspapers. We use it to fill space. We call it filler material."

"But that was a piece of creative writing I worked very hard to produce. The Chicago editor paid good money for it, but I retained all rights to the story. Are you not legally obligated to pay me for it?"

The editor laughed nervously, glanced at a colleague hunched behind a desk nearby, and walked with busy attention in that direction. He just got up and walked away, leaving me sitting there like an office fixture. They had nothing to offer me, not even common courtesy. They turned their backs on me and went on with their work. It was obvious they viewed me as an intruder and troublemaker. I left *The Hellespont Herald* feeling sick to my stomach and weak from hunger. In the shade of an elm tree I sat on a bench to rest.

I had always been poor but any situation in which I wouldn't have enough to eat had never occurred to me. It was beyond the range of my experience, not the sort of thing my family had ever worried about. Life was often hard as I was growing up, but somehow we had enough to eat and never had to beg for anything from anyone. I was vaguely ashamed of myself for sinking so low.

Though I don't like to admit it, I began to feel I would rather be dead and have it over than endure it. I thought of throwing myself in the nearby river, but as soon as the thought came to me I rebelled against it. My reason told me the misery I was suffering wouldn't last forever. I had but one life to live and happy or not, I would live it as long as I could. Also I had some money in my pocket, not a lot but some. I wasn't entirely broke. I couldn't be arrested as a vagrant. Notwithstanding, I spent several days in Troy and came close to starving.

I lived on peanuts in the shell bought a pennyworth at a time from a street vendor. The man was tall and swarthy, thin as a rail, dour in manner and appearance, but talkative and generous. He said with a thick accent that his name was Alexander Kouropoulos. He had relatives in the old country and was proud to be Greek. Though I was in a predicament that didn't allow for irony or humor, it pleased me to find a Greek in Troy. In Homeric legend Troy was the mighty city of King Priam, besieged for ten years by the Greek army during the Trojan War and finally conquered through trickery. The town in New York had Greeks such as the saturnine vendor, and more affluent Greeks who owned and operated restaurants. I had no money to visit any of them for a meal and no energy to find them and ask for a job.

I was down and out, not in a big city where opportunity was just around the corner, but in a struggling little town on the Hudson and Mohawk rivers near the state capital. I walked along the towpath beside the river and looked into the swirling water and once more had dark thoughts of self-destruction. As before, it was not a solution I considered seriously. When I was eleven and caught stealing raw potatoes from a green grocer's cart and a policeman threatened to throw me in jail, my anguish had been so great I wanted to die. In my present predicament I would die only if I starved. Circumstance would have to kill me.

I found a patch of grass and lay down for an hour, the June sun warming my face. I wanted to rest longer, even spend the night there, but knew a cop with a billy club would demand I move on. I was fearfully tired, had a dull ache in the pit of my stomach, and a leaden dread of what the next day would bring. Troy seemed oblivious to whether I lived or died. Now I realize the town went about its business without even knowing I was there. I was desperate in that town but too proud to ask anyone for help.

Then one sunny day when my belly button was scraping my spine, I chanced upon a traveling photographer who needed an assistant. Geoffrey Barnes had grown up on a farm in Pennsylvania, had tried to wrest a living from it, and knew all about hardship. A slightly built man with a large head and hollow chest, he seemed to have too much energy for his thin legs. He was a nervous man always on the move. He didn't talk a lot but anything he said made sense.

We went to a tavern and ate thick summer sausages with beer and thick slices of tough but tasty bread. The food was very simple and very good. We talked about the job I would do.

"I won't be able to pay you even a living wage," said Barnes apologetically, "but I can assure you of one thing, you won't go hungry. We must eat well to work well, and I will see to that."

"That's fine with me. I'm down on my luck and will work with you for food and shelter. Before winter comes I hope to get back to my family in the South. How long have you been a photographer?"

"For about five years. I've had some bad luck too, but found that work can numb pain and help one forget."

"Oh, I can agree with that. Any number of preachers will tell you that work is man's salvation. They say if you find your work and do it, at the end of your life you won't have to ask if you were happy. Did bad luck hit hard when it came your way?"

"My wife and son died of diphtheria," he answered, hesitant and laconic. "It was not a good time for me but worse for them. They suffered terribly. Couldn't breathe, couldn't swallow. And then came heart and nerve damage and they were dead. We worked a farm in Pennsylvania, in Amish country. I sold everything but two horses and a wagon and started traveling."

"I'm sorry for your suffering and loss, Mr. Barnes. Your story is sadder than mine."

"Call me Geoffrey, please. What's done is done. We can't undo the past. You ate only two sausages, friend. Take another and have some more beer. We have traveling to do and work."

It was a good summer for both of us. Barnes was probably the best boss I ever had. He saw to it that I ate well, slept in a good bed at night, and had decent clothes to wear. In time he paid me a small salary that I saved for the future. I finally managed to go southward before winter came. Mama was ailing with arthritis and little sis was sickly looking, but both were glad to see me and cheerful. As expected, my old daddy was hale and hearty but bitter with few words. Brother Luke was in jail. I went looking for work, but times were hard. I found nothing and left soon afterwards to wander again. In Norfolk a sailing ship needed a sailor. Its name was *Sea Cloud*. I signed on, but that's another story.

32

One Autumn Night

People often say young men are able to travel great distances without hardship. It isn't true. As human beings we are subject to the same vagaries of weather and circumstance as anyone else. Most of the time we manage quite well; at other times we don't. Once in autumn I found myself in a very unpleasant situation. I had just come into a town without even knowing its name, and night was coming on. I knew not one living soul in the town and had only a few cents in my pocket, not enough for even the meanest night's lodging. Walking swiftly against the chill of a late-October evening and simply following the pavement, I was soon looking at steamships docked at the waterfront. In daylight the scene was surely bustling as boisterous men worked the wharves. The place was silent as night was coming — lonely, dark, and deserted.

I wandered among the buildings and warehouses and thought how good it would be to find something to eat and a place to sleep. And then it occurred to me in the world we live in today it's easier to feed the mind than to feed the body. Just about every town has a free library where one may read and relax in comfort all day and sometimes well into the evening. The libraries have an abundance of books to satisfy the hunger of anyone's mind but not even a cup of coffee to warm an empty stomach. One can become well-read in a good library while suffering from a lack of proper nutrition. I've been told the mind of a hungry man is always sharper than that of the well-fed man. If that were so, the lean and hungry would be the leaders of nations, not the well-groomed, self-satisfied politicians with pot bellies and fat faces.

Rain was beginning to fall, and winds from the northeast were howling. Waves had built in the water and were smashing against the wharf. On the tall ships under the dark sky I could see shadowy figures moving about. I felt a pang of envy, for they had full bellies and a place to sleep. Lying on the beach away from the ships was a rowboat with its bottom upwards. For a moment I thought of the shelter it could provide while I slept. Then realizing the sand was cold and my clothing thin, I walked on with teeth chattering. I came to a large crate, lately unloaded from a vessel, and found a girl not older than eighteen behind it. She was crouching on the sand, her clothing getting wet and her dark hair shaggy and wet. With slender hands she was digging under the crate with fury and didn't see me as I approached and stood near her.

"What are you doing?" I asked. "And why?"

A muffled scream came from the girl. Quickly she stood up and stared at me. I wanted to apologize for startling her in that quiet, dark place but waited for her to speak. She shook the sand from her hands, wiped them on her skirt, and spoke with a question.

"Do you want something to eat too? Dig away then. I think maybe the crate has food, bread and maybe sausages. I'm getting a whiff of food though I can't be sure."

I began to dig. A moment later she was helping. We worked in silence. I gave no thought to the criminal code, the moral impact of what we were doing, the legal proprietorship of the crate, or any of those things that seem important to most people. I was thinking of one thing only: would we find edible food inside. My stomach was scraping my backbone and crying out to be fed. Finding something to eat had become all important. My companion was suffering from hunger too. I could see it in the pallor of her face and the furious digging.

"It could have a bottom of heavy boards," she said at last. "If so, we won't be able to break them. It might be easier to break the lock."

In minutes I found the lock half covered with sand and wrenched it off with a heavy rock. A little door opened and the girl scurried inside.

"Anything in there?" I asked.

"Some bottles, an old lamp, many wool overcoats, what looks like a small machine of some sort, a tin box, and a bucket."

My heart sank. An overcoat might keep me warm but do nothing for my belly. Just as hope was fading, she exclaimed: "Hey, wait! There's something in the tin box! It has some stale bread that looks edible and what looks like a canned ham."

Out she came with two loaves, and we freed the ham with my pocket knife. I was working on the ham and bread when she exclaimed, "The watchman's coming! We gotta get out of here, man, and fast! No time to go back in for overcoats."

Not getting an overcoat, especially a wool one, bothered me. The night was getting colder and I was dressed almost for summer. She was wearing only a skirt and sweater and needed a coat too. We were not dressed for the chill of night but we couldn't risk getting caught.

"We can hide under that rowboat on the beach," I said, pointing. "It'll be dark under there and cold, but dry maybe. We can eat and rest under the boat and maybe sleep."

In the wind and rain we ran for the skiff and squeezed under it to find dry sand and relative warmth. The rain grew violent and pelted the boat's bottom, our roof, so hard we had difficulty hearing each other as we tried to get acquainted. She placed the ham on the bread, and in the damp darkness we had a feast. With our bellies full a complacent fatigue took over, and we began to rest but without comfort. The girl curled up against one side of the skiff and I on the other. I think we tried to sleep but the howling of the wind wouldn't allow it.

"Why is life so unfair?" she groaned without expecting an answer. "Who cares whether we live or die? If the owner of this boat should find us dead when he comes to go fishing tomorrow morning, do you think he would give a damn?"

"He wouldn't like finding two ripe corpses under his boat," I said, trying to make a joke. "Might spoil his day just a little."

She made a little sound that wasn't laughter. I could

tell she was inexpressibly sad. I didn't know whether speaking would make her feel better or worse, but made up my mind to say something.

"I can see that things are not right with you. Who battered you? Who or what hurt you and left you like this?"

"Nathan did it all," she explained without emotion.

"And who is Nathan?"

"My fiancé," she replied hesitantly. "He's a baker. We lived together."

"Did he beat you?"

"When he was drunk, yes!"

Then suddenly, quite rapidly, she began to talk about herself and the love affair that went wrong. Her name was Elizabeth but he called her Liz. His name was . . . she decided not to mention his name. He had done things for which he could be arrested, and she didn't want him punished. When sober he was a good man, she insisted, getting up early in the morning to bake goodies that made life pleasant for people. But the job eventually got to him and he drank too much and beat her when life treated him harshly. That was bad enough, but the final insult came when he began to chase after other girls.

"It was a terrible insult. I know for a fact I'm better looking than any slut he ran after, and I loved him when they didn't. I couldn't take it any more. And so about a month ago when he didn't come home for a couple of days, I went looking for him and found him drunk as a skunk in a run-down dump with another woman."

"That's always a bad situation, a stew with sour ingredients."

"She's a known drug addict and ugly as sin, but there he was with that bitch instead of me, sitting on a dirty couch in his underwear. I lost my temper and called him every dirty name I could think of and got for my trouble a hard smack. Then later he locked me out of the house and told my employer I was no good. So overnight I found myself with no home and no job, nothing to eat and no place to sleep. I was forced to find shelter and food wherever I could."

"And so you drifted down to the waterfront? What did you hope to find in this place? Sailors are notorious for treating women like dirt."

"I wasn't looking for no sailors. I would starve before selling myself to a sailor. But what's gonna happen to me now? No food, no shelter, only the clothes on my back." She began to whimper.

The rain had stopped but the wind continued to howl, and the night hours grew colder. My teeth danced a jig of pure misery. Elizabeth huddled against me for warmth. Even in the darkness I could see gleams of hope in those young eyes when she spoke of no hope. She said Nathan had given her a very painful black eye.

"Men are devils!" she plainly said. "I hate men! I guess I hate you, but maybe you're not a devil. You're warm like red devils are supposed to be, but the warmth ain't devilish at all. It's good. So are you a devil?"

"The last time I checked I was a man, a traveling man often hungry, but not as hungry as when we met. I'm an Irish Traveler."

"Oh, I've heard of them. They're crooks and roam the

countryside and steal from farmers and treat women badly."

"Some do. Not all."

I began to shiver with no control. I groaned and ground my teeth. My stomach was turning sour. Maybe the bread or the ham was spoiled. She said I was warm and yet I felt terribly cold. She could feel a quake wracking my body and asked in a quiet and soothing voice whether I was sick. I believed someone else was speaking, not Elizabeth who had just declared an undying hatred of all men.

"Why didn't you tell me you were cold? What a dunce you are laying there silent and sick. You should have told me. The boat is keeping the sand dry. Stretch out on it and I'll lay on top of you and keep you warm like a blanket. Now put your arms around me and squeeze me tight. You'll be warm very soon now. And then I'll turn my back to you and the night will pass as fast as you can bat an eyelash. Just see if it won't. You were turned out of your place too? We're comrades now."

With those words she comforted me, cured me when I was sick. At a time when she thought her life was over she reached deep into her woman's heart to give another human being all she could give. She encouraged me. She made me strong. And who was she? A young woman, scarcely more than a girl, warming me with her body. A wretched, battered, haunted creature warming me even more with her words. It had to be a dream, an oppressive dream. But no, impossible to think that. The wind howled, the rain began again and pelted the skiff with water as hard as pellets. The sea a few yards away churned and splashed convulsively. Under the small boat we embraced with the passion of lovers but only to stave off the cold. It was real. No dream, however bizarre, was ever so bittersweet as that reality.

Without pause Elizabeth was uttering calm and soothing talk as only women can do it. It was kind and sympathetic talk that revealed amazing strength of character, bright intelligence, and rare resiliency. I could only groan in response to the music she made. It didn't matter. She wasn't looking for chatter from me. She began to kiss me, kisses warm and wet all over my face. She ran her fingers through my hair and breathed reassuring thoughts into my ear.

"There, there, you funny traveler. Don't be alarmed. It's nothing. You'll be fine tomorrow. If you want, you can be my man. I'll find a place for us. I'll find a job. I'll help you find a job. We'll have a good life."

Her quiet, persuasive whispers were cellos and alto violins fused in harmony, music from afar and hypnotic. We slept a few hours and awoke to a sunny autumnal day. In the good weather we crawled from beneath the skiff, shook off the sand, and walked into town. We had no money for breakfast, but a kindly grocer gave us apples. We sat on a bench and munched them before taking leave of each other. She kissed me goodbye on my left cheek, her hands gently stroking my face. Her warm breath was sweet. It smelled of lilacs in bloom.

For a year wherever I went I looked for Elizabeth. I hoped to find her and live with her and love her as no man has ever loved. I even returned to the beach where I met her but never saw her again. I asked if anyone remembered having known a young woman named Elizabeth, and I described her in detail. I asked people in the town if they knew a man called Nathan, or maybe Nate, but got no positive response from anyone. Maybe, after all these years, that remarkable young woman is dead. Yet as long as I live she lives within me.

33

Things Fall Apart

The November weather wasn't good the day I walked all the way to the poorhouse. Owned and run by the county, it was some distance from the room I had rented in Kelly Junction. The poorhouse was now called "the County Farm" because that sounded better to genteel ears. Also it had 160 acres of rich soil. The people sent there, if they expected to eat, were required to work the land. Several carefully tended gardens supplied fresh vegetables, and the farm had an apple orchard, a potato patch, and a cornfield. Women who knew how to cook worked in the kitchen preparing meals and canning fruits and vegetables for winter. Some like my sister weren't able to work outside or in the kitchen, and that placed them beneath the residents that could. On the lowest rung of the social ladder, the pecking order, they were pariahs in an institution that was itself a pariah. Scut work filled their days.

From a distance, the stone building of three stories was impressive. It appeared to be a wealthy plantation owner's mansion, or maybe a country manor in the

English countryside. Those who erected it thirty years before I got there were apparently well funded. The establishment looked rich and appealing as I approached, but this was engraved in stone above the main entrance: *"Remember us, for we too lived and loved and laughed."* That bizarre inscription, striving to sound poetic, referred to the inhabitants in the past tense. Poor wretches in that place were seen as no longer part of the living world.

Inside I expected to be greeted by an official who would ask about my business there and politely answer questions. There was no such person anywhere. In the wide hallway beyond the vestibule I saw people shuffling along in night clothes even though it was late in the morning. I could see a counter off to one side and a desk behind it cluttered with papers, but no one working. I wandered in the hallway to get my bearings and merged with the sleepwalkers. Within minutes an old woman began to talk to me in a wheezy, low, confidential voice as if she didn't want anyone but me to hear. Tugging on my sleeve, she pulled me over to an alcove where we sat down in wicker chairs.

"I'm old and gray and sixty-seven," she began in gravelly tones that became sort of chirpy the longer she spoke, "but I don't deserve this. They brought me here two months ago, or maybe two years ago, because I was down and out with no family. They called me a pauper. I asked them am I lazy or crazy, am I blind or lame? I can work for a living and pay my way. Just help me find work and leave me be. The man just laughed at me and the woman, hustling me to a tiny hole they called a room, spoke with syrupy but phony kindness. I have to share the room with another old woman, a very old woman. She babbles all day and coughs her head off all night, and she stinks."

The woman was intense despite her years and struggling to understand what had happened to her. She wanted me to listen and perhaps understand in some way. I began to feel sorry for her.

"What happened to your family?" I asked in the same quiet tone she had adopted. "Couldn't you go live with a daughter or a son? Are you a widow now? Do you have no friends or relatives?"

"I was married to a good man and we raised a good family, but as the years pass, you know, things fall apart."

"No, I don't know. What do you mean by that?"

"I mean the little things that made a good life for us just fell apart, dissolved like a wedding cake in the rain. We had three daughters and three sons, and we raised them every one. Worked for them summer and winter, night and day. But when they got to their teens they turned their backs on us and drifted away. Then the Lord Almighty came one day and took my dear John away and I was alone. My son Charlie was unemployed and not able to make ends meet. He came to live with me and brought with him his snotty little girlfriend."

"Well now, that's good to hear. Things got better then? You were not alone any more. You had another woman to keep you company. You had someone to chat with when Charlie went looking for work."

"No, things didn't get better. Charlie couldn't keep a job even when he was lucky enough to find one. And try as I might I could never please that girl Ethel. We couldn't get along at all, and I really don't know why. It was fussin' and cussin' all the time. I got bone tired of it and let them take over the house and pay the rent. I went to live with Susan, but Susan's place was tiny and crowded somethin' awful. Her husband, his two unmarried sisters, and three children lived there. I could see right away there wasn't no room for me."

"So what did you do then?"

"I went to live with my boy Tom but that didn't last neither. His five children were soon all over me, and he expected me to care for them night and day. I tried to be firm with them and teach them some manners, but he got huffy when they complained. He said he was the boss of all the children, not me. So I wrote to Becky to get away from Tom, but she said the climate up north was too cold for an old woman."

"Now I understand. None of your children wanted you 'cause you were in the way and interfered with their lives."

"I guess you might say that, but I can tell you one thing. All the time they was growing up I was never in the way. It was always 'Mama do this, Mama do that, Mama find my shoes, Mama comb my hair, Mama go buy us something good to eat. We're hungry, Mama, cook us some rice and beans. Feed us, Mama!' Well, to make a long story short, Charlie took steps and I ended up here, and I don't deserve it. I just don't deserve it. Nobody old or young should be in this place."

Her name, she said, was Helen. I think I caught her last name as Hopkins but couldn't be sure. She was so slight and frail a puff of wind was ready to double her up and turn her over, ready to blow her away like thistle in a storm. Though I could see her health was not the best, her senses were keen enough and she had feelings her loved ones hurt. They made her suffer. She wanted to know if I was new to the place. Before I could explain why I was there, she drifted away to tell her story to a tall and lanky old man. He had a bad leg and shuffled along in bedroom slippers, staring straight ahead. She was holding on to him and talking as fast as she could. He was clicking his tongue, snapping his fingers, and not listening to a word she was saying.

I went on down the hall into what they call the common room. All the residents who couldn't be working seemed to be in that room. It was filled with an assortment of people I'd never seen before. In rags and tatters and night clothes, many were short and paunchy. Others were walking skeletons. Some were old and wrinkled and wearing on haggard faces either a fixed smile showing one or two bad teeth or a scowl. Here and there in the chaos and misery I found little spots of what appeared to be happiness. A young man with stringy hair falling to his shoulders was playing an invisible fiddle, smiling soulfully, and dancing to the music. At best it was a dull, animal happiness delusional and detached from reality. Most were miserable. Beside a window a woman sat looking into a small mirror she held in her hands. She was examining her face closely and crying hysterically. Each time she saw a pimple, discoloration, wrinkle, or some small imperfection, she sobbed loudly. I passed nearby. Her face was aging but clear and clean.

Most of the residents in this poorhouse, this "County

Home" as some would have it, were grotesquely thin. Some were so emaciated they looked like leathery cadavers; others were so obese they could barely walk. Here and there a tottering old man or woman in night clothes and slippers lurched forward to accost me, and in their effort almost fell to the floor. Outside in plain view, a man and woman in flimsy attire were searching through a pile of garbage. They were greedily eating whatever they could find and squabbling like animals over a kill. The crisp air of late autumn carried inside the sounds they made. I stood at the window and stared at the ruined gold of once-worthy lives. The trees nearby were barren of leaves and swaying in the wind.

In the common room a severe-looking woman I took to be a nurse was seated behind a counter. I believe at one time in her life she was pretty, but her prettiness had no grip on time and was doomed to fade away like the colors of autumn. Her aquiline nose and black eyes were in a cheap magazine. Looking only at the illustrations and flipping the pages with a rhythmic jerk, if she noticed me at all she paid no attention. I stood at the counter to speak to her, expecting her to say something. She didn't. I waited for her to speak. She didn't even look at me. An illustrated magazine filled with gray and static pictures was more important to her than a living soul wanting help. I cleared my throat, hoping to get her attention, and spoke first.

"I'm here looking for my sister. I was told she's living here but don't know for sure. Her name is Lena and she's probably blind."

The woman flipped her magazine shut, placed a thin,

blue-veined hand on it, and looked at me with tired eyes. Slowly she began to speak. In the midst of a rising tide of incoherent babble, I could barely hear her. An old woman was screeching, "You hit me! You hit me! How dare you!" An old man in the rigid stance of a preacher in a pulpit was loudly reciting what sounded like biblical verse. A young man was singing a throaty ballad and pretending to conduct an orchestra. All three had drive and energy, but in the stupefying atmosphere that pervaded the place a poisonous torpor wrapped around them.

"I don't know a blind resident by that name," the nurse was saying through the din. "I've been here thirteen years and ran into several blind women, but don't know anyone named Lena. Did you go to the main office? They might be able to help you."

"I said she's *probably* blind. Not entirely blind maybe but close to it. She was losing her sight even as a little girl."

I thanked the woman and for reasons that gradually became clear I began to feel sorry for her. She had worked there a long time, and what did she get for all the dreary hours she put into the place? I could tell by just looking at her. She got a tired, sullen face surrounded by kinky hair turning gray. She got a frowsy and soiled white frock they called a uniform and probably had to wash and iron it herself. She got toil and boredom, stooped shoulders and callused hands, bad teeth, aching joints, and terror from angry residents. She had spent the best years of her life in a warehouse designed for sick and deranged people. The respectable citizens of her county had labeled them paupers and wanted them off the street. The vocal, fat-cat politicians took it upon themselves to hide them away. And without hesitation they hired this woman at small wages to look after them many hours each day. To preserve her sanity, she lost herself in cheap magazines whenever she could.

"I'm wondering," I said, "what the rules and regulations are for this place. I hear institutions have all kinds of regulations."

"Oh, we have a long list of rules for the governance and good order of the County Farm," she replied. "I took the time to read through most of the rules and it seems to me they're very reasonable. This ain't a prison, you know. It's a home for the poor. You can't call it a hotel, that's for sure, but we try to make it tolerable."

"It's more like an asylum or hospital than a home," I said with some emotion, "and to call it a prison wouldn't be inaccurate. Some of the people milling around in this room don't have their full wits about them, and some are plainly sick. Also, as far as I can tell, not one man or woman in this place has the freedom to leave it."

"Well, sir," she retorted with warmth, "it *is* the county poorhouse, and it was never meant to be a fancy resort. People sent here are maintained by public funds, and I'm sure you must know Kershaw is not a wealthy county. I think I might have a copy of the rules in a drawer somewhere. Would you like to see them? Most people don't bother to ask, but every station is supposed have a copy."

She rummaged in a drawer and found the document. It had a long title I took pains to remember. It went something like this — *Rules and Regulations and Bylaws for the Governance and Good Order of the County of Kershaw Farm in the State of South Carolina.* I read through some of the rules and they didn't seem totally harsh, but even as I read I knew many were being ignored. One rule in particular caught my attention: "*When any person dies, the female assistant shall immediately take the clothes of the deceased, cause them to be washed and mended, and deposit them neatly folded in the storeroom near the laundry.*" That same rule applied to the clothing of inmates who died in prison.

Other rules said all persons who could work would work. Any person claiming to be sick to get out of work and found to be well by one of two physicians who came once a week, or any person causing a disturbance of any kind, would be sent to the lockup. In solitary confinement, he or she would be fed bread and water until fully compliant. Any person late for dinner without a valid excuse would forfeit the meal, and no person would sing or talk loudly at dinner. Any person found to have a contagious disease would be kept in "fullest isolation" — solitary confinement — until well again or dead. And the clerk claimed this was not a prison? Many of the rules were exactly the same as for prisons.

I wished the poor woman well and went in search of the main office. As I walked down the dark corridors past numerous cramped little chambers, I could tell the sanitation of the place was less than perfect. In spite of what the rules dictated, no attempt was being made to ventilate the rooms and corridors properly. I could sense a clammy dampness in the air, and strange odors merged into other odors the farther I went. The unhealthy atmosphere of the place brought on visions of my dear sister falling victim to diphtheria, dysentery, croup, cholera, typhoid, bronchitis, pneumonia, consumption, and kindred disorders. Though I could find no evidence to refute her remarks, the woman had told me the death rate was fairly low in that selfless, benevolent, altruistic home funded and operated by the good citizens of Kershaw County. All I had seen convinced me otherwise. The poorhouse was a Bastille where paupers and other undesirables went to die. I feared if my sister had indeed come there, she was no longer among the living.

I went through a maze of corridors before reaching the main office. As my uncertain luck would have it, I got there just as the chief clerk was closing for the day. He was a self-important little man in his middle fifties with big ears and a fringe of gray hair on either side of his head. His round blue eyes above pale cheeks blinked behind round spectacles and looked watery and weary. He appeared to be filing some papers. I stood at the counter separating his work space from the public and waited for him to finish. When he turned to tell me the office was about to close, I could see his arms were long even though his torso and legs were short. He spoke with a southern drawl typical of the region.

"We're closing, sir. Come back tomorrow. We open at seven sharp and we close at five sharp. Your watch will tell you it's past five."

"I know you want to get home, but I'm wondering if you can tell me quickly if my sister lives here. I'm in town again after being away for a time and was told she was sent here maybe two years ago."

"Yes, I do need to get home sir. My old mama ain't well and I have to leave her every day to come here and work. I can't help you today, sir. Come back tomorrow. The office is closed."

"I've heard you have a ledger with all the names of the inmates. Will you take just a minute to look at it?"

"If your sister is living here, sir, she's a *resident*, not an *inmate*. We don't use that word here. The rules forbid it."

I was being pushy and knew it. I was a bit upset by what I had seen and was trying to seize the moment. I had come to the place to find my sister, or to find she was no longer there. I spent most of the day in the county poorhouse and found nothing but pain and suffering and heartache. Though I protested, the officious little man took me by the elbow and ushered me out of his office. In the dreary hallway with its stench of vomit, urine, sweat, and other odors I heard a female voice howling. A male voice bellowed in response, "shut up, you ol' bag, shut yer goddamn mouth!" The woman responded with shrill laughter. It was high-pitched cackling devoid of mirth. I walked back to Kelly Junction in the rain feeling sad. Every person in that place was falling apart and crying. I felt like crying too.

34

A Gift for Lena

I was in Kelly Junction again and wanting my sister to live with me. Several weeks passed before I was able to go looking for her. After I found a job and a place to live, I heard from a distant relative that when the family fell apart she might have gone to the county poorhouse. So early one morning I went there hoping to find her. Already a number of people were waiting in the public room with its long counter, and for nearly an hour I waited with them. When I told the clerk why I was there, he smiled wanly and rummaged under the counter. He pulled out a ledger bound in faded green and almost as wide as a newspaper. He placed the heavy volume on the counter and opened it. On its pages were many names. I asked how many but got no answer. On pain of losing his job, he was careful not to answer my nosey question.

He found the O section and placed his stubby finger on O'Connor, obscuring the name. Then when the finger moved away, I read "Sarah O'Connor, 8 mos." In smaller script beside it were the words, *"Wife of Liam O'Connor, occupation unknown."* There was no doubt about it. My old gentle-hearted mama, wracked by pain in all her joints, died in the poorhouse after being there eight months. I felt a little weak in the knees when I saw that. Later I reasoned if Mama was alive in the poorhouse eight months before passing, Lena was probably with her.

"Does this tell me," I asked, "that my sister never lived here? I have it on pretty good authority she came here too."

"Well, it don't say she did and it don't say she didn't. Just says a Sarah O'Connor came and went. Did you know her?"

"She was my mama, and the mother of two other children."

"I take it the one you call Lena was her daughter. I don't see no Lena above Sarah on this alphabetical list, but this is an old ledger. Gimme a few minutes and I'll see if I can't find another one more up to date." He rummaged under the counter a second time and came up with the same huge ledger looking newer.

"I think I'm gonna have to ask you to sit over there 'cause visitors ain't supposed to be looking at the records. Rules, y' know."

I found a wooden chair, one of those folding types, beside the flyspecked window and sat down. For half an hour or more I waited for the clerk to tell me something, wondering why it was taking so long. Beside me in another chair was a grim-faced young woman who had come to visit her elderly parents. To pass the time we began to chat. The old folks had a good marriage and a good living, she told me, until her papa fell off a wagon at work and broke a leg. She paused and put a handkerchief to her nose. Her dark eyes brimmed with tears that stained her pallid cheeks.

"Well," she went on, "instead of paying for his hospital bill and waiting for him to get well again, his boss fired him. Mama tried to keep the wolf from the door by sewing, but that was only seasonal work. So with every passing day they slipped deeper into poverty. When they couldn't pay their rent or buy food to stay alive, they were forced to apply for beds in the poorhouse. Because so many others were ahead of them on the waiting list, they starved before being admitted and came into this place walking a tightwire 'tween life and death."

I asked why didn't she take them into her own house and look after them. She wiped away a tear before answering. She lived with her husband and four children in two rooms and couldn't find the space for another bed even if they could have bought one. Her husband was a pipefitter, she said, and often didn't have steady work and sometimes drank too much. The woman was no older than thirty but looked fifty. She lived in another part of the county north of Kelly Junction, and it seemed to me her life was harder than mine had ever been. In a sad place she was telling a stranger a sad tale. Before I could hear the end of it the clerk called me back to the long counter.

"I found the entry," he said. "A woman named Lena O'Connor came here with a woman named Sarah O'Connor. They were admitted at the same time nearly three years ago. The older woman was infirm with severe rheumatism but able to mop floors. The daughter was blind and not able to do farm chores or housekeeping chores. She was put to hackling flax and picking oakum to help pay her way. The record shows she's still here and still able to work."

I had been a sailor and knew all about oakum and picking oakum. Sometimes on idle days at sea, especially when becalmed, some of the crew was assigned the task of tearing apart old tarry ropes strand by strand to get a fibrous material used to caulk a vessel's timbers and deck planking. It was an ornery task that blistered your fingers and made them so black even turpentine couldn't clean them. Now I was hearing that delicate Lena, struggling all her life to see more than shifting shadows, was blind and doing that kind of work. For a roof over her head, a rickety cot to sleep on, and coarse food to mitigate a gnawing hunger, she was picking oakum or hackling flax. With no little misgiving I asked the clerk where I might find her.

"I'm not sure," he replied, "but I think the woman could be living and working in the East Wing. Just follow the yellow stripe."

I followed the stripe, walking briskly through dark and dreary corridors in the midst of sick and demented people. Like ghosts from another world, they shuffled along staring straight ahead, each of them wearing and sharing an unchanging grimace of pain and confusion. As if mesmerized, they moved in cloth slippers and night clothes with stiff arms pointing downward. A tall, emaciated man with a long white beard and crazy eyes walked with arms akimbo as if daring the others to bump into him. All of them moved slowly and methodically. The sound they made was like the chant I had heard in my youth at church before the sermon began. One or two tugged at my clothing to gain my attention. Others pressed themselves against the wall to let me pass.

After forty minutes I found the East Wing and my sister. She was sitting at a table in a barren room in front of a pile of oakum. The hour was early, but her long hard day of unceasing labor had already begun. I stood in the doorway looking at her, recalling what she looked like in her youth and trying to see a fresh and delicate girl in the thin and worn woman. I stood in the narrow hallway for several minutes, observing the figure inside the room. I'm sure my jaw was slack, and I was staring in disbelief. My favorite person, so clean and uplifting, had turned into a blind old woman before her time.

Her pallid face was drawn and pockmarked. Her frame was so frail she looked as though she would break at any moment. She sat stiffly upright in front of the oakum, her thin hands kneading the stuff skillfully and rapidly. She seemed to be looking not at her work but at the blank wall in front of her. Yet I could tell she was blind and seeing only darkness. All the time I had known her she was going blind, and now sitting straight and prim on that hard chair she was without sight but not insight. As a child she had peopled her shadowy world with happy persons and sunny events, and maybe she was doing that now. She had a way of making a dreary world a tolerable place. A little smile flickered across the thin, cracked lips as she turned to face the doorway.

Sensing my presence, she invited her unknown visitor to speak. Struggling to put down feelings that welled up inside me, I didn't know what to say. For a fleeting moment I was sorry I had gone in quest of Lena. Maybe

I was bringing more harm to her than good. Maybe for me to come back into her life would disrupt any peace of mind she might have found. Deep feeling rose in my throat and tumbled out.

"Lena? Your brother Leo is speaking! I'm home from my travels and living in Kelly Junction. I've been looking for you."

The mindless, automatic movement of her fragile hands stopped abruptly. The head on the long neck slowly turned, and her hands went back to their work. She was uttering softly something I didn't recognize. I think she was saying, "Billy? Billy?" That name had no meaning for me, and I repeated my name. It had no effect on her. She went on saying . . .

"Billy? Billy? Is that you? I will get it done before noon, I promise. Two fingers on my left hand are blistered and hurting, and so I have to go slower than usual. But I'll make my quota by noon. I will, I will."

And then she began to sing in a flat monotone a little song we sang when we were children but somehow different:

Rock a bye Billy in the treetop,
When the wind blows the cradle will rock,
When the bough breaks the cradle will fall,
And down will come Billy, ol' Billy and all!

She had changed the words of the ancient rhyme and was mocking her taskmaster, predicting doom for him. Her unseeing eyes were wide open and a sly smile shaped her lips.

I was beside her now, lightly touching her shoulder, and I could feel a tremor running down her neck and across her back. She reached out, caught my hand, and buried her face in it. Her warm affection was the signal I needed to let me know she understood. Not until later did she tell me her sense of smell let her know I was truly her brother. Before speaking she held my hand to her face.

"My prodigal brother returns!" she cried with a theatrical flourish. "Roaming the world, the wanderer comes home again! I can't believe it, I really can't believe it. After straggling across the wild deserts of the world, my Leo is finally home again!"

"No," I said to her, "no deserts unless you see the rolling ocean as a vast desert. I went to sea. In all my life I never saw a desert."

"You've never seen a desert, Leo? I see them all the time! And they're not all bad, you know. Some bad people put me and Mama in a desert, and I thought the sun would burn us to a crisp. Mama put up a fight but died all dried up in the desert, and they left her bones to bleach in the sun. Ah, but Lena found a way to survive! I can shut it all out, and then I see blue skies and feel a cool breeze on my face and hear birds chirping. I hear music too, Leo. I often hear the most amazing music in the middle of the night and even when I'm working."

"I can see that very active imagination you had as a child is still with you, Lena. I'm glad you never lost it."

"Oh, Leo, please understand. I'm not always a dreamer lost in a world that never was. Sometimes I think about life and the mystery that surrounds us in the here and now. Sometimes I ask myself: *Who are you and why are you here and where are you going?* And then I laugh because it sounds like gobblegook! Didn't Mama used to call it that?"

"I think you mean *gobbledygook*. Our old daddy talked a lot of nonsense, and Mama called it gobbledygook."

She was laughing now and I was laughing with her. Then as we began to talk about home and childhood and family, a burly attendant in a white coat appeared in the doorway looking perplexed. I tried to explain I was the woman's brother, absent from her for many years, but he didn't understand or care to understand.

"You may be her brother, sir," he said with a firmness that startled me, "but you are seriously breaking the rules. You're interfering with her work and causing her to fall behind. If you stay here longer, you'll get your sister in trouble. We don't allow relatives of residents in the workplace. How did you get in here anyway? You must go, now!"

Without a chance to say goodbye, with no opportunity to assure Lena I would see her later, I was hustled out of the room and down the bleak corridor to the main entrance. The attendant was large, rough, and strong. I was in no mood to resist him.

I could hear my sister calling, stricken and disconsolate, "Don't you hurt him, Billy! He's my brother! Don't you dare hurt him!"

She was as weak as a fly in a web, and yet she was cautioning big and burly Billy to go easy on her brother. The spirit of the girl I remembered lived on in the blind and rapidly aging woman.

I later found out that Billy was notorious for his rough treatment of residents. He felt it was his calling to bully and brutalize paupers of both sexes. He wasn't confined to a specific wing of the place but had free run of the entire farm. He had misbehaved for a decade and remained unpunished. The rules and regulations of the place emphasized humane treatment of residents. They didn't seem to apply to Billy.

For more than three tortuous months I wrestled with bungling bureaucrats and finally achieved something positive. Even now I'm not sure how it happened, but I was able to get Lena out of that place to live with me in Kelly Junction. I found a place with two bedrooms and for the first time in all her life she had her own room. I'm happy to report that she breathed free air again. Each day for her was an adventure that brought her joy. She often sat in a large rocking chair by the window looking down on the street. More than once I could see a familiar smile flicker across her face as she sat there. I asked her once what she saw in the street to make her smile.

"More than you will ever know," she replied.

Lena had one year and five months to enjoy warmth and sunshine in my place. Even as the end days approached her capable hands were never idle. She made my rented rooms a very pleasant home. She made for me a book with blank pages I later used as a notebook. She even prepared simple meals we shared together. Life in Kelly Junction is no longer the same without her. I feel lonely as I write this, and I think when spring comes I'll be traveling again.

35
Walking Westward

"Hello, dear sir, you are walking westward?"
"Yes, indeed yes! I should be in nightmare
Were I to walk easterly in this place."

I'm an old bookkeeper, or in the more up-to-date term, an accountant. I have lived all my life in Philadelphia, and for many years I've worked for Gruenwald and Trueblood in the business district. I began my tenure with them at twenty-one, and now when I'm old enough to retire I work from eight in the morning until six at night. I eat my lunch at my desk from a brown paper bag and take half an hour to do it. We have what the younger folk call a break room, but I never use it.

I began with a salary of not more than . . . well, I won't say exactly, but I will tell you this. Though I worked hard and did my job dutifully, I received only small increases in pay and not one promotion in all my years with the firm. While others got hefty raises, mine invariably was so small it was laughable. Once when it was smaller than usual I thought of walking directly into the boss's office and telling him if he pretended to pay me, I would pretend to work. But of course I didn't do it. I'm not a confrontational person. I simply suffer in silence.

I suppose the bosses made it harder for me because I kept to myself and lost myself in my work. I didn't gather with co-workers at the water cooler to laugh and tell jokes and listen to gossip and exchange slaps on the back. I went to my tiny office in a far corner of the building and remained there all day. My boss would barge in from time to time, always cheerful and mouthing, "How goes it, Howard?" Wearing a flinty smile that showed a golden tooth, he would dump another load of work on my desk. Just about every day I was the last one to leave the building.

Then out of the blue came a warm Saturday in late summer. On that day I left work earlier than usual. My eyes were adjusted to the yellow light of the dim corridor leading to the street, and when I stood on the sidewalk in sunlight I had to close them for a minute. I could feel my eyelids twitching in the light and warmth. It was a different experience for me because on most days the sun was low in the sky when I left work. For thirty years I spent the entire day bending over the books, scratching tiny figures in a big ledger with dusty covers, and doing the job as best I could. At times when there was occasion for pause I would allow myself to dream a little. What would I do if I had the income of my boss, that brusque and burly man with the paunch who walked the floor with a fiercely quizzical look? The dream never lasted longer than a few minutes, for the work was always demanding attention.

Well, to dream was a waste of time anyway. I lived

alone in two rooms. I had a comfortable bedroom, a sitting room with a window, and a little alcove for a kitchen. My father died when I was quite young and so did my mother, and because I was an only child I had no brothers or sisters who might come to visit and no friends. Once when I was much younger I got to know a sprightly young woman I liked very much. We talked of marriage and even made plans for a simple wedding, but it never happened. To this day I don't know why. Later I met a girl with freckles and red hair, and she told me she really liked me.

"You're not pushy, not overbearing like some fellows I know. You speak humbly and softly, and your words are weighty with thought."

"I have reason to speak harshly about many things in my life," I said to her, "but you bring out the softness in me. As for weighty words, well you flatter me when you say that. I'm not a thinker."

She liked my response and nestled close to me. I began to feel a pleasant warmth when we met to spend time together. We talked of a future together, but she didn't like living in Philadelphia and wanted to move to a warmer climate in North Carolina. In time she moved away and I was alone again. No other woman ever said she liked me.

Now on my way to work I stop at a little bakery just about every morning and buy a sweet roll and a pint of milk. I eat the roll and drink the milk while walking so as to get to work on time. In all the years I've worked for Gruenwald and Trueblood I was late only twice, once when my ancient alarm clock failed to go off and once when a blizzard was brewing. To my amazement but not to my surprise, the boss docked my pay for tardiness. I would have gained nothing by complaining.

The years went by all alike one after another. I did my work hour after hour, left at six or later with tired eyes and a headache, had a spare dinner in a small eatery near Independence Hall, went home and tried to read for an hour before bedtime. I soon realized I had no harvest of memories to draw upon when days were dull.

Events occur in the lives of others, either planned or unexpected. Rarely did anything of note happen in mine. Thirty years rolled by as similar to each other as drops of water from a leaky faucet. Thirty years came and went with nothing to celebrate. Thirty years of suffering from indigestion, sleeping fitfully, and working without recognition. Years I spent breathing stale air in a cold and tiny office day after day.

But this day, dazzled by the blazing sun, I decided to break the chain of habit. I would not go directly to Ellen's Eatery and then home. I would stroll westward along Market Street until the sun went down and darkness cloaked the street. When tired I would enter a restaurant better than Ellen's and treat myself to a good dinner. Maybe I would order a glass of wine and splurge for once. Then with a full belly and feeling warm and comfortable, I would make my way home.

So with these thoughts in mind I strolled among a crowd of people walking jauntily past brightly illuminated shops. The weather was warm and pleasant, and the girls in their summer dresses were sweet and attractive. Arm in arm they walked, skipping almost and laughing, their feet hardly touching the pavement. I felt for the first time in a very long time an air of tranquility, even a kind of joy that gladdened a heart too soon grown old. It made me feel at peace with the world.

The sun turned into a gigantic red ball and sank rapidly, leaving the western sky aflame with pink and red, yellow, orange, and purple. In the gathering twilight I began to feel hungry and went into a restaurant for dinner. It was served by a slim waiter in black and white at a little table with a candle. I had French bread, beef au jus, potatoes, asparagus, and a salad. I washed it all down with a glass of burgundy and was drinking my after-dinner coffee when the waiter left the bill. I paid it, and true to my intent to splurge I gave him a generous tip.

On the pavement again, I felt young and alive and continued my stroll. A warm and still night had fallen over the city of brotherly love to bring out many people seeking adventure and pleasure. In the street was a steady flow of noisy traffic. On the sidewalk were young and happy couples striding with a sprightly step, often hand in hand. And why not? The summer air bore kisses riding on soft and gentle breezes.

In time I grew tired of walking and sat down on a bench to rest and catch my breath. A slender girl not more than seventeen ambled up seductively and sat down beside me.

"Good evening, my well-dressed, good-looking, mature gentleman," she purred as she moved closer and took my hand in hers. "I can see you're out tonight for adventure."

A bit taken aback, I managed to reply. "You are mistaken, dear girl. You've chosen the wrong target this evening. I have no desire whatever to purchase anything you may be selling."

"Oh, come off of it, old daddy!" was her petulant reply. "Don't be an old fuddy-duddy. I can tell you haven't been with a woman for years. I can make you feel young again."

I walked away shaking my head and feeling sad. I thought of that scene in *Candide* with Paquette saying: *"I was turned out of doors quite destitute and obliged to continue this abominable trade. It brings death to the living, and I verily detest it!"* Only yesterday I had finished reading Voltaire's incisive work, and now in real life I was experiencing its powerful depiction of human depravity.

A few yards away in shifting shadows stood another woman, older and not so attractive as the first. Certain I had money and seeing me as an easy mark, she lost no time accosting me.

"There's a bench over there in the park, sir. Will you come with me and sit beside me and talk to me about wine and roses and moonlight? You are lonely and so am I. We have a need to console each other."

"What brought you into this line of work?" I asked softly. "Will you please tell me? I really and truly want to know."

"I'm sick and can just barely walk about but have to earn money somehow. If I don't get enough for rent, my landlady will turn me out of the house. I won't survive on the streets. I'll die like a mangy dog in a junk yard. Come with me, dear sir, to the park."

"I'm not able to go anywhere with you. I'm old and have no money. I spent it all on dinner. I have but two quarters. Will you take them?"

"No, I will not! Twenty dollars I would take but not fifty cents! I'm not a two-bit whore, old man! Piss on you!"

In a huff she strode away. Her legs seemed quite strong. I couldn't be sure she was sick at all. I believe it was all a sham.

Other women of the night were near and speaking persuasively in words dripping with honey. I had become a mark in this street with shops on one side and a shadowy park on the other. The sun had gone down, a brief twilight had quickly passed, and the night had become very dark. I found another bench and sat down, wearily heaving a sigh. I couldn't deny I needed a woman in my life. For years I had wanted the companionship of a young woman, but not that kind. I wanted to marry, have a wife and home and children. I wanted to come home to noisy children, not two little rooms shrouded in deadly silence.

I had to admit the woman claiming to be sick was right. I was lonely and my life was empty. Then suddenly, as I sat there in the gloom of night, the hard facts of my existence snapped into focus and became painfully clear. It was not a revelation, not an epiphany as they say in books, but clear thinking for once. One simple phrase described it all: I was *a pye-dog pariah.* Some people, and I was one of them, seem to have no luck in life and living becomes a burden. The social pariahs of this world are doomed to live in pain. Try as they might they can't escape the monotony of living day after empty day.

The people in this section of Philadelphia, laughing as they strolled quickly by, were intoxicated with life and living. They were laughing and joking, snuggling close to one another, and paying no attention to me, a stranger in their eyes, a feeble old man. Alone and beginning to feel uncomfortable, I looked at them as though viewing happy people in a warm house from outside in the cold of winter. Tomorrow I would be alone again. I might try to come out of my shell and chat with co-workers at the water cooler, but I didn't know how. Try as I might, I wouldn't be able to make a truce with fate or fortune and improve my condition. I rose and had trouble breathing. I felt very tired. I found another bench and sat down. Maybe I slept all night, I don't remember.

The next day I woke up in a hospital. The nurse in attendance said I had suffered no damage sleeping in the park through a mild summer's night. She advised me to be careful should I decide to do it again. Violent gangs in the city of brotherly love were known to have very little brotherly love, and they were on the prowl in public parks. I was lucky none had bothered me. She said I was fully capable of returning to my usual routine. That meant walking eastward. My heart sank.

36
Appleseed Lane

Lance and Beatrice Evans were in the third year of their marriage when they had to make a big decision. The leaders of Lance's company chose him as one of nine employees to open an office on the west coast. In the new location they would work to make their tool company well known in California. Hesitant to move away from his family and friends — he had grown up in Chicago — Lance thought he might turn the offer down. But after a long discussion with his wife, who emphasized the benefits of a new job in a new place with more pay, he let it be known he would go. A week later the company threw a party to see the five men and four women off. A week after that the group put down roots in Pasadena. The new branch quickly began to flourish in the city of sun and flowers.

Then one day as Lance and Beatrice were shopping, they happened to run into a young man whom Lance had known in high school. His name was Gordon Paige. At that time the fellow was a nerdy little guy with narrow shoulders, a long neck, and a pimply face. After a decade his body had taken on muscle, his skin had cleared, and he was much better looking. His blue eyes twinkled as he spoke to Lance after many years. The man of business remembered that he and another kid had taunted Gordon with "Gordo," a nickname meaning fat in Spanish and really not applicable to the thin and awkward teenager. The boy didn't like the name, and he liked the bullying even less.

"Well, if it isn't Gordon Paige!" Lance declared with surprise. "Beatrice, say hello to Gordo! I knew him years ago in high school."

"Glad to meecha, Bee. And Lanny Boy, you still calling me Gordo? Well, no bother. No bother at all. Just happy to be acquainted again."

"A pleasure to meet you, Gordon," said Beatrice in that soothing voice of hers. "As a friend of my husband, you're my friend. We live on Appleseed Lane. If you care to visit, the house number is 1912."

"Umm, 1912 Appleseed. Got it! Just add a hundred to *1812 Overture* and think of Johnny Appleseed! That energetic nurseyman planted seeds all over hell and creation. Found symbolic significance in apples! And the Russian's celebratory music, well you know — boom!"

"Yes, I see," Lance curtly replied. "Nice to meet so far from home."

"I'll be seeing you and your wife soon, old buddy," Gordon called as the couple ducked into a nearby shop.

And he did see them soon. One afternoon in that special light that Pasadena enjoys he dropped by unannounced. Lance was at work but Beatrice was home. They sat on the patio in back, drank tall glasses of iced tea, and talked. Beatrice detected a unique assortment of words coming from Gordon's mouth and rather liked the man. He said he was lonely and friendless in the sunshine of southern California. The remark brought sympathy from the young woman, and she said he could visit them any time he felt like it. So unannounced, Gordon routinely came every other day bearing little gifts.

Beatrice liked the attention he was giving her in her new home. He was always courteous and friendly and gave her no cause to worry. However, Lance began to feel uncomfortable when he heard his old classmate was spending time in his home almost as if he lived there. He wasn't a jealous person. He knew his wife could never be unfaithful. But Gordo coming so often bothered him, particularly when he came one day with koi for the little pond they had in the backyard. In high school Lance Evans had harassed Gordon Paige daily. Everyone knew Gordon hated the popular teen. Now it appeared he wanted to forgive and forget the dreary past and cultivate an adult friendship.

"I'm puzzled by his attitude," Lance admitted, "and I really don't want the guy coming here when I'm away at work."

"He's harmless," Beatrice countered. "Just a lonely guy in a new place looking for human companionship."

"Doesn't he work somewhere? How does he manage to come here in the middle of the afternoon just about every day?"

"He tells me he inherited property and money from an uncle but plans to work as an accountant with an insurance company."

"A likely story! The guy is a liar, Beatrice, and not to be trusted."

"We'll find out soon enough. He invited us to his home, believe it or not, and it's located in Bel Air where the millionaires live."

A week later the couple traveled from Pasadena to Bel Air. They found themselves in a large and elegant mansion set back from a street with palm trees. They were there for dinner in a room illuminated with crystal chandeliers. Impressed, they waited to be served exotic food. They would be drinking champagne with the dinner, but on the table was a pitcher of beer, glasses, and empty plates. Gordon explained that even though a servant had caused delay in the preparation of the dinner, they would soon be eating. He was making small talk when his phone rang. Abruptly he left the table to answer it. His guests heard a soft mumbling from another room that went on and on.

"Something isn't quite right here," exclaimed Lance. "I can feel it. I really believe that guy is trying to put something over on us."

"Oh, don't be so suspicious, dear," Beatrice replied. "So he had to answer a phone call. What isn't right about that?"

"I don't like what's going on at all. We come to this big, empty, silent house for dinner and sit idle for an hour. Then he leaves us to chatter on the phone for another hour. I'm gonna tell that nerd to get lost, to leave us alone. I never was his friend and don't intend to be now."

"Don't lose your temper, Lance. The man seems a little strange, I agree, but I think he means well."

The two sat at the table smelling stale beer for what

seemed an eternity. Then smiling broadly, Gordon returned. By then Lance was angry and told him in no uncertain terms to stay away from his wife.

"She likes you, Gordo, but I don't like you and never will. Stay away from Beatrice when I'm at work. Don't come to my house any more."

"I'm sorry you feel that way, old boy, but of course I'll do what you say. I thought we might have a delicious dinner to foster friendship, but things didn't go the way I planned. I'll see you out."

The next day, walking in the garden that featured a fish pond, Beatrice knelt beside the pool and found the koi dead. A dozen large ornamental carp were floating belly up in the water, a shocking sight. Someone or some thing had deliberately killed them. Alarmed and upset, Beatrice called her husband at work. Gordo had installed the fish. Maybe in angry revenge he had poisoned them. Lance assured his wife he would look into the matter and get an explanation.

Leaving his office, he drove to Gordon's house to confront him. He parked in the driveway of the sprawling house and rang the doorbell. When he got no answer, he rang again and then a third time. The massive door appeared to be slightly ajar, and he pushed it open to enter. On the shiny hardwood floor were letters the mailman had left. Lance picked them up, glanced at them, and realized with amazement that another person owned the house. Gordo was an interloper, a pretender. The house didn't belong to him, nor did anything in it.

Several days passed and the couple heard nothing from Gordon Paige. Then one evening while Lance was working late and Beatrice was preparing for bed, she thought she heard a thumping sound in another room. Later as she tried to sleep she began to feel she was not alone. The next day the feeling persisted. She half believed that while her husband was working long hours, someone in her home was spying on her. When the suspicion left her unable to sleep, she got a prescription for sleeping pills. She began to feel at ease again, chiding herself for being silly. Bowing to her husband's demand, Gordon was out of her life. In the morning mail came a letter of apology, saying he wouldn't bother them again even though he was "willing to let bygones be bygones." That puzzled her. What could he mean?

"I wish I knew," Lance asserted. "The guy is crazy, loony. I wish to god we had never bumped into him that day we shopped. The letter has an address miles away from Bel Air. We won't answer it."

Four days later Lance's sister came from Chicago to spend a week with them. Jenna was talkative and spilled the beans. In high school Lance and a boy named Reginald had bullied Gordon without mercy. They falsely reported that Gordon was homosexual and had tried to molest them. That brought misery to the boy and more bullying. To make matters worse, his conservative father was prone to believe the accusations. His mother was supportive but indecisive. Gordon slipped into profound depression and tried to kill himself. The local newspaper reported he jumped off a bridge and was drowning when a fisherman in a boat nearby brought him to shore. School officials identified his tormentors but did nothing to remedy the situation. They heaved a sigh of relief when Gordon went to another city to live with an uncle.

On hearing the full story from Jenna, and hearing too that her husband had been dishonest and manipulative in business and could lose his lucrative job, Beatrice packed her bags and went home to Chicago. Lance Evans was left alone in the pleasant house on Appleseed Lane. He spent his days pretending to work and his evenings steadily drinking until he passed out. Every evening he received a taunting phone call from Gordon Paige.

The man boasted that he, Gordo, had made love to Beatrice for hours on end when Lance was working. She was uninhibited and passionate, he claimed, and she loved only him. They would marry, he said over and over, as soon as her divorce from a man she never loved was final. In the lonely house on Appleseed Lane, a contrite and desperate man couldn't sleep or eat. He went to bed soused and found it hard to get up in the morning, With the approval of his boss in Chicago, the man in charge of the Pasadena operation reluctantly fired Lance Evans, citing dereliction of duty. Beatrice got her divorce and Gordon got his revenge. Beatrice married a car salesman in Chicago who was seldom at home. Gordon died in a car crash on a freeway. Lance lived on into his "golden years" but not with ease. Not one of them, not even lovely Beatrice, lived happily ever afterwards.

37

A Nightbird Warbling

The day had come when I would see my old friend, Gideon Fernwood, after a long hiatus of twenty-three years. It was no surprise when he invited me to visit him at his home in another state, for by then we had revived our friendship. In our youth as classmates in high school he had been a close and dependable friend. We met often to gorge ourselves on greasy doughnuts and discuss how we might change the world even before we entered college. Later as university students we established a rapport that became the basis of a long friendship.

One or two teachers saw potential in us, believing we had in our possession something called intellect. They said we had the promise of a good future if we worked hard and abstained from drugs and alcohol. We managed to do that as he majored in German while I studied philosophy. Later he switched to scientific studies to prepare for a medical career. The divergent paths we had chosen put us miles apart, and the friendship we cherished dwindled in a year or two and dried up.

In time we lost sight of each other, and for twenty

years we lived in different worlds with different friends, activities, and responsibilities. Then I heard from a mutual friend that he had married, was practicing medicine in California, and was apparently becoming a well-known figure in the medical community. He had specialized in psychiatry, and I could see him treating neurotic celebrities in southern California and raking in tons of money. An early dream of his was to become a millionaire before reaching thirty.

Some years later when we began to rebuild the friendship, slowly with a phone call now and then, I learned that he was no longer living in Los Angeles but in a small town in northern California near extensive vineyards. He said he had indeed treated Hollywood celebrities in a flourishing practice but quickly grew tired of his daily routine. He described his patients as shallow, thin as paper with no mental or moral depth whatever, and often intractable. He said in time he came to despise his work in that locale and so looked for greener pastures. That decision took him to a modest practice in northern California.

I learned that he had married quite suddenly a stunning blonde who had come to Hollywood from Idaho to act in the movies. Though she aspired to become a star in the movie firmament, things didn't pan out that way. Her career had stagnated, she wasn't getting younger, and she wanted to be a mother. So off they went to northern California to begin a new life in a house they bought on the outskirts of a town called Aqua Fria. It was a spacious dwelling, I was told, and they were able to take in her grandfather even as children came like clockwork.

I remembered Gideon as clever, witty, and eager to learn. He was a fast and voracious reader. In his home he had books on every subject you can imagine. He read scientific works but also a novel now and then, and he mastered German and French to read the literature of those languages. He was an introspective person always thinking. Whether he would be the same when I met him face to face after many years I didn't know. Would he be the person I remembered: lively, witty, and light-hearted? Would he be the enthusiastic dreamer I had known, or would I find him wrapped in torpor induced by age?

We met at the airport. I was sitting in the terminal reading Descartes when a man I must describe as corpulent ambled up to me on short, fat legs exclaiming, "Dexter! Dexter Shellenberger! Is that you?" I had seen him coming but had not recognized him. Gideon had always been slim and sinewy, priding himself on fitness.

We embraced as old friends do and shook hands. Looking him over, I said with no effort to conceal my bluntness, "I can see at a glance, Gideon, that you are no longer thin."

Laughing loudly, he asked, "What did you expect? It's the result of good living, Dex! And it's been many years since last you saw me!"

"Indeed, and the years have surely brought change."

"You've changed a bit too, my friend, more somber perhaps? A bit more crusty living with the works of dry-as-dust philosophers? With me it's been good living, good food, and good family! I must confess my kids and wife are the sun and moon of my existence."

I looked at him closely, trying to discover in this fat

and florid man the features that made him different and interesting in youth. The sharp, intense face I remembered now featured bulging red cheeks, a large nose, and sagging jowls. His pale blue eyes had not changed, but I no longer saw that intense expression of long ago that seemed to probe the mystery of human reality and penetrate to the heart of things.

"If the eyes of a person reflect the quality of one's thoughts," I was thinking, *"the thoughts in that round and balding head are lame at best. Once I saw fire in those eyes. Now I see embers."*

And yet his eyes, rimmed in red and made smaller by the fat of his face, were warm and friendly and clearly those of a happy man. As we stood looking at each other, he suddenly announced, "These are my oldest children! I want you to meet Hannah and Robert." A girl of seventeen and almost a woman came forward, looked at me shyly, and smiled. A boy of fifteen, awkward and hesitating, shook hands with his father's friend and mumbled something I couldn't decipher.

"Ah, these are your children," I murmured politely. I couldn't think of anything else to say.

"Yes! Of course!" he replied, laughing. "Aren't they handsome?"

He said that proudly with an abundance of satisfaction. "And I have three more at home. Five altogether! Five happy, boisterous, full-of-life children! They bring untold joy to my dear wife and me. I hear you remained unmarried, Dexter."

"I did indeed," I said with some hesitation, "but not by

choice, my friend, rather by circumstance or by a dearth of suitable women."

In all the years of our separation I had met women of all stripes but not one with the qualities I was looking for in a spouse. Entering middle age as a confirmed bachelor, I lost entirely the desire to marry and have a family. So I couldn't quite understand how my friend, in his youth so awkward around women, had married a stunning young woman and sired a large family. When he was twenty or more he was still finding it difficult even to speak to a female. At that time he had said, perhaps justifying his reticence, that a man can live as fully as any other man without a woman in his life. Now he was married with five children.

We scrambled into his small car of foreign make, I in the front seat with the driver and the two brittle teens in back. They sat in silence and so did I while their father talked. It was late afternoon in late summer, and the town was dull and sleepy. Nothing moved in the streets except a car now and then and a dog chasing a beleaguered cat. Here and there someone on the sidewalk waved to us, and Gideon returning the salute told us the person's name. It seemed he wanted me to know that he was a personal friend of everybody.

We were soon moving along a narrow road toward what he called his ranch house. It was a squat little bungalow, or so it seemed to me, but suddenly grew larger as we approached. It was set back from the road and had a spacious lawn with trees and shrubs.

"This is where we live," said Gideon, pausing to hear what I might say. "We call it our homestead. I own the place free and clear and the children will have it when their parents pass on."

"It looks very agreeable," I said, "well-built and comfortable with plenty of space around it."

A woman of some girth appeared in the driveway, dressed for company. She was no longer the beautiful blonde starlet a mutual friend had told me about some years earlier. A portly lady of uncertain age, she was clean and pleasant but emitting an aroma of profound motherhood. She exhibited nothing to remind me that she was once a young woman parading her femininity in second-rate movies. Preoccupied with her children, husband, and household, she had become a genial matron.

"Giddy has told me so much about you!" she exclaimed. "I really believe I know you already. I've heard all about the good times you had as teenagers, how much he liked the fun you had together!"

In the living room were three blonde and plump children ranging in age from seven to eleven. They were neither sitting nor occupied with toys, but standing rather stiffly against the wall as if for review by some gentleman of the military.

"Ah! So these are the three children you mentioned earlier?"

"Indeed, yes!" Gideon roared with pleasure. "Let me introduce each one of them. The smallest is Herbert, we call him Herbie. The biggest is Gertrude or Gerty, and this little fellow is Gideon Junior. I didn't want a junior but gave in to please Lucy. The movie people of years ago called her Greta as more glamorous, but her real name is Lucy."

The children stepped forward one by one, bowed as in a Japanese movie, and scrambled away to another part of the house. Sitting by the window in an overstuffed chair was a man, a very old man with a trembling hand. Though his large and liquid eyes were staring at me, he said nothing. Lucy Fernwood — she insisted I call her Lucy — said with a sprightly gesture, "This is my grandfather, Dexter. His birthday was two weeks ago, and would you believe it? He's eighty-nine!"

She moved in close to the old man and shouted in the large left ear. "This gentleman is Giddy's long-time friend, Papa. Say hello to him!"

The thin old man tried to greet me, perhaps even to welcome me, but managed only to mutter a string of words that made no sense. As though I were in the act of departing, he waved to me. He tried to smile, I think, but it appeared more like a grimace.

Coming in from outside, Gideon was chortling with pleasure. "I see you're becoming friends with Papa! Grandpapa I should say. That old man is a treasure to us, a source of unending delight for the children. They laugh at every little thing he does, and of course he doesn't mind at all. He's a treasure, Dex, a real treasure, but greedy as a bear."

"Now, now Giddy, dear," Lucy interposed. "Surely you know Dexter doesn't want to hear all the little details regarding Papa."

But Gideon was speaking even as she was speaking, emphasizing the habits of the old man and how on a daily basis he delighted the children with his antics.

"I tell you he's greedy. He's so greedy he wants to

gorge himself senseless at every meal. You have no idea how much he would eat if we allowed it. We have to be centurions, unbending taskmasters, to keep the old darling from killing himself. He looks at the apple pie my wife puts on the table as if it were a pretty girl of fifteen. He lusts after food, and always wants too much. We rein him in but he gets angry and mutters nonsense. You never saw anything quite so funny."

I was shown to my room to freshen up before dinner. My window looked out on a wide expanse of green grass and golden wheat and ripe vineyards. It was a pleasant scene, and I imagined life in that house was just as pleasant. When I heard the tinkling of a bell, I went downstairs for dinner. Lucy guided me to my chair in the dining room. One of the children wheeled in the old man in a special chair and placed him at the head of the table. I gathered he was too infirm to walk. With shining eyes and trembling lips, he stared at two desserts on the table. Lucy and her daughters had made a chocolate cake of four layers slathered with thick brown icing. Beside it sat a scrumptious and very sugary cherry pie. I had a fleeting thought they had done the baking to impress me. Or did they do it to tempt the old man for a special show?

Gideon was sitting at the opposite end of the table, rubbing his palms together and smiling broadly. "You will be amused by what will soon take place," he said to me loud enough for all to hear. The children, understanding the drift of his comment, began to giggle. Their mother was smiling, and their father began to yell in the old man's ear.

"This evening, Papa, we have two desserts! Chocolate

cake and cherry pie! Look at them, Papa! Cherry pie and chocolate cake!"

The pocked and wrinkled face of the old man turned bright with excessive eagerness. The tired old eyes flamed like struck flint. His thin lips began to quiver, and spittle dribbled onto his shirt.

"Now look at the spectacle he's gonna make," Gideon whispered.

And indeed it was a spectacle. He didn't like the soup and refused to eat it. However, for the sake of his health he had to eat it, and Hannah the eldest daughter, began to force feed him with a spoon too big for his mouth. Trying not to swallow the soup, he sputtered the gray liquid all over the table. The children roared with laughter, and I could hear a chortle or snicker coming from Lucy. Vastly amused, Gideon ceased his laughter to ask a question: "Don't you think he's a natural-born clown? He's so funny! He keeps the entire family in stitches!"

Papa the Clown, emaciated and hungry, demanded the attention of every person at table. He stared at the steaming dishes of food with supplicant eyes. More than once he tried to seize a dish in trembling hands and pull it to him. The family put the roast beef close enough for him to smell, almost within his grasp. They laughed when he couldn't clutch it. He muttered inarticulate grunts and groans and begged with drooping eyes. In greedy eagerness and frustration he slobbered on the napkin tucked under his chin and hurled it to the floor. The family was viewing his behavior as a comical theatrical performance. That scene of mindless elder abuse amused them greatly. For me, and I like to think I'm not overly sensitive, it was grotesque and tragic.

At last they put a tiny piece of roasted meat on his plate, and he gobbled it down with undiluted gluttony to get another piece as soon as possible. They gave him potatoes and gravy and green beans to go with his meat. Ravenously he cleared his plate, scraped it with a bony finger, and licked the finger. He groaned with beggar eyes for more, but the man of the house said to him firmly: "You've eaten too much already, Papa. There is nothing more for you." The old man took the remark as a reprimand and began to cry. He cried while the children laughed.

I found myself unable to sit there and do nothing. "Give the man as much as he wants," I said at length. "It's obvious he hasn't been eating enough and is wasting away. For God's sake, Gideon, feed the old fellow! He's hungry. Your table sags with food and he goes hungry. Feed him!"

The prominent physician sensed my anger but replied calmly. "No, my dear friend, if he were to eat as much as he wants it would hurt him dreadfully at his age. I'm a doctor, I must remind you, and know these things. If he were allowed to eat all he wants, he would die in a week."

I wanted to explode with an epithet underscoring his appalling stupidity, his lamentable lack of human kindness, but held my tongue. Perhaps he and his family meant well when depriving Grandpa of the one remaining pleasure he had left, but I couldn't help but see it as a cruel form of elder abuse. Both Gideon and Lucy insisted they were looking after his health, extending his life. But what life? To eat was the only pleasure left for the old man, and they were starving him so that he might live a month or two longer. I felt the least they could do was show him a little kindness until he died, and that meant giving him food to satisfy his craving. But Gideon was a doctor, a physician he preferred to be called, and knew better.

After dinner I excused myself and went up to my room and packed my things. I had come to spend a few days with an old friend but decided I would leave as soon as morning came. I knew I would never see him again. I sat at my window looking at the grain and grapes in moonlight and felt sad. A nightbird was warbling in a nearby tree, singing perhaps to lull his mate asleep. And I thought of my friend who was no longer my friend. I thought of him and his five children living in a cruel and bizarre world they had made for themselves and wondered what had happened. What terrible chain of freakish events had caused my friend to lose that invincible intelligence I so admired when we were young? What had caused him to lose that instinctive sense of knowing at once the difference between right and wrong? My last impression as I drifted off to sleep was of Gideon and his wife sleeping like grizzly bears in a lair. I could see them pressed against each other snoring blissfully. And I wondered what the next day would bring.

38

Daddy, Wake Up!

Outside the sun was shining through misty clouds, and the snow that had fallen during the night was beginning to melt. November had been a blustery month, and the weather in December was cold. Martha Hudson, organized and efficient, had already bought Christmas gifts for her husband and two children. Henry Hudson, a troubled long-distance trucker, was home for the holidays. The children had learned to be wary of him but were excited to be out of school more than a week. Martha encouraged her family to set up a Christmas tree and look forward to exchanging gifts. But as the big day approached, an event took place that crushed completely the woman's dreams of a joyous Christmas.

Morning had come, but the curtained room was dark. In front of the fireplace was a large overstuffed chair that shut away the heat and much of the light from the two children huddled in the back of the room. The boy, Adam, was eleven and his sister, Abigail, nine. They were good-looking children, boisterous and happy most of the time, but now quiet and timorous. Both were staring at the back of the armchair and whispering in an overflow of emotion.

"It's all right, Abby," said the boy. "Our daddy ain't gonna bother us no more at all. He's soaking up warmth from the fire and sleeping like a bear. We don't even have to whisper, but I guess it's better we do."

"Oh, let's do be careful," said the little girl. "We can't make a sudden noise and wake him up. You know how angry he gets when that happens. I don't like it when he's angry."

"Are you afraid of him?" the lad of eleven asked. "I ain't afraid."

"No, stoopid, I'm not afraid of my own daddy. But I do know he likes to be the boss in this house, and Mama says he's always angry 'cause he works too many hours and don't like his job. She says he works hard but can't make enough to pay the bills and can't find another job, and he has a mean old boss he really hates."

"I guess what you say is true enough, but he ain't my daddy no more. He's a killer, Abby, a murderer. He told me so himself. He came in my room just as I was waking up and said, 'I killed your mama, boy. I killed your mama. She made me angry and I killed her. I didn't mean to do it, didn't want to do it, but did.' And I went and looked and her bed was a mess, the white sheets red all over, and the wall splattered with little red drops. I cried out, but Mama didn't answer. Her face was very pale with a lot of red on the left side, and I was pretty sure it was blood, and that means she's dead."

"Maybe that red is from spilled cherry cider. She likes cherry cider even better than apple cider, but I think apple is better. Maybe it's red ink. I heard her say a few days ago we're drowning in red ink."

"It's blood, stoopid. Not cider, not red ink, not paint neither. It's blood, *her* blood, and maybe some of his too. His right hand got all bloody, and he was shaking a little, and he stared at me with a strange look, and I thought he might kill me too. But he came down to the living room and built a fire and sat down and went to sleep in that chair We gonna be dead if we wake him and so we gotta be quiet."

"I don't believe you, Adam. I just don't believe you! Daddy wouldn't hurt us, and I don't believe he did something bad to Mama. He's just tired and needs rest. Mama says he wears himself out on the road mile after mile trying to make a dollar."

"I guess he's tired all right, sure looks it. But he's not your daddy no more. He killed your mama, Abby. He's a murderer and we can't call him Daddy no more."

"My daddy didn't kill nobody! He gets angry and he kicked our dog, but he wouldn't kill nobody. He wouldn't kill my mama. If he wanted to kill somebody, it wouldn't be her. He would shoot his mean old boss and shoot him real dead."

"You have to believe me, Abby. Mama is dead, and you can't call him Daddy no more 'cause he did it. I would take you up to see her, but the stairs squeak and we can't make a noise, not even a little one." The Bible says, *Thou shalt not kill*, but that man killed. So he'll go to hell for it. And you will too if you call him Daddy."

"Does the Bible say, *Thou shalt not call a murderer Daddy?*"

"No it don't, but if you do you'll burn in hell for it."

"I don't want to burn in hell! All my life even when I was little I always wanted to go to heaven. I do so want to go to heaven!"

She was only nine and she had a firm belief that heaven was a very nice place high in the sky, or above the sky, with golden streets and fleecy houses. White-robed angels with magnificent wings flitted about from place to place or relaxed drinking mint juleps in a perpetual garden of ease and delight. They were free of all earthly problems and created celestial music on golden harps. Their faces of pearls and roses glowed with kindness, and when not doing anything else they sat at the feet of God Almighty. He had a long gray beard and very kind eyes.

"If you wanna go to heaven, you must do what I tell you," said the boy. "You gotta stay here and keep watch on that man. If he wakes up, I want you to run to a neighbor's house as fast as you can and tell them your dad murdered your mom. Then tell them to call the police."

"What if they don't believe me?" asked the girl. "Mama says grown-ups almost never believe anything a kid tells them."

"Then you just stay at their house 'cause I'm gonna find a policeman right now, right this minute, and you stay here."

"And what will the policemen do when they come here?" Her eyes were wide with wonder, and she thought her brother was handling the situation very well.

"Oh, they'll put handcuffs on him and take him away and give him a trial and find him guilty and kill him for his crime, and he goes to hell to burn forever. I learned all that in school."

"What? What did you say? They gonna kill him 'cause he killed our mama even when he told you he didn't mean to do it? And then you say he's going to hell and get burned?"

"Yes, of course. The Bible says an eye for an eye and a tooth for a tooth, and that's just another way of saying a life for a life. The man in that chair is a murderer and he's got to pay for what he did."

"Don't call the police, Adam. Please don't call the police!" She had forgotten to whisper and was almost screaming.

Alarmed, her brother put his hand over her mouth and told her to shut up or run the risk of waking up the killer.

"Our telephone don't work no more. Otherwise I would of called before now. I'll go and ask a neighbor to call. If I don't get a policeman here quick, I'll go straight to hell and so will you."

"Please don't say that, Adam, please don't!" The little girl was sobbing now. "We must go and talk to Mama. I know she wouldn't want Daddy to be killed for something he didn't mean to do and go to hell."

"I told you not to call him Daddy, you stoopid girl. And I told you Mama's dead and so you can't talk to her. If you don't believe me, come and see for yourself."

The master bedroom was cold and quiet and seemed awfully big to both of them. Abigail touched her mama's shoulder and shook it. She got no response. She touched the woman's face, all bloody from a blow to the head, and found it cold. She cried out to be heard and so did Adam.

Only an echo replied. Both pinched her cheek and nose to know she wasn't sleeping. Her eyes were closed and she appeared to be in peaceful sleep, but after touching her they knew she was dead.

"Did she go to hell when she died?" the girl asked faintly.

"No, of course not! She was a good woman and she went to heaven. Only bad people go to hell, the people that break the commandments and do bad things. That man sleeping in that chair in front of the fire will go to hell because he did a bad thing."

"If Daddy goes to hell he won't be with Mama any more, or with us if we go where mama's gone. I don't want him to go to hell!"

"Now don't start that again, Abbey! I'm off to find a policeman. If Dad wakes up, don't you tell him where I went. If he finds out he'll run and hide and maybe get away with murder. But even if he does the devil will take him sooner or later."

"I don't want the devil to take him! He's my daddy and I don't want the devil to take him." Again she was almost screaming. "Maybe he only hurt Mama and she's gonna wake up all right tomorrow."

"Your head is harder than a rock!" the boy scolded. "I'm disgusted with you, Abigail, just plain disgusted!"

"I don't care! Daddy don't deserve to go to hell."

She heard the door bang shut and she knew she was there alone with her mother dead upstairs and her father a murderer and sleeping in the living room. On tiptoe she went into the room and lay down on the carpet. She could see the top of his head as he reclined in the chair, and she imagined she heard him snoring. But then she realized the only sound in the room was the occasional crackling of the wood-burning fire. She wanted to creep closer to the fire but couldn't because she feared he might wake up and confront her. She would have to tell him her brother had gone to call the police, and that would make him angry. She feared his anger. Some nights she had covered her head with her pillow when she heard him calling her mother names. She couldn't understand why he did that, for Mama was always saying he was a good man but troubled. So she lay on the carpet and quietly sobbed, quietly because she didn't want to disturb him.

She recalled what her brother had said. Her daddy was a murderer and would be killed because he had killed. He would be executed, Adam had said, using the big word, and would go directly to hell. Her mama was already in heaven, he had said. Daddy had been fond of dear Mama and wouldn't like to be in a different place, and the little girl knew her mama wouldn't like it either. If the police didn't get him to be executed, maybe he could avoid going to hell. Wouldn't that be better for all concerned? She took a deep breath, screwed up her courage, ran over to the sleeping figure, and cried out to him as loudly as she could.

"Wake up, Daddy! Wake up! The police are coming and you'll be killed for killing Mama. It's an eye for an eye, the Bible says. And you'll go to hell. Wake up! Wake up! The police are coming! I don't want you to go to hell. Run away from here as fast as you can and hide."

When two policemen arrived with their hands on their sidearms and a triumphant little boy not far behind them, they heard the shrill cry of a little girl, "Wake up, Daddy, wake up! The police are coming!"

The fire had dwindled to scarlet embers and the room was cold and dark. A frenetic entreaty from a frightened little girl was bouncing off the dreary walls: "Wake up, Daddy, wake up! The police are here!"

But her daddy had chosen not to wake up.

39

Leaving a Footprint

Jonathan Blue labored all his life to be recognized as a novelist of ideas. He died at forty-six not certain any reader would remember him. He was buried in the midst of wild flowers in a modest cemetery on the outskirts of a small town in France. If you go to that alien ground and examine the plain and simple tombstone to read the weathered inscription, you will be reminded of a life bravely lived though not entirely well. His place of rest is silent and solitary. It is far removed from England and London and the fictional world he passed on to later generations. Leaving the lonely place, you will view the broad expanse of the Bay of Biscay and look into Spain.

Tired to the bone, sick and near death, Blue wanted to go home to England. He wanted to breathe native air, rest and read, and no longer live as an exile. It didn't happen. Before he drifted away on a cloud of soft reminiscence, the Reverend Josiah Cobble chattered quietly for almost an hour. Driven by righteousness and a sense of moral duty, the good parson spoke of religion and the saving of souls. In a solemn ecclesiastical ceremony that Blue would have found disturbing had he been well and alert, the man murmured a benediction and blessing.

"My good and gentle friend," he said, leaning in close and placing his palm on the dying man's forehead, "you are going home."

"May God's will be done," he reported Jonathan Blue as replying. "Now, if you will, please let me rest."

That dramatic scene as described by the parson was later called a fabrication, a blatant lie in more pungent language. It was vehemently disputed by all the people who had been close to Blue. Even the middle-class family in Harrogate, staunchly religious and accepting scripture without question, found the parson's pronouncement hard to believe. Gabrielle knew that for most of his life her complicated husband had been a militant atheist. During their four years together, he softened somewhat into agnosticism but never expressed any belief in heaven or hell or one almighty god. He had said to her more than once that we make for ourselves our own heaven or hell, and death ends it all. Everlasting life after death? Mumbo jumbo, balderdash!

Though Cobble was respected as a dedicated god-fearing man, his declaration couldn't be taken with even an atom of truth. A sudden, deathbed conversion was not in the cards for Jonathan Blue. Lying there and looking at the ceiling, he heard little of what the parson was saying. His thoughts were on the past.

It was time to examine the life he had lived and sort through it. To waste his last hour listening to a parson chatter about religion was unthinkable. In shining water he drifted calmly in the boat he had wanted since childhood but never got. Although fate had made him a stranger to both his sons, he hoped their lives would be longer than his and better. He couldn't know that a savage war would kill one of them in his prime. He remembered Will, his brother, who at twenty had died too soon. Was he cheated by chance or decimated by some arcane power that lurks in darkness?

He thought of Muriel, his first wife, who died at twenty-nine. In bleak misery she had surrendered to a pernicious force that slowly consumed her. His thoughts went to the untimely death of his father. Thomas Blue had been a vigorous man who put his work and family before himself, and yet his life for whatever reason was cut short. Jonathan Blue remembered the man's last words: *"Break, break, break on thy cold grey stones, O Sea!"* And he remembered he was able to finish the line: *"And I would that my tongue could utter the thoughts that arise in me."*

The private thoughts that flowed like torrential rain into the corners of his fevered mind he did not utter. In an instant he spanned the years of endless labor. The grueling toil he viewed as so important throughout his life now seemed unimportant. At one time he could name by title in chronological order all the books he had published. And he could recall with photographic accuracy a scene or event in a specific book. Now to remember and repeat even three titles as he approached the end was too much work and of no real importance.

Only the beginning was important, the days of youth and dreams and bright hope. Where were they now, those wonder days of promise and fulfillment? Where had they gone? And so fast? What had happened to the hope that sustained him when times were hard? Pain and disease had abruptly taken its place, and he couldn't understand why. What good had come of the struggle? What did it all mean? In a world insensate, unconscious, indifferent he knew his moment in time had no meaning whatever. He came and went and that was all.

A small planet spinning in space spawned life. On that same planet life in all its forms would end. The meaning of life could be found only in the living of life. The only meaning anyone had found was the instinctive will to live one's life, and that he had done. It mattered not how long he had lived nor how well. He had come into the world to produce, and that he had done. He did his work, grumbling at times to be sure and often without grace, but he had labored prodigiously. And the labor had produced fruit. He had created something vital that others in a later time would perhaps notice. He had done what he was meant to do. He had married, had children, had worked hard at what he knew best, and had produced. Could any person ask for more? He was not seeking salvation in this moment of crisis, only a vague feeling of satisfaction.

The idealism of his youth and the brave, resurgent idealism he felt with Gabrielle now seemed of little value. The idealist had wanted more than life could offer. The realist clamored for life as he found it but lost it too soon. Vaguely he felt there was something better than the realism he had placed in carefully crafted novels. Had he found this better thing in the grand historical novel he was leaving unfinished? In this last hour the fog was lifting, and he was beginning to see into the heart of things. He was ready to discover something of indisputable significance; of that he was certain. In the blatant glare of sunlight on fog he sought to see the thing as in itself it really was. But in an instant that kernel of truth at the center of it all shifted shape and dissolved.

The nightingale that sang all night in back of his house he vividly remembered. Was the bird delivering a cryptic message? It sang with urgent intensity and seemed to know more than he knew. Surely the bird had something to tell him, but the message in birdsong he couldn't decipher. Was there meaning somewhere that he had missed, or was the bird no messenger at all? The nightingale sang because nature urged it to sing and had nothing to do with him. That thought came as a flash of truth in heavy darkness. The parson had insisted he would see radiant beings clothed in light at the end of a tunnel. Blue saw nothing of that.

He thought of head and heart, of reason and intuition. He couldn't be positive that reason was worth anything at all in the conduct of life. He had reached the conclusion that life was a meandering river, alive and flowing through frost and sun but without awareness of what it touched. So in a world of mechanical cause and effect what was the good of reason? Perhaps feeling was all that mattered. He remembered the violence of his emotions with Muriel, the warmth of his loins with Christine, and the pounding of his heart with Gabrielle. With all three the life force had made him a puppet on strings, and yet a puppet with feeling. The times he had surrendered to youthful passion he had felt a phenomenal vigor, and his mind had worked with burning clarity. Yet in maturity he had found that self-control and self-respect could be as passionate as the surrender to passion. It was the lesson Gabrielle had taught him. During the last four years of his life he had loved that delicate and deserving woman as no man had loved. She had loved him too, unconditionally, and he gained spiritual strength from her.

Now these recollections, so airy in their lack of substance, taxed his strength. Yet relaxed he was, more relaxed than he had ever been, not weary and worrisome but completely relaxed and without pain. In the distance a soothing male voice from a figure no longer in focus was talking, consoling, cajoling. But his words mingled with the murmuring of a stream, and they bubbled along as leaves in the stream. He thought of the rivers he had loved in his youth. Quiet rivers and tumultuous rivers, all with energy and beauty. Somewhere in the room he heard an oily voice mumbling something about living and life, dying and death, and he made no effort to understand.

Once in Italy he had stumbled upon a rare old sage in a village north of Rome. The man had endured eighty winters, losing all sense but gaining an echo of wisdom. In one brief utterance he demolished the epic narrative Blue had carefully crafted in a thousand pages: *"You were born, my son, and you will die. You will live for a season to struggle and suffer and die. You cannot ask for more."* It was wisdom unvarnished, inviolate truth. Yet it stirred within him red-hot embers of rage.

Now as he lay dying, the sage's words tweaked his tongue like piquant wine. Of one thing, as Reverend Cobble spoke of life and death, he could be certain: living was painful, dying was not. He no longer feared that passage into the night. It merely completed the process that began when he was born. It was all a pattern just like the pattern on the ceiling that would soon give way to another. The rivers he had walked beside in wonder told him that everything in a temporal world was in flux and would pass. His time had come, his moment had moved on, and some other person would fill the next moment.

Any footprint he had made during his brief existence was now yielding to other prints. *Footprints on the sands of time!* Who was it who said that? He opened his eyes and looked at the ceiling. The pattern there seemed to pulsate for an instant, move downward, and swing upward again. The pale eyes intensely viewing it all began to blink. His lips moved wryly. As the parson spoke of God and everlasting life, the author of more than twenty novels was appealing instinctively to gods older than the god of Israel, older than any of those in the cradle of civilization. In the fever of his last moments he mumbled a prayer to them all: "Let there be peace in the valley for me."

Sitting beside him and holding his hand — she had entered the room moments before the end — Gabrielle in unspoken grief nodded and smiled and tenderly kissed the blank face.

40
Growing Old

"What is it to grow old?
Is it to lose the luster of the eye?
Yes, this and more!"

We were two gentlemen sipping coffee after dinner at the Cordon Bleu in Atlanta. We had just finished a delectable dinner when my friend exclaimed, "Ah, I am growing old, John! Only yesterday on a warm summer evening like this I would have wanted activity, adventure, a love affair. I would have felt full of life, randy, and eager, but now I feel only that excellent escargot dissolving gracefully in my ample stomach. Life is really so very short, you know, so short it makes one sad to think about it. And yet I do think about it and weep."

Philip was in his late fifties, already turning bald and fleshy. In his youth he had been a good athlete, but now in what we like to call middle age his step was no longer light and bouncy. He had resigned himself to a sedentary life and to the inescapable fact that time in the lives of all of us moves at breakneck speed to make us old and tired before we know it. I am older than Philip by three years, and though older I've resisted the urge to accept the dour thoughts my friend was expressing.

"Well," I said as the waiter refreshed our coffee, "I too am growing old. It's a condition not one of us can possibly avoid, but I try to do it without paying much attention to it. I've always felt strong and vigorous and I intend to keep on feeling that way. I see my face in the mirror every morning, and the changes are so subtle I detect no shocking aberration at all. I should have to abstain from looking into mirrors for a couple of years, and maybe then I would begin to feel as you do."

"Reluctantly, John, I must agree with you. With robust good health you are aging, my friend, but without noticing a slow decline. I'm able to read the script old Father Time is writing on your face better than you. And to be honest, the lines are gentle and unassuming for the most part, but a little rough around the edges. In time, I dare say, an awakening will come to you, as it has to me, with the force of revelation."

"You would be boring, Philip, if you were not so open and frank. You do have that peculiar ability to see into the heart of things and know them for what they really are. I hope you never lose it."

"Well, thanks, old friend, I like you too."

"As for *revelation* as you put it, coming to terms with my own mortality is the way I would put it. It's already happened and I must admit it wasn't a pleasant experience. It was quite painful in fact, but slowly I got over it. At least I hope I did."

"Now you arouse interest, even my curiosity," Philip retorted. "Why don't we take a little walk? The evening is perfect for walking and talking, and I want to hear all about your unpleasant experience. Let it be a story about dastardly Time and what it does to a man."

"Then I shall begin! And no interruption, please. Enjoy that cigar of yours, walk with me, and listen. Comment if you please at the end of my story. Censure me for being foolish, if you are so inclined, but listen now.

"Like all men, I've known a few women in my time. But one was as special as any woman can be, and I loved her as soon as I met her. It happened twenty-three years ago in New Orleans. I was a young lawyer sent by my firm to settle a property dispute involving several parties. Mary Ann Lafitte was twenty-six, a schoolteacher, and single. In a way we were adversaries in the legal dispute, but when she sat beside me one evening at dinner we quickly became the best of friends and more. The dinner was held to bring divergent parties together for informal discussion. When it was over I asked if I might see her home. We walked and talked all the way to her house. It was a beautiful summer evening like this one, and she told me all about herself.

"She was a very complete young woman, tall and slender, with a musical voice so enchanting I heard it long after I left her. In my hotel room I drifted into slumber thinking about her. I awoke to a warm and sunny morning wondering how she would spend her day. Then as luck would have it I saw her shopping with her aunt, exchanged a few words with her, and spoke with her again on the phone that evening. One thing led to another and before long we found ourselves 'going steady' as we called it in those days. She had no school work to fill her time, being off for the summer, and most of my work with legal briefs was done in the evenings. So in fine though humid weather we walked the quaint streets of the Latin quarter and later frolicked in the large pool of my hotel.

"The first time I saw her at the pool I was reminded of the nymphs and sirens of classical legend, so beautiful her shining skin and so enticing. Her face had appealed to me at first glance and delighted me. Now her body in a swimsuit was having the same effect. In every way her physical dimensions were perfect, and I felt I had found the woman I was born to love. I was smitten, I tell you, smitten. I longed for her with a terrible ache of sinew and soul. It was torture and yet thrilling. Subtle and varied facial expression, dark hair lifted by the wind, brown eyes speaking a special language, the way she moved that shapely body entranced me. Even the way she wore her clothes delighted me.

"I fell in love with her. I loved her beyond reason. She was elegance personified — freshness, femininity, youth, and mystery in one small package. I found seductive beauty in the curve of her jaw, the arch of an eyebrow, the hesitant flutter of sensitive lips framing a word, and the siren call of her body. I could never be certain she loved me as ardently as I loved her, and yet our affair sizzled for three months. Then my firm called me back to Seattle. Overwhelmed by emotion, I had to leave her. The thought of her, even the scent that surrounded her, excited me day after day. Two thousand miles away I belonged to her as completely as when lying beside her. And yet, even though her image was ever before my eyes, my love in time became a tender memory.

"Twenty-three years aren't many in a lifetime, you will agree. The years go by so rapidly one doesn't feel them slipping away. Yet they fly away like sparrows on the wing, like swallows in twilight, like geese in autumn. They disappear like those phantom horsemen of story who ride a chill wind after sunset and vanish with the color. So completely they disappear one sees nothing of them, not even a shadow. Then pausing to consider what has happened, one can't understand the thing at all. For a time, basking in self-imposed delusion, it seemed to me that only a few months stood between me and that delightful summer in Louisiana. Only a few months separated me from that rarest of women I was so fortunate to meet and love with abandon.

"In October of last year my firm required me to look into a transaction in Mobile, Alabama. The dispute resolved, I rented a car and drove from Mobile to New Orleans to visit once more the angel-woman of my dreams. If I could find her and be near her for only a few minutes, it would be worth the long trip. Over the years I had lost her entirely, but now while driving I was thinking maybe not. Maybe alone but quietly content she was waiting for me. I went to her house to find strangers living there. I asked at several businesses if anyone knew her. I called the high school where she had taught and asked about her.

"'Why, yes,' said a woman's voice, 'you are using her maiden name. Mary is married now, married Pete Hawkins. She's the principal of our school but currently out of her office. Hold on please.'

"I waited for maybe ten minutes. Just as I was about to hang up a woman came on the line. She was not a young woman and she spoke with a distinctive Southern accent and a nasal twang. 'This is Miz Hawkins,' she said with a ring of authority. 'What can I do you for?'

"We arranged to meet the next day, a Saturday, in the same park we had enjoyed years earlier. I got there first. It was autumn and chilly. I found a bench and sat down and pulled up my collar against a light breeze. Presently I saw a large woman with a little girl stumping toward me. She carried herself well but was certainly a heavy-set matron. She had a broad face, sagging jaws, and spectacles perched on a prominent nose. She greeted me loudly and sat down heavily, puffing a little because she had walked faster than usual to be on time. I looked at her and she looked at me and we could think of very little to say.

"So that was she! That big and square woman with fat legs and yellow hair was my nymph! That plain and dowdy woman with the nasal twang and the brassy manner, my ideal love! Behind her thick glasses tired brown eyes blinked. Her mouth wearing a dab of lipstick twitched and hung open. Her big hands, as she reached out to draw the little girl close to her, were those of a man. She had become the happy mother of two little boys and one girl. Already the little girl was being groomed to take the place of that beautiful young woman I had loved with foolish abandon in my salad days. Life was moving too fast for me, faster and more dangerous than a bullet. Driving back to Mobile, I could barely see the road through misty eyes that ached."

"We just passed a cozy bar," said Philip offering solace. "Why don't we go back there and have a drink? I really believe you could use a stiff one, old man, a double. I'm paying."